THE CITY

After reading English a[...]
Yorkshire Television as a Script Editor on *Emmerdale Farm*, where he became Series Producer. He also spent several years in the Drama Department, first as Script Consultant then Producer, before leaving ITV to write full-time. He has been a regular contributor to *Midsomer Murders* and recently scripted the last ever episodes of *A Touch of Frost* which topped the ratings. He lives in Ireland with his family.

# MICHAEL RUSSELL

## *The City of Shadows*

**AVON**

AVON

A division of HarperCollins*Publishers*
77–85 Fulham Palace Road,
London W6 8JB

www.harpercollins.co.uk

A Paperback Original 2012
2

A catalogue record for this book is
available from the British Library

ISBN-13: 978-1-84756-346-0

Set in Minion by Palimpsest Book Production Limited,
Falkirk, Stirlingshire

Printed and bound in Great Britain by
Clays Ltd, St Ives plc

MIX
Paper from
responsible sources
FSC® C007454

For Anita

I have been here before,
    But when or how I cannot tell;
I know the grass beyond the door,
    The sweet keen smell.

*'Sudden Light'*
*Dante Gabriel Rossetti*

# PART ONE
# Free State

*In the back drawing-room there was a quantity of medical and electrical apparatus. From the ceiling, operated by pulleys, was a large 170 centimetre shadowless operating lamp hanging over a canvas covered object – when the cover was removed it was found to be a gynaecological chair with foot rests. The detective sergeant found a specially padded belt that could be used in conjunction with the chair. Among the objects found in the drawing-room was a sterilising case, in the drawer of which were wads of cotton wool. In the office there was a cardboard box containing a dozen contraceptives and a revolver.* The Irish Times

# 1. The Phoenix Park

*Dublin, June 1932*

The moon shone on the Liffey as it moved quietly through Dublin, towards the sea. The river was sparkling. Silver and gold flecks of light shimmered and played between the canal-like embankments of stone and concrete that squeezed it tightly into the city's streets. By day the river was grey and sluggish, even in sunlight, darker than its sheer walls, dingier and duller than the noisy confusion of buildings that lined the Quays on either side. Its wilder origins, in the emptiness of the Wicklow Mountains, seemed long forgotten as it slid, strait-jacketed and servile, through the city it had given birth to. It wasn't the kind of river anyone stood and looked at for long. It had neither majesty nor magic. Its spirit had been tamed, even if its city never had been. From Arran Quay to Bachelor's Walk on one side, from Usher's Quay to Aston Quay on the other, you walked above the river that oozed below like a great, grey drain. And if you did look at it, crossing from the Southside to the Northside, over Gratton Bridge, the Halfpenny Bridge, O'Connell Bridge, it wasn't the Liffey itself that held your gaze, but the soft light on the horizon where it escaped its

3

walls and found its way into the sea at last. Yet, sometimes, when the moon was low and heavy over the city, the Liffey seemed to remember the light of the moon and the stars in the mountains, and the nights when its cascading streams were the only sound.

It was three o'clock in the morning as Vincent Walsh walked west along Ormond Quay. There was still no hint of dawn in the night sky. He had no reason at all to imagine that this would be the last day of his short life of only twenty-three years. He caught the glittering moonlight on the water. He saw the Liffey every day and never noticed it, but tonight it was full of light and full of life. More than a good omen, it felt like a blessing, cutting through the darkness that weighed him down. It was a fine night and surely a fine day to come. Turning a corner he saw lights everywhere now, lighting up the fronts of buildings, strung between the lampposts along the Quays, illuminating every shop and every bar. Curtains were drawn back to show lamps and candles in the windows of every home. The night was filling up with people. The streets had been empty, even fifteen minutes ago, when he'd set off from Red Cow Lane, but suddenly there were figures in the darkness, more and more of them now, in front, behind, crossing over the bridges from south of the river, all walking in the same direction: west.

A stream of Dubliners moved along with him, flowing in the opposite direction to the Liffey, growing at every tributary junction that fed into the Quays. Men and women on their own, quiet and purposeful; couples, old and young, silent and garrulous, some holding hands like lovers and some oblivious of one another; families pushing prams and pulling stubborn toddlers, while youngsters of every age raced in and out of the throng with growing excitement. There were young men who walked in quiet, sober groups, some fingering a rosary, and others full of raucous good humour; women and girls, arm in arm in lines across the street, gossiping and giggling as eager, teasing, endless words tumbled out of their mouths. Occasionally the whole population of a side street decorated with flowers and banners erupted out to join the flow of people moving towards the Phoenix Park. Vincent Walsh glanced back to see the first pink glow behind him in the sky. The new day was coming. And it was as if everyone around him had that same thought at once, as if all those footsteps, already full of such happy anticipation, were moving even faster now, more purposefully and more exuberantly forward, to the gates that led into the Park.

The noise was suddenly much louder. Everyone was talking. The sense of being a part of it all, of belonging to it all, of being absorbed into this hopeful stream of humanity, was irresistible. It wasn't something Vincent wanted to resist. He was fighting back tears, even as his face beamed and smiled in response to the joyful faces around him. This was how he wanted to feel; it was how, when this day ended, he knew he could never be allowed to feel. As they all poured through the Park gates together it was quiet again for a moment. Abruptly the night had opened up around them. Dublin, always so closed and crowding in on itself, was gone. There was only the rhythmic sound of thousands of feet on grass and gravel, and the sight of thousands of shadows amongst the trees of the Phoenix Park.

*

As full daylight came, the tramp of feet and the clamour of voices grew louder. Vincent had tried to sleep but he didn't really want to. His heart, like everyone else's, was beating to the sound of those feet and, like everyone else, he couldn't tire of simply watching the arriving masses. From a stream to a torrent now, melding to form great banks and squares of humanity as far as the eye could see. By eight o'clock the cars and the coaches were coming too, from every corner of Ireland. Someone said there must be a million already, a million people there to bear witness to the real presence of Christ in the Eucharist. Someone said the Eucharistic Congress was the final victory for Ireland, after hundreds of years of faith in the face of persecution, flight and famine. Someone said, and at some length, that for anyone who thought there was no such thing as democracy, here was enough real democracy to right the whole shipwreck of the world. Someone said even the angels looking down from the gold bar of heaven could see them there. Someone said it was the greatest loudspeaker system the earth had ever known, stretching fifteen miles through the Park and into the city. Someone else said the angels should have no trouble hearing so. And in front of the crowd, close to where Vincent was sitting, was the high altar that would be the focus of a million devoted faces that day. It shone in the morning sunlight, radiantly white against the dark phalanxes of the faithful, with its two great arms of pillared colonnades, echoing the colonnades of St Peter's in Rome, reaching out to hold a million people in a joyful embrace.

There was really no plan. He knew the block of seats where the priest would be giving communion. They'd talked about it, weeks before, the last time they'd been together. They had talked about everything that night, everything that mattered to them, everything they felt passionate about, everything they'd ever dreamed about. Vincent had never felt closer to anyone. He had never felt such belonging. He had never felt such an all-possessing love. The priest didn't meet him the next day, or the next, or the next. He'd promised he'd be there, waiting in his car in Smithfield, but he didn't come. And there'd been no more letters. But it was understandable. The Eucharistic Congress meant so much work for any priest, every priest. Today he would see him. He would be at the Pontifical Mass. The priest had been so proud, so excited about serving so close to the high altar. And Vincent would find him. It would happen. Irrespective of tickets and passes and seat allocations and stewards, it would happen. There would be a million people in the Phoenix Park, a million people full of hope. And no hope was stronger than Vincent's. If he had had doubts as he set out in the darkness that morning, he had breathed in the intoxicating faith that was all around him now, and he had been consumed by it.

Vincent had been watching a group of stewards and workmen as they struggled to unload a trailer of heavy benches in front of the high altar. People were already being moved back from the areas reserved for the great and the good. They would have no need to arrive before dawn and stand there all morning. He spoke to the big man who was so cheerfully in charge.

'Is there anything I can do to help?'

'There's still benches to be shifted. We can't have the bigwigs standing up, not when they've brought their arses with them to sit on.'

He worked through the morning, carrying benches and chairs and lining them up in rows. He brought plants and flowers to the colonnades of the high altar. He fetched kettles of tea for the stewards and the labourers, and he picked up their litter. The more he worked, the more he let himself sink into a sense of belonging that was utterly unfamiliar to him. The Eucharistic Congress had seemed a long way from him a week ago, even though it was the only thing anybody was talking about. It filled Dublin and Ireland and the hearts and minds of everyone in it. But it had had nothing to do with him until now, except as the chink of light that offered him a way to find the man he loved. Now it felt different. He didn't forget why he was there, not for a moment, but he hadn't expected to be absorbed into the day like this. Suddenly it was his day too. He had contributed his sweat to it. And when the work was done and a hush of anticipation descended on the Phoenix Park, the steward he'd first spoken to slapped him on the back.

'You may stay at the front, lad. You've done more than your share.'

The cavalry came first, lances held high, escorting the carriages and the cars that brought the world's cardinals, archbishops and bishops to the high altar. They were followed by politicians and ambassadors in tails and top hats, businessmen and union leaders, and the banners of almost every society, association and club in Ireland that could come up with a halfway decent reason to be there. They were led by the graciously waving hand of Éamon de Valera. Ten years ago he had gone to war with the independent Irish state he helped wrest from British rule, because it wasn't independent enough. Then, if some of

the Irishmen he had fought be
caught him, he would have been
municated by the Church during
the War of Independence, when
another because of the six cou
British rule, and an oath to the
took any notice of, even in Lo
returned triumphantly from the
he was the president of the Free

Meanwhile a purple and crimson thread of prelates made its way through the thousands of robed priests in front of the altar. For seconds it was so quiet that the birds could be heard singing in the trees; there was the cry of a solitary gull sailing overhead. Cardinal Lauri, the Papal Legate, read the Pope's words to the crowd. 'Go to Ireland in my name and say to the good people assembled there that the Holy Father loves Ireland and sends to its inhabitants and visitors not the usual apostolic blessing but a very special all-embracing one.' And as the Mass started Vincent simply walked to where he wanted to be, where he had to be. 'Introibo ad altare deo.' I shall go unto the altar of the Lord. He answered the Cardinal's words with words he had not spoken in many years. 'Ad Deum qui laetificat iuven-tutem meam.' To God who giveth joy to my youth. Once he had spoken those words as an altar boy. But slowly, painfully, not even understanding why at first, he had seen all the words he knew by heart come to feel like someone else's. They couldn't belong to him any more, and worse he couldn't belong to them. But today they were his again. He held them close, like childhood friends. He hadn't understood how much he wanted them to be his again.

...ents in the Mass when he felt the happi-
...hood that had been ripped away from him
...ciousness of who he was. Was it really impossible
...a way back when he could feel like this? Suddenly
...realised that the time had come. The Cardinal had
...elevated the host that brought Christ's presence into the
life of every one of the million men, women and children
now on their knees. Three thousand priests moved out into
the crowd with the Eucharist. And for the first time that
day, there was doubt in Vincent's mind. He had still not
seen him. He had looked and looked, hoping, believing.
Only now did he feel fear, a growing fear that despite
everything the priest was not there, that something had
happened, that he was lost in a crowd that was a quarter
of the population of Ireland.

But then he saw him, shockingly close, moving forward
with the chalice, along the line of kneeling figures towards
him, just as the passionate voice of John McCormack soared
up from the high altar, where he stood in the red and gold
and black velvet tunic of a Papal Count. 'Panis Angelicus.'
Bread of Angels. The bread of angels becomes the bread
of man. O miracle of miracles. The priest was too absorbed
in what he was doing, too full of the sanctity of the moment,
even to see anyone he served the host to; each kneeling
form, hands clasped in prayer, each tongue protruding to
take the bread of the angels. And it was almost as the priest
reached him that Vincent took the note from his pocket.
'I will wait for you after. I will wait for you. Vincent.' He
had written more at first, much more, over and over again,
but each time he had thrown the note away. There would
be time to say all that. And there would be ways to say it
without any words. He was shaking now as the priest stood

in front of him. 'O res mirabilis!' As the host left his lover's hand and rested on his tongue, Vincent pushed the tightly folded note at him. The man stared down. It was a look first of nothing more than broken concentration and surprise, but it was followed by confusion, and then fear.

The kneeling figure looked up at the priest with an expression of almost beatific devotion. The moment lasted only seconds, though for both men it seemed much longer. For Vincent it was as if the million people in the Park were no longer there. For the priest it felt as if a million pairs of eyes were looking into his soul, horrified by what was there. He moved on abruptly to offer the host to the next communicant. Vincent closed his eyes in a prayer of thanks. He had seen neither the confusion nor the fear on his lover's face. He hadn't seen the tightly folded note, screwed instantly into an even tighter ball, fall to the ground to be trodden underfoot, unread. And as the Mass ended and a million people went in peace, Vincent Walsh simply sat and watched them go – the people, the cars, the carriages, the politicians, the priests and the prelates. He watched until the stewards and soldiers and policemen were leaving too. He watched until long after he knew that his faith in that day was not going to be fulfilled, until long after all the hope that he had shared with a million people that day had drained away.

There was darkness in the sky now. The policeman had been eyeing him on and off for over an hour. He walked towards Vincent with a look of distaste.

'It's time you were away from here.'

'I was waiting for someone.'

'I don't see anyone left to wait for. You heard what I said. Off.'

'He still might –'

Vincent stopped. The world he had forgotten about since the early hours of that morning, looking down at the shimmering, moonlit waters of the Liffey, the world he really lived in, the world in which he was a permanent and unwanted stranger, was there in front of him again. Even those words, 'He still might –', said in the way he'd said them, were enough. This guard he had never seen before already knew him. The expression of contempt and disgust was palpable, already like a punch, like the real punches that had so often come with that look in the past. It wouldn't be the first time they had come from the police officers of the Garda Síochána.

'If you want the shite kicked out of you, there's a few of us would be happy enough. Are you up for that?'

Almost anything Vincent said would provoke a beating. He knew the look too well. There was a group of gardaí, smoking close by. They were watching him too. It was the same look. He got up and turned away, without another word. He walked back through the Park, back to the river, back along the Quays. Everywhere there were people. They still filled the streets, more and more of them as he got closer to the city centre, where the parades and processions had continued all afternoon. The whole place was full of people celebrating this day that had been like no other. But for Vincent Walsh it was a day like every day again; like every day had been for years.

\*

He walked into Carolan's Bar. He nodded in response to the greetings, but there was nothing behind the smile he

12

forced out of himself. He stepped in behind the bar. For a moment Billy Donnelly said nothing. Then he picked up a bottle of Bushmills and half-filled a tumbler. He thrust it into Vincent's hand. Billy didn't need an explanation. Hadn't he known the outcome?

'What else did you expect? I told you.'

'You're a fecking clairvoyant, Billy.'

Vincent put the glass to his lips. He didn't want it but he drank it.

'Jesus wept, Vinnie. If I'd a pound for every man here was fucked by a priest and never saw him again, I'd be the richest man in Ireland!'

'You don't know anything about him.'

'I've met his sort in every jacks in Dublin. We all have.'

'You're a gobshite.'

'I am and I wouldn't know an angel if he was up my arse. It's why I'll never get to heaven. Go on, forget about working tonight. Get off and see some of your pals. Or take the bottle upstairs and shout at the moon.'

'I'll be better doing something, even listening to a bollocks all night.'

Billy grinned. He reached for the Bushmills again and refilled the tumbler. Vincent drank it down in one. He'd the taste for it now. He turned back to the bar and grabbed one of the empty glasses thrusting towards him.

'Another pint if that's the sweet nothing's all over with now!'

'In the glass or will I pump it straight into your great, gaping gob?'

'If that's what's on offer I'll have the pint afterwards so.'

Vincent laughed with everyone else. The cramped bar at Carolan's smelt of stale beer and sweat and cheap

13

aftershave. Once in a blue moon Billy Donnelly decided the place had to be cleaned properly, and for the next week it smelt so strongly of Jeyes Fluid that when the smell of the stale beer, sweat and aftershave returned, it was like the breath of spring. Vincent looked around at the noisy crowd of regulars; the screeching queens with rouged cheeks; the swaggering boys always giggling too much; the big men with moustaches and muscles and paunches; the tweed-jacketed pipe smokers who jumped every time the door opened and kept their wedding rings in their pockets. It wasn't a place you could really say you belonged, but it was safe. It shut out a world where belonging was out of the question. The Guards knew what Carolan's was and most of the time they left it alone. But there was a price for that. They paid a visit now and again, just to drink Billy's whiskey and to remind him and his customers they were there on sufferance. And if the Guards wanted information, they got it. A sign behind the bar read: 'Don't say anything, Billy's a fucking unpaid informer'.

That night Vincent Walsh laughed a lot and kept on laughing. He kept on drinking and drank too much, and Billy Donnelly was happy to let him. There were a lot of bad things that could happen to a homosexual man. Falling in love came high on the list. The kind of love that didn't go away the next time you had sex was the worst. You had to train yourself not to care if you wanted to survive. And behind the laughter Billy could see that Vincent believed in something no one in Carolan's Bar had any right to believe in. Love was still burning in his eyes. It would be a long time before he let it go. Billy knew. He had been to the same place. Twenty years ago a doctor had pumped his stomach and saved his life. There were days when if he'd

14

met that eejit of a doctor again he'd have beaten the bastard senseless.

It hadn't been such a bad evening in the end. Carolan's was at its loud and irreverent best. The sound of laughter and the caramel-brown anaesthetic had numbed Vincent Walsh's head and put his heart in a box, at least till the morning. They worked hard at laughter in Carolan's. It was the language in which everyone spoke about everything; politics and the price of bread, sex and family squabbles, memories and dreams, religion and the litter in the streets, joy, sorrow, desire, bitterness, hope, resentment, love, hatred, grief; every ordinary pleasure and irritation that life delivered. Outside they spoke another language. And it was someone else's tongue. The last recalcitrants were pushed, cajoled and kicked out into the street. Vincent started to pick up pots. The silence was as sobering as the prospect of washing the stinking glasses and emptying out the filthy ashtrays. Billy bolted the door shut.

'We'll have the one we came for and let the glasses wash themselves. There won't be a saint in heaven lifting a finger with the day that's in it, so why the fecking hell should we?'

Vincent smiled at the comfortable predictability of the words. Every night of Billy Donnelly's life there was a reason why it was just the wrong time to wash the pots. He had no need of high days and holidays to put off till tomorrow what he was supposed to do today. It was often well into the next afternoon before what passed for clearing up in Carolan's got underway. If you really wanted a clean glass for a morning pint you were better off bringing your own. But as Billy went behind the bar to twist the cap off another bottle of Bushmills, Vincent carried on collecting glasses. Yes, at some point he would go upstairs to the room in the attic and force himself to go to sleep. Not yet. So Billy poured two more glasses, humming the tuneless tune to himself that always indicated no more conversation was required. Then there was a loud hammering on the front door. Billy sighed, walking across the bar with his most forbidding landlord's scowl.

'Now which old queen thinks we can't get enough of her company?'

He unbolted the door and pulled it open.

'Didn't I tell you to piss off –'

He stopped. A tall, thin man in his forties stood in the doorway, smiling amiably. He walked in without a word, followed by three others, a little younger. Under their coats and jackets they all wore the blue shirts that marked them out as members of the Army Comrades Association, demobbed Free State soldiers and assorted hangers-on, who thought they'd knocked the bollocks out of Éamon de Valera in the Civil War, only to see him president of Ireland now. The Blueshirts modelled themselves on the Blackshirts and Brownshirts of Mussolini and Hitler, at least as far as shirts were concerned. Their political agenda hadn't got any further than brawling with the IRA in the streets, but in the absence of IRA men to pick a fight with, and with drink taken, a bit of Blueshirt queer bashing wouldn't have been out of the question. Didn't they pride themselves on defending Ireland's Catholic values above everything else? But what struck Billy Donnelly immediately was that these Blueshirts weren't drunk, in fact they were coldly sober.

'Now, you wouldn't deny us a drink, Billy, not on a night when we should all be throwing our arms around each

16

other with the holiness of it all. And when it's starting to rain out there too.'

Billy didn't know these men, whatever about the familiarity. He glanced back as the last one shut the door and bolted it, smiling. Billy knew that smile; he was a big man who would enjoy what he was going to do.

The older Blueshirt walked across to the bar. He picked up one of the glasses of whiskey Billy had just poured out. He sauntered back towards Vincent. Two of the others went to the bar and started to help themselves to drinks as well. They wouldn't be sober long. The big man stayed put.

'And you're the bum boy. Vincent, is it?'

Vincent didn't move. He still held a tray of glasses in his hands.

'You've no business in here.' Billy's voice was firm. But he was puzzled. He didn't know why this was happening. If they'd been drunk it would have been easier. He could handle drunks, even queer-bashing drunks. Nine times out of ten they wanted a drink more than they wanted the pleasure of pulping some queers. The thin-faced Blueshirt turned his attention back to Billy. He moved closer to him, pushing him backwards.

'Were you at the Mass today, Billy?'

Billy said nothing. The man's easy, conversational tone wouldn't last. He knew that. He knew what was coming when the man stopped talking.

'I hear Vincent was. Did you pray for Billy, Vincent? Because the old bugger needs all the prayers he can get. "Quia peccavi nimis cogitatione verbo, et opere: mea culpa, mea culpa, mea maxima culpa." Right?' And with each 'mea culpa' he slammed his fist into Billy's chest, forcing him back against the door. 'Get down on your knees, Billy. Say some prayers.'

Billy was coughing. He was in pain. Vincent took a step towards him but the publican shook his head furiously, choking. The Blueshirt by the door walked over to him. He put both hands on his shoulders and pushed him down hard, till Billy had no choice but to bend his knees and kneel.

'If we put a white surplice on you, wouldn't we take you for an altar boy so, Billy boy?' The thin-faced Blueshirt smiled down at him.

'The Guards aren't going to like –'

'They turn a blind eye to you and your sodomite clan most of the time. That doesn't mean they wouldn't think someone had done Dublin a favour if you were floating in the Liffey tomorrow morning. Once in a while you need to be reminded what being a queer is about. Why not now?'

Billy knew, just like Vincent earlier, that there was no reply he could give that wouldn't provoke more violence. The older man turned to where Vincent still stood with the tray of glasses. He put down the glass of whiskey he was holding, very slowly and very deliberately. It was a simple act, but the very precision with which he placed the glass on the table was menacing.

'You defiled the Eucharist today. Did I hear it right?'

He stretched out his hand and held Vincent's wrist in a tight grip.

'Is that the hand?'

'I don't know what you're on about.'

'There was a time it would have been cut off for that. I'd do it now.'

Billy was struggling to get up off his knees, determined he would take the beating himself if there had to be one.

'Jesus and Mary, what is it you bastards want? Get out of here!'

The Blueshirt next to Billy slammed a fist into his stomach. He collapsed on to the floor. The man's foot came down hard on his chest.

The older Blueshirt still held Vincent's wrist.

'A grand day for blackmail was it then, Vincent?'

'I told you, I don't know what you're fucking gabbing about!'

Suddenly the man stopped smiling. He swung Vincent against the wall, knocking the tray of glasses out of his hands. They smashed all around him as he fell to the ground. The Blueshirt bent down and dragged him back up by the throat. Vincent was bleeding. There were cuts on his face, his hands, everywhere. Spots of blood were starting to show through his shirt.

'All I need is the letters.'

Vincent stared at him. He knew now. It made no sense, but he knew.

'Do you understand what I'm gabbing about now, bum boy?'

He let go his throat. Vincent leant against a table to get his breath.

'Give me the letters and we'll be gone. That's not so hard, is it?'

After a pause Vincent nodded. He straightened himself up. The Blueshirt smiled again. No, it wasn't hard. He picked up the glass of whiskey he had put down so deliberately and drank it, slowly, in one go.

'Amen!'

He turned back to Billy, still on the floor, clutching his stomach.

'And we'll have something for our trouble, Billy boy. Go on lads.'

19

The other three Blueshirts moved to the bar and started to take bottles of spirits from the shelves. They were going to clear them. The thin-faced man turned to Vincent again. He hadn't seen Vincent's hand tightening round the neck of a broken glass on the table beside him. Nobody had.

'Where are they?' demanded the man.

He didn't see the bottle coming either, as Vincent summoned every ounce of fear and force and love in his body and pushed the splintered glass into the Blueshirt's face. As the man cried out in pain, Vincent was already through the door that opened straight on to the stairs. The other Blueshirts, racing from behind the bar they were pillaging, were too late to stop the bolt on the inside of the staircase door shooting home. The older man was screaming now; he was momentarily blinded by the blood pouring down his face. The others wrenched at the door. It wouldn't take long to break through it. It was just about as rotten and rickety as everything else in Carolan's Bar.

Vincent Walsh was already at the top of the first flight of stairs. He didn't stop. He carried on running up the narrow, twisting staircase that led to the top of the house. He pushed open the door to the tiny room that was his home. An iron-framed bed, a lopsided chest of drawers with a drawer missing, a hat stand with a few clothes, a wash basin and a jug, a paraffin stove, a pile of second-hand books. There was no lock on the door but he slammed it shut behind him and pushed the chest of drawers a few feet across the room against it. He turned to the bed and reached under the mattress. He pulled out a small bundle of letters, four blue envelopes.

He looked at the letters for a moment, unsure what to

do, knowing he only had seconds to decide. He pushed them into his pocket. Then he climbed on to the bed. In the sloping roof above it was a small, square window. He pushed it open and pulled himself through, out on to the roof.

Thick cloud hung over the city and there was a steady drizzle now. The slates were wet underfoot; many of them were loose. But Carolan's Bar was tucked tightly into the side of a more substantial Georgian building. As Vincent scrambled and slid down the roof, his fall was broken by the parapet wall next door. He climbed over it, into the lead valley on the other side. He had been here before. He had lain in that wide valley on hot summer nights sometimes, when his room was too stifling to let him sleep. He heard the angry, vengeful Blueshirts as they burst into the room above, but in the seconds before one of them appeared at the window, Vincent had run along the lead valley to the back of the Georgian house. He had disappeared.

\*

It was raining heavily now. It had been for several hours. The city was silent. The day's celebrations had gone on long into the night and they had faded away, finally, with a reluctance that wasn't hard to understand. Tomorrow ordinary life would return. And the rain itself seemed to carry that message. Vincent Walsh was soaked to the skin. The cuts that covered his body had long since stopped bleeding and the bruises could have been worse. There were plenty of times they had been worse. But pain and fear didn't matter. What mattered was that he had saved the

21

letters. And in saving them he had saved the man he loved. Even if he never saw him again, even if the priest never knew about it, Vincent believed he had done something that made him worthy of the love he felt. This was the romantic notion that had grown in his head as he walked the streets of Dublin, pushing out the real world again, as it had been pushed out twenty-four hours before, walking along the Quays to the Park. Perhaps it was all his head could find to keep the truth out of his heart. He would have to leave Dublin, for a while at least, but he could come back when things had quietened down. There would always be a place to stay with Billy. He knew that. It didn't matter. One day, one day he would meet the priest again. One day he would be able to tell him everything.

There was almost a spring in Vincent's step as he turned the corner into the street that led through Smithfield Market to Red Cow Lane and Carolan's. He was still wary, but it was four hours since he'd scrambled down the pub roof and made his escape. There'd be no one there now, except for the publican. He was sure they wouldn't have hurt Billy; it was him they wanted. But he wasn't as sure as he'd like to be. He walked more quickly. Then, as he stepped out across the echoing emptiness of Smithfield, he stopped. There was a car ahead. He recognised it immediately. Finally he knew that everything that had happened since he had set off to walk through the night to the Phoenix Park had been right. The faith he had found had been real. It was the priest's car. He had come after all, after everything. Hadn't there been the great procession in O'Connell Street that evening? A grand reception at the Mansion House? He had come when he could. Vincent didn't move. He was smiling, smiling like an idiot. The car headlights blazed into his eyes. The engine started up. He was still smiling as he walked forward again. The car moved forward too, picking up speed. A puzzled frown was all that Vincent Walsh had time for as it came towards him, faster, louder. There wasn't even time for fear before it hit him.

The rain was much heavier now. He could feel it on his face. The pain that had blasted through his whole body as the car smashed into him was there, somewhere, but it was a long way away. It was a pain in a dream that didn't quite seem to belong to him. It was the rain on his cheek that he could feel most, running down to his lips, into his mouth. He didn't know that his own tears were there too, mixing with the rain. He didn't hear the car door open. He didn't hear the footsteps coming towards him across the cobbles. His eyes opened for only a second, level with the pool of water his face was lying in. No moon shone through the heavy clouds, but inches from his eyes the water shimmered in the headlamps of the car. He registered the golden ripples spreading over that oily, muddy puddle. He felt he was struggling to wake from a deep sleep and couldn't. All he could see was light, water and light. He didn't even register the figure that was crouching down beside him now, cutting off that golden light. He would never register anything again.

# 2. Merrion Square

*Dublin, December 1934*

The woman was obviously preoccupied. As she stepped off the pavement to cross from Kildare Street to the Shelbourne Hotel a horn blasted at her. She stepped back abruptly. A taxi, turning in from Stephen's Green at speed, swept past without slowing. A string of abusive words cannoned back at her in the broadest of Dublin accents. She smiled, pausing to catch her breath. Even those insults carried the flavour of a Dublin she had missed far more than she was ready to admit. She looked down Kildare Street and back to the Green. She crossed and walked on past the Shelbourne, her head up now, determination in her eyes. She was doing what she had to do. It wasn't easy, but she wasn't supposed to be afraid of things that weren't easy. She wasn't supposed to be afraid of anything. She stopped for a moment, by the entrance to the hotel, looking up. A man was leaning out of an upstairs window, where a flagpole carrying the Irish tricolour, green, white and orange, extended over the pavement. There was a second pole beside it and the man was unfurling another flag. She knew the colours even before it dropped down beside the tricolour; red, white and black, and at the centre the swastika. She glanced round, expecting other people to be surprised, but no one else had noticed. She walked on quickly. She had other things to do.

The woman was in her early twenties. She was tall. Her hair was almost black, flecked in places with red. There was a warmth about her dark skin that could almost be felt, as if it had known a fiercer sun than ever shone in Ireland, even on the best of summer days. It was a sun that certainly didn't shine on grey and soft December days like this one.

The purpose in her step was firm and unwavering as she walked along Merrion Row. She moved to avoid a crowd of winter-pale faces, bursting noisily out from a pub. She caught the breath of beer. It was another memory, almost comforting, but she wasn't here for comfort. She turned into Upper Merrion Street. It was quieter. The flat fronts of Georgian houses gave way to the pillared buildings of government at Leinster House. She saw the trees that marked out Merrion Square. What preoccupied her was the tall terraced house at number twenty-five, with the closed shutters and the green paint peeling from the door, and the big room at the end of the long unlit corridor where the man who smiled too much did his work. Briefly her pace slowed, but only briefly. There was no real fear in her about what she had to do. The fear was about the darkness that might lie on the other side of it.

'She's back, your dark-eyed acushla.'

It was the fat policeman who spoke, squeezed uncomfortably into the driver's seat of a black Austin 10, exhaling smoke from a Sweet Afton, the last of a packet of ten he had bought just before he'd parked the car two hours earlier. They were several hundred yards along from twenty-five

Merrion Square. Detective Sergeant Stefan Gillespie, sitting in the passenger seat, opened his eyes. He wasn't tired, but closing his eyes and feigning sleep was one way to stop Dessie MacMahon talking to him. He had already taken an hour of Dessie's problems with his innumerable in-laws; gougers and gurriers the lot of them, and all the worse in drink, which they were in a lot it seemed. But Detective Garda MacMahon was right. It was the same woman. They had watched her make the same journey yesterday. They had watched her pass the house at twenty-five Merrion Square twice before she made herself mount the steps and knock on Doctor Hugo Keller's door. They had watched her go inside, watched her emerge fifteen minutes later, and watched her hurry away again. They knew why she was back now.

'She was making the appointment yesterday. This'll be it I'd say.'

Dessie drew on his last cigarette one more time. Stefan nodded, his eyes fixed on the woman. She wasn't what he'd expected. Even yesterday she didn't seem to fit. That was the only way he could put it. There had been nervousness and uncertainty then. That made sense. Now she had her head high. It was more than grim determination though. It was in the way she held herself. As she paused for an instant at the bottom of the steps, she tossed her hair back, sweeping it off her face. There was nothing there that said shame. He could almost feel anger in that determination. There was something more too, something like pride. They were all words that didn't belong here, words she couldn't have any right to, doing what she was doing. And suddenly he found himself conscious of her as a woman, elegant, tense, beautiful. He hadn't really noticed it yesterday. He frowned. It was a squalid business and that was the end of it. He didn't like the intrusion of feelings that challenged that simple fact. The woman went inside the house and the green door closed behind her. The smell of sweat and smoke that came from Dessie swept over Stefan Gillespie again. There was a job to do and they needed to get on with it. As he turned, Dessie was grinning.

'Your woman's a looker. You wouldn't blame the feller who wanted to give her a go.'

It would have been an exaggeration to say that the fat policeman had read his sergeant's mind. It wasn't even close. But it was still a lot closer than Stefan was comfortable with.

'We'll give it a few minutes, Dessie.'

'I need a piss first.' Garda MacMahon opened the car door and squeezed out, dropping his cigarette end in the gutter with the other nine. He walked quickly through a gate into the square, in search of a concealing tree. Sergeant Gillespie got out of the car himself and took a welcome breath of air. He was taller than his colleague and thinner, quite a lot thinner, and where Dessie was balding he had a mop of thick, brown hair that was shapeless rather than long, as if he didn't remember to get it cut very often, which he didn't. He looked younger than his twenty-eight years and people often assumed he was the garda rather than the sergeant. He put on his hat. It was colder than he'd thought. He stood looking towards the house. The dark-skinned woman was making him uneasy. It wasn't a job he'd feel good about at the best of times, but it was more than that. He felt like getting back into the Austin and driving away. He pushed the thought from his mind. At least he wouldn't have to sit there all afternoon with

Dessie and his family rows and the smoke from another packet of Sweet Afton. Detective Garda MacMahon came back from the square, still buttoning up his fly.

The two policemen walked to the house. Stefan mounted the steps and rapped on the door. After a moment, he knocked again. It opened a crack. A middle-aged woman in spotless nurse's uniform looked out at him.

'Yes?' It was supposed to be a question, but as yesses go it meant something much more like 'no'.

'We'd like to speak to Mr Keller.' He took off his hat.

'He's not in just now.'

'We can wait.'

'He's not here. And he sees no one without an appointment.'

'Then I'd like to make an appointment. Now would be fine.'

Detective Sergeant Gillespie took his warrant card from his pocket and held it up. The woman's first instinct was to slam the door in his face, but Dessie MacMahon had anticipated her. With surprising speed for his size he moved forward, past his sergeant, and put a foot and a portion of his not inconsiderable torso against the fast-closing door. He applied his weight in the opposite direction to the nurse, pushing her and the door firmly back into the hall. He had slammed her against the wall quite hard, but even as the two policemen walked into the house she had recovered her breath sufficiently for her furious and now panicking voice to fill the echoing hallway.

'Hugo! Doctor Keller!'

'You think he might be back then?' said Dessie, grinning.

A door at the far end of the long hall opened. A small, rather avuncular man stood with the light behind him, peering through the thick lenses of his glasses as if he couldn't really make out who was there. But if there was concern beneath that puzzled look it was well hidden. There was already a half smile on his face, even as Detective Sergeant Gillespie started to walk towards him. He knew what the two men were. He had absorbed that information and accepted it. He was not a man who bothered about the inevitable. He didn't move as the detective approached him; instead his smile broadened. Stefan had only seen Keller at a distance before, going in and out of the house. He was always well dressed; today was no exception. Even though he was in shirtsleeves, the shirt was gleaming white; the yellow bow tie was perfectly tied; the braces had a floral pattern that was bright, almost loud, yet expensively tasteful; the suit trousers had knife-sharp creases; and his black shoes were spotlessly clean. By now Keller's benign smile was irritating the detective. It was altogether too pleasant to be anything other than extremely unpleasant. Wherever it came from the effect was to make him want to wipe the smile off the man's face with his fist. But even as that thought flashed through his mind he had an unsettling picture of Keller getting up from the floor and wiping the blood from his mouth, with the smile still there, broader and more unctuous than ever.

'Hugo Keller,' said Stefan flatly.

'Doctor Keller.' The German accent was stronger than he had expected. But he knew German accents. Austria, probably Vienna.

'It's Mr Keller I think.'

'My doctorate is from the University of Graz. You may not know it, but it's the second oldest university in Austria. Doctor Keller is correct.'

'In Wien hat jeder streunende Hund ein Doktorat, aber sie sind noch immer Hunde, nicht Ärzte, Herr Keller.' He stressed 'Herr'. It was true. In Vienna every dog in the streets had a doctorate in something. They were still dogs, not doctors. The smile wavered on Keller's lips. This wasn't quite the Dublin detective he had anticipated. Contempt might not be so wise.

'I am Detective Sergeant Gillespie. I will be conducting a search of your premises. I believe you have instruments here that have been used to procure miscarriages, contrary to Section 58 of the Offences against the Persons Act, and I believe you are, even now, engaged in procuring a miscarriage for a woman. You will be taken into custody, Mr Keller.'

'Naturally, Sergeant. I'll get my jacket.'

He turned back into the room. Stefan followed. He passed an open door on his right, a small office full of books and files. He paused, looking in, registering it. The nurse had composed herself now. She brushed back her hair and walked past him into the office. Unlike her employer the look on her face was familiar; it was fear. He watched her as she sat at the desk.

'Please don't try to leave,' he said quietly.

'Why should I?' Despite the fear, this was her territory.

He carried on into the back drawing room of the house. It was a startling change after the dark corridor, with its stained wallpaper and blackened ceiling. The room was bright and clean and looked as if it had been transported there directly from an expensive private clinic. But while Stefan took this in his attention was fixed on the dark-haired woman he had watched enter the house. She stood in the window, framed by the sunlight that had momentarily broken through the grey December clouds. It shone through her hair in a gauze-like haze. For a second the startling brightness made him blink. And then it was gone. She was looking straight at him. Now, more closely, he saw there was indeed neither fear nor shame in her dark eyes. There was anger, and it seemed to be directed at him.

'If you'd wait in the hall, Mr Keller.' He didn't look round.

'I'm sorry, my dear.' Keller smiled a slightly different smile at the woman. It was kinder and more reassuring than the one he had for Garda sergeants. He picked up his jacket from the back of a chair and pulled it on. 'I don't know if you heard any of that, outside in the hall. This gentleman is a policeman, a detective. My advice would be to say nothing, but that's entirely up to you of course. You need offer no explanation for why you are in this room, as he well knows.' He walked to the door. There was a mirror on the wall and he stopped to straighten his bow tie. Stefan Gillespie hardly noticed him go out. His eyes were still on the woman at the window.

'Can you tell me who you are, Miss?'

She shook her head, but only in irritable and frustrated disbelief.

'You couldn't have done this on another day, could you?'

He just looked. Nothing at all about this woman was right.

'How long has this man been doing this, procuring miscarriages, whatever it is you call it? How many years? It's just what I needed, you and your great policeman's boots stomping in before I'd even got started!'

'I need your name. I'm sure you know why I'm here.'

The woman gazed at him and shook her head again. All

at once the anger was gone. He saw something else in her eyes now. It was a mixture of contempt and suspicion. She looked at him as if he was the one in the wrong.

'No, I don't know why you're here. I think I'll reserve my judgement on that, Sergeant. In the meantime I shall take Mr Keller's advice about keeping my mouth shut. You may be his best friend. So I shall say nothing.'

*

Pearse Street Garda station was the main police station for the South City, built for the old Dublin Metropolitan Police in 1915, the year before Padraig Pearse was executed after the Easter Rising, when the road was still Great Brunswick Street. It took up the corner of Townsend Street, looking towards Trinity College, a grey, austere building that echoed the Scottish-castle style of architecture popular with insurance companies, all chiselled stone and mullioned windows. The DMP was only a memory now, except for two small corbels supporting the arch over the main entrance; the sour faces of a DMP officer and a helmeted constable still looked down in disapproval. As stations went it wasn't a bad place to work. The offices upstairs were brighter and cleaner than most of Dublin's Garda stations, but downstairs the cells smelt like they always smelt – of stale sweat and urine and tobacco.

Stefan Gillespie sat in a room on the ground floor, close enough to the stairs for the odour of the cells to hover in the air. A bare table separated him from the dark-haired woman. The room was bare too, lit by a naked bulb. There was a window high in one wall, no more than a foot square,

32

the glass painted over with the remains of what once must have been whitewash. She had still given him no information and no explanation. She denied nothing, admitted nothing, said nothing. He didn't even know her name. She returned his gaze with quiet self-assurance. He was the one who kept looking away to scribble something he didn't need to scribble on the sheet of white paper in front of him. She was beginning to make him feel she was the one running this.

'You're from Dublin, thereabouts anyway. The leafier parts I'd say.'

She didn't answer.

'You've clearly been out of the country though.'

'An accent and a suntan, I can see you're nobody's fool.'

She didn't need to smile to make him feel foolish.

'Do you realise how much trouble you're in?'

'As a matter of fact I don't.'

'I can see you're an intelligent woman. You're not what I expected.'

He knew those last words were another mistake.

'You were expecting some sort of idiot, were you?'

'That's not what I meant. '

'Idiot enough to be pregnant. Well, how idiotic can a woman get?'

'Sooner or later you're going to tell me who you are. You know that as well as I do. The only thing that can help you in this situation is to cooperate with us as fully as possible. It's Mr Keller we want, not you.'

'I'm sure even he knows you've got him. What do you need me for?'

She reached across to the packet of cigarettes on the table. They were Stefan's. She hesitated, looking at him. He shrugged. She took one and put it between her lips. He pulled the lighter out from his pocket and flicked it, then stretched over and lit the cigarette with what he hoped was an appropriately reassuring smile. But if he thought the woman's silence was about to end with this small act of human contact he was mistaken.

'Thank you.'

She drew on the cigarette, then shook her head.

'I can't do what I went there to do. And that's your fault. I'm not sure where that leaves me. Well, apart from being stuck here in a police station with you. That's all I've got suddenly. I want to see what happens next.'

'What happens? This is about a life, a life that would have ended this afternoon. It's about God knows how many other lives that have ended in that back room.' He was speaking the words he was supposed to speak now, but he knew they didn't sound like his own. He knew too that this clever, unfathomable woman would understand that immediately. And she did.

'Yes, it is about a life. I know that already. I wish I didn't.'

Stefan saw something else in the woman's face now. It was sadness, a deep and uncertain sadness. He also saw that it had nothing at all to do with why they were here. Whatever she was talking about it wasn't the conversation he had just felt obliged to start. The interview was still going nowhere. He was not controlling this. She was. The words 'stuck-up bitch' were in his head. He'd had enough. He got up, pushing the cigarettes at her.

'I'll leave you the fags. It'll be a long night.' He went. Let her stew.

As he left the room he found himself smiling unexpectedly. He remembered another time he had walked away from a conversation with a woman and thought the same thing – 'stuck-up bitch'. It was nearly six years ago. A pub in Nassau Street. Maeve. Seven months later he'd married her. And now she had been dead for nearly two years. One year, nine months, eight days. He had thought about that night in Nassau Street a thousand times in those months, waking and sleeping. He had relived it as he had relived every moment of their lives together. But he had never smiled about it in quite the same way before. It wasn't that the woman from Merrion Square reminded him of Maeve. Perhaps she reminded him of something about himself he had forgotten. Instead of feeling angry she made him want to laugh. These thoughts came at him out of nowhere. He pushed them away. He saw Dessie MacMahon walking towards him, with a bacon sandwich and a mug of tea.

'Has Keller phoned his solicitor?' he asked.

Dessie nodded, taking a bite of the sandwich.

'But he's still not saying anything?'

'No. He's very polite about it though.'

'Is the solicitor on his way?'

'He didn't say.'

'Stick him in a cell for the night and see how polite he is about that.'

Garda MacMahon took another bite of the sandwich.

'What about the nurse?' said Stefan.

'She's still giving out, but it's the same story. Nothing to say.'

'The evidence is all in Merrion Square. I don't understand how Keller thinks he can explain that away by keeping his mouth shut and grinning.'

'Do we give him another go, Sarge?'

'No, I've had enough. Just lock the three of them up for the night.'

He wasn't sure that would wipe away Hugo Keller's smile. It looked like it was painted on. He was too cocky. He seemed to think he was untouchable. The nurse would keep insisting that she was just a nurse. He didn't believe her, but Sheila Hogan was hard. She wouldn't talk till there was something in it for her. The dark-haired woman was different. She had no place in this. Twelve hours in a police cell might bring her to her senses.

It was dark in Merrion Square as Detective Sergeant Gillespie approached the house again, but it looked brighter now than it had in daylight. The shutters were open and all the lights were on. The front door was open too and a uniformed guard stood on the steps. Stefan smiled a greeting.

'How's it going, Liam?'

'Great, I can never get enough of standing around in the fecking cold.'

Stefan went in and moved down the hall to the back drawing room. A man in his late fifties was sitting on the edge of the couch, writing notes. Edward Wayland-Smith was the State Pathologist. He was tall, overweight, bearded, dressed in tweeds that made him look like he had just been blasting pheasants with a shotgun or pulling fish from a stream with a rod and flies. There was a silver-fresh salmon in the boot of his car to say he had been.

'He's certainly got some extraordinary equipment here. You wouldn't find better in any hospital in Ireland. Well, in most hospitals you'd be grateful to find anything at all.' He continued to write as he spoke, not looking up. 'Nota bene!' he announced, finally raising his eyes.

'Suspended from the ceiling a 170 centimetre shadowless operating lamp. You also see a state-of-the-art gynaecological chair; German, almost brand new I'd say, with some very clever modifications. There's a well-equipped workshop in the cellar too. It looks like your man Keller was making his own equipment, or at least improving on what he'd got. Ingenious, some of it. He must be rather bright, certainly not your average backstreet abortionist. There's also an X-ray transformer of very high quality. I haven't seen one like it in Ireland. It's a modification of another continental piece of apparatus. I've made a full inventory, which I will have typed up tomorrow. You have looked at the office I assume, Sergeant?'

Stefan nodded. 'I'd like you to make a note of the books.'

'It's done.' Wayland-Smith got up and walked out to the hall, turning back the pages of his notebook as he did. He went into the office. He stood beside a bookcase, scanning his notes, then pointing at some of the books.

'They are mostly standard medical texts, nothing out of the ordinary.'

'Except that Mr Keller was a quack posing as a doctor.'

'Well, I've encountered no shortage of highly qualified colleagues I'd describe as quacks posing as doctors. It's unfortunate that there seems to be no law against that. In several books you'll see sections on abortion and miscarriage have been marked and quite heavily annotated. I've recorded those. There are also a number of books dealing very explicitly with sex, in ways that might shock even a policeman, some in German that would not be readily available on our island of saints and scholars, and would normally be sent back whence they came with much sprinkling of holy water. It seems clear Mr Keller was handling a lot of what the profession likes to refer to, in a hushed whisper, as "women's complaints". Again it's not your run-of-the-mill abortionist. He certainly had no problems writing prescriptions that were acceptable in any chemist in Dublin. A Merrion Square address never fails to impress. There are very detailed financial records, almost proof in itself that the man is not a real doctor. Never any names though. All very discreet. And all very expensive from the look of it. He was certainly earning more than I do. Oh, and there's a revolver too. German, I think'

'It is. I've seen it,' replied Stefan.

'And a box of contraceptives, also German.' Wayland-Smith smiled.

'Yes, Dessie's recorded all that.'

'Splendid! You'll have the opportunity to prosecute the man simultaneously for the provision of contraceptives and for attempting to deal with the consequences of not using them in the first place. Good stuff, eh?'

'You don't like this very much.'

'I don't like the state asking me to count contraceptives for a living, no. But then I don't like what Mr Keller does very much either. Who does? However, as a doctor I have always found it gratifyingly simple that virtually all of my patients are dead. Nothing to like or dislike. And that brings me to an observation about the cellar. Have you been down there?'

Stefan shook his head.

'Dessie took a quick look. More medical equipment.'

'There is also an unusually large stove. I'm not an expert on plumbing, as several plumbers I've been fleeced by will testify, but a cursory glance suggests it isn't connected to the heating system. I would say the stove is more than adequate for disposing of whatever it was that Mr Keller may have found it necessary to dispose of in the course of his work.'

Sergeant Gillespie stepped into the black hole that was the stairway down to the cellar. He fumbled for a light switch. There was a dim glow over the stairs as he walked down into the darkness beneath the house. At the bottom of the stairs he found another switch. This illuminated the whole cellar more brightly. He saw a workbench and rows of carefully ordered tools, neatly stacked boxes of screws and bolts, coils of wire and electrical hardware, medical equipment in various states of repair. It was a place of strange calmness and order. Beyond the workbench, through a brick arch, was the cast-iron stove Wayland-Smith had seen. Stefan approached it through the arch. Coal was heaped up on one side, carefully stacked timber on the other. He could feel the heat from the stove now. He picked up a cloth that lay on the ground and opened the door, letting go of the handle sharply as the heat reached his hand. The stove was blazing fiercely, so much so that he had to step back. He turned, hearing someone on the stairs. Dessie MacMahon, flushed and sweating, was roaring down at a speed that was rarely seen.

'I don't know when I last saw you run. Confessions all round?'

The fat detective was still struggling to get his breath.

'I wouldn't want you risking your life for less,' laughed Stefan.

'They're gone.'

'Who's gone?'

'Two fellers from Special Branch walked into the station

half an hour ago, asking about Keller. Seán Óg Moran, you'd know him, an arse-licker who'd crack his mammy's skull if someone told him. And a sergeant called Lynch. I've maybe seen him, but I'd know the smell anyway. He'll have a trench coat in the car. Straight out of the IRA and into the Branch.'

'I know Jimmy Lynch. You're right. A flying column man. If there was a landowner to shoot he'd have sulked for a week if he didn't do it.'

'First thing I heard they were in with Inspector Donaldson and there's shouting and bollocking going on. But it's your man Lynch doing the bollocking. Next thing they're going out of the station with Keller and the nurse and the woman in tow. I asked them what they were doing. And I told this Lynch you weren't going to like it. He said you could fuck yourself.'

'A way with words too. But what the hell is it to Special Branch?'

'They took them off in a car.'

'What about Inspector Donaldson?'

'I don't know what your man Lynch told him, Sarge, but the words head and arse were in there somewhere. After that the inspector said the case was closed. Forget it. It's out of our hands. Then he went back in his office and shut the door. I'd say he'll still be in there with the holy water.'

'Did he ask for any paperwork?' Dessie shook his head. 'Course he didn't,' continued Stefan with a shrug. 'If Special Branch dumped a body on his desk and told him to have it in court on a drunk and disorderly the next morning he'd only stand up and salute. Did Hugo Keller say anything?'

'No, but I reckon the cute hoor looked happy enough.'

'And not exactly surprised. He never expected to stay locked up.'

The thought hadn't occurred to Dessie before, but Stefan was right.

'What about the woman?'

'She did say something, when she was going out the door. "I told Sergeant Gillespie I wanted to see what happened next." Are we the only ones not in on this, Sarge? The Branch? What the fuck is going on here?'

Stefan didn't know what the fuck was going on, but he'd find out.

Inspector James Donaldson was a small, precise man who wore thick-lensed glasses that made his eyes look disconcertingly bigger than they were. He disliked disorder. He also disliked detectives. Quite apart from the fact that they were rude, ill-disciplined, sloppy, generally drank too much, and had the ability to turn the word 'sir' into an insult, they were the ones who were guaranteed to bring disorder into his police station. They thrived on the chaos he hated. And there were times when Stefan Gillespie or Dessie MacMahon knocked on his door that he had to resist an overwhelming urge to turn the key in the lock and pretend he wasn't there. Normally Inspector Donaldson sought refuge from the disorder that went with being a policeman in his faith. He attended Mass every day at the Pro-Cathedral at eleven o'clock, and when he returned to Pearse Street Garda station, with the incense still in his nostrils, he had just enough spiritual calm to get him through the rest of the day. But the events of this particular day meant that he had little calm left. If it wasn't enough to have his own detectives treating him like an eejit he now had detectives walking in off the street, pulling criminals out of his cells and telling him, in front of his own men, that if he didn't like it he could stick his bald head up his arse. And they were from Special Branch too. Those fellers were a law unto themselves. They were supposed to protect the state from the people who wanted to destroy it. That was mostly the IRA of course, but these days you were hard pressed to tell whether a Special Branch man had worked with Michael Collins and his crowd bumping off British agents during the War of Independence, or with the anti-Treaty IRA bumping off Free State soldiers and policemen during the Civil War. What was guaranteed was that they'd done their share of bumping off somewhere along the line. They were thieves set to catch thieves after all. You didn't want to cross them. They did what they liked.

The raid on Hugo Keller's abortion clinic had been a rare thing at Pearse Street, an operation instigated by Inspector Donaldson himself. He was the one who had gathered the first intelligence. Well almost. The facts had been presented to him at a Knights of St Columbanus meeting, and as treasurer he had no choice but to act. It never occurred to him that there was a reason the so-called Doctor Keller could operate with apparent disregard for the laws of the land, among the real doctors and consultants in Merrion Square. A blind eye was being turned at a much higher level than James Donaldson. Now, for his pains, he had not only been humiliated by a Special Branch sergeant, his own CID sergeant was standing in front of him, berating him because Special Branch had just walked off with the prisoners.

'Why didn't you kick the bastards out?'

'I wasn't in a position to, Sergeant,' replied Donaldson defensively.

'We hadn't even put a case together. You were the one who pushed for this. You ordered the raid. Then you let Keller waltz out of here.'

'It's not in our hands any more. Special Branch will deal with it.'

'How is inducing miscarriages anything to do with Special Branch?'

'That's not my business. Or yours.'

'Keller knew.'

'What do you mean?'

'The expression on his face. When we walked into the surgery. When he sat in the cell and didn't say anything. When he phoned his solicitor. Who didn't bother to turn up. I'll bet he made the call to Special Branch though.'

'It's clear there are other issues here, Sergeant. Quite possibly issues of state security. We can't expect Special Branch to reveal that sort of thing.'

'That sort of thing my arse, sir.' There it was, that 'sir'.

'That's enough, Gillespie. I'm not happy about this either. They were extremely heavy handed. I don't like it any more than you do, but it's done.'

'And what about the woman?'

'They took her too. There's no more to say.' Donaldson wanted Gillespie to get out now. He had had enough. But Stefan wouldn't let go.

'I don't know what was up with that one. There was something. And it didn't have anything to do with being in Keller's clinic for an abortion.'

'I have no idea what you're talking about. Leave it alone!'

Stefan had no idea what he was talking about either. He was angry about what had happened for all sorts of reasons. Somewhere it wasn't much more than territorial. He'd been pissed on and he didn't like it. He knew how Special Branch detectives loved to throw their weight around. But why was he so wound up? It was Donaldson who had insisted on the raid. Now it was someone else's problem. What did it matter? It was the woman. She mattered. He didn't know why, but she was still there, still in his head.

The telephone on Inspector Donaldson's desk rang. He picked it up.

'What does she want? What? All right, I'll talk to her.' The inspector put on a smile as he waited a moment. 'Hello, Reverend Mother, how are –'

The cheerful greeting was cut off abruptly, and it was clear that what he was listening to was a tirade. He tried to speak several times but the words barely escaped from his mouth before they were cut off. 'She was here –' 'The case is no longer –' 'I gave no instructions –' 'I didn't know –'

Stefan turned away. It was probably the right time to make his exit.

'Stay here!' Donaldson hissed after him.

He stopped and turned back to the desk. The inspector glared.

'I'll send Detective Sergeant Gillespie across right now!' He slammed down the phone. It wasn't over yet. It was always the damned detectives.

'That was the Mother Superior at the Convent of the Good Shepherd. This woman, the one having the – the one at Merrion Square.' Abortion was not a word Donaldson found easy to say. 'Those bollockses from Special Branch dumped her over there. Now the Reverend Mother is blaming me for it. Well, why wouldn't she? The only name the woman knows is yours. So it all comes back here, straight back on to my desk as usual, Gillespie!'

'What did they take her there for?' said Stefan, puzzled.

'The woman's pregnant, isn't she? And I assume she's not married!'

'How do I know, she didn't even give us a name!'

'It doesn't matter. It's not our business any more.' Donaldson changed tack abruptly. He was about to give every good reason why the woman should have gone to the convent. Wasn't it where the police took women like that? 'I don't know what's wrong, but the Reverend Mother wants her out of the place. She's beside herself. And she thinks I'm responsible. You brought the woman in here, Sergeant. You go and sort this bloody mess out!'

# 3. Harold's Cross

The Convent of Our Lady of Charity of the Good Shepherd lay south of the Grand Canal in Harold's Cross Road, behind high walls. As Stefan Gillespie drove in through the black gates, two nuns closed and bolted them shut, then disappeared into the night. The house was Georgian. Once it stood in its own park; an avenue of fifty chestnut trees lined the drive. The park was gone now. The trees came down; roads and houses had spread out where the lawns and shrubberies had been; and when the nuns came, the walls went up. Low brick buildings, almost windowless, extended out from the old house to the back and sides now, shutting it in. But the great windows still filled the front, looking out over the cobbles to the gates. They were all dark now. The only light came from the front door where another nun waited for Stefan.

As he walked towards her, the small, neat woman looked at him accusingly. 'Reverend Mother is waiting for you.' She turned abruptly. He followed her in. His footsteps echoed loudly on the tiled floor of the dimly lit hall. What light there was came from two small table lamps. An elaborate glass chandelier hung from the high ceiling, but it carried neither candles nor bulbs; it was never used. An oak staircase led up from the centre of the hall to a galleried landing and darkness. Darkness and silence. There was a faint smell, not altogether unpleasant. It reminded Stefan unaccountably of one of his grandmothers. His eyes were drawn to the floor, polished so ferociously that it was the only part of the entrance hall that really reflected any light. It wasn't only praying that kept the women on their knees here.

The nun led him through a door behind the great staircase. Beneath her long skirts, reaching almost to the ground, he could see her black shoes, shining like the floor, oddly similar to a pair of regulation issue Garda boots. Yet while his footsteps filled the silence of the place, the nun made no sound at all. He smiled. If he hadn't seen those polished boots he would have been tempted to consider the possibility that she was on wheels. A long corridor stretched ahead, still only dimly lit. On either side were doors, evenly spaced, firmly closed, each one bearing a number in Roman numerals. The smell was stronger now, and more unpleasant. At the end of the corridor the nun took a key that hung from her robes, beside her rosary, and unlocked a heavy door that led outside. She held it for him as he walked through, back into the cold night, though it felt barely colder than the house they had left.

There was a courtyard with high wooden gates. Across the courtyard was a long, low, factory-like building. The windows were more brightly lit here and where they were open there was steam billowing out into the frosty air. Stefan could hear the sound of women, shouting and laughing. The nun quickened her pace and led him inside. They were in a laundry. Women of all ages were working, some barely in their teens, some in their twenties, others middle-aged and older. They all wore the same grey, smock-like dresses. They were washing, starching, wringing, hanging up clothes, ironing, folding, packing clean linen into wicker baskets. The smell that had seemed like a pleasant childhood memory in the convent's entrance hall was overwhelming now and almost made him retch. Soap, endless quantities of pungent, fatty soap, mixed with starch and steam and laundry water rank with the human body's odours. This was not a place many men saw the inside of, but he was a policeman. He knew who these women were. Unwed pregnancy was not on the statute books as a crime in the Free State but every one of them was serving a sentence. As for the babies they'd borne there, those that survived were long gone, sent away for adoption or to industrial schools, with no knowledge of where they came from. He had never been past the hallway of the convent before, but as a guard in uniform he had brought girls here often enough; sometimes from a courtroom, sometimes straight from a police cell, because there was nowhere else to take them.

As he followed the nun the length of the building, he was assailed by whistles and shouted propositions. Black-robed nuns appeared as if from nowhere to discipline the laughing women. By the time he reached the end of the laundry, order had been restored. The nun brought him into an office where the Mother Superior stood, fingering her rosary beads with a ferocity that had nothing whatso-ever to do with prayer. Two startlingly large sisters, who wouldn't have disgraced a rugby front row, stood shoulder to shoulder before a closed door on the far side of the room. Mother Eustacia looked at Detective Sergeant Gillespie with profound irritation.

'Are you responsible for this?'

'Responsible for what, Reverend Mother?'

'I see, you're a fool as well as an incompetent.'

'I understand there's been a mistake.'

'Yes, a mistake. You do know this woman isn't pregnant at all?'

He was thrown by this unlikely non-sequitur.

'The reason she was in custody –'

She cut him off.

'We haven't been able to examine her. We did try. I have a nun in the infirmary now as a result of the subsequent assault. However, she seems as aggressively confident about her condition in that respect as she does about everything else. I am, therefore, inclined to believe the woman.'

He was still puzzled. It didn't make much sense of soliciting a miscarriage from Hugo Keller, let alone getting arrested for doing it.

'Why did you bring her here, Sergeant?'

'I didn't bring her here, Reverend Mother.'

'I don't care which clown drove the car! She gave your name.'

'As far as I know she was brought to the convent by Special Branch. A Sergeant Lynch I think. Or maybe someone else. They've got so many incompetent fools there it's hard to pin them down. Women's welfare isn't their usual line of work, although they do specialise in dirty laundry.'

She looked at him, tightening her lips.

'You'll keep a civil tongue, Sergeant. Just get her out of here!'

'Did she tell you who she is?'

'Yes, Sergeant, she certainly did. And what she is!'

49

The Mother Superior offered no explanation and he could see that she wasn't about to enlighten him. She nodded at the two nuns who were standing guard in front of the closed door. One of them opened it. In the small, cell-like room beyond the woman from Keller's clinic sat on the edge of a table, smoking a cigarette. Her hair was dishevelled. Her clothes were torn in several places. She stood up and walked out into the office. Stefan could see that there was a bruise on her face. As she passed them the guardian nuns, despite their size, looked distinctly uncomfortable. It wasn't physical fear. It was as if her proximity threatened them in some almost spiritual sense. The woman smiled with the insolent confidence she had shown when he was trying to question her at Pearse Street Garda station.

'Do you know what she is?' said the Mother Superior darkly.

'What . . . she is?'

'A Jewess, Sergeant!'

Mother Eustacia spoke the word as if she was still struggling to believe it. Stefan was unsure what would be an appropriate reply. He was mildly surprised; simply because it was information he had no reason to know. He glanced from the Reverend Mother, who was staring at him with wide-eyed indignation, to the woman, who was smiling. She seemed to be enjoying this. The look in her eyes made him want to laugh.

'Well, in that case it's even more of a mistake, Reverend Mother.'

The woman moved closer to him, drawing on the cigarette.

'I'm glad they sent you, Sergeant. I didn't like the other two.'

'Did they do that?'

She wasn't sure what he meant. Then she glanced down at herself, realising what he was looking at. She laughed.

'Oh no, the sisters tried to give me a vaginal examination.'

The two big nuns gasped and then both crossed themselves. Stefan was startled, not so much by the words as by the matter-of-fact tone. Well, it was no more than a description of what had happened after all. But it wasn't how a woman should speak, not anywhere, let alone here. The Reverend Mother pinched her lips more tightly.

'You won't shock me, young lady. I've known too much of the foulness of the human heart to be shocked by anything you can say.'

'I'm sure. From what I've seen, you'll be quite the expert.'

Mother Eustacia processed ahead of Sergeant Gillespie and the woman, with the small nun on wheels beside her, back through the laundry. Work continued all around as they walked, but the eyes of every one of the grey-clad laundry workers followed the figure of the woman. Her hair was still a mess; her clothes were torn; her face was bruised. But she walked with her head upright, her dark skin still somehow reflecting the warmth of a sun that would never find its way in through these windows. As they approached the door to the courtyard the small nun who had brought Stefan in scurried ahead to unlock it. The Reverend Mother turned to the woman. Her anger and indignation were undiminished. The very way this woman carried herself was another insult. But there was one weapon Mother Eustacia had left that would put her firmly where she belonged. She fixed her eyes on the

51

woman, and with a look of almost infinite compassion she prayed for her.

'Almighty and eternal God, who dost not exclude from thy mercy even Jewish faithlessness, hear our prayers, which we offer for the blindness of that people; that acknowledging the light of thy Truth, Christ, they may be delivered from their darkness.'

'I'm afraid I prefer my darkness to your light.' The woman looked back at the laundry, at the pasty-faced girls and women, still working, but all watching her so intently. 'You evil old bitch.'

Mother Eustacia slapped the woman hard across her face, with all the irritation, anger and humiliation she had felt welling up within her. But the woman barely blinked. She laughed as if the Mother Superior had just handed her a victory she hadn't realised she even wanted. And there wasn't a split second between that laugh and the sound of her hand striking the Reverend Mother's face in return, quite as hard and quite as full of anger. There was complete silence in the laundry. No one spoke. Work had stopped. Every eye in the laundry was on Mother Eustacia, though the Reverend Mother seemed unaware of anyone else now. In her long years as the mother of this convent she had slapped many, many women, but no one had ever dared to hit her back. She turned slowly towards Stefan.

'What are you going to do, Sergeant?'

'I'm going to do what you told me, Reverend Mother. I'm going to get her out of here. As requested. For the rest, I think I'd call it quits.'

He grabbed the woman's arm and pulled her away. The nun on wheels was holding the door to the courtyard open, bog-eyed and fearful as she still stared at her Mother

Superior. No one else moved. Then there was a sound. It was a clap. It was followed by another clap, and then another. Then there were more. The sound of slow clapping, from every girl and woman in the laundry, filled the building. The nuns turned back to their charges, shouting at them to stop. But they kept on. The Reverend Mother walked slowly back towards the office, as if she didn't hear the noise at all. The women's clapping grew even louder now. They would suffer for it, of course; but it would be worth it. Nothing would erase this moment.

As Stefan drove out of the convent and the high gates closed behind them, the woman brushed her hair back from her face. She looked at him, smiling, as if this sort of thing happened every day.

'So, am I under arrest?'

'I don't think so.'

'I'm glad you know what you're doing.'

'What I want to know is what you're doing.'

'I'm not sure any more. I thought –'

She stopped. For the first time he felt her mask slipping.

'Do you know what happened to Hugo Keller?' asked Stefan.

'You mean you don't know?' She sounded surprised.

'No.'

'Those nice guards were going back to Merrion Square with him.'

'Did they say that?'

'He did. He was the one giving the instructions.'

Stefan drove on. Dessie always said that when things didn't make sense, sometimes it was better left that way. It smelt like one of those times.

'So where are you taking me now, Sergeant?'

'I need a drink. You too. It's not every day you're beaten up by nuns.'

He expected her to bounce back a sarcastic remark; she had before. But she said nothing. She looked straight ahead through the windscreen. Then she put her hands to her face and sobbed, in almost complete silence.

*

*Saturday. Dear Tom, Today I've been busy doing so many things I'm not sure what they all were. Some days are like that. But Christmas is coming, that's the main thing. There's the biggest Christmas tree you ever saw in O'Connell Street. They were there putting the lights and the decorations on. It'll be something to see I'd say. The windows in Clery's are full of toys. And boys from St Patrick's were singing carols in Grafton Street. Tell your grandfather. The day you come up with Opa and Oma we'll go and see it all. I hope the new calf's getting better. Don't worry about her. It's no more than a bit of scour, and she'll be tearing about again in no time.*

Stefan put his pen down and looked up to see the woman watching him. He hadn't seen her come into the bar. He had driven her back to her home in Rathgar so that she could repair some of the day's damage. Now he was waiting in Grace's, a pub close by. It sat at a busy road junction, south of the Grand Canal that marked the boundary between Dublin's inner and outer suburbs, between streets where nothing ever grew and avenues wide enough for trees. The avenues of red-brick Victorian terraces fanned out all around Grace's Corner, quiet and tidy, substantial and well-ordered. There was space here, and there was air, and on clear days, looking to the south and east, the round tops of the Dublin Mountains rose up in a ring, not far away.

The woman smiled. She was herself again. But make-up hadn't quite covered the bruise on her cheek from the struggle in the convent.

'You look a long way away.' She sat down opposite him. There was a glass of light ale waiting for her. She picked it up and drank, still watching.

'Not that far really, just West Wicklow. I was writing to my son.'

'Oh.'

'Oh?'

'I suppose that's not what I was expecting from a policeman.'

'Having children?'

'No, I meant –' She laughed. 'All right it was a silly thing to say.'

He folded the piece of paper in half and put it in his pocket.

'How old is he?'

'Four, nearly five. I'm up here and he's down the country with his grandparents. I try to write something for them to read him most days. It doesn't amount to much. Still, it makes me look for something in a day that's worth saying to a child. It's not always that easy to find.'

'No. There won't have been much today.' She smiled, but behind it he could see the thing he couldn't get hold of about her. Was it sadness, loss?

'How often do you see him?'

'I get down every Sunday I'm not working. It's the best I can do.'

She wanted to ask more. She wondered why his son didn't seem to have a mother. At that moment it felt as if they were two people who'd just met, sitting in a pub, starting to ask questions about each other. He wasn't much older than she was. It felt ordinary in a way that nothing had for a long time. The pub felt ordinary too, in a way that she found reassuring. It was nearly two years since she had sat in Grace's Lounge with the friends she grew up with, saying goodbye to them. The dark mahogany shone as it had always shone, so did the brass. There was the sound of familiar laughter, the smell of beer and cigarette smoke and furniture polish. The same watercolours of the same racehorses lined the walls; the same prints of the Curragh and Leopardstown, Fairyhouse and Punchestown. She wanted everything else to be the same, everything that couldn't be. The feeling caught her unawares. And the guard sitting opposite her was unaccountably part of it. She didn't know why he was so easy to talk to. But it didn't matter how easy or how hard the conversation was. That wasn't why she was there.

'You look better now anyway,' he smiled.

'Hannah Rosen. That's my name.'

'I'm glad you've got one, but it doesn't tell me much. It doesn't tell me why you wouldn't say who you were before. It doesn't tell me why you solicited a miscarriage when you're not pregnant. Or why you and Herr Keller were carted off by Special Branch, with him giving them orders. It doesn't tell me why I don't know anything about any of this, and you do.'

'I don't know much, really. I'm trying to work backwards.'

'I'm a simple soul, Miss Rosen. Why not start at the beginning?'

She looked at him, hesitant, still not quite sure she could trust him.

'Whatever it is you wanted from Keller, you didn't get it, did you?'

She shook her head, watching him before she continued.

'I've been away from Ireland for quite a long time. It's almost a year and a half. In Palestine, I live there now. I'm probably going to stay there.'

The last words were spoken more reflectively. They weren't for him at all. Clearly Palestine wasn't a simple issue for her. But whatever issue it was it couldn't have much to do with Hugo Keller and the Garda Special Branch.

'I came back to Ireland for a reason. I came home because –' She had made her decision now. She liked him. She would trust him. 'My friend, my oldest friend, Susan Field is – missing. She's disappeared. She's been gone for over five months. No one's heard from her. No one knows where she is.' She paused. Stefan just nodded, but didn't say anything. She went on.

'Susan and I have been friends since we were children. We grew up together in Little Jerusalem, in Lennox Street. We went to school together. We did everything together once. And all the time I've been in Palestine we've written to each other. A lot – I mean every few weeks. Her letters stopped coming at the end of July. I didn't think there was anything wrong at first. I knew there was something, well, a problem – we still told each other everything. I thought that must have affected her. I thought she might not want to talk about it for a while. But somewhere I knew that wasn't true. She would have written. There would have been even more reason to write if she was in trouble, not less. And then I got the letter from Susan's father.'

Before she had been holding his gaze as she spoke, but now she was looking away from him. She was trying not to show how painful this was.

'He said she'd disappeared. She'd been missing for almost six weeks then. None of her friends knew anything. The Guards couldn't find any trace of her. They were still searching. He had to tell me – and he had to ask me –'

She met his eyes again now.

'He had to ask me if I knew anything. I told him. But it didn't make any difference. It was as if Susan had just walked out one morning and vanished off the face of the earth. The Guards, well, after all the weeks of looking for her, or supposedly looking for her, all they could come up with was that she'd taken the boat to England, and simply run away.'

'Is that what Mr Field thinks?'

'I don't know. I think now he's . . . almost forced himself to believe that. If he doesn't, then what does he believe? She was twenty-three, Mr Gillespie. She was bright and full of life and independent and utterly bloody-minded. The idea that Susan would ever run away from anything is mad.'

'You said there was a problem. What was it?'

'Susan was a student at UCD. She was always very clever. But however clever you are you can get yourself into stupid situations. She had been having an affair with a man at the university. He was a lecturer. It started last year. She went into it with her eyes open. She made a choice.'

'He was married?'

'No, he was a priest.'

'So that was the problem . . .'

'It was one problem.'

'Just tell me about it, Miss Rosen.' He could see she needed to talk.

'Well, I suppose . . . it was all very exhilarating at first. Susan needed that. She was always searching for excitement,' Hannah smiled fondly. 'But after a while it started to feel . . . claustrophobic. They couldn't go anywhere. They couldn't be seen together. And then she realised she was pregnant . . .'

'That's where Mr Keller comes in?'

She looked at him, trying to gauge his response, then she nodded.

'Who else knew she was pregnant?' he asked.

'The priest. I don't know . . .'

'What about her parents?'

'Her mother died five years ago. I'm sure she'd have talked to her if she'd been alive. Mrs Field was the heart of that family. Maybe too much. Susan always said she took the heart with her when she went.' Hannah stopped, thinking about the past as much as the present. 'Her father's never been the same. I suppose he's turned in on himself. He's the cantor at the Adelaide Road Synagogue now. That's his life, all his life. She couldn't tell him. And her sisters are married. They've left Ireland. Things change, don't they? It's funny, I was always jealous of how close they all were.'

Stefan let her find her way back to the present before he continued. 'A boat to England's a common solution. It happens every day.'

'Not Susan. And there was already a solution, wasn't there?'

'She'd made arrangements with Keller?'

'It was the priest who knew about him. He did the arranging.'

Stefan couldn't hide his look of surprise. It seemed to irritate her.

'I didn't mean to shock you, Sergeant.'

'Shock would be overstating it, Miss Rosen.' He smiled wryly.

'Anyway, he knew where to go. He told her it was a proper clinic too, with a proper doctor. And he was going to pay for it all, she said.'

'A gentleman as well as a scholar. It's not what you'd expect.'

'I don't know. How do priests usually deal with these things?'

'I don't know either, Miss Rosen. I'm very rarely on my knees.'

'That's reassuring at least.'

'So Susan wrote to you about the abortion?'

'I had one letter telling me it was happening. Then she wrote to me again, the day before she went to the clinic. That was at the end of July. She was going on the twenty-sixth. I didn't know it when I got that letter of course, but she disappeared the day after she sent it. And that's all there is. No one knows where she went. No one's seen her since.'

Stefan took this in.

'Did she seem distressed about what was happening?'

'I don't think so. And I'd have known, even if she'd been putting on a brave face. It was something she had to do. She wasn't jumping for joy, Sergeant, but I'd say the strongest feeling she had – was about drawing a line under it.'

Hannah dropped her head as she had done before, when she felt she was talking about Susan's feelings in a way that didn't quite fit a conversation with a policeman. Her hair fell forward each time and she brushed it out of her eyes, looking back up at Stefan with a slightly awkward combination of forthrightness and reserve. And each time, as their eyes met again, he was conscious that she was trusting him with her feelings as well as the facts. He somehow knew she didn't do that easily. It happened of course, when people had no one else to talk to, when they'd bottled things up inside that they couldn't tell anyone. As a policeman you relied on that sometimes. But this was different. At least he wanted it to be different. The sound of conversation and laughter all around him in Grace's had faded away completely. Hannah spoke softly, but by now her words were all he heard. And he was conscious that he didn't want her to stop talking to him.

'So, do you think this abortion happened?'

'Why wouldn't it? She said she was going the next day.'

'Isn't it something she might have changed her mind about suddenly?'

She shook her head.

Stefan decided to take that at face value for the time being.

'What did she tell you about Hugo Keller?'

'She just knew what he did and that he did it in Merrion Square.'

'And the priest set it all up?'

'I told you. He was paying for it.'

'So who is this priest?'

'I don't know. I haven't found him yet.'

61

He took note of the determination in those words; she would find him.

'So your friend, who told you everything, didn't tell you his name?'

'When it started she almost liked the cloak and dagger element. It was as if she was breaking all the rules at once.' There was the hint of a smile again, as Hannah thought about the friend she knew so well. Then she shrugged. 'And she had a genuine desire to protect him. She was in love with him. She wanted to protect herself too.' Hannah laughed. 'Susan liked breaking the rules but she hated getting caught. She wouldn't have called herself a practising Jew, but the idea of what people would say – an affair, with a goy, who was a Roman Catholic priest.' She stopped. She wanted to keep laughing about her friend's foibles, but all of a sudden it felt like another way of hiding her fear. Even what she was saying didn't seem so funny now. 'It wouldn't have been nice. We Jews may have been the victims of everyone else's prejudice, but we can find plenty of our own, Sergeant.'

'When you contacted Mr Field, what did you tell him?'

'I told him what she'd said in her letters.'

'The affair, the abortion, the priest?'

'Yes.'

'And he passed the information on to the Guards?'

She nodded, slowly.

'That couldn't have been easy for him.'

'I talked to him last week when I got home. He didn't want to see me really.' She paused. 'I don't know which was worse, his daughter disappearing, or what he found out about her afterwards, from me.'

'Isn't that a bit harsh?'

'Why shouldn't it be?'

'All right, so what happened?'

'The Guards didn't come back to him for weeks. He went to Rathmines every day, and every day they said they'd be in touch when they had any information. Only there never was any. In the end they told him they had no reason to suspect foul play. Do you have a manual for those phrases? Anyway, it was the same story as before, there was only one conclusion. Susan couldn't face him after what had happened. She did what that sort of girl does. She got the boat to England. But they did think, sooner or later, she'd contact him. That sort of girl usually does – eventually.'

'Did they talk to the priest? Did they talk to Keller?'

'No. The priest was a figment of her imagination, or just a lie. The man must have been married and she made up the priest because she couldn't deal with the shame. A Jewish woman wouldn't understand what the vow of celibacy really meant, and how unlikely an affair with a priest was, you see. As for abortions, the inspector said Mr Field could rest assured such things didn't happen in Ireland. That was, sadly, why some women, now what was it again, oh yes, why some women took the boat to England.'

Stefan made no attempt to explain away what had happened. He couldn't. He didn't want the contempt in Hannah's voice directed at him.

'What were you going to ask Mr Keller?'

'If my friend had arrived for her abortion, what happened then, oh, and who the priest was who paid for it all. That would have been a start.'

'And do you imagine he'd have told you?'

'I don't know. That's when you walked in.'

'I don't think your conversation with Keller would have lasted long.'

'Why not? I'd just paid him for an abortion. I would have been happy to say that very loudly and very publicly. All I needed was information.'

'The events of this evening make it clear Mr Keller isn't without friends. He's also a criminal who keeps a revolver in his desk drawer.'

'I hadn't thought about him shooting me. Perhaps I should have.' She was laughing at him. It didn't seem there was much she was afraid of.

'So you've got a man, the priest. An appointment for a miscarriage. Let's assume she went. You don't think he'd have gone with her?'

'They'd stopped seeing each other. She didn't say he was going.'

'Then there's Keller, who's unlikely to tell anybody anything. And Susan, who no one's seen since July. It's hard to know what it really says.'

'I think I know.' She held his gaze, unwavering now.

'What's that?'

'It says Susan's dead.'

He didn't answer. Instead he reached across the table and took Hannah's hand. She nodded. It was answer enough. She had known for a long time now, however much she had tried to persuade herself it couldn't be true. Even as she spoke the words she still hoped Stefan would tell her she was wrong. And it would have been easy for him to. It was what he was meant to do as a detective, at least till there was evidence to prove otherwise. And there was no evidence at all, of anything. Not that anyone had really looked for any yet. But he had a sense of where looking was going to lead already. It was the total absence of facts that made pushing aside Hannah Rosen's simple statement hard. Hannah knew her friend. It wasn't a fact but it was as close to one as made no difference. He couldn't tell her he didn't understand what Susan Field's silence was. It was the silence of the grave.

# 4. Stephen's Green

The lights were still on in the house at twenty-five Merrion Square. It was almost ten o'clock. The uniformed officer Stefan Gillespie had left there was still on the steps. Garda Liam Dwyer had the collar of his coat turned up, his cap pulled down. Smoke hovered in front of his face. He was cold and hungry and pissed off. He should have ended his shift three hours ago.

'I can't let you go in, Sarge, sorry.'

'Who says?'

'Sergeant Lynch. It's a Special Branch operation now.'

'A serious business then, Liam. Is he inside?'

'They've gone for a pint.'

'I can see why they would. It's thirsty work keeping the nation safe.'

'No one goes in. That's Sergeant Lynch's orders.'

'So what's Jimmy Lynch up to in there?'

'How do I know? I'm out here.'

'There's no fooling him, is there, Dessie?'

'He's got Special Branch orders, he needs to be on his toes, Sarge.'

'You can piss off, Dessie. I've been here since this afternoon.'

66

'Maybe they'll bring you back a bottle of stout,' laughed Dessie.

'I hope you're not thinking about putting in for any overtime from Inspector Donaldson when you get back to Pearse Street.' Stefan shook his head with a look of mock concern. 'He's not happy about those two at all, especially Detective Sergeant Lynch. I'd say he had the holy water out when they left the station, and maybe the bell, book and candle. Will we go back and tell him you're taking your orders from Special Branch now, Liam?

Garda Dwyer felt that a little more cooperation would be no bad thing.

'They've been looking for something, Sarge,' he said quietly.

'Jimmy and Seán Óg?'

'And the German feller. They were turning the place inside out.'

'You know what they were looking for?'

'I can't see through the front door, not being a detective.'

Stefan smiled, but ignored the sarcasm.

'Where's Keller now?' he snapped.

'He went with them, Sarge. Not to the pub though.'

Stefan could see he knew where Hugo Keller was.

Dwyer smiled. 'Any fags? I'm on my last one.'

'I'm sure Dessie's got some, Liam,' replied Stefan.

Begrudgingly Dessie MacMahon pulled twenty Sweet Afton from his pocket. As he opened the packet, Stefan took it and handed it to Dwyer.

'Hey, I've only just bought those!'

Liam Dwyer lit a cigarette from the stub in his mouth. He put the packet of Sweet Afton into his pocket and dropped the stub to the ground.

'You're not the gouger they crack you up to be, Dessie.'

'So Keller's not with Lynch?' Stefan returned to the matter in hand.

'He was off to the Shelbourne for a drink. There's a Christmas party on, every German in Dublin. Jimmy Lynch said they'd see him back here.'

'Well, it's a pity we didn't know there was a party. I'm sure the inspector would have told us to back off on the raid if someone had said. But they're always the lads for a bit of Christmas spirit in Special Branch.'

'How much longer do I stand here, Sarge? Can't someone take over?'

Stefan laughed. 'You'll have to ask Sergeant Lynch that, Liam.'

The Shelbourne Hotel was warm and welcoming. Two flags still flew over the brightly lit entrance, looking out on to Stephen's Green – the Nazi swastika and the Irish tricolour. As Detective Sergeant Gillespie and Garda MacMahon entered the frayed-at-the-edges splendour of the Shelbourne lobby the top-hatted doorman smiled. He also gave a quick, warning glance to the porter at his desk. He knew who they were. Detectives didn't just call in there for a drink. The porter emerged from behind the desk with the same barely disguised combination of welcome and wariness.

'Anything I can help you with, Mr Gillespie?'

'There will be, Anto. When I've worked out what it is I'll tell you.'

They walked towards the doors that opened into the dining room, which had been taken over for the evening by the German Christmas party. Stefan stopped and peered into the room. It was festooned with red and white and black swastika flags and red and white Christmas decorations. Inside there was a buzz of loud and cheerful German conversation. Men, women and children filled the tables and milled around amidst the debris of an almost completed meal. Just then a loud 'Ho, ho, ho!' boomed across the lobby. As Stefan and Dessie turned, they saw a fat, bearded figure in red, with a bulging sack over his shoulder, heading towards the dining room and the party. He was accompanied by a middle-aged elf in green and gold and a Brunhilde-like maiden, flaxen plaits and all, in German peasant costume. They also carried sacks of presents. The two detectives stepped back. Santa Claus and his companions burst into the dining room to the sound of applause. Children clustered round Santy as he fought his way through the crowd. Stefan turned to the porter, still hovering a little way behind them.

'Hugo Keller, do you know him?'

'Mr Keller, of course.'

'Is he in there? I can't see him.'

'He'll be in the bar. He was just now.'

They moved on towards the Horseshoe Bar.

'It's hardly likely Keller isn't going to notice us,' remarked Dessie.

'I'd say you're right.'

'But aren't we meant to be leaving him alone? Inspector Donaldson said the case is dead. And didn't Lynch tell us to keep our noses out of it?'

'Which case is that?'

'What do you mean which case is that?'

'This is about a missing woman. Susan Field. Twenty-three. Student at UCD. Lived in Little Jerusalem. Sixteen Lennox Street. She disappeared five months ago. We're trying to trace her last known movements and find out who was the last person to see her. It's a cold trail though. It's bound to be after all this time. I've got a hunch Herr Keller might be able to help us.'

'And where did all that come from?'

'Hannah Rosen. She's a friend of Susan Field's.'

'The woman –'

'The woman we arrested at Keller's house, the one who wasn't having an abortion after all, and the one DS Lynch dumped on Mother Eustacia.'

'It doesn't sound much like leaving Keller alone.'

'But this is a different inquiry altogether. We only want some help.'

'What's this missing woman got to do with Special Branch?' Dessie didn't like the sound of it. When Stefan started following his nose you never got much sense of where it would lead. But experience had taught the guard that it usually meant trouble. There didn't seem any doubt about that here.

'Nothing I should think. We don't want to tread on those fellers' toes.'

As they pushed their way into the small bar it was packed. People were spilling out into the hallway. Inside much of the conversation was in German, loud and enthusiastic and fuelled by large quantities of highly proofed Christmas cheer. The detectives squeezed through to the bar, Stefan apologising in festive German. Dessie caught the barman's eye.

'A hot whiskey.'

'That'll be two!' called Stefan.

The barman poured two whiskeys and topped them up with hot water from the kettle. Stefan was trying to locate

70

Keller. Dessie took the drinks and moved his hand towards the wallet in his jacket pocket. It was a gesture. He didn't intend to pay and the barman didn't expect him to. He simply waved his hand. It was on the house. It always was. Stefan pushed his way through the noisy crowd again, exchanging more Christmas greetings in German as he went. Then he stopped, close to a corner table where Hugo Keller sat with two other people. There was a sharp-featured, middle-aged man with balding, close-cropped hair and thick-rimmed circular glasses, and a younger man, with a shock of dark hair, wearing a brown suit that bore a small swastika emblem on one lapel. The two older men were arguing. It wasn't comfortable and it certainly wasn't festive. But they spoke quietly and it was impossible for Stefan to pick up even a few of the words. The younger man sat back, smoking a Turkish cigarette, with an expression of impatience. Keller became aware someone was watching him. He looked up.

Hugo Keller was surprised, but it was only seconds before the same look of supercilious self-confidence he had shown when he was arrested reappeared. The other two looked at Sergeant Gillespie too. They had no idea who he was. Keller fired some kind of explanation, unheard over the melee. The older man in glasses looked even more ill-tempered. He was distinctly put out by the explanation. The three got up abruptly. Stefan smiled at the abortionist and raised his glass. 'Fröhliche Weihnachten!' The Christmas greeting spread through the bar, until even the three men trying to leave were forced to respond to the people around them wishing them a Merry Christmas. Hugo Keller was only a few feet from Stefan, who was still irritated by the smirk of invulnerability that hung about his smile. 'Did you find what you were looking for, Herr Doktor Keller?' He stressed 'Doktor'. The smirk disappeared. Stefan had thrown these words out on a whim, but he had got something back. Whatever was being searched for at twenty-five Merrion Square, it hadn't been found. Then Keller was gone. The detectives downed the whiskeys and pushed their way back through the crowd to the hotel lobby. As they extricated themselves at last from the bar, the three Germans were ahead of them, just turning into the dining room.

People were stepping aside for Father Christmas and his entourage, now emerging from the party, their task completed. Chriskindl continued to call out 'Ho, Ho, Ho,' and 'Herzliche Weihnachtsgrüsse!' He reached into his pocket and handed small Nazi lapel pins to anyone sitting in the hotel lobby or passing through it. He grabbed Stefan's reluctant hand and thrust one into it. The policemen carried on to the doors that opened into the party. All around children were playing with their gifts from Santy, at the tables, on the floor. Several of them ran out into the lobby chasing a boy who held a model fighter plane over his head, all making rat-tat-tat machine gun noises.

In the restaurant, waiters were ladling out mulled wine. Someone started playing the piano. After only a few notes an abrupt and almost complete silence descended on the noisy gathering. A boy of nine or ten was lifted up on to one of the tables. He started to sing. As he did, everyone in the room who wasn't already standing, rose. Detective Sergeant Gillespie was one of the few people – besides the partygoers – who understood the words. They had nothing to do with Christmas, but after some of the day's events they made him feel very uncomfortable. 'Deutschland erwache aus deinem bösen Traum! Gib fremden Juden in

72

deinem Reich nicht Raum!' Germany wake from this fearful dream. Give Jews no room to live and scheme. Germany arise, our battle cry. Our Aryan blood shall never die! There were tears in watching German eyes. Even Dessie MacMahon, who understood not a single word, was captivated by the boy's perfect voice.

'Let's go, Dessie,' said Stefan abruptly.

As they turned, he beckoned the porter over. He looked back into the room once more, pointing to where the two men who had been with Keller stood, watching the boy as he sang, with the same rapture as everyone else. There was no sign of Keller now. He didn't seem to be there any more.

'So who are the two fellers who were with Mr Keller, Anto?'

'I don't know the young one, Mr Gillespie. He's something to do with the German embassy though. But everyone knows the older one. That's Mr Mahr, Adolf Mahr. He's the director of the National Museum. We know him very well in the Shelbourne.' There was just a hint of condescension. Anybody who was anybody ought to know who Adolf Mahr was.

Stefan nodded. He knew the name well enough, even if he didn't know the face. Was it *The Irish Times* that had called Adolf Mahr 'the father of Irish archaeology'? Or was it Éamon de Valera? Mahr was an important man. He was certainly a friend of de Valera's, which made you an important man now, whatever you did. He was also head of the Nazi Party in Ireland.

Then all at once the whole dining room erupted into song as the first verse was repeated, with everyone singing now – Adolf Mahr and the man from the German embassy too.

The sound seemed to fill the Shelbourne Hotel. 'Germany arise, our battle cry. Our Aryan blood shall never die!'

Stefan and Dessie walked out on to Stephen's Green.

Dessie was still humming the tune he'd heard inside.

'I'll say that for the Jerries, they know how to throw a party.'

Stefan was aware that he was still holding something in his hand. He looked down at the small brass lapel pin Santy had given him. It was the size of a farthing, a black swastika on white enamel. Round the edge was a circle of red with the words 'Deutschland Erwache'. Germany Awake.

Neither of them had noticed the fair-haired man sitting in a leather armchair by the porter's desk in the Shelbourne lobby. As they left he was still reading the same page of *The Irish Times* he had been reading when they stepped inside the hotel. Folding the newspaper and tucking it under his arm, he sauntered out after them with a nod to the porter, whistling the music that still echoed from the dining room. He stood on the steps, watching the detectives walk to the corner. Dessie MacMahon crossed over and continued along Stephen's Green; Stefan Gillespie turned into Kildare Street. The fair-haired man walked to the same corner, lighting a cigarette. He waited until Stefan had left the lights of the Shelbourne behind and then followed him.

Kildare Street was almost empty. The National Library and the National Museum were dark, along with the buildings of government they framed at Leinster House. On the other side of the road the offices in the flat-fronted Georgian terraces were dark as well. A few taxis trundled up to Stephen's Green in search of customers. A man walked past with a Yorkshire terrier. A young couple, slightly drunk, crossed the road, arm in arm, giggling, as Stefan made his way home to Nassau Street. A lot had happened, but very little about the day made sense. Keller, the clinic, Hannah Rosen, Jimmy Lynch and Special Branch, the Convent of the Good Shepherd, Susan Field. As he passed the National Museum the unlikely company Hugo Keller kept struck him again. Why had a Special Branch detective sprung him from custody, only to deliver him to the Shelbourne for a conversation with a German embassy official and the director of the National Museum? And what about the missing woman? Was he right to trust Hannah Rosen's instincts? Was it really so unreasonable that a pregnant woman couldn't face an abortion and just ran away? For a moment the questions faded, and he smiled to himself, thinking about Hannah again. He remembered not wanting the conversation with her to stop. Perhaps he should have felt more uneasy about that, because it had nothing to do with what they were talking about. Yet he wasn't. He was thinking about her in ways he still only associated with his dead wife. And there was nothing wrong with it. There was an exhilaration in him now that he had almost forgotten. But none of that had anything to do with why he trusted Hannah's instincts. That had to do with being a policeman. Since leaving Hannah in Rathgar, the sense that something very nasty had happened to Susan Field had only grown in him.

The wall of Trinity College, with the tall trees behind it, stretched ahead of him as he reached Nassau Street. It was noisier here. The pubs and restaurants were still turning out. There were taxis and trams; there were Christmas decorations in the shop windows; there was the breath of beer and whiskey in the cold air. He unlocked the narrow door squeezed in between O'Dea's optician's and Duval et Cie's Parisian Dyers and Cleaners. The two rooms in Nassau Street he rented from James O'Dea were above the optician's shop, on the first floor. The room at the front looked out over the gardens of Trinity. Mr O'Dea had told him, as if he should be paying extra, that if you stood on a chair you could see over the wall. In the year he had spent at Trinity he knew the gardens well enough. In fact the college gardens were the only thing he'd ever really liked about the place. But he never did have any desire to stand on a chair in the window to look at them. As he opened the door on to the steep staircase, the fair-haired man had stopped at the corner of Kildare Street. He watched Stefan Gillespie go in.

Stefan was surprised to see the light on in the hall. It wasn't very welcoming; a bare bulb, no shade, and only twenty-five watts. But the optician didn't usually let the lights burn late. He had a habit of taking the fuses out at night so none of his tenants could leave them on and waste his money. Late home always meant feeling your way up the stairs and along the landing in the darkness. But now, when Stefan reached the turn in the stairs, he could see the door to his room was open. Someone was inside.

He leapt the remaining stairs and raced across the landing. He stood in the doorway. The room had been turned inside out and upside down. The drawers had been tipped out, the sofa was on its back, books had been swept off the bookcase on to the floor; the contents of the kitchen cabinet were everywhere. Then he heard a sound. There was someone in the bedroom. He moved more quietly now, across the room to the door by the window. But even as he took the first steps, he sensed there was someone behind him, someone who must have heard him coming. He didn't have time to turn round. Hard wood hit his head. And he collapsed, unconscious, to the floor.

There was darkness inside his head and a dull throbbing pain. Before full consciousness came, he felt as if he was struggling to climb out of that darkness; when he tried to move his limbs nothing happened. Then his eyes opened abruptly and adrenalin pumped the realisation of danger through his body. He knew his attackers were still there. Cold water was dripping down his face. There was the smell of whiskey. A round, red face looked down at him, so close that for a moment he saw only the eyes. A hand poured water from a jug. As the face retreated he saw the mouth open into a grin of uneven, tobacco-stained teeth. He was being pulled up by his shoulders from the floor. For an instant he was upright, but only for an instant, before he was pushed into an armchair. Detective Garda Seán Óg Moran looked down at him. The grin was instantly replaced by a look of vacancy, as if the guard had just shifted into neutral, and was simply marking time. Stefan turned his head. It hurt. And it would hurt more. He already knew who he'd find looking at him next. There was a smile on Detective Sergeant Jimmy Lynch's pinched lips too. Or maybe he'd just bitten into a lemon.

'You should have said, Jimmy. I'd have had the kettle on.'

'I wanted it to be a surprise.'

'I'll have to see if I can a find a surprise for you some time.'

'They say you're quite the clever lad, Stevie.'

'I've been cleverer.' He raised his hand to touch the back of his head.

'I told Inspector Donald Duck to keep his fucking nose out of Special Branch business, and yours. Did the holy bastard not pass that on to you?'

'He did say something. Maybe I wasn't paying attention.'

'I can say it louder.'

Lynch looked round. Moran stepped forward.

'If you told me what Special Branch business it was –'

Seán Óg's fist hit his face full on. It may have been luck that it wasn't harder, or maybe the detective garda knew how to judge these things. If it had been harder, it would have broken Stefan's nose. As it was he could feel the warm trickle of blood; seconds later he tasted the salt on his lips.

'That's a lot clearer. It'll be a matter of national security then.'

'No, it'll be a matter of how far Seánie can push your nose into your face if you don't do what your inspector said. I can't stand insubordination. That's right, isn't it, Seánie?' Lynch smiled. Moran's yellow teeth showed again; his shoulders moved up and down several times; a snort of laughter.

'I'm missing something, that's the thing, Stevie.'

For the first time, Stefan didn't reply. For the first time, Jimmy Lynch was giving him information about what he was doing here.

'I want everything you took from Keller's,' he continued.

'You've got it.'

'I don't think so.'

'Inspector Donaldson gave it to you. Dessie said you took the lot.'

The pinched lips became a little more pinched and Lynch's smile screwed itself into something less assured. The expression wasn't very different, except that the lemon he'd bitten into now was even sourer than the first. But it told Stefan more. Lynch had come here believing something had been taken from Hugo Keller's clinic, something that wasn't with the other evidence. That's what the two of them had been looking for in his room. Whatever it was, the Special Branch sergeant wasn't sure Stefan had it after all now. It wasn't difficult to be convincing; he had no idea what Lynch was talking about. The Special Branch man was becoming uneasy; to go any further he would have to reveal what he was looking for. But he had spoken to Keller. He knew what Stefan Gillespie had said in the Shelbourne.

'Why did you ask Keller if he'd found what he was looking for?'

'Because you pissed me off. You'd get a lot of that, I expect.'

'You piece of shite.' Garda Moran moved forward again. But a look from his sergeant stopped the blow that was about to follow. Lynch was dimly aware that his interrogation was giving more than it was getting back. And he was right. Stefan knew Keller must have phoned Jimmy Lynch from the hotel. That's why he was turning the place inside out. He also knew he needed to persuade Jimmy he was wasting his time before things got worse.

'Some arsehole walks off with my prisoners and a case that might not have done me any harm at Garda HQ. I get a bollocking from my inspector for doing my job. I wanted to find out whether anything else was coming my way. Why would I take any notice of Donald Duck? So I went back to Merrion Square. I wanted to know what was going on. Wouldn't you?'

Here was something Lynch understood; begrudgery and self-interest.

'I thought you'd be at the Shelbourne with Keller, that's all, Jimmy.'

The Special Branch sergeant got up from the chair. It was a movement that told Garda Moran the interrogation was over. He could relax. Seán Óg was not a man who took pleasure in inflicting physical violence on people; it was just his job. And now, for the moment anyway, the job was finished.

'Will we go back and try the woman again, Jimmy?'

The detective sergeant frowned, his mind elsewhere. Stefan Gillespie was no longer relevant. He nodded at Moran, then turned to go to the door.

'No chance of you lads helping me clear the place up so?'

'You've got the message now, Stevie?' Lynch glanced back.

'Oh, yes, loud and clear, Jimmy.'

And with that he was gone. Moran followed. Stefan pulled himself up out of the armchair, gasping at a sudden surge of pain. Seán Óg was still in the doorway. He smiled awkwardly, almost childishly. This time the stained teeth were hidden. The smile was entirely genuine now. He had done his job, that's all. And naturally, there were no hard feelings, why would there be?

'Thank you, Sarge.'

Stefan felt he had no option but to return the smile. No, no hard feelings. The Special Branch detective closed the door. As the footsteps sounded down the stairs the door swung open again. The lock was on the floor. Also on the floor was a half-bottle of whiskey. Stefan bent down – grimacing – and picked it up. He unscrewed the cap and drank what was left.

# 5. Clanbrassil Street

The next morning Stefan Gillespie walked along Nassau Street, still aching from the attentions of Seán Óg Moran, to the telephone kiosks in Grafton Street. The city centre was quiet; it was Sunday and still early. He got through to the number in Rathgar that Hannah Rosen had given him. A man answered. It was an elderly voice, cautiously polite; it would be her father. When he gave his name as Detective Sergeant Gillespie, he could feel the coldness at the other end. It was the palpable wish that whatever was going on simply wasn't going on. Stefan doubted that Hannah would have told her father very much of the previous day's events; it felt like even the little she had said had been too much. When Hannah came to the phone, he couldn't pretend he wasn't pleased to hear her voice. There was a slight awkwardness as the conversation began. He asked her how she was. It wasn't an unreasonable question after everything that had happened. Her answer sounded a lot more brusque than he either expected or wanted.

'I'm fine. Have you found anything out?'

'Not about Susan.'

'When are you going to talk to Hugo Keller?'

'I'm working on it.'

'What does that mean?' There was a hint of exasperation already. She wanted results and it felt like he was fobbing her off. He was. He didn't have any information about her friend, and after the Shelbourne Hotel and the visit from Jimmy Lynch last night, his head was full of things he couldn't even tell her, let alone explain. He couldn't explain them to himself yet.

'I wanted to see the letters, that's all. Susan's letters to you. I wondered if you could bring them in to me? I haven't got that long today —'

When he had decided to phone her, he had only half worked out why. He did need to see the letters of course, and the train journey to Baltinglass, travelling home to see his son for the day, would be a quiet opportunity to read them. It wasn't just an excuse to meet her, but it was partly that too.

'I can come into town.' She wanted him to have the letters; at least it meant something was actually happening. But she also wanted to see him.

'I won't be here this afternoon. I thought —'

'I can come now. Are you at Pearse Street?'

'No. Maybe I could meet you somewhere.' He hadn't planned on going into the station anyway. It was his day off. But after last night he felt that the less anyone, especially Inspector Donaldson, knew about what he was doing, the more likely it was that he would be allowed to do it.

He left the phone kiosk and carried on up Grafton Street. He turned into the little alleyway that led past the stone arch into St Teresa's Church. There were a few early Mass-goers heading that way. He could read their thoughts as they looked at his bruised face and blackened eyes. He would be better off going in through the arch and getting down on his knees than walking past. He was unaware that the fair-haired man who had been looking at the Christmas display in Switzer's turned into the alley after him, following him as he walked on to Clarendon Street and Golden Lane, then along Bull Alley, past St Patrick's Cathedral and into Clanbrassil Street.

The ancient cathedral was very still. It would be another hour before the great bells started to ring for the Eucharist, calling the scattered remnants of Anglican Dublin to worship in what had once been the public heart of the city. In the new Ireland it was already a forgotten backwater; the power was somewhere else now. It brooded over Dublin like a befuddled, senile uncle whose past life it wasn't quite decent to talk about. As a child Stefan had lived on the other side of Clanbrassil Street, in the Coombe, before his father's promotion to inspector brought a move out of the cramped flat to a suburban terrace in Terenure. For four of those years he had gone to the cathedral's choir school. He had sung in the choir stalls at matins and evensong and the Sunday Eucharist. Matins would be over now. As he glanced across at the great stone tower, he could see the light of the stained-glass windows he had once looked up at, day after day. He heard a snatch of half-remembered music in his head; Stanford's maybe. 'To thee all angels cry aloud.' He walked on towards the noise and bustle of Lower Clanbrassil Street, a narrow, crowded corridor into the city from the suburbs to the south that was always busier on a Sunday than anywhere else in Dublin.

It was the smell of bread that reminded him how he had walked home each Sunday after the Eucharist with

Sam Mortimer, each of them eating a warm bagel from Weinrouk's bakery. Mr Moiselle had always baked the bread there, but the smell of yeast and baking bread was only the first of the smells in Clanbrassil Street on a Sunday morning. He breathed it in now and other smells followed almost immediately. There was blood from the meat and poultry, slaughtered before dawn, hanging outside Myer Rubinstein's butcher's shop; the smell of new milk and sour cream from Jacob Fine's dairy; through the open door of Doris Waterman's grocer's a pungent mix of salami and garlic sausage, salted fish and herrings, spices and pickled cucumbers. He had walked along Clanbrassil Street from time to time since he knew it as a child; as a student at Trinity in the brief, unhappy year he spent there; and as a recruit to the newly formed Garda Síochána soon afterwards, in an unforgiving uniform, to the sound of whistles and laughter from shopkeepers and their customers amused by his youth. But he had always been on the way somewhere else. He had never stopped. Today he did. He stepped into Weinrouk's bakery, catching the sharp mix of words that was as pungent as Clanbrassil Street's smells; the familiar voices of Dublin, the thick accents of Poland and Lithuania, and all the overlapping voices in between, loud and laughing and argumentative, peppering the English Dublin had made so distinctively its own with Yiddish.

The voices felt stranger today than they had when he was a child; then they had been too commonplace to be remarkable. Then the Yiddish simply sounded like another kind of German. His own home was a place where English and German were spoken. His mother had been determined that he should have her language too; she called it hers, even though she had been born in Dublin like him, because words were something precious to her.

In the crowded bakery he bought a bagel and the loaf of bread that he had often brought home for his German grandmother on those Sunday mornings. He would bring one back to Baltinglass for his mother today. The bagel was warm, as it always had been; he remembered that. At the counter, beside him, were two girls, aged around eight and ten, very neatly dressed, their hair in pigtails. He was surprised that Mr Moiselle spoke to them in German, not very good German it had to be said, though it may have been better Yiddish. As he handed a bag of golden, plaited loaves across the counter, he gave them a small, miniature version of the loaf. He had baked some for his grandchildren and there were two left. 'Plaited like your hair!'

Stefan walked out behind the two girls. At the kerb was a black car he hadn't noticed before. A man and a woman sat in the front. The man got out and opened the back door. One of the girls held up the miniature loaf. 'It's a present from Mr Moiselle.' She spoke in German. The girls clambered on to the back seat. As the man shut the rear door and turned to get back into the car he suddenly looked up at Stefan. And Stefan recognised him now, from the Shelbourne the previous night; it was Adolf Mahr. The director of the National Museum wasn't sure, but he knew he recognised this man from somewhere. He nodded politely, clearly registering the bruises on Stefan's face but too well-mannered to show it. 'A beautiful morning,' he said.

'It's not so bad,' replied Stefan. Mahr smiled, amused by the Irish understatement that meant, yes, it really was a beautiful morning. As the car drove away, Stefan saw there were several other people watching it head up past St Patrick's, apparently glad to see it go. He wasn't the only one who thought a Jewish baker's an odd place for the leader of the Nazi Party in Ireland to shop.

He walked on, taking the hot bagel from its bag and eating it as he had eaten as a child. Crossing the street he looked back, waiting for a horse and cart to pass. A fair-haired man stopped quite abruptly to take out a packet of Senior Service. He hunched over his hands, lighting the cigarette. There was something strange. Maybe it was the abruptness; there couldn't be that much urgency about a cigarette, even if you were gasping for one. And the man stood out somehow. Hanging about in Clanbrassil Street, among people whose most natural activity was hanging about in Clanbrassil Street, he looked like he should have been sitting in a pew in St Patrick's Cathedral. And Stefan knew he had seen him before. The man drew on his cigarette and crossed the road, with a studied casualness that was in peculiar contrast to the abruptness of only seconds earlier. Stefan smiled. They were the actions of a man who was following someone, and wasn't very good at it.

'How's the bagel?'

He turned round. 'Good.' He hadn't seen Hannah approaching.

'So much better when I was a girl. Mr Moiselle was a baker, not a businessman then.' She stopped, staring at his face. 'What happened?'

'I accidentally trod on someone's toes.'

'Does that mean you're not going to tell me?'

'Taking one consideration with another –'

'I see, a policeman's lot –' She was still puzzled. 'Has it got something to do with Susan's disappearance? Is that why you won't –'

'Yesterday was a strange day. Someone needed to mark his territory.'

She shrugged off the lack of communication with a smile. If he wasn't going to tell her any more, she wouldn't ask. But he saw it had been registered. It wouldn't be forgotten. For now there were other things to do.

'Shall we have a cup of tea?'

'I can't. I've got to catch the train. I'm going down to Baltinglass.'

'Oh yes, of course, your son.'

He nodded. He didn't say any more, but he was glad she remembered.

'I've got them here,' she said, taking a small bundle of letters from her bag. She handed them to him and he put them in his pocket. She watched as if she didn't want to let them go. He saw how precious they were to her.

'I'll let you have them straight back. I'm sorry, I do have to go.'

'Are you going to Kingsbridge?'

'Yes.' He glanced at his watch.

'I'll walk a little way with you.'

She was the first to move, touching his arm tentatively as they walked on. It was barely for a second, but it was a gesture of intimacy nonetheless. She was brighter again now, chatting quietly about nothing in particular.

'I'm going to see my aunt. She's always complaining Ma and Pa never call in. They do, all the time, and she always comes home with them after shul, but she likes to tell us about our airs and graces now that we live across the canal.

We moved from Lennox Street when I was sixteen, but she's not a great one for new topics of conversation. When I get there she'll complain about me coming too, because I didn't tell her I was!'

He smiled, enjoying her voice. They walked on in silence.

'Do you know who Adolf Mahr is?'

She looked surprised. It was a strange question. 'Yes.'

'As director of the National Museum or as Nazi Party leader?'

'I don't suppose the Nazi role's common knowledge everywhere, but some of us have better reasons to know about these things than others. Irish Jews don't find it reassuring that all the Germans the government employs have got their own little Nazi Party here. I don't remember seeing a swastika in Dublin before I left. Yesterday there was one outside the Shelbourne.'

'He was here just now. His car was outside the bakery. There were two girls buying bread. His daughters, presumably. It seemed a bit odd –'

Hannah laughed.

'Some things are so awful even the most devoted Nazi has to put aside his deepest prejudices. Irish bread. Even the master race can't stomach it.'

'Bread?'

'He comes every Sunday. It's the nearest he can find to a Vienna loaf in Dublin. But he can't go inside the shop because it's Jewish. So he sends his daughters. Everyone knows. Susan told me in one of her letters. It's a standing joke. Mostly people laugh about it. I don't know how funny it is –'

He felt an uncomfortable sense of connection, not with Hannah, but with Adolf Mahr. It was what his grandmother used to say. 'They can't make bread. They don't know how. For God's sake, once a week let's have good bread!' They walked on without speaking. Her mood had changed.

'Was that just an idle question?'

'What?'

'About Adolf Mahr.'

He was right; she didn't miss much.

'The German community had a Christmas party last night, at the Shelbourne. It's why the Nazi flag was flying. He was there with Keller.'

'That's nice for Doctor Keller. He's got a lot of friends.'

'It does seem like it.'

'Is that why you were beaten up?'

He shrugged. It wasn't exactly the truth, but he couldn't deny it.

'I suppose it proves you're not one of his friends too.' She stopped. 'I'm going this way. Have a good day with your son. It's going to rain though!' As she turned, smiling, she touched his arm again. He watched her walk away, sensing that she hadn't wanted to go. Or maybe that was what he wanted to believe, because he didn't want her to go. It was a long time since he had felt like this, and he wasn't at all sure how good his judgement was.

When Stefan Gillespie turned away from the ticket window at Kingsbridge Station, he saw the tall, fair-haired man again, sitting on a bench, reading the *Irish Independent*; the man who had stopped so abruptly for a cigarette in Clanbrassil Street; the man he was now convinced was following him. And as the man turned a page and leant back – just as he had turned a page and leant back into a leather armchair, in the entrance to the Shelbourne Hotel the night before, Stefan remembered that was where he had first seen him. There were still fifteen minutes to go before the train left for Baltinglass. He walked across the station concourse, back towards the street. He stood close to the entrance, looking at a rack of newspapers and magazines. Outside, a taxi drew up. A man and a woman got out. As the man paid the driver, Stefan walked briskly out of the station. He opened the taxi door and got in.

'Straight across the river, over the bridge. As quick as you can.'

The driver pulled away with a sour glance in the mirror.

'And where am I going then?'

Stefan looked through the back window. The fair-haired man had just emerged from the station, looking up and down, his eyes fixed on the departing taxi. There could be no doubt at all; the man was following him.

'If you're in a hurry, you'll want to tell me where you're going, sir.'

'Just turn round at the other end and drop me back at the station.'

'What the fuck is this? There's a bloody minimum fare –'

Inside Kingsbridge, the fair-haired man was at the ticket office window, talking to the clerk who had sold Stefan his ticket. He was unaware that the man he had been watching was now watching him. He walked to a platform where a train was disgorging passengers. He looked for a moment, then moved to a hoarding and ran his finger down the printed timetable. Stefan was right behind him now. The man turned. As he did, Stefan grabbed his shoulders and slammed him up against the hoarding, very hard.

'Baltinglass, that's where I'm going. Why do you want to know?'

The response wasn't what he expected. The fair-haired man grinned.

'You're back.'

'And you're not very good at this.'

'I didn't think I was doing badly. It's a shame about your nose.'

'It's Jimmy and Seán I owe that to, but any friend of theirs –'

'Friend would be overstating it. You're going to miss your train.'

Stefan took his hands from the man's shoulders. He looked over to the platform, where a few passengers were now boarding. Smiling amiably, the man brushed the shoulders and lapels of his coat. He held out his hand.

'John Cavendish.'

'You're not Special Branch.' Stefan ignored the proffered hand.

'Oh, I'd say you're a better detective than that, Sergeant.'

The Tullow train pulled out of Kingsbridge. It wasn't a corridor carriage and they had the compartment to themselves. No one would hear; that mattered to Cavendish. He had made Stefan wait on the platform till the last minute.

'I'm a bit like you, Sergeant.'

'What does that mean?'

'I'm not supposed to be doing this.'

'What is it I'm not supposed to be doing?'

'I don't know what Sergeant Lynch would make of you

91

meeting Miss Rosen today. I assume you've been warned off Keller.' He tapped his nose. 'Well, you didn't have that when you left the Shelbourne last night.'

'Are you going to tell me who you are?'

'I'm actually Lieutenant John Cavendish.' He reached into his pocket and took out a leather card case. He pulled out a neatly printed card.

Stefan looked down at it. He shook his head, stifling his laughter.

'I'm sorry, am I missing a joke?' frowned the lieutenant.

'You're with G2?'

'More or less.'

'And you give out cards saying Military Intelligence?'

'Well, someone had them printed up,' he grinned amiably.

'And more or less means –'

'Not leaving undone those things that ought to be done simply because our political masters have instructed us to leave them undone.'

'This could go on for some time, couldn't it? And I'd say I'll still have no idea what you're talking about. So why are you following me?'

'I did think you were working with Lynch.'

'Does it look like I am?'

'No. I don't know what you're doing. I don't know why you arrested Hugo Keller, only to have Special Branch pull him out of a cell in Pearse Street and take him home. I don't know who Hannah Rosen is or what she's got to do with Keller. I don't know why you met her today when you've been told, in a variety of ways I imagine, to lay off Herr Keller now. But I'd hazard a guess that Lynch is looking for something he thought you had.'

'And is that what you're after too, Lieutenant?'

Cavendish looked at him, saying nothing. He had been thrown into this conversation abruptly and unexpectedly. Whatever about the nonchalant smiles, he had blown what was meant to be a simple surveillance.

'It's not my business, Lieutenant. I don't want to get between you and Special Branch. You'll have important work to do, following one another round Dublin. I just arrested an abortionist when nobody wanted me to.'

'What happened to the evidence you took out of Merrion Square?'

'Lynch has got it.' Stefan smiled. 'Except for what's missing.'

'And what is missing?'

'Give me a clue. I might have seen it, who knows?'

'What the hell does that mean?'

'It means it would take a lot more than a punch in the face from Jimmy Lynch's bulldog to make me give up something worth having. So what's your offer? You don't look like the shite-kicking sort, Cavendish.'

The soldier didn't reply. He was trying to get the measure of Stefan. He wasn't sure about him. Was he joking? Was he really hiding something?

'Look, I haven't got it, Lieutenant. I don't even know what it is.'

'So what are you doing then?' persisted Cavendish.

'My job.'

'And where does Keller come into your job now?'

There seemed no reason not to tell the truth. It wasn't a secret.

'I'm looking for a woman who disappeared earlier this year. The last thing she did was go to Merrion Square for an abortion. That makes Hugo Keller the last person who saw her, the last I know about anyway. That's what I'm doing. So what about you? Why don't you tell me what you and Special Branch are looking for? Did Keller keep a list of his customers?'

'That would be some of it,' replied the lieutenant.

'I guess there'd have to be more to interest Special Branch?'

Cavendish's silence gave him his answer. Then the officer smiled.

'So what do you know about Hugo Keller, Sergeant?'

'As a posh backstreet abortionist, he's got some unusual friends. And he seems to generate a surprising amount of activity in unexpected places. What with Special Branch dancing round him, not to mention the director of the National Museum, who happens to be the leader of the Nazi party the Germans have set up here, and now Military Intelligence, I can't decide whether he's a national treasure or a threat to national security. Which is it?'

The lieutenant didn't answer. 'So, who is this missing woman?'

'I doubt she's going to be of any interest to G2 or to Special Branch. She's just a woman no one's seen for a long time. I'd be surprised if she's alive. I don't know how, or why, but that's what I think. That's what I was talking to Hannah Rosen about. It's what I intend to talk to Herr Doktor Keller about, whether it goes down well with Military Intelligence, or Special Branch, or the German embassy, or my inspector or anybody else.'

'Well, if determination was all there was to it, Sergeant –'

'Meaning what?'

'Adolf Mahr drove Keller to Dún Laoghaire last night

and put him on the mail boat. He'll be in London by now, I'd say on his way to Germany.'

Lieutenant Cavendish got out at Naas, where the train took the branch line that led along the River Slaney and the western edge of the Wicklow Mountains to Baltinglass. And as the train set off again Stefan Gillespie took out the letters Hannah Rosen had given him. Immediately he found himself in a world that was complex, intense and unfamiliar. Naturally enough, the letters between two old and close friends were full of epigrammatic references to people and events he could know nothing about, both in the lives they had shared in Dublin and in the lives they now led in Ireland and Palestine. As a detective he had tried to piece together the jigsaw of a stranger's life before, but this had an intimacy that at once absorbed him and made him uncomfortable. Susan Field almost certainly wrote as she spoke. Her words tumbled over each other and took tangential, unlooked for directions, sometimes finding their way back, circuitously, to what she had started speaking about, sometimes leaving the original thought behind, never to return. Several times she made him laugh out loud – once when she described sitting in the gallery of the Adelaide Road synagogue on a Saturday morning, mesmerised by a man who had fallen asleep below, wondering how long it would be before the growing intensity of his snores would be loud enough to compete with the cantor's recitation of a psalm; another time, when she kept patting the packet of cigarettes in her coat pocket to reassure herself that soon, very soon, she would be outside the synagogue drawing in the invigorating smoke that was all the more desirable because it was forbidden on the Sabbath. It reminded her, she wrote, of the time she and Hannah, just seventeen, tore along the South Circular Road after shul to light a cigarette in a doorway, only to meet the pious and disapproving faces of Mrs Wigoder and Mrs Noyk. He could feel the vitality of Susan Field in her breathless words; it brought him closer to the loss that consumed Hannah. It wasn't hard. His own loss wasn't buried very deep.

The letters were punctuated by words Stefan didn't quite understand, but every so often there was something familiar about the closeness of a community that was both a part of the world around it and at the same time engaged in its own private rituals and habits. Catholic Ireland was a public event, but his own childhood, especially the teenage years, when his Sunday mornings still belonged to the Church of Ireland, didn't feel very different to some of Susan Field's memories. There was the same mix of boredom, irritation and impatience; there was the same sense of something apart. He looked out of the window, seeing the water of the Slaney for the first time, and to the east the round-topped Wicklow Mountains. He played no part in all that now. He couldn't remember when he last sat in the church by the river in Baltinglass. Yet he still knew that what his father always said was true; it wasn't just a more private way of looking at the world; it was about keeping your head down. His parents still did keep their heads down.

By the end of the first few letters Susan Field's swirling narrative had moved from the past to new excitement about being at University College Dublin. He knew her better here. And he still felt the closeness between her and Hannah. There was a letter that ended with a paragraph of invective about a priest who was lecturing on medieval philosophy.

He was arrogant, supercilious and never listened to what anybody else said. Fierce intelligence and blind faith. Didn't the first mean you shouldn't be a prisoner of the second? How could you argue with someone whose ideas admitted no doubt? In the letters that followed, her irritation with the man she started to refer to jokingly as 'John' was replaced by an admiration that was already about something else altogether. She had done more than find his doubts.

*He came to the pub with us. I don't know why. He never did before. I started arguing with him, mostly about how his lectures infuriated me. But he wasn't as stuffy as the stuff he spouts. I don't mean he doesn't believe things I could never believe, but he was so much sharper and funnier than in college. He's full of questions about what he believes after all. He's obviously committed to being a priest, but he said he wasn't sure he would have become one, if he'd thought the way he thinks now. Anyway, we ended up talking on our own, after the others all went. And when the pub closed we walked round Dublin for hours and hours, just talking and talking. I think he's probably a bit of a mess underneath. I quite like that really!*

Soon the world of the family and friends Hannah and Susan shared had almost disappeared from the letters; so too had the references to what Hannah's letters must have contained about her life in Palestine. Stefan was very aware of that. He found himself scanning the later letters, not for the pieces of the jigsaw he was actually meant to be putting together, but for the pieces of the other one, the one that was about Hannah Rosen. Sometimes there was still a glimpse of that, buried among her friend's preoccupations.

*When I met John tonight we didn't talk very much. We finally did what we'd both wanted to do at the end of that first night, when we walked through Dublin. You always tell me I use the word love too easily. You don't even like using it when you're talking about Benny, and you're marrying him! Tell me which of us is the more confused? Anyway, I'll pretend I'm not talking about love even if I am. You're the only person I can say all this to. I quite like how secretive and exciting it all is. Sounds a bit daft of course. I know you'll think so! But then you've got a nation to build. You've got to be serious. I don't suppose it'll last long – after all he is a priest! It'll get a lot less exciting once guilt catches up with him. But just now he hasn't got time!*

As the letters went on they were less and less about excitement and more about unhappiness and isolation – from her family and her community, even from the friends she had at UCD. It seemed to Stefan as if some of the things Susan said suggested that Hannah reciprocated those feelings at times – not of unhappiness perhaps, but at least of uncertainty. Soon, however, there was scarcely any room in Susan Field's letters for anybody else, even her best friend. And then, in middle of it all, she found out she was pregnant.

*Well, I told him. He started on about leaving the priesthood and meeting his obligations. God, the only thing worse than the mess I'm in is the thought of a lifetime with a man who's 'meeting his obligations'. I just shut him up, but then he surprised me. He asked me if I wanted to keep the baby, and when I told him I didn't, he said he'd help. There's a man in Merrion Square, a proper doctor I think, German, all very private and swanky. He knows somebody John knows. I don't know how. I can't say I care. I've seen him and it's all very easy. It'll be sorted out next week. John and I won't see each other again. He's leaving UCD. It seems a long time since we felt happy with each other. I'm not sure we ever did, whatever we told ourselves.*

The last two letters were much shorter. The animation that had filled the others, even when she was writing about unhappiness, had been drained out of her. There was only emptiness. Now she just wanted it over with.

*Merrion Square tomorrow. I don't know what then. It was all about nothing in the end. In between I seem to have lost touch with all the things I cared about. I can't even remember what they were. I'm a long way from everyone. I wish you were closer, Hannah. I suppose the blues are inevitable. But they'll go, I guess. By the way, if I use the word love too much, you don't use it enough. If you don't love Benny, then making the desert bloom and filling it with babies won't be enough. I don't know so much about myself any more, but I know that about you. Anyway, here I go!*

That was the final letter. It was dated the twenty-fifth of July. The end was bleaker than Hannah had made it sound. He knew what darkness was, and he could feel it in Susan Field's final letter. There was a time when he had thought about walking away from it all. In Ireland the boat to somewhere was always an option; for some it offered new hope, for others it was the final expression of despair. He had even thought about another journey once, the darkest journey. For the Greeks you took a boat for that one too. It had been no more than a thought that he left behind. He had his son Tom to pull him out. What did Susan Field have? In that last letter it didn't feel like very much.

# 6. Kilranelagh Hill

As the train pulled into the station at Baltinglass it followed the road and the River Slaney, black now under still thickening cloud. Beyond the river, Baltinglass Hill rose up above the town, a great pyramid of green. Three thousand years ago the people who lived there had buried their dead on its slopes and had looked down from the stone fort at the summit, as a new people arrived. The newcomers had probably followed the river too. And then the people who watched from the fort were gone, even the words of their language had disappeared, unremembered for thousands of years. They left only the ring of stones on the hilltop and the megaliths that once covered their dead.

Stefan put Susan Field's letters into the inside pocket of his overcoat. He looked across the river at the hill he had climbed so many times as a boy, and at the ruins of the abbey that had stood below it for a thousand years, sitting next to the small Church of Ireland church that had replaced it. The abbey was not quite forgotten, but it was another place of tumbled stones and unremembered words; it was where the dead were buried now, his grandparents and his great-grandparents among them. The train juddered to a halt with the grinding of steel on steel and a long, weary hiss of steam.

In front of the wooden station buildings, a tall, bearded man in his sixties stood on the platform. Next to him, tense with anticipation, his eyes fixed on the train, was a boy of four. The old man had Stefan Gillespie's dark eyes and so had the boy. David Gillespie and his grandson Tom waited, and then Tom ran forward as a carriage door opened and his father got out. Stefan folded his son into his arms and lifted him up, laughing, for no reason other than that Tom was laughing, with the simple happiness of seeing him.

'Jesus, you're a weight, Tom Gillespie! What's Oma feeding you?'

'Will you carry me then?'

'I will not!' But he carried him a little way along the platform anyway, till they reached David. Inevitably Stefan's father was looking quizzically at his face and the evidence of the beating. 'And I'd a run in with a feller before you say anything else about it. It's nothing but bruises so.'

'Did you lock him up, Daddy?' asked Tom, impressed.

'Well, not exactly. It was sorted out.' He laughed. His father just nodded, suspecting there was more to it than nothing but bruises, but he asked no questions. It was clear Stefan wouldn't be saying any more.

'Tom was at Mass with the Lawlors. He wanted to stay and walk back with you. And I fancied a bit of a walk myself. We had nothing better to do, did we, Tom?' It was a two-mile walk from the farm on the saddle of land behind Baltinglass Hill and another two back up again.

Tom took his father's hand as they walked to the road.

'Is the trike in the window at Clery's still, the way you told me?'

'When did I tell you that?'

'You told me last week, and the week before.'

'And the week before, ever since you saw the picture in the paper.'

'Is it there though?'

'I'd say it is.'

'Do you look every day?'

'I maybe miss the odd one.'

The town began just beyond the station. The buildings closed in on either side of the road and shut out the fields along the River Slaney; the blank, stone walls of the mill on one side and low two-storey houses and shops on the other. As they crossed over the bridge the water from the mill race made the river noisier and more urgent, though as it spilled out on the other side it resumed its leisurely course. Again the hill rose up, this time over the wide main street. Here some of the buildings were higher; the bank, the solicitor's. There were occasional splashes of colour on the rendered fronts of the small-windowed shops and houses, but mostly they were grey, and mostly the grey plaster was crumbling. In the square, next to the statue of Sam MacAllister, who had died in the hills beyond the town in the last days of the rebellion of 1798, was a Christmas tree, yet to be decorated. Beyond the square was the Catholic church. It marked the eastern end of the town as the abbey ruins did the western. But the business of the churches was done for this Sunday. As grandfather, father and son walked through Baltinglass a Sunday silence hung over it. The shops were shut. And for those who were not at home, the pubs – as was their way – were curtained and shuttered, looking in on themselves, and not out on the world.

They were soon through the town and among the fields again, walking away from the river now and beginning the climb to Kilranelagh Hill and the farm that had belonged to Stefan's grandfather; where his own father had been born, and where David had returned when the Dublin Metropolitan Police had become, inescapably, part of a war that he wanted no part in. They talked about the sow that had farrowed last week and the six new piglets in the sty, and the geese being fattened for the Christmas market, and the one they'd picked out, the fattest one of all, that they'd eat themselves. They talked about the calf that was ill with scour that Tom had prayed wouldn't die – it was better now and out in the orchard field with its mother, though she still hadn't the milk for it and Tom was giving the calf the bottle himself. There was the window that Tom didn't want to talk about at all, that he and Harry Lawlor had smashed, knocking tin cans over with Harry's catapult. There was the book Opa was reading him now, about Eeyore and Piglet and Winnie the Pooh, and there was the rhyme he could sing from it to a tune Oma had made up on the piano. They always used the German words for grand-mother and grandfather; the other grandparents, Maeve's mother and father, were Grandma and Grandpa, but Stefan's mother and father were always Oma and Opa, just as his mother's parents had been to him. They talked about the speckled hen Oma was cooking for the dinner, the one Opa had to kill after Tess the sheepdog chased it into the hay barn and it broke its leg. And they talked for the fourth time and the fifth time about the tricycle in the window of Clery's department store in O'Connell Street, with a trunk behind you could put things in, that Tom had seen the picture of in the newspaper. He'd cut the picture out and put it by his bed, next to the photograph of his mother and father and his collection of books and stones and tin soldiers. It had been on three lists he'd sent up the chimney, despite warnings that it wasn't a good idea to overdo it with Santy.

There was a steep track into the farmyard from the road up to Kilranelagh Hill. There was the smell of dung and hay. A long stone barn stretched towards the house on one side of the yard. They heard the sound of the cows inside, calling for food. On the other side of the yard stood a rusty, corrugated shed, full of straw. Quite suddenly, something black and white hurtled through the barn door, barking and snarling furiously. Tess stopped at Stefan's feet. She looked up at him and abruptly turned away, trotting back into the barn with just one backward glance to tell him that her job, a quite unnecessary job as it happened, had been done. Then as Tom opened the door to the kitchen there was the smell of the dinner. Stefan walked across the room and put his arms round his mother. Tom held up the paper bag his father had brought and took out the loaf of bread that was in it.

'We've got some bread for you, Oma, some special bread!'

Helena stared at her son's battered face. He put his finger to his lips.

'It's from Weinrouk's. Do you remember it? I'm sure it's still Mr Moiselle who makes it. Remember? When did you last have a loaf like that, Ma?' She smiled. She remembered very well. She had more to say, about the bruises, but that would have to wait. She looked back down at the pots on the stove. She spoke quietly, not wanting to let her concern show to Tom.

'Father Carey's here. He's been waiting.'

The sitting room was dark. It looked out on to the farmyard through a window that let little enough light in on a summer's

105

day. Now the clouds were black over the farm and over Kilranelagh Hill above. It wasn't a small room, but it was lined with bookshelves that crowded the heavy furniture into the centre. The priest was by the fireplace, crouching down, almost on his knees, pulling out a book. He rose as Stefan Gillespie entered the room.

'You wanted to see me.'

Normally the word 'Father' would have been added to this, and in a man he liked Stefan would have had no problem with that polite expression of respect, even though Anthony Carey was barely two years older. But there was neither liking nor respect, and the feeling was thoroughly reciprocated in the cold and cautious eye the priest cast in his direction.

'It's about the boy.' No name, just the boy.

'You'd better sit down.'

The priest made no attempt to sit down. Instead he walked to a table at one side of the room where he had made a neat pile of the books he had already taken from the shelves. He put the one he was holding on top of the pile. Then he noticed the bruises on Stefan's face. He gave a sour grin.

'A rough night, Sergeant?'

'A rough customer. I do meet them in my job.' The reply was curt. He had no intention of explaining himself. He waited for the priest to continue.

'It's about his schooling,' said Father Carey, businesslike now. He had a thin, angular body and somehow his voice had the same spiky quality.

'We've already talked about that,' replied Stefan shortly.

'I felt he should begin school at St Tegan's this September, you remember I'm sure. You weren't happy about that at the time of course.'

'I didn't think he was ready. He'd have been the youngest one starting. He's still only four. He'll go next year. I don't see there's a hurry.'

'The particular circumstances –'

'I thought this was settled. I spoke to Father MacGuire –'

'I was away then.' Father Carey smiled.

The smile expressed what both men knew – that Stefan had chosen to speak to the parish priest when the curate was away, precisely because he was. Father MacGuire was an older, gentler, easier man altogether.

'I have now taken over from Father MacGuire as chairman of the school's board of management. It's a lot of work for the parish priest. We both felt that I would have more time and energy to devote to it.'

'The school year's begun now anyway. There's a term gone.'

'My feeling – my strong feeling – is that Tom should be at school.'

'Next year he will be.'

'As I've said, the particular circumstances really do argue against that, Sergeant Gillespie, as far as the Church is concerned. He is a Catholic living in a home that is not Catholic. I have a responsibility to ensure that he does not suffer in a situation that is, from the Church's point of view, extremely unsatisfactory. The lack of a Catholic home makes his presence in a Catholic school all the more imperative. He should start after Christmas.'

'He's very young. He's still – after his mother's death –'

'Your wife has been dead for two years. It's hardly a reason for the boy not to go to school. In fact it's her absence, the absence of a Catholic mother, that makes it all the more important that he does go and go now.'

'He goes to Mass every Sunday with the Lawlors.' There was nothing to be gained from telling the curate that Tom's mother had no time for the Church at all. It was a mixed marriage, and in order to be married they had to agree that their children would be brought up as Catholics. That was simply how it was. Death did not release Stefan from the contract. But the easy, familiar way the priest threw Maeve into the conversation, a woman he hadn't known, was about more than that. He knew it irritated Stefan, and it did now. Stefan said nothing, struggling to hold his temper.

'I've never been in here before.' It was an abrupt change of subject. Father Carey looked round the room at the crowded bookshelves with a mixture of amusement and contempt. 'You're quite the reader so,' he said.

'Is there something wrong with that?'

'I've been looking at your . . . library.' The final word was said with a patronising smile, but he was serious. 'I'm not easily shocked, Mr Gillespie.'

'I'm sorry, I'm not with you.'

'This is in German,' he announced, picking up the book that was on top of the pile with a look of distaste. 'But not hard to decipher, even for me. Isn't it *The Communist Manifesto*? Would I be right about that?'

'It was my grandfather's. He studied philosophy, at university in Munich. All his books are here. And why wouldn't they be?' Stefan knew the priest was going to test his temper in every way he could. He was already angry, angry with himself as well as Carey. He was explaining away the presence of a book instead of telling the priest to get out of the house.

Father Carey put down the book and frowned at the rest of the pile.

'Voltaire, Hobbes, Locke, Darwin, Martin Luther. I've picked these out. I'm sure there are others. All these are on the Vatican's Index Librorum Prohibitorum. As a great reader, I hope you'll know what that is.' The words continued to express disdain for the idea of Stefan reading anything at all.

'I think I can work it out. But there's not a book here you couldn't walk into any public library and pick up. What are you trying to say?'

'That may or may not be true. But this is not a library, is it?' The curate walked across the room to another bookshelf. 'This is a house in which you and your parents are bringing up a Catholic child. Yet I see books, many books, that I wouldn't even want a Catholic child to touch.'

'He's four, for God's sake!'

'They're certainly not all books your grandfather brought from Germany though. I've heard of this, *Point Counterpoint*. It's by a man called Aldous Huxley. I think you'll find it's a book that the State Censorship Board has actually banned. Hardly an ancient, inherited tome. A souvenir of your Trinity days perhaps? You were there, *briefly*, weren't you?'

'You're very well informed about banned books. I'm not.'

'I make it my business to be, Sergeant. As a policeman you should make it yours, since owning Mr Huxley's book breaks the law.' He moved sideways, running a finger along a line of books. 'Then there are the bibles.'

'Perhaps they'll cancel out *The Communist Manifesto*,' Stefan ventured. The attempt at a joke didn't help. It didn't disguise his animosity.

'You won't be familiar with the catechism,' said the priest coldly.

'Familiar would be overstating it.' Stefan walked to a bookshelf and looked along a row of books. He took out a small, grey Catholic catechism.

'You think you're a clever sort of man, don't you, Gillespie?'

'I'm trying to keep my temper, Father Carey.'

'Protestant bibles, several Protestant bibles, in English and German. This German one, I presume, is Luther's.' The priest spoke the name as if he was referring to a pornographer. 'The catechism asks a question of the faithful: What should a Christian do who is given a bible by Protestants or by the agents of Protestants? The answer is that it is to be rejected with disgust, because it is forbidden by the Church. If taken inadvertently, it must be burnt immediately or handed to a priest so that he can dispose of it safely.'

'I know burning books is the coming thing in Europe, but I don't think it's Ireland's way yet. I'm sorry. Tom starts school next September, as we agreed. That's all there is to say.' He had had enough. He wanted to bring the conversation back to the reason the priest was there and put an end to it.

'I won't be leaving it at this. It won't do, Sergeant.'

'This is my parents' house. It's my home, my son's home. Please go.'

'You don't understand your position.'

'What?'

The priest's eyes roamed round the room again. Wasn't it obvious?

'Am I supposed to see an acceptable home for a Catholic child here?'

'I've asked you to go.'

'The child is already motherless, the idea that he should grow up surrounded by all – all this . . .'

Stefan's determination to hold his temper was failing. He stepped forward. He would make the curate leave. The expression of grave concern on Carey's face turned quite abruptly to a smile. It was the smile of a man more pleased with the job he has done than he expected to be. Briefly his smug, angular features reminded Stefan of the self-satisfied, knowing face of Hugo Keller; here was another man who knew he was untouchable. Stefan had the same desire to wipe away that smile. And the priest could read it. He held Stefan's gaze, almost challenging him to go further; one step further would do it. But the moment was gone. And the priest could read that too.

'Watch that temper, Sergeant. You're not in the Garda barracks now.'

Father Carey picked up the black fedora that sat on the table beside the books. He stepped round Stefan with a curt, businesslike nod, and left.

For a moment Stefan didn't move. He turned to the window and looked out. The black figure strode through the farmyard, across the cobbles to the road, the fedora, slightly too small, perched on his head. All of a sudden, out from the barn, low to the ground, came something else black, with a flash of white round the collar. The sheepdog aimed itself at the priest, barking furiously. She wasn't going to bite but he didn't know that. He turned and kicked out. The dog changed direction effortlessly; now she was behind him, snarling and yapping. The curate's very black and very polished boot kicked again. The dog slithered back on her legs. As the boot touched down it landed in a pat of watery dung. Father Carey cursed. He looked up to see Stefan watching from the window. He turned towards the road angrily and walked on, faster than before, conscious of the dog slinking along behind him, no longer barking, her teeth bared, her lips curled in snarling, silent disdain. The sheepdog didn't like the priest very much either; but unlike Stefan Gillespie she had nothing at all to fear from him.

*

Above the farm, higher up on the bare slopes of Kilranelagh Hill, was a graveyard. It was a wild place, full of tumbled stones and brambles and tussocks of thick, uncut grass. The only sounds there were the wind and the rooks and the screech of the foxes at night. It had been a cemetery as long as anybody could remember. When the mountain townlands were full of people and the churches in the valleys were not their churches, this was where the dead came. There was no church here of any denomination, though there was a place of worship. Where the graveyard disappeared, almost unnoticed, into the surrounding gorse, there were two great stones that had marked the way out of this life for three, four, five thousand years. Now there was a neat and lovingly tended Catholic cemetery above the river in Baltinglass, but this was where Maeve Gillespie had once told Stefan she wanted to be buried. Neither of them could have known in that idle conversation, one day on the slopes of the mountain, that the time for her burial would come so soon.

She had loved the farm from the first time he brought her home to meet his mother and father. She was the one who said they'd live at the farm below Kilranelagh, when he had only thought of a house in the suburbs of Dublin. And when she was gone, with such brutal and aching suddenness, he knew it was where she would have wanted Tom to be. He couldn't live on his own in Dublin with his father. It felt right that he was here. Or if it wasn't right it was the best Stefan Gillespie could do. The future was uncertain. Two years on from Maeve's death he still felt he was unable to see beyond the next week. For now, the farm was where his son was safe and happy. Tom's happiness was all that mattered. And Maeve was safe too, here among the tumbled stones and the raggedy tufts of grass on Kilranelagh Hill.

Husband and son stood over the grave. Someone had left a single white lily a few days earlier. The dead were closer here than they were in Dublin. Neighbours did not forget. Tom clasped his hands tightly together and talked to his mother. There was a prayer, but when that was said he opened his eyes and whispered all the small, important happenings of his week, and gave her yet another description of the tricycle in Clery's window. As they walked back down the hill to the farm the rain that had been threatening all afternoon began to fall. They ran all the way, but by the time they burst into the warm kitchen they were drenched to the skin. They sat by the open range drinking tea and eating Weinrouk's white bread, with butter and plum jam, before Stefan went out to the barn with David to milk the cows. When they came back in his mother was in the sitting room, packing books into boxes. 'They'll come to no harm in the attic, will they?'

That night Stefan Gillespie didn't sleep very easily. The rain lashed hard against the roof all night. He lay in the small bed across from Tom, listening to his son's slow, contented breathing. Tom could start school after Christmas. The books could go into the attic. All they had to do was let Father Carey have his way. Tom would be all right. But the day had taken Stefan to some strange places. In some way all the dissatisfaction and unease he felt about his own life was being stirred up, all the things he'd locked away behind what he simply had to get on with; the Gardaí, the money he needed to earn, the support he had to give his parents, and Tom, always Tom. Yet, when he fell asleep it wasn't any of that he was thinking about. As his eyes closed it was the dark-haired woman, Hannah Rosen, who filled his mind.

# 7. The Mater Hospital

The room was at the rear of the terraced house in Lennox Street, looking out over a small yard and the backs of another row of houses. There was a neat pile of cardboard boxes, stacked on the floor. Two suitcases sat on the bare-mattressed bed. The bookshelves were empty, as were the wardrobe and the chest of drawers. There was no sense that anything was being thrown out, but everything had been put away. It was part of a process Stefan knew too well himself. For a long time after Maeve died her clothes simply stayed in the bedroom where they were. He cleared the dressing table, but only by putting brushes and combs and bottles of make-up into the drawers. Then one day he had to do more. He packed everything into boxes and old suitcases and carried it into the attic at Kilranelagh. It was all still there, but he knew he would have to take the boxes and the cases down soon. He would take out the few things he wanted to keep; the rest would go. There was a time. That time would eventually come for Susan Field's father too.

Stefan didn't know what he was looking for; something real or just something to give him more sense of who this woman was. He opened a cardboard box and saw the things he expected to see; brushes and bracelets, brooches, powder, make-up. There were clothes that gave off the faint, stale smell of old scent. There were books. There was an album with photographs. He was struck by the photograph of a man and a woman with three small girls; they were feeding swans by the Grand Canal. One of them was Susan. He turned to see her father standing in the doorway, his hands clasped tightly in front of him. Brian Field didn't really want to watch all this.

'You can wait downstairs, Mr Field. I won't disturb anything.'

The small, nervous man, grey-haired, grey-skinned, nodded and went away, relieved that he wasn't needed. Stefan looked back at the photograph album. He found a picture of two girls in school uniform, twelve or thirteen, their arms round each other, laughing. Behind them were the blurred bars of a cage. It looked like Dublin Zoo. He easily recognised Hannah Rosen beside Susan Field.

Half an hour later Stefan came downstairs. He had found nothing that helped him. Mr Field was sitting in an armchair in the cluttered front room, looking out through the net curtains at nothing. He stood up. It was clear that the detective's arrival had made him uncomfortable. He moved in front of the fire, standing with his hands clasped tightly behind his back now. He didn't want the conversation that Hannah Rosen's stubbornness was forcing on him. His daughter's disappearance was in a box and he had closed the lid as far as he could. He knew Hannah thought Susan was dead, but he still didn't believe that himself. Shame played a part in it. He felt shame for his daughter, as well as grief and loss. He couldn't bring himself to contemplate Hannah's dark, insistent questioning. He didn't want to go there with her. There was enough shame to explain why his daughter might have run away.

When Brian Field's father, Abraham Breitfeld, arrived in Dublin from Kiev in 1896, via Warsaw, Hamburg, Amsterdam and Manchester, he had worked as a peddler, tramping the roads of South Dublin, Wicklow, Carlow, and Wexford. After three years he opened a grocer's shop in Clanbrassil Street. He moved his wife and his children from a tenement in Malpas Street to a flat over the shop. Two years later he bought the terraced house in Lennox Street, just north of the Grand Canal, in the part of Portobello that became known as Little Jerusalem. It was the first year of the twentieth century, the year of Queen Victoria's last visit to Ireland, and the year Abraham Breitfeld became Abraham Field. He had brought with him from Russia a view of the world that adapted very easily to his new home. The English were the Russians, the Irish were the Jews; Queen Victoria was the Czar. He was immediately a staunch nationalist. Though his English was never very good, his children could not only speak it perfectly before they went to school, they could even read Irish, when the Irish friends they played with in the street could barely understand a word of it.

Brian Field still lived in his father's house. His children had grown up in it and his wife had died in it. When his friends made the move over the Grand Canal to leafy Harold's Cross and Terenure, he stayed where he was. The business was sold now and his life was devoted to something else. He was the cantor at the Adelaide Road Synagogue. His children were grown up; Judith was dead. He had a daughter in New York, a daughter in London, and had long known that when Susan left he would be an old man on his own. There would be no woman to light the Shabbat candles in the house in

117

Lennox Street any more. In recent years Susan had done it, but more often than not she hadn't been there. Now she was gone altogether. He still had the memory of the noisy family at the table. It was a painful memory. It wasn't a long walk to shul; that was what had come to matter. It was only when he sang in the synagogue that he didn't feel old.

Absence was in Jewish blood in the same way it was in the blood of the Irish. People were always going. That's how it was. His father's brothers and sisters were in Poland and Germany and England and South Africa and America; they had left their parents in Russia and never seen them again. Mr Field had always known Susan would go, sooner or later, like her sisters, to Palestine perhaps. That was why she wanted a degree, so that she could teach there. He'd never been comfortable with the young Zionists she used to bring home. He enjoyed the arguments, but there was too much socialism and communism flying around for his taste. He didn't really notice when she stopped bringing anybody home at all. He was too busy at the synagogue.

'There's nothing more I can tell you, Mr Gillespie.'

'She has a sister in London.'

'Yes, in Finchley.'

'Would she have contacted her?'

'Susan's nearly ten years younger. Rachel has a family now.' It wasn't an answer; it was empty evasion. It was a man trying not to think.

'What does she say about it?'

'We just don't know, Sergeant, none of us know.'

'She must think something.'

'I went to the police again, when Rachel came over, but there was nothing more to find out. Susan was living her own life. She lived in the house, but we hardly saw each other. Sometimes she was here, sometimes she wasn't. I know she was very unsettled. I should have talked to her, I know I should. Rachel felt the only thing we could do was wait –'

Stefan took a small photograph of Susan Field from his pocket. He had found it upstairs in one of the boxes. It was a head-and-shoulder shot, taken not long ago. Her hair was cut short; she wore a dark, tailored jacket.

'Can I borrow this? I'll get a copy made.'

'Yes, of course.'

'I will do my best to find out what happened to Susan, Mr Field. Would you mind if Hannah Rosen looked through her things? She might see something I can't see. She knew Susan. If there was anything out of place –'

The cantor nodded, but there was really no hope in his tired eyes, only growing resignation. He had already waited too long to look for anything now, let alone hope.

'Is there anyone else she was close to? Anywhere else she could have gone? Was there anyone else she knew in England?'

Mr Field shook his head. 'We talked to everyone we could think of.'

Stefan waited. He could see that the old man was holding back tears. But there were still questions he had to ask, however difficult they were.

'You know she was going to have an abortion?'

Brian Field shrugged, pushing away the tears.

'It's what she said to Hannah, in her letters. I didn't know before.' He turned his eyes back to the window. 'I knew she was unhappy. I didn't know why. And if I'd asked her she wouldn't have told me. That's how it was.'

'What about the man who was the father?'

'I know what Hannah told me.' The words were short and curt.

'Do you think Hannah was the only person Susan confided in?'

He turned back towards Stefan and nodded again.

'Yes. It doesn't say much for us, does it, Sergeant?'

Bewley's Café in Grafton Street was quiet. It was still early. Breakfasters were lingering over morning papers and the waitresses were laying the tables for lunch. Hannah Rosen and Stefan Gillespie sat over empty tea cups. He had asked her to go to Lennox Street to look through the belongings in Susan Field's room. There was at least a chance she might see something significant that would have meant nothing to him. He had talked about the letters. He had tried to piece together what they said about the time leading up to Susan's disappearance. Now he had faced the most difficult part of the conversation; telling her that Hugo Keller had left Ireland. There would be no opportunity to ask any questions about the day Susan Field went to the clinic in Merrion Square now, or even to confirm that she really did go there. Hannah saw how uncomfortable he was and that did something to curb her anger, but she also knew he wasn't revealing everything. She had talked easily before; now there was distance. It wasn't mistrust, but it was doubt.

'When did you find out he'd gone?'

'Yesterday, after I saw you.'

'From the Special Branch man, Sergeant Lynch?'

'No, I haven't seen Lynch again.'

It was an answer, but she could hear it wasn't the full answer.

'You just heard?'

'He'd been released. There were no charges against him. There was nothing to stop him leaving the country. He took the mail boat on Saturday.'

'He wasn't wasting any time then.'

'That's how it looks.' Stefan shrugged.

'You think that's just a convenient coincidence?'

'I don't know what you mean.'

'You're the detective, aren't you? You're the one who was going to ask him what happened when Susan went to see him. Isn't there something a bit odd about the fact that he's suddenly not here any more? No questions, so no answers, when that's the last place we definitely know she was going.'

He couldn't even begin to talk about Hugo Keller and Adolf Mahr, or about the spat that was going on between Special Branch and Military Intelligence. He didn't know what any of that meant anyway, and if he found out it was hardly likely to be information he could tell anyone else, even Hannah. There were a lot of things going on that might explain Hugo Keller's abrupt departure. It certainly seemed as if the leader of the Nazi Party and the Garda Special Branch wanted him out of the way. Whether that had anything at all to do with Susan Field's disappearance five months ago it was impossible to say; it was hard to believe it could do. It really did feel like a coincidence, but even while Stefan thought that he questioned it. As Hannah had put it, it was a very convenient coincidence.

'You're not going to tell me everything, are you?'

'I am going to find out what happened to Susan.'

She smiled. 'All right. That'll have to do. For now. I'll have to put up with it and trust you. But don't lie to me, please. Will you promise me that?'

121

'I'm not going to lie.'

She looked at him for a long moment, then nodded.

'The letters did help though?' she said.

'I'm sure it won't be hard to identify the priest.' He was trying to find something positive to say, a way to leave all the secrecy and evasion behind.

'It's the only place left now, isn't it? Now that Keller's gone.'

'It's one place.' He was silent for a moment. There was a question about the letters, Susan's last letters, that was still in his head.

'There are things in the letters . . . I'm talking about how she felt, the last few times she wrote. She was in a very dark place. It doesn't always sound like that. She was still making jokes, but you know what I mean.'

Hannah was surprised. 'I'm not sure I do.'

'She was very unhappy, more than that,' Stefan continued.

'Is this mail boat territory again?' She was tight-lipped.

'No. Dark places can be dangerous.'

'Is that from the Garda psychology manual?'

'When I'm not a guard I'm a human being. Only part-time of course.'

He let his irritation show and it seemed to make her rein in her own.

'Are you telling me you think she killed herself?'

'I need to look at it all. I have to try and understand her. You can only have so much emptied out of you sometimes. Not everyone can take it.'

Hannah was looking at him harder as he spoke. She could see that he wasn't trying to explain anything away. He was talking about himself.

'I've thought about it, of course I have,' she said more

calmly. 'I still think I know her though. I don't believe she ever had suicide in her head.'

'All right,' he replied. 'When will you go to Lennox Street?'

'I'm going straight there.' She was pleased to have something to do.

They got up and walked through Bewley's to the street.

'Do you live in Dublin?' Hannah asked unexpectedly.

'I've just got a couple of rooms. It's not much, but it's better than the Garda barracks. That's where you're meant to be if you're single –'

'Your son's in Wicklow though.'

They came out into Grafton Street and stopped.

'He lives with my parents. My wife died.' He said it simply enough, because it was a simple fact about his life. He was used to saying it.

'I'm sorry. I didn't mean to pry – I hadn't –' She looked away.

'It was two years ago.'

'It must be hard for him, you being away.'

'It's hard for both of us. But you do the best you can.'

They were very ordinary words, but she felt their weight.

'Phone me at Pearse Street when you can.'

'Yes, I'll phone you later.'

He smiled and walked quickly away. She watched him go, until he finally disappeared into the crowds further down Grafton Street, then she turned to walk up to Stephen's Green to get the tram to Lennox Street.

*

Stefan Gillespie walked through the empty rooms at twenty-five Merrion Square. There was nothing to see that hadn't been seen. It was a mess, what with the searching downstairs and hurried packing upstairs, and more policemen than you'd wish on anybody. But of course there was nobody to care one way or another now. He could sense that Hugo Keller wouldn't miss what he had left behind. There was valuable equipment in the clinic and the basement; that was money. But upstairs only a few rooms had been inhabited. Stefan had no sense that this was a home. There were no pictures, no photographs; the furniture was no more than functional. He was standing in the room that had been Keller's bedroom now, looking out at the gardens in the middle of Merrion Square. On the unmade bed were clothes that had been pulled from the wardrobe and chest of drawers and never packed. Dessie took out a packet of Sweet Afton and slowly extracted a cigarette.

'Liam Dwyer was still on duty when your man came back from the Shelbourne. Jimmy Lynch was with him. About half an hour later a car came across the square from the German consulate. Keller brought a suitcase out and Jimmy did the honours with another one. Then the car took Keller off. I'd say they must have driven straight to Dún Laoghaire for the mail boat.'

'Who was driving?'

'From what Liam says, probably your man Adolf Mahr.'

It didn't make much sense, but it wasn't a surprise.

'If I was director of the National Museum, I'd have classier pals,' continued Dessie.

'But if you want a job done you're maybe better doing it yourself.'

'You mean getting him out, Sarge?'

'He knew he'd be going, I'd say the moment we walked in here.'

Dessie waited for a moment. 'You'd think after us and Special Branch the place deserved a rest.'

'And what's that supposed to mean?'

Garda MacMahon lit the cigarette and held it between his fingers, not smoking it, just smiling. Stefan knew the expression well enough. It always gave Dessie a little bit of pleasure to know more than his sergeant did.

'I was in O'Donaghue's for a pint on Sunday, on my way home like.' He drew on the cigarette. 'And I thought I'd walk back through the square afterwards. Jesus, I swear to God there was two more of them at it in here.'

'At what?'

'They were searching the place. They weren't the best. They had the sense not to turn the lights on, but they were flashing a torch all over the place. They broke in at the back. There's a window into the cellar smashed.'

'It couldn't have been Lynch. He's got the key.'

'No, they weren't Special Branch.'

'So who were they?'

'I walked down Fitzwilliam Lane and waited for them to come over the back wall. From the laughter you'd think they were at it for a lark. They went into Baggot Street, and along Fitzwilliam Street, and into a house in Fitzwilliam Place. I've got the number here –' Dessie fished in his pockets.

'One of them was a tall, fair-haired feller?'

Dessie's lips tightened round the cigarette. He drew the smoke deeper into his lungs. The pleasure of being one up on his sergeant was short-lived.

'He was watching us at the Shelbourne. I don't know the other one.'

'Who are they?' Dessie waited for an explanation. It didn't come.

'I couldn't tell you what they're doing or why they're doing it. Let's say they're freelancers. What did you find out about Keller's nurse?'

'She's a couple of rooms off Dorset Street, but when I was in O'Donaghue's for that pint the little dark feller, Max he calls himself, reckoned Sheila Hogan spent much more time here. She'd be in the pub with Keller a lot, always at it they were, arguing, the two of them. Then back here to make up. That's only Max's opinion and the man's a hoor for the gossip.'

Stefan walked to a table that stood at one side of the bed. Papers were piled up on it. There were tumblers and empty beer bottles, and an ashtray heaped with cigarette ends. There was a small mirror, and next to it a brush and a comb and a powder compact. It was a makeshift dressing table. He opened the drawer and took out a pair of crumpled silk stockings.

'She wouldn't buy those on what he paid her, not as a nurse anyway.'

'Beat me to it again, Sarge. Will we talk to her, then?'

'Where is she now? Dorset Street?' Stefan asked.

Dessie smiled, stubbing his cigarette out, finally ahead of the game.

'She's in the Mater Hospital. It seems she fell down the stairs.'

Sheila Hogan's face was swollen and bruised; her arm was in plaster. She was propped up on pillows in a ward full of women who were a lot older than her; most of them without the strength or the desire to do anything other than lie flat. Mixed with the smell of hospital antiseptic was the smell of old age. As Stefan Gillespie approached the bed the first thing he saw in the nurse's eyes was fear. It wasn't just any fear; it was the fear that he was going to hit her, there and then, lying in the hospital bed. She already knew he was a guard before she recognised him from the raid at Merrion Square. He could see it was that way round. Nobody was born with the instinct to spot a policeman and know what he was. You needed a reason to learn that.

She said nothing as he introduced himself again.

'I need to ask you some questions.'

'How many more answers do you want?'

'I didn't have a chance to get any before.'

'Didn't your friends tell you what I said?'

'You mean Sergeant Lynch. You've been talking to him then?'

She didn't reply, but he knew who'd put her in hospital.

'That'd be before you fell down the stairs, would it? Just before.'

There was something else in her eyes now; defiance, contempt.

'Did he find what he was looking for?'

'You'd be better asking him.'

'You know Hugo Keller's gone? Germany probably.'

'I wouldn't blame him. If I had somewhere to go, I'd go myself.'

'Come on, Sheila. You were playing doctors and nurses in more ways than one in Merrion Square. I know there's fellers who keep stockings and knickers by their beds, but I wouldn't have put Hugo down for that game.'

'Maybe he'd surprise you.'

'Did he tell you he was going?' asked Stefan.

'What's it to you?'

'Not a lot. But then it wasn't much to him. You, I mean.

127

He didn't stop by on the way to the boat to pick you up, Sheila. He'd have been sitting down for a beer on board I'd say, about the time you fell down the stairs.'

'With a bit of luck it choked him.'

'He didn't even say goodbye then?'

'This is the only goodbye I got.' She lifted her plastered arm and gestured at her battered, blackened face as best she could.

'We've got something in common then. Sergeant Lynch and his friend called on me too. They thought I must have taken it. I don't know if it was a guess, or maybe it was what you told them the first time round?'

'Is it sympathy you're looking for, Sergeant?'

'I don't really know what Jimmy Lynch wants, but if I haven't got it and you haven't got it, maybe we're both done with falling downstairs.' He waited for a response. There wasn't one, just the same look of contempt. He took the photograph of Susan Field from his pocket and held it up to her.

'Did you ever see this woman?'

She looked at the photo and shook her head.

'She'd have visited Keller.'

'A lot of women did. I'd hardly remember them all.'

'It was about five months ago.'

'I'm not saying she didn't. I'm saying I don't remember her.'

'Susan Field.'

She shook her head again.

'I do know the name's not in the appointments book, Sheila.'

'You think they use their real names?'

'The last thing we know about Susan Field is that she

was going to Merrion Square, to see Hugo Keller for an abortion. She'd an appointment. The twenty-sixth of July. She hasn't been seen since. She's disappeared.'

'That's not my business. I don't know her.'

'How many abortions did he do in the last six months?'

'I don't know.'

'Come on! It can't be that many.'

'There were people he didn't want me to see. Special.'

'What do you mean special?'

'It's not hard to work out, is it? Important people, people with money, politicians from over the road in Leinster House. Bigwigs who want extra privacy. People who wouldn't like to walk into a hospital with a dose of the clap, or let anyone know whose wife they got pregnant. Important people.'

'I don't think there was anything very important about Susan Field, except to the people who loved her. All they want to do is find her.'

'Maybe she doesn't want them to.'

Her words were cold. It didn't tell Stefan that Sheila Hogan knew more than she was saying, but if she did it was very clear sentiment wasn't going to open her mouth. He put the photograph back in his pocket.

'They change their minds,' she said. 'They don't always turn up.'

'What would you think if I said the man who sent Susan Field to see Herr Keller, to get the abortion, was a priest? Would that surprise you?'

'I wasn't paid to be surprised.'

'So has that happened before?'

'You'd have to ask Mr Keller. I wasn't paid to ask questions either.'

'I wish he was around to ask, Sheila. He wasn't a great talker, then?'

'There were two things he wanted me for. The second one didn't involve a lot of talking, not the way he did it anyway.' There was a disdainful sneer on the nurse's face again. It could have been for Hugo Keller, but Stefan felt it was for men in general. And he wasn't excluded.

'This book of Keller's, the one Jimmy Lynch is looking for, the one neither of us knows anything about, is that what he kept in there? Names, addresses, appointments? The things he didn't want anybody to find out?'

He threw this at her, not expecting an answer, but hoping for more than he'd got from Jimmy Lynch or Lieutenant Cavendish. Whatever the book was, it had to contain answers to some of the questions he couldn't ask Keller face to face now. All he wanted to know was whether there was anything in it about Susan Field. But Sheila Hogan had nothing to give.

'If I knew where it was I wouldn't be in here, would I? You think I give a toss about anything of Hugo Keller's? I've got him to thank for this. I don't care about any fecking book or any fecking women or anybody else. He can screw himself as far as I'm concerned. If ever I saw him again it'd be to spit in his eye. If you want to take the message I can always spit in yours.'

# 8. Kilmashogue

When Stefan came out of the Mater on to Eccles Street, Dessie MacMahon was there, waiting for him in the black Austin. A body had been found in the Dublin Mountains. The State Pathologist was already on his way there.

'Do we know what they've got?'

'Bones, that's all Mr Wayland-Smith said. Oh, and *she* was in, looking for you. About an hour ago.' He didn't need to be more specific.

'What did she want?'

'She left a couple of books. And there's a note.'

Dessie reached over to the back seat as he pulled out into the traffic.

'Drive, Dessie! I'll do it.' Stefan lifted up two thick, heavy volumes. One was still quite new; the other was well-used and thoroughly dog-eared.

'She was a while writing the note. I didn't read it,' grinned Dessie.

'If we want to get to this body alive you'd be better looking where you're going,' snapped Stefan. As Dessie drove on, whistling quietly in amusement, he unfolded the note that was tucked into one of the books.

*Just back from Mr Field's. The only thing that struck me were Susan's books, well, she never read much when we were at school. Most of them were for her UCD course. But look at what's written at the front of these.*

He registered the title of the first book as he opened it, *The Dawn of Modern Thought: Descartes, Spinoza, Leibnitz*; on the flyleaf was a name, a place, and a date, 'Francis Byrne, Pontifical University, Maynooth, 1932'. The other book was *The Revolt of the Angels* by Anatole France. Inside, on the flyleaf, in the same handwriting was written, 'Read it and give it a chance, your good friend Francis'. He didn't think either book would impress Father Anthony Carey very much. He looked back at Hannah Rosen's note.

*I called in at the UCD office in Earlsfort Terrace this morning, asking about courses. I mentioned Francis Byrne. He turns out to be Father Francis Byrne, a lecturer in medieval philosophy last year. He left UCD about six months ago. The woman said she thought he'd gone abroad somewhere.*

Stefan was both pleased and irritated. Hannah couldn't walk around Dublin questioning people as if she was still barging into Hugo Keller's clinic. But she had found something, a new place to start. The priest was that place.

All night the rain had poured down the wooded slopes of Kilmashogue, already sodden with weeks of wet weather. On a bend in the steep road up into the Dublin Mountains, where the embankment had been weakened by the felling of trees, it had collapsed part of the hillside and thick, sticky mud was blocking the track. The body had been found by a dog belonging to one of the workmen who had come up in a tractor to clear the road. The soil that had covered the shallow grave had been washed away in the landslide and the body with it. Now there was only a cold drizzle. They were standing in the low cloud that covered the mountain. On a fine day you saw the whole of Dublin laid out below and the sea beyond, stretching away to meet the sky. Today there was only the wet mist and the pile of earth across the road and, just above it, something almost indistinguishable from the black earth that Wayland-Smith was scraping at as he knelt in the mud. Detective Sergeant Gillespie and Garda MacMahon stood over him. A little way off two gardaí were smoking with the workmen who had discovered the body. The dog, tied to the tractor now, whined and barked intermittently, his only thought how to get back to the bones that had been so rudely dragged away from him. Wayland-Smith was scraping at a skull now, the eye sockets packed with soil. Other bones were visible just below it. Three ribs stood out – they were the colour of the wet earth, brown and yellow and black.

'It's hard to say how old. There's a lot of peat, which would keep things fresh for longer. It's quite well preserved in parts. There's even some skin coverage in places. And there's some hair on the skull.' He leant forward, using a trowel to prise what looked like more mud from the body. 'As well as several pieces of clothing that haven't really broken down yet.'

'So not that long?'

'Two to five years. No longer than seven. Male I think.'

'Any idea of his age?'

'Adult clearly, but not old, twenty or thirty from the teeth.'

'He's a mess.'

'Quite an unusual one.'

'Why?'

'The bones didn't get like that lying here. It looks as if someone took a sledgehammer to them. So the question is, was that before or after he died?'

Three wet hours at Kilmashogue produced nothing more. The bones were scraped and dug out of the hillside, wrapped in sacking and loaded on to the workman's trailer to be brought to the morgue. Dessie drove the Austin back into town, while Stefan went with Wayland-Smith in his shooting brake. There was little to say about the body. There was no obvious means of identification yet, though the discovery of a wallet where a trouser pocket had once been offered some hope. There was also a small round hole in the skull, close to the temple, which suggested a bullet.

It was what they might have expected. Nobody looked for bodies in the mountains, but they were there, from the War of Independence and the Civil War that followed. IRA men executed by the Dublin Metropolitan Police's G Division; informers executed by the IRA; victims of the Black and Tans; landowners shot for being too English and farm workers shot for being too Irish; anti-Treaty IRA men dragged into the night by pro-Treaty IRA men and pro-Treaty IRA men killed by old comrades; and in the midst of all that self-righteous, brutal murder not a few who were on the wrong end of old scores dressed up as something to sing about in years to come. These were the bodies most people preferred to forget about, bodies no one in the Irish Free State really wanted to find, let alone the Garda Síochána.

If the body at Kilmashogue looked like one of those there would be a slim file and no further investigation.

134

They would know when Wayland-Smith had finished the post-mortem, but that wasn't why Stefan was sitting in the estate that always smelt of fish. It was the doctor's role as a lecturer in the medical faculty at University College Dublin that interested him. The doctor's reputation as a pathologist was exceeded only by his reputation as a man who knew everybody who was anybody, especially in the academic world. He was a snob, but that made him a walking *Who's Who* of Ireland.

'I'm looking for a priest,' said Stefan quietly.

'Are they hard to find on our isle of saints and scholars?'

'As it happens it's the scholarly element I'm interested in.'

'I wouldn't leap to any metaphysical conclusions about our body.'

'I'm looking for a priest who's teaching at UCD.'

'You won't find many in my faculty. Medicine's not a strong point.'

'But you know who's who.'

'Do I want to know why you're asking me this, Sergeant?'

'How often would students encounter priests in the university?'

'Where do you want to start? We've got a selection of bishops and monsignors on the senate, some admirable, some excruciating. There are various senior figures in the faculties; and the chaplains of course.'

'He'd be lecturing in philosophy,' continued Stefan.

'Metaphysics without God, mumbo without jumbo.'

'Thirties or forties. Not older.'

'The fact that a priest might be lecturing doesn't mean he's on the staff. He could be coming in from Maynooth, or a seminary, especially if it's the kind of philosophy that counts the number of angels on an Irish pinhead.'

'I think he might be interested in something more modern.'

'Ah, he's been teaching banned philosophers and you're on to him!'

'This relates to our friend Herr Keller and his abortion clinic.'

Wayland-Smith stopped smiling.

'I thought that was dead in the water.'

'This is about a missing woman, not Keller. But there's a link between him and the woman, possibly a link between both of them and the priest.'

'On the face of it that would be extremely unlikely I'd have thought, Sergeant.' His voice was flat. He didn't like the conversation's direction.

'Father Francis Byrne.'

The State Pathologist said nothing, but Stefan could see the name meant something to him. Wayland-Smith knew who Father Byrne was.

'You know him then?'

'I know of him.'

'You sound like you don't like him.'

'I'm not too keen on the company he keeps.'

'What do you mean?'

The State Pathologist hesitated for a moment.

'Whatever this is about, it sounds unpleasant, very unpleasant. Father Byrne has powerful friends; I think you should know that. One very powerful friend in particular. I'd be careful asking questions that associate him with an abortionist, unless you're sure of your ground. Even then –'

'I just want to talk to him. Apparently he's out of the country now.'

'Do you know who Monsignor Robert Fitzpatrick is?'

'The Association of Catholic Strength?'

'Your man Byrne is a protégé of his. A clever fellow from what I know, which isn't much, and very personable. I've met him once or twice. Fitzpatrick was trying to get him on the General Board of Studies last year.'

'This isn't about university politics.'

'Nor is Monsignor Fitzpatrick. He's about politics and influence in a much bigger arena. And the kind of politics he's about aren't very palatable, to some of us at least, though they're becoming rather more so to others.'

'I'm looking for a woman who was a student of Father Byrne's.'

'Who else knows about this, Gillespie?'

'Dessie.' Stefan gave a half smile. 'I'm not spreading it about.'

'You haven't mentioned it to Inspector Donaldson?'

'I'm sure I will do.'

'He'd be a man who thinks quite a lot of Monsignor Fitzpatrick.'

'I'd say he would.'

'So he won't like it. And he won't be the only one.'

'I imagine Monsignor Fitzpatrick would know where Father Byrne is, wouldn't you? That's all I want to find out. Hardly a contentious question.'

'A priest, a woman, an abortion clinic! That's your starting point?'

Stefan Gillespie shrugged. 'I didn't choose where to start.'

\*

Monsignor Robert Fitzpatrick had a large house at the Stephen's Green end of Earlsfort Terrace, between the Alexandra College for the Higher Education of Ladies and a small, private nursing home. The other side of the road was taken up by the long stone facade and the vaguely classical, pillared entrance to University College Dublin. A crowd of students, noisy even from where Stefan was standing, was flooding down the steps. He watched them from across the road; mostly they were men, but there were several women, much the same age as Susan Field would have been.

Two brass plaques, on either side of the front door of the house, announced the monsignor himself and the Association of Catholic Strength, of which he was the president and prime mover. As Stefan walked up the steps the front door was open. He entered a hallway that was lined with posters. He recognised one of them immediately; it decorated the wall of Inspector Donaldson's office. A man in a military uniform stood with an upraised sword in his hand. 'Soldiers Are We!' Next to it, on another poster, a farmer stood in a ploughed field, deep in thought; on one side of him was a hammer and sickle, on the other a cross. 'Workers of Ireland: Which Way?' A staircase stretched up ahead. To the left, another open door looked into a room lined with books and religious pictures; it was a shop. To the right, there were double doors, one of them open. A man was speaking, loudly and passionately. Stefan went in. He saw that it was a meeting room, lined with rows of chairs and, if not packed to overflowing, full enough for a quiet afternoon. A piece of paper was thrust into his hand by a middle-aged woman who smiled enthusiastically and whispered a cheerful welcome. 'Please, do take a seat.' He sat down on the chair nearest the door.

The walls were decorated with the posters he'd seen in the hall. At the front of the room a man in his early fifties stood at a table speaking. On either side of him sat men and women who looked as if they had been born to sit on committees and were fulfilling their destiny. He knew the speaker must be Monsignor Fitzpatrick himself, in a clerical collar and a black suit noticeably more well-cut than the usual threadbare priestly uniform. If he had any doubts the look of rapture on the faces of several of the elderly women in the room would have been enough to confirm it. But the audience was by no means all elderly or middle-aged; there were students from across the road as well, all listening intently. And as Stefan took in the words he began to understand the discomfort Wayland-Smith had shown earlier, about exactly what it was that Monsignor Robert Fitzpatrick represented.

'There is war going on, a war that no one sees. And we are here because we understand, because we do see, because we must take the side of Christ's Church in this war that puts the very existence of His Church in peril. Has not the veil of the temple already been rent in Russia, where blood and darkness fill the land, where the hounds of atheism are in full cry, supplanting the True Messiah with the false messiahs of communism and capitalism? And who are the leaders of this diabolical army, all-powerful through their control of the world's finance and industry? You don't know? Even your Church does not tell you? Yet their plans are in plain sight, for the destruction of all belief in God and dominance over His creation: *The Protocols of the Elders of Zion*!' He held up a book, brandishing it before his audience. He crossed himself and many of his listeners did the same.

'The armies of Judeo-Masonic communism have invaded every corner of human life, proclaiming a doctrine of illusory freedom and equality that puts atheistic man in revolt against God, as Satan once rebelled. The pity of it all is that once God offered the Jews a glorious role as the harbingers of spiritual grace. They refused that gift and down the centuries they have devised a scheme of destruction that is coming to fruition in our century. Didn't Jewish financiers and Freemasons start the world war? Wasn't every leader of the hideous revolution in Russia a Jew? Aren't Jewish bankers plunging the world into economic chaos? The clock stands at one minute to midnight and still, even in the Vatican, the chimes of midnight are unheard. But in Germany Herr Hitler has heard. God has given Germany a great leader in a time of peril. There is no hope in democracy! It has had its day. Some in the Church see Herr Hitler as our enemy. They are wrong! Shut out that siren song. Lash yourselves to the mast of faith. Steer towards the light!'

The priest sat down, mopping his brow with a gesture that told the audience how much had been drained out of him. Applause erupted and soon the whole room was on its feet. Stefan stood too, dragged up by the movement of those around him. As Monsignor Fitzpatrick rose again there was a reverential silence. Heads were bowed in prayer and as the prayer ended, the audience filed out, some clearly moved to silence, others talking enthusiastically. Stefan waited as people left. At the front of the room the committee members talked to the monsignor for a few moments longer, and then they too filed out. The middle-aged woman who had pointed Stefan to his seat was collecting up the leaflets and papers left behind on the chairs.

'We're finished for today.' She smiled warmly as she approached him. 'But you will let me know if there's any information you want.'

'I was hoping to have a word with the monsignor.'

'He gets very tired after these meetings. Inspiration takes its toll.'

'I won't keep him long.'

She smiled a motherly smile. He liked her. She made him feel as if he was at a cake sale to raise money for new kneelers for church pews. She moved down to the table where the priest was gathering his papers into a black leather briefcase. As she spoke to him he looked round and smiled at Stefan. Then she came back, still clutching her bundle of creased leaflets, and headed for the door. Stefan walked towards Fitzpatrick and stopped.

'We haven't seen you before, have we?' said the priest.

The smile didn't survive Stefan's explanation of who he was.

'And why exactly would you have questions to ask me, Sergeant?'

'It's a colleague of yours I wanted to talk to, Father Francis Byrne.'

Monsignor Fitzpatrick's brow furrowed.

'I gather he's not in the country now,' continued Stefan.

'I understand that to be the case.'

'I need to contact him.'

'For what reason?'

'It has to do with his teaching at UCD.'

'I was Father Byrne's immediate superior there. He has worked with me for a long time. I'm also a member of the university senate. I can't imagine Father Byrne's path crossing yours. But if there is anything you have a good reason to know about, I'll do what I can to help you.'

'I'd like to know where I can contact him. The university

doesn't have a forwarding address, other than yours. Am I right that he's in Germany?'

There was no answer; the shutters were up.

'As for any questions, they're of a personal nature.'

'And why would the Gardaí have personal questions to ask of a priest who was in my pastoral care until very recently, Sergeant Gillespie?'

'All I need is an address, Monsignor.'

'Are you suggesting Father Byrne has done something wrong?'

'I'm not suggesting anything.'

'Then I think you need to make yourself plainer.'

'You do have an address for him.'

'I can contact him if I feel it's necessary.'

'Can I ask when he left Ireland?'

'It was some time in the summer. August, I think.'

'When are you expecting him back?'

'I don't know that I am expecting him back.'

'Can I ask why he left?'

'Why he left is the business of the Church.'

'He isn't working for you now?' Stefan persisted.

'No.'

'He was living here when he left Ireland though?'

'This is none of your business, but since you are determined to be intrusive, I will tell you that before Father Byrne left for Germany, he and I had not been on the best of terms for some time. He lived here and he worked for me. It was my influence that got him the post as a lecturer that he seemed – eventually – to find more important than his duties as a priest. As his obligations to me became a burden to him, it was inappropriate that he should remain here. I suggested he went back to the seminary at Maynooth.

However, Father Byrne took the unusual course of taking a flat somewhere.'

Stefan had to hold back a smile at how much venom the man in black had squeezed into the word 'flat'; it was the Fall of Man and Sodom and Gomorrah in a single, apocalyptic syllable.

'Did his students ever come here, Monsignor?'

'A lot of people come here. You've seen that yourself.'

'I suppose I mean friends, rather than just students.' He was treading on dangerous ground, but the resentment Fitzpatrick clearly felt towards Francis Byrne made it worth pushing. The monsignor had a high opinion of himself and his importance; it was something else Stefan could use.

'I find myself in a very difficult position, Monsignor Fitzpatrick. I have an investigation to pursue, a very serious one, and a very sensitive one. A woman is missing. She was a student at UCD and Father Byrne was one of her lecturers. He had a friendship with this woman, a close friendship. I have good reason to believe he was one of the last people to see her before she disappeared. I'm sure you would want him to help us if he could.'

'I don't like the words close friendship in this context, Sergeant.'

'They're words that need go no further, Monsignor.' Stefan left the sentence hanging in the air. He didn't need to say anything about the possibility of scandal for Fitzpatrick to see that he had to give something.

'Father Byrne was sometimes less careful in his relationships than he should have been.' The priest spoke slowly and carefully. 'I don't suggest that there was ever anything unpriestly about his behaviour, but he did perhaps regard himself too much as part of the university rather than as

143

a man apart, which is the path of the priest. There were things Francis and I shared that we share no longer. I understand your problem, Sergeant Gillespie, but it has nothing to do with me. I'm sure if there is anything Father Byrne can do to assist you in your search for this woman he will. If you write to him, he will, of course, reply. My sister will have his address.'

He picked up his briefcase. It was clear he would say no more. He stood for a moment by the table, suddenly looking slightly lost. Then he turned and walked out without another word. Stefan thought that behind the irritation and indignation tears were beginning to well in the priest's eyes.

As Stefan came out of the meeting room, the woman was still there, standing in the doorway of the shop. The footsteps of the monsignor could be heard, climbing the stairs. The woman was looking up after him. She turned to Stefan, an expression of concern changing quickly to a smile.

'My brother says you need Father Byrne's address, in Danzig.'

'He's not in Germany then?'

'Isn't it Germany anyway? Or don't they want it to be? I can't remember. It's something like that. But it's very simple, you can address letters to him at the cathedral in Oliva. He's working for the bishop there.'

The monsignor could have told him that easily enough. There was more going on between Robert Fitzpatrick and Francis Byrne than not seeing eye-to-eye. There was real hostility, at least on the monsignor's part. Stefan thanked the woman and turned to go. She pushed a leaflet into his hand.

'Your wife should read it too.'

He came out into Earlsfort Terrace. It was cold and almost dark, but he was pleased to breathe fresh air. As he walked back towards Stephen's Green he screwed the leaflet into a tight ball and dropped it into the gutter.

# 9. The Gate

At Pearse Street Garda station there was a note on Stefan's desk. Wayland-Smith wanted to talk to him at the morgue. As he turned back to the door Inspector Donaldson was there, eyeing him, with the strained expression that meant he knew he wouldn't relish the answers to the questions he had to ask.

'What's happening with this body at Kilmashogue?'

'I'm just going to find out if Doctor Wayland-Smith's got anything.'

'Was he killed?'

'I don't suppose he buried himself.'

Donaldson pursed his lips impatiently.

'Is it going to be an active investigation or not?'

'If there's anything to act on.'

A shrug was not what the inspector wanted either.

'You know what I mean, Sergeant. How long was the body up there?'

'He's not sure. It could be two or three years, or it could go back to the twenties. We'll find out. It doesn't smell like some old IRA job to me.'

James Donaldson would go a long way to avoid a conversation about the Civil War or the IRA, but a death you couldn't investigate because of 'all that' was in many ways preferable to a murder you had no choice but to investigate. Whenever he couldn't get a straight answer out of Stefan Gillespie it usually meant trouble. He could smell it now. The kind of trouble his detective sergeant brought into the station like old dog shit on his shoes.

The black mottled bones had been laid out like an archaeological exhibit in a museum, on the white marble slab at the centre of the big room in the mortuary. The scent of carbolic didn't altogether hide the reek of putrefaction that was not just in the air but in walls and floor and ceiling. It got you as you walked through the doors, a strange sweetness that caught at the back of your throat. The State Pathologist stood over the skeleton they had brought back from the mountainside, with an expression of almost tender concern. He spoke, as always, in the businesslike, dismissive tone that seemed to imply this was a job and nothing more, but his eyes showed something else. Two things in fact; that the dead mattered and that he would enjoy telling Detective Sergeant Gillespie everything he had found out.

'A young man, in his twenties or thirties; nothing to contradict my judgement there.' Wayland-Smith walked slowly round the slab. 'A number of broken bones. Now he's been scrubbed up rather more broken bones than I counted up at Kilmashogue. You'll see the left arm, multiple fracture of the humerus; broken ribs here and here, along with the sternum; in both legs, femur left, tibia right. He has suffered severe trauma. The fractures indicate it happened quickly, and with some force. A fall from a considerable height or, more likely, something hit him. The injuries would be consistent with a traffic accident for instance.'

'And that's what killed him?'

'It was certainly enough to result in death. But I can't say it did.'

'And what about this hole in the skull?'

Wayland-Smith smiled. It was the question he was waiting for.

'Certainly not a bullet. I didn't think so.' The words 'of course' hovered in the air. 'It could have happened during the accident, collision, whatever we choose to call it. Maybe something sharp, a protruding metal spike, narrow in diameter, hammered into his head by the force of impact.'

'Which might have killed him?'

'Again I can only say something of that sort would have had the potential to. With no soft tissue and no exit on the other side of the skull I can't know how far the projectile went into his brain. I don't much like the idea anyway.' He peered down at the hole. 'And it still seems remarkably neat, don't you think, if we're talking about smashing and hammering? There's nothing about it that strikes you as in any way familiar, Sergeant?'

'You mean you know what it is and I should know too?'

'Doesn't your family have a farm?'

Stefan nodded and waited. Wayland-Smith enjoyed these moments.

'I'm sure you've seen the butcher arrive to stick the pig.'

He turned and walked to a table close by. He picked up a heavy pistol, wood and grey metal, square and clumsy. Stefan was puzzled by the weapon; it looked like something that had been cobbled together from other guns, but as the State Pathologist held it up he recognised what it was.

'A Messrs Accles and Shelvoke captive bolt pistol,' proclaimed Wayland-Smith. 'Not a pretty thing. I borrowed it from the slaughterhouse which is, in the absence of cadavers, the source of carcasses, usually pigs, for my anatomy students. The skulls always come with a neat, round hole, where the animal has been, as we like to say – to show what nice fellers we all are – humanely stunned before slaughter. Now, if we take a pig's head –'

In a gesture that was unashamedly theatrical, he picked up a piece of oilcloth to reveal a pink pig's head, sitting on a large white plate; it only needed an apple in its mouth to go into an oven. He cocked the pistol and held it to the pink, bristly skin, just above the eyes, and fired. The blank cartridge discharged violently in the echoing mortuary; there was the smell of cordite. They were both deafened for several seconds. 'There are pistols that operate by means of compressed air,' shouted Wayland-Smith. 'It's all I could find, I'm afraid.' He put down the pistol and pointed at a small hole. 'Remove the flesh and we'd have a match for the hole in our friend's skull.'

'Which may or may not be the cause of death,' said Stefan.

'Yes. The function of the gun is to render an animal unconscious so that its throat can be cut for bleeding. I don't know if that killed him. But between whatever smashed into him and the bolt from the stunner piercing his brain, we can at least say death couldn't have come as a great surprise.'

'So when did it happen?'

'1932. Some time in June or July.'

'Now you're showing off.' Stefan hadn't expected that much.

Wayland-Smith gestured at several dark shapes sitting on a sheet of white paper. Beside them were the remains of the dead man's leather wallet.

'I've cut open the wallet. There are several pieces of what was originally paper. Naturally most of it has perished, but the conditions have preserved some things rather well. I've done as much as I can to clean up the scraps and dry them out; much more and we'd simply destroy the things. There's a little corner of a ten shilling note. It might get you some sort of date if you can find a serial number, but not terribly useful unless it was a new note. Some of the paper has simply congealed into papier mâché. You won't do much with that. And then there's this, which I think has two clearly discernible words, if you look here, and part of a date as well, just here.'

He handed across a magnifying glass and Stefan bent over the scrap of blackened paper. After a moment he could make out some letters and what looked like a number, all slightly darker than the surrounding brown.

'It's a three, or an eight?'

'One or the other I think.'

'And that has to be July, doesn't it? But no year.'

Wayland-Smith shrugged cheerfully and pointed. He had more.

'Do you think that says "the word" or "the world"? I'd go for "world".'

'Yes, I think you're right,' said Stefan, smiling slowly as he looked up at the State Pathologist. It was his turn now. '*The Way of the World*.'

'What do you mean, Sergeant?'

'William Congreve. I saw it at the Gate, a couple of years

ago. I suppose it would have been summer. It's July thirty-two. A theatre ticket.'

\*

Dessie MacMahon heaped a third spoonful of sugar into a steaming cup.

'Jesus, you'd want to keep your back to the wall in that place!'

'But your virtue's intact.'

'Sure that'd be telling!' Dessie grinned and gulped the tea. It had been his first visit to the Gate Theatre. Even if he'd got no further than the box office and front of house manager, its exotic reputation could not go unremarked. Closer examination of the ticket in the dead man's wallet had confirmed the date and the name of the play. It had also revealed a seat number.

'They thought I was joking them when I wanted to know who'd bought a ticket for a play two years ago. This front of house feller, Sinclair, was rolling his eyes at the woman in the box office like I was an eejit straight from the eejits' home.' Dessie grinned and drank some of the tea.

'But?' asked Stefan.

'Hmm?'

'There's a but.'

'The date on the ticket wasn't any old date, Sarge. It was the first night.' He was pleased with himself. 'When they put the thing on after –'

'I know what it is, Dessie.'

'That'll be why you're a sergeant so.' He drained the cup. 'Anyway, most people there wouldn't have bought tickets. They'd have been invited.'

'So there would have been a list?'

'There would.'

'And?'

'They're going to see if they can dig it out. I wouldn't say it's the best organised place. You wouldn't expect it to be, would you? The arty type.'

Stefan surveyed the debris piled on Dessie's desk. Garda MacMahon laughed. Suddenly they both sensed someone watching them. They looked round to see Inspector Donaldson in his usual position, in the doorway, debating whether he really wanted to walk in and have a conversation with Detective Sergeant Gillespie or whether it could be left for another day.

'This body's a nasty business. I've just seen the autopsy report.'

'Very nasty, sir.'

'Are you any nearer identifying him?'

'We've got something.'

'What about this woman you're looking for?'

'Susan Field.'

The inspector hesitated. This was what was really on his mind.

'I understand there's a connection with the man Keller, Sergeant.'

Donaldson sniffed uncomfortably, but it had to be said.

'There is. We know she was going to him for an abortion.'

The word still offended Inspector Donaldson and he thought he'd seen the back of it. 'Didn't they look into her at Rathmines? They didn't find anything.'

'There's more evidence now, and more reason to be concerned.'

'They concluded she'd gone to England,' persisted the inspector.

'I'm not convinced of that sir. There's no evidence at all. It's an assumption, just that. The abortion is still the last thing we know about Susan Field. Of course, if Keller was still here we'd have someone to talk to about it.'

Stefan and Dessie gazed blandly at Donaldson, waiting for him to say something. He was the one who had allowed the Special Branch detectives to pull Hugo Keller out of the Pearse Street cells. But as far as the inspector was concerned it wasn't his business any more, and that was the end of it.

'You'd better take that up with Special Branch.'

'It didn't go down well last time.' Stefan pointed at his bruised face.

'Is that some kind of accusation, Gillespie?'

'It should be. What do you think, sir? Shall we have a go?'

Stefan glanced at Dessie and Dessie tried hard to keep a straight face. Inspector Donaldson bristled. If there was any truth to the suggestion that Detective Sergeant Lynch had something to do with Gillespie's injuries it was between the two of them. Lynch was a thug; Gillespie ought to have known better than to cross him. No one would thank James Donaldson for poking his nose into Special Branch's sewer and he had no intention of doing so.

'I suggest you get on with your job and put personal matters aside.'

He was pleased with that; it came very close to sounding like leadership. But there seemed no need to cross the threshold into the CID office now. He turned and walked away. The soles of his always highly polished shoes echoed loudly and decisively along the corridor. Dessie looked at Stefan.

'You haven't told him there's a priest in it somewhere?'

'Hasn't the man got enough to worry about?' laughed Stefan.

The telephone rang. He reached across the desk and picked it up. The voice at the other end was an odd combination of the punctilious and lazy.

'Is this the CID office? I'm afraid my front of house manager took the number, but not the name. His best suggestion was that I ask for the fat detective who smokes Sweet Afton. I don't know how many fat detectives you have, and perhaps they all smoke Sweet Afton; however it may give you a clue and, given your line of work, that should be more than enough.'

'Is that the Gate?'

'Faultless! You see, I didn't underestimate you.'

'I'm the thin one who doesn't smoke Sweet Afton.'

'It's about the first-night ticket. We have a name for you.'

Crossing over the Liffey and on to O'Connell Street Stefan Gillespie looked at the Christmas window full of toys at Clery's. Tom's tricycle was there. He had paid the deposit at the beginning of November and a little more at the start of December. When his wages came next week he would be able to find the rest. It was a long walk to the far end of the wide street, past the statue of O'Connell the Liberator, past the GPO, past Parnell and the incongruous Nelson's Column. The other Christmas windows went unnoticed. His mind was full of things that didn't connect with each other. He hoped the Gate Theatre would at least show him a way forward for the body on the hillside at Kilmashogue.

The theatre made up one side of the Rotunda Hospital, where its grey eighteenth-century facade turned sharply into Parnell Square. A small door, almost unnoticeable until you reached it and fell up the steps, led into a dark and narrow corridor, more like the entrance to a Georgian town house that had seen better days, as most of the houses in this part of Dublin had, than to a theatre whose reputation was not measured by its size but by the grace and the compassion it brought to its cramped and untidy quarters. When you walked into that corridor and up the steep steps, to an auditorium that seated barely three hundred people, you had done more than enter a theatre. If there was anywhere in Dublin where the writ of the city's squinting windows didn't run, it was here. The Gate was an island. Its founder, Micheál Mac Liammóir, an actor who gave his life's greatest performance as an Englishman triumphantly playing an Irishman, had made the play the theatre's only purpose and in doing had created something more than a theatre. The Gate had ignored Dublin and had made Dublin, a city that was nothing if not contrary, love it for that. Along the way, almost unnoticed, it had given lungs to a city that, despite all its passions and its furious energies, was wheezing and consumptive and in constant need of God's clean air.

Detective Sergeant Gillespie sat in the Green Room, high-ceilinged, and small like everything else; the walls were dark, green as they had to be, lined with photographs of actors and productions. Light poured in from a high Georgian window on to the street below. When the door opened he knew the man who came in. He had sat in the auditorium here with Maeve; it seemed like a long time ago now. Was it five years? *Diarmuid and Grainne*; love and death. Micheál Mac Liammóir had been Diarmuid. The actor shook Stefan's hand firmly, fixing his gaze hard for some seconds. It was a look that told Stefan he would be judged here, and precisely what he would be told would depend on that judgement. It was as obvious as that.

'Your colleague said very little. I didn't speak to him myself. But I imagine this is something rather serious. I think you should tell me more.'

It was an odd start to the questions Stefan was there to ask, but he sensed this was a place where he would find honesty and trust reciprocated.

'We have the body of an unidentified man. We don't know the circumstances of his death, but they are, for the moment, suspicious. I can't say any more than that. The fragment of a theatre ticket was found in a wallet buried with the man. So far it's the only thing that's given us any chance of identifying him. For now we're assuming the ticket was his.'

Mac Liammóir didn't waste time showing surprise or shock.

'Well, we've dug out a list of people who were invited to the first night of *The Way of the World*. The ticket in question was given to a young man called Vincent Walsh. I didn't know him well myself but he did work here as a dresser from time to time. He was never on our permanent staff.'

'Was the ticket used?'

'No. There's always someone ticking off the names of guests at a first night and Vincent Walsh's name wasn't ticked. I presume he didn't come.'

'Would you have expected him to?'

'He was very close to our wardrobe master, Eric Purcell.

He was his guest.' He pronounced all his words with an unusual, almost mannered care. He spoke the words 'very close' quite slowly, watching Stefan's eyes again. It was not a statement but a question. 'Do you understand?' He did. He also understood that the best answer to the question was to say nothing. Mac Liammóir would decide if that answer was the one he wanted to hear.

'I have spoken to Eric. He can remember the evening very clearly. He was expecting Mr Walsh and he was rather upset when he didn't arrive. As it transpires he didn't see his friend again. No one did. He simply disappeared. Of course, that makes some sense now. You will want to talk to Mr Purcell.'

Stefan nodded. Mac Liammóir left the Green Room for a moment and returned quickly with a man of around forty. He looked nervous and as they were left alone, the nervousness seemed closer to fear. Stefan recognised the species of fear precisely. Eric Purcell was a small man whose effeminate features and movements were a part of his being; he would have encountered policemen in very different circumstances, without the protection of the Gate's walls. He would have had reason to be nervous.

It was obvious that Purcell was upset; it was obvious that Vincent Walsh had mattered to him, in a way that already told Stefan the world the dead man had inhabited. And because of that it wasn't surprising that the wardrobe master knew very little about the dead man's family. He knew Vincent had had a mother and father in Carlow, and that's where he'd grown up. They had a shop there; Purcell thought it was a tobacconist's. That was all. As far as he knew, Vincent Walsh hadn't kept in touch with his parents.

'I thought something was wrong, Sergeant.'

'You expected him to be at the first night?'

'He'd never have missed it. It wasn't just the play. I got him a little bit of work here when I could. I'd told him there was something in the offing.'

'Did you try to contact him?'

'I did. But he'd gone.'

'Gone where?'

'People go, don't they?'

'Who told you he'd gone?'

'He worked at Billy Donnelly's, Carolan's, in Red Cow Lane. He'd a room there. It was Billy who said he'd left. Well, why wouldn't he? There isn't much to stay for.' It was clear Vincent Walsh's disappearance had left a bitter taste. It was all the more bitter now that Eric Purcell knew the anger and hurt he had harboured for so long afterwards had been unjustified.

'What made you think something was wrong?'

'I don't know. I just thought Vincent was better than that.'

'When did you last see him?'

There were tears in the wardrobe master's eyes, of grief and guilt. He hesitated. Stefan could see there were things Purcell didn't want to say. He had been gentle enough with him at first. Now he needed to be tougher.

'Mr Purcell, your friend didn't meet a happy end. He was killed. And when he was dead someone took him out to a mountainside, dug a hole and dumped his body in it. I want to find out who did that. I need your help.'

'I'll help if I can.'

'You remember the date?'

'Yes.' He had made his decision; to stop feeling sorry for himself.

158

'I couldn't tell you the date off the top of my head, but it's easy to remember the day. It was the night after the Eucharistic Mass in the Park. He pulled me out of bed, hammering on my door at one o'clock in the morning.'

'Did he often do that?'

Eric Purcell shook his head. It still wasn't easy. He was fighting the old habits of self-preservation that told him never to say anything to the Guards, about anything, about anybody. Stefan knew that and he waited.

'He'd been at the Mass in the afternoon, then he'd been working in Carolan's. When the pub closed some fellers came in, Blueshirts, a gang of them. They started roughing up Vincent and Billy the way the Guards – I'm not saying – I mean it happens sometimes, you'd know yourself, Sergeant.'

Purcell assumed Stefan wouldn't think there was anything out of the ordinary about a couple of queers being beaten up. It wasn't as if it was entirely unreasonable. Didn't the police have a go at it now and then too?

'So what happened?'

'He got away, and eventually he turned up at my flat.'

'Was he hurt?'

'There was a bit of blood, a few bruises.'

'Did he stay?'

'He left after a couple of hours. He was worried about Billy.'

'What did you talk about?'

'I don't know.'

'Your friend gets you up in the middle of the night. There's blood on his face. He's been beaten up. He stays a bit, then he goes back to the pub where he was attacked. You're worried about him. But you've arranged to meet

159

him here the next week. Then he doesn't turn up. He's just gone. You never see him again. And you don't remember what he talked about?'

'He didn't say very much. That's the truth. He didn't want to talk.'

'So what did he do?' persisted Stefan.

'Nothing really. I cleaned him up. I washed the blood –'

'Did he know these men, the Blueshirts?'

'No, I don't think so.'

'So did you just sit there and look at each other?'

'He wrote a letter.'

Stefan looked at him, surprised.

'He wanted an envelope. He had some papers in his pocket. I didn't really see. He put them in the envelope with a note. Then he wanted a stamp, but I didn't have one there. He asked me to post the letter the next day.'

'Did you?'

The wardrobe master nodded.

'Did you look at the address?'

'It was addressed to Billy Donnelly.'

'Which was where he was going when he left?'

Purcell nodded again.

'Didn't that strike you as odd?'

'It wasn't my business.' Grief was still there; so were old jealousies.

'Did he say anything about this letter?'

'No. He seemed a bit happier when he'd written it though. He laughed when he gave it to me. He said they wouldn't look in the same place twice.'

'Did you know what he meant?'

'No, I told you, he didn't want to talk about what happened.'

Stefan Gillespie believed him. He believed him all the more because of the note of bitterness he could hear, even though tears were still in Eric Purcell's eyes. Vincent Walsh had mattered to him, perhaps more than he had mattered to Vincent. When Vincent was in trouble he'd knocked on the wardrobe master's door; he needed help, but he didn't offer trust in return.

'What's going to happen to him? I mean his body.'

'We'll contact his parents now. He'll be buried in due course.'

'I'd like to know when.'

'I'm sure Mr and Mrs Walsh –'

'I doubt they'll be inviting his friends, Sergeant.'

Walking down the stairs on his way out of the Gate, Stefan was surprised to see Wayland-Smith sprawling in an armchair by the box office, frowning over the crossword in *The Irish Times*. He laughed, finally seeing something he should have seen immediately, and wrote in the answer. He got up.

'My car's outside. It seemed quickest to come here and get you.'

'What's happened?'

'They've found another body at Kilmashogue.'

*

It was almost dark as Stefan Gillespie and Wayland-Smith stood on the road below the woody mountainside again. The rain had gone now. It was a clear, crisp December night. Below them the great sprawl of Dublin was just starting to disappear into the darkness. The lights from the tractor and the State Pathologist's estate shone on the heap of earth and rock that still slewed across the track. It was only when the workmen had started to clear the landslip that they discovered the second body. It lay in several pieces where it had broken apart as it tumbled down the slope with the soil that had covered it; a leg, an arm, the torso and head. Black skin still held some of the bones in place, barely, like a wet paper bag about to split apart; other bones had already lost most of their flesh. It was immediately clear, to Stefan as well as to Wayland-Smith, that the body had been buried far more recently than the first. The jaw and the face were already almost a skull, but on the top of the head there was still skin and hair. It was long hair, a woman's. The pathologist turned to a guard behind him, who held a small cardboard box.

'So show me.'

The policeman moved forward, stepping up on to the mound of earth, opening the flaps of the box. Stefan needed to shine a torch in to see. It could have been no more than earth and leaves, muddy, compressed; it could have been the carcass of a young rabbit, the fur stripped away, rotting. But the tiny skull was human. It was a foetus. Wayland-Smith crossed himself. It was a gesture Stefan didn't expect; he was conscious that he had never seen the State Pathologist make it over any adult corpse before. He moved closer to the torso and the head of the woman, stumbling in the slippery mud. He bent down, shining the torch on to her skull. He brushed away the mud on the forehead. There was something, quite small, blacker than the blackened skin; it was a round hole. Wayland-Smith squatted down beside him.

'She's been dead no more than a year, maybe less.'

He took the torch from Stefan and bent nearer the head. The work of the soil had nearly removed the smell of putrefaction from the dead flesh, but this close it lingered. Stefan coughed as it hit the back of his throat. Wayland-Smith took a pencil from his pocket. He poked it into the hole.

'I'd say so too, Sergeant. It's our captive bolt pistol.'

In the light from the torch something glinted in the mud. It was tiny. Stefan brushed it with his finger. It glinted more. He eased it away from the wet earth. A thin black cord came with it, circling the vertebrae that were all that was left of the neck; a silver chain. What had glimmered in the torchlight was silver too, barely half an inch in size. It was a Star of David.

Detective Sergeant Gillespie sat in the Austin outside the house in Lennox Street. It smelt, as always, of Dessie MacMahon's Sweet Afton. Usually that irritated him, if he bothered to notice it, but for now it seemed to drive out the smell of rain and soil and death that he had been breathing for the last twenty-four hours. Inside, Hannah Rosen was telling Susan Field's father that his daughter's body had been found. Stefan had not been on the wet plot of earth at Kilmashogue very long before he knew. It was scarcely an hour later that her handbag had been found, still full of the ordinary business of her life; comb, lipstick, pens and powder compact. There was a purse packed with shillings and pennies and threepenny bits and bus tickets, and there was a cheque book from the College Green branch of the Hibernian bank. The name inside the cheque book – still clearly legible – was Susan Field's.

Hannah had not been surprised by the fact that her

friend was dead of course. Instinct had already told her that. But the circumstances threw her back into the kind of bewildered disbelief that made acceptance hard. Faced with death, knowing is never enough, not at first. She had known but she didn't believe. And now her heart, for a short time at least, had to fight the truth, in the futile, painful battle that can only be lost. Stefan could see it in her face; he had fought that battle once himself. He hadn't told her everything. There was still too much he didn't understand. Now there was more. How did the murder of Susan Field relate to the death of Vincent Walsh, dumped on the same hillside two years before, his bones broken and smashed, his head spiked like an animal in a slaughterhouse, just as Susan's head had been spiked?

It was only a few minutes before Hannah came back out to fetch him. He went into the house. Brian Field stood by the fireplace, hands clasped tightly behind him, like the last time Stefan was there. It felt as if the cantor had been standing there all that time, knowing he would come back to say, no, she didn't go anywhere, Mr Field; her bones are scattered on the mountainside. Stefan expressed his sorrow for the old man's trouble, with the handshake that always accompanied those words and, as ever, when the words were said and the hand-shaking done, there was nothing else to say.

'I should see her,' said Brian Field very quietly.

'She's been in the ground a long time, Mr Field. I'm not asking you to identify your daughter now, not from the remains. It might be best –'

'I should see her.' He simply repeated the words. 'I should see her.'

'I'll go with you.' Hannah put her arm through his. All

at once the composure on the old man's face was gone. There was a look of anguish.

'Her sisters –'

She tightened her grip on his arm.

'We'll telephone. Rachel can be here from London in no time.'

The cantor shook his head slowly; he didn't want to telephone.

Stefan recognised what he saw in that anguish. He remembered it well enough. Each person you tell makes death more real; each word of telling takes away the little breath of life that still survives inside your heart.

They stood over the body as it lay on the mortuary slab. They were the only people in the building. There were no questions to ask. Not now. It was the necessary business of death. Brian Field's fingers trembled as he took the blue kippah from his pocket. He put it on his head. He trembled again as he tried to fix it there with a hairgrip. Hannah took it from him and slid it on. He seemed unaware she was doing it. Stefan's eyes were fixed on the hairgrip. It was exactly the same as the two lined up on his desk, with the compact and the lipstick and the purse and the pens and the comb from Susan Field's handbag. And then quite suddenly, strong and clear, somewhere between singing and speaking, the cantor's voice filled the mortuary. 'Yisgadal v'yiskadash sh'mei rabbaw. Amein.' May his name be exalted and sanctified in the highest. 'B'allmaw deev'raw hir'usei.' In the universe created according to his will. 'V'yamlih malhusei b'hayeihon uv'yomeihon. Amein.' May his kingdom swiftly come in our day and in the days of the house of Israel. Amen. As he continued, each amen was echoed more quietly by Hannah. Stefan watched her. He could feel how much it mattered to her. Sometimes you didn't have to believe it for it to matter.

Stefan and Hannah sat in Neary's in Chatham Street and said very little. She didn't talk about what had happened to Susan, only about their friendship, half-remembered events, unfinished stories, times and places and people she was trying to bring back, just for a moment. Some of the time she said nothing at all and for a while he felt he had to speak. When he tried to ask her about herself, about Palestine, about what she did, where she lived, her replies didn't tell him anything. Eventually she shook her head and laughed.

'You don't have to say anything when there's nothing to say.'

'I'm sorry. I should know that. It was always my line.'

'How do you mean?'

'When Maeve died, and afterwards, for ages. I couldn't move for people talking to me. It was as if they'd organised themselves into shifts. One went and there'd be someone else. If it wasn't my mother or father, it was a stream of neighbours, or some cousin or aunt I hadn't seen for years. "Whatever you do, don't leave him on his own. And keep him talking!"'

'It's only because people care.'

'And Jesus, how they care! They all felt so bad about how I felt I ended up comforting them! I swear I'd never seen some of them in my life.'

'That's a terrible thing to say!' she said, still smiling.

'Sometimes people need to know when to shut up.'

'So are you going to shut up now?'

'If that's what you want, Hannah.'

'I suppose I'm running away from all that a bit.' She was more serious again. The strain in her face couldn't be hidden by a smile for very long. 'All the people I know, the people we grew up with. It's like you said. They'll be in and out of Lennox Street tomorrow, and we'll sit and say the same things, over and over. I will do it, of course I will. I will sit there. But not tonight.'

Stefan nodded.

'Sometimes it was easier being with people I didn't really know.'

'That's not what I meant, Stefan.'

He was aware it was the first time she had called him that.

'It doesn't feel like I don't know you.'

Stefan reached out and took her hand. She held his hand tightly.

'It doesn't for me either. It hasn't from the first time we met.'

'Time, please! Let's have you two out of here!' The barman's voice boomed across the room in their direction. The glasses were rapidly snatched off the table. They looked round, laughing. The bar had been full when they came in two hours earlier. Now they were the only people left.

As they walked out of the pub towards Grafton Street it was bitterly cold. The long street of Christmas shop windows was almost empty now.

'Do you want to get a taxi, Hannah?'

He was already turning towards Stephen's Green and the taxi rank.

'No.'

'I'll walk home with you then.'

'I don't think I'll go home,' she replied quietly, gently, her eyes fixed on his. She was shivering. She put her arm through his, pulling herself closer to him. It was not what he expected, but it wouldn't be true to say he hadn't thought about it, and suddenly it seemed not unexpected at all. Perhaps it had been clear from the beginning, to both of them, and now there was a need for comfort that had pushed away all the reasons why it wouldn't happen. There was nothing they needed to say to each other. They turned away from Stephen's Green and walked on, down towards Nassau Street.

# 10. Red Cow Lane

The next morning Stefan Gillespie took the train to Carlow Town. It was a journey to a familiar place; the nearest big town to Baltinglass. Until Naas, the railway followed the route he took going home, but where the line branched away towards the Wicklow Mountains, he carried on now to Kildare Town and the flat plain of the Curragh and down into the neat pastureland of County Carlow. He fixed his mind on the day's work, but it wasn't easy. It was one thing to tell himself he expected nothing from Hannah after the night they'd spent together; it was another to believe it.

Her mood had been very different that morning. The questions about Susan's murder had come faster than his answers. Why was he holding things back? Why was he trawling the streets of Dublin when he should be on the boat to England by now, across the Channel, and on a train to Danzig? Wasn't it the priest he needed to question about Susan above everything else? And he knew it was. He also knew why nobody, from the Garda Commissioner down, would be rushing to buy his train ticket. He was investigating the deaths of a woman and a man that a lot of people, his superiors among them, would rather had lain undiscovered on the mountainside at Kilmashogue. Then, quite abruptly, the questions had stopped. She had to go. She walked across to him and kissed him. She rested her head on his shoulder. It was an expression of support, and something more, of tenderness. And then the room was very empty. She was gone.

As Stefan looked out from the train at the green fields of Carlow, Hannah Rosen was making tea in Brian Field's kitchen, steeling herself for a long day talking to all the people who would come through his door. But in her head there was another conversation going on. Lying in Stefan's bed that morning, before he woke up, listening to the sounds of Dublin outside, she knew how much this was still her city. The ease she felt with Stefan, even in the face of her best friend's death, went deeper than she wanted to admit. She could never tell Benny what she was feeling, and not only because of what had happened between her and Stefan. He would be hurt by that, but he would understand. What he wouldn't understand were her thoughts as she listened to Dublin, rattling and clattering and cursing beyond the window of the scruffy room in Nassau Street. The creation of Israel drove Benny Jacobson with a relentless passion that left no space for sentimental attachments to the past. And she was full of those attachments now. That was the betrayal he wouldn't forgive. This was still where she belonged. Her head had made a decision about what her life should be; her heart had not.

Stefan went straight from Carlow Station to the Garda barracks in Tullow Street to pay his respects to Superintendent Flynn, who wanted to be remembered to his father and seemed in quite the mood to settle down for a chat about country policing and metropolitan crime.

That is until he got the whiff of unnatural practices in his nostrils and found his presence elsewhere was more urgently required than anticipated. Stefan would want to talk to the parents, of course. Wouldn't it be best if he got on with it? He knew the town like the back of his hand – there was no need for the superintendent's officers to get involved, was there? Stefan just smiled. No, there wasn't.

He walked the length of Tullow Street and turned into Dublin Street at the bottom. The tobacconist's was on the left. He remembered it, but when he walked inside the memory was much stronger. The smell of the place, a comfortable smell of sweetness and smoke reminded him of his grandfather. He had bought Christmas presents for him there, a half ounce of tobacco, some pipe cleaners. But the moment Mr Walsh showed him through the shop into the living room behind it, the warmth was gone. There was only empty space, somehow not quite filled by the table and the two wooden chairs, the two-seater settee and the armchair, and the heavy mahogany sideboard that was too big for the room. It was a dark room and although the day was cold, there was no fire in the grate. There was a photograph of a wedding on the mantelpiece – Mr and Mrs Walsh's – and on either side of it were oval framed photographs of two couples who must have been Vincent's grandparents. Above the fireplace too was a black-framed picture of the Sacred Heart. 'Blessed be the home in which my heart is exposed.'

Somehow it felt less like a home than the shop had. That was where they spoke to people. Stefan could feel that when Mr and Mrs Walsh walked back through the door from the tobacconist's there weren't many words. No one ever said much in this room. He learned that Vincent had been their only child, yet there was no photograph; when he asked for one they looked at each other uncertainly, as if they weren't sure where to find such a thing. Mrs Walsh made no move. A slight nod of her head gave her husband permission to act.

He went to the sideboard and opened a door, with the key that was in the lock. The lock was stiff; the door was rarely opened. He took out a biscuit tin with a picture of the Rock of Cashel on the lid. He opened it carefully and looked through the contents, hunched over the sideboard. He produced a small cardboard frame with a photograph in it; R & F Beard, Photographers, Tullow Street, Carlow. It was a picture of a young man of sixteen or seventeen. He wore a dark suit jacket, a white collar that was too big for him, and a striped tie. He wasn't smiling. There was a similar photograph of Stefan on the wall in the kitchen at Kilranelagh. He had gone to the photographer's shop in Tullow Street the summer before he started at Trinity College; his mother wanted a photograph of him in the dark suit that looked so much like Vincent Walsh's. He had sat in the same chair, in front of the same stained sheet in Mr Beard's studio. Mr Beard would have said the same things and made the same jokes. Stefan promised he would return the photograph as soon as he could. Mr and Mrs Walsh didn't reply.

His questions were answered with as few words as were needed. They had not seen their son for over three years. He had left home to work in Dublin in the summer of 1930. He had come home twice. The last time had been Christmas, 1931. He went back to Dublin that Stephen's Day and it was the last contact they'd had with him. There was nothing to find out here. They could have understood nothing of their son's life. They knew just enough to ensure it was never spoken about. Stefan could almost feel, through the years between, the long silence that final Christmas must have been for all three of them. As he walked from the shop out into the street, it was as if the ghost of that Stephen's Day past, when Vincent Walsh had left his home for the last time, still hovered in the tobacconist's doorway. Whatever the shop had meant to Vincent then, once it must have held the sounds and scents and images of a childhood that wasn't always silent and empty and cold.

They hadn't asked about his body. Stefan didn't have to explain that there was nothing for them to see or identify, nothing he would want a mother and father to look at. He told them they would be able to make funeral arrangements before long, perhaps in January. They nodded. They would do what they needed to do. There would be no wake. There would be no line of customers and friends and neighbours and family to follow the coffin the few hundred yards along Dublin Street, past the pillared court house into College Street, past the seminary; or to sit with it in the Cathedral of the Assumption overnight. The Mass for the Dead would be spoken to a handful of people. Vincent Walsh would be buried with as much shame as sorrow. Afterwards, his mother and father would sit in the room behind the shop and say nothing. They had mourned for their son long before his death.

\*

Dessie MacMahon was a lot more comfortable in Carolan's Bar than he had been at the Gate Theatre. Apart from the fact that Billy Donnelly didn't need to be asked to put two hot whiskeys in front of him and Sergeant Gillespie, you knew who was who in here, and more to the point, who was what.

Any man you found drinking in Carolan's was queer and that kind of clarity seemed to Dessie to be only proper. Besides which, you could treat them like queers. A bit of craic was fine. Didn't some of them have a way of making you split your sides sometimes? But up at the Gate you needed to watch yourself. You couldn't know who was queer and who wasn't and nobody seemed the least bit bothered about it. That couldn't be right. However, as Stefan questioned Billy Donnelly, the publican was less forthcoming about Vincent Walsh than he was with the drinks. He took the news that Vincent's body had been found with hardly a change in his sour expression. Maybe his eyes closed for just a moment, but it was hard not to feel that this didn't come as news at all.

'He was living here?' said Stefan.

'He worked for me. He'd a room upstairs.'

'How long?'

'Maybe a year.'

'You knew him well then.'

Billy looked across the bar at the last of his departing customers. It was barely one o'clock and the pub never did do much daytime trade, but the presence of two detectives was enough to frighten off what there was.

'You're costing me money. Are you stopping long?'

'Tell me about the night of the Eucharistic Mass,' continued Stefan. It was not a question Billy expected, and if the news of Vincent's death hadn't seemed to surprise him very much, those words clearly did. He frowned.

'You'd quite a night of it, I hear.'

'I'm not with you, Sergeant.'

'There was a gang of Blueshirts here, beating the shite out of you.'

'Is that right?'

'Was there a reason for that?'

'Sure, why would they need a reason?' It was the kind of answer Billy Donnelly would have given at any other time, and at any other time he would have laughed. He smiled, but his voice spoke wariness and caution.

'It was just you and Vincent Walsh, Billy?'

'If you say so, Mr Gillespie. It's a long time ago.'

'Vincent got away from them?'

Billy didn't reply. He'd picked up a glass and a towel earlier and had been drying the same glass for some time, unaware that he was doing it.

'Did he?' insisted Stefan.

'If I'd had the legs on me I'd have done the same.'

'So when did he come back?'

The publican stopped drying the glass.

Stefan could see he was trying to work out an answer.

'He was worried about you. That's what I'm told. He was on his way back here by two in the morning.'

'I didn't see him.'

'You didn't see him come in?'

'He never came in. I didn't see him again.'

'What about his things?'

'He'd a few clothes, a few books.'

'You've still got those?'

'What do you think this is, the left-luggage office? I kept hold of his things for a while, but when I saw he wasn't coming back I got rid of it all.'

'Did you get the letter he sent you?' Stefan was watching him closely.

'What letter?'

The response was quick, controlled; perhaps he was anticipating the questions now. But neither Stefan nor Dessie had any doubt that Billy Donnelly knew all about the letter, and that it had arrived. However, they could get nothing more out him now. There was no letter. He knew nothing about any letter. Yet the letter mattered and Stefan knew it. Vincent Walsh's words still rang in his head. 'They won't look in the same place twice.' If Vincent had died that night they were some of the last words he ever spoke. They couldn't be explained, but they certainly couldn't be cast aside.

As the two detectives left, Billy Donnelly could feel the sweat, cold on his back where it had been hot only seconds before. As he went to pour himself a drink, Dessie MacMahon reappeared at the door. He had remembered something.

'Weren't you in the Joy for a stretch last year?'

'Six fucking months.'

'What for?'

'What's it to you?'

Dessie grinned. He had a memory for these small things. 'Attempting to procure an act of gross indecency at a urinal in Upper Hatch Street, but as it happened the feller was a guard, wasn't that the story, Billy?'

Two fingers ushered Dessie out. Billy stood in the empty bar. He hadn't forgotten Vincent. He never would. The drink was the first of many.

*

Inspector Donaldson had been reading Stefan Gillespie's report for almost ten minutes. It wasn't a long report. It deliberately avoided any facts that could be avoided and it made no attempt at theories or opinions. It described the discovery of the two bodies and the bare details of Wayland-Smith's examination. Vincent Walsh and Susan Field had been identified, and although the circumstances of their deaths could not be determined, there could be no question but that the deaths were indeed suspicious. Something like two years separated the two events. Nothing linked them except the place of burial and the State Pathologist's opinion that damage to both skulls could have been caused by a captive bolt pistol. Donaldson had already pencilled in the word 'speculative' above the word 'opinion'. There was considerable information about the probable movements of both Vincent Walsh and Susan Field close to the time of their disappearance. The inspector had crossed out the word 'probable' and replaced it with 'possible'. He turned the pages of the report over several times more, not because there was anything else to read, but because he didn't want to have the conversation he knew had to come next. Nothing was going to make this trouble go away.

'The man Walsh,' he said, finally looking up. 'How reliable do you think these people are? Purcell, I mean, and the publican, Donnelly?'

'I'd say Purcell is telling the truth. Billy Donnelly knows more.'

'I know Donnelly. The other one's a queer too, I presume?'

'Purcell doesn't have any reason to lie.' Stefan knew exactly what Inspector Donaldson meant. You couldn't believe anything a queer said.

'Lying is a way of life with these people. At any event there doesn't seem to be anywhere else to go. The man disappeared. He hasn't seen him since. Or are you suggesting Donnelly was involved in the death somehow?'

'Like I say, I think he's got more to tell us.'

'And if he hasn't?'

'Sir, four men attacked the pub the night Walsh disappeared.'

'Oh, yes, the Blueshirts.' Donaldson smiled. He didn't believe it.

'I've no reason to doubt that,' Stefan continued. 'Your man Purcell could see Vincent Walsh had been beaten up. And what the hell has Billy Donnelly got to gain from a story like that, two years down the road?'

The inspector sniffed. The Blueshirts, under the leadership of Eoin O'Duffy, the first Garda Commissioner and almost the first man President de Valera sacked on taking office in 1932, had been banned a year ago. They had threatened to march on Dublin in the same way Mussolini's Blackshirts marched on Rome. After the ban the sale of blue shirts had declined rapidly, and the movement had faded away. But there were plenty of Gardaí whose sympathies lay with O'Duffy and the march that never was, and James Donaldson had been one of them, however quiet he kept about that now.

'Cat fights are common enough in the queer fraternity I'd say. The man wouldn't want to be pointing his finger at friends, even after all this time.'

'I think I need to take the Blueshirts seriously, sir.'

'I don't know where you'll find any Blueshirts now, but you might want to remember that the majority of them were ex-soldiers who served this country well, whatever the views of the current regime. I would be careful about stirring up the past, and on the back of what's probably a pack of lies.'

'Susan Field.' Stefan wouldn't let Donaldson avoid this any longer.

'We've been here already, Sergeant. I'm well aware that it comes back to Keller.'

'I can't question Keller. I don't know where he is. I did speak to Sheila Hogan, his nurse. But that was after Jimmy Lynch had had a go and put her in the Mater.'

Donaldson ignored the last remark.

'Didn't she say she'd never seen the woman?'

'That doesn't mean a bloody thing. There was a foetus.'

'I know that Gillespie. Obviously you've established the woman was pregnant.'

'She wrote a letter that said she was having an abortion!'

'Yes, there are questions to ask, Sergeant, I do accept that. And I will pass a request up the line for the German police to try to locate Herr Keller.'

Stefan looked at his tight-lipped superior and shook his head.

'He was driven to Dún Laoghaire by the head of the Nazi Party here. With friends like that, not to mention our own Special Branch, I don't think we'll hear much back. That leaves us with one witness – Father Byrne.'

Inspector Donaldson might sideline the references to Adolf Mahr and Special Branch, but Byrne was another matter. However much he wanted to ignore it he knew he couldn't. And so he had already tackled the problem.

'I understand that and I have spoken to Monsignor Fitzpatrick.'

Stefan was surprised. The smile on Donaldson's face was troubling.

'You should have asked me before speaking to him your-self.'

'I wanted to find out where Byrne was. It was the shortest route.'

'That wasn't a decision for you to make, Gillespie.'

'It was a simple question, sir.'

'It was a series of scandalous allegations against a priest!'

'I have good reason to believe Francis Byrne was the man Susan Field was having an affair with, that he was the father of her child and, according to her letters, that he was the man who arranged for her abortion with Hugo Keller. He also paid for it. That makes him one of the last people to see Miss Field alive. And he left the country within a few days of her disappearing.'

It was more troubling that the inspector seemed untroubled by this.

'As I said, I have spoken to Monsignor Fitzpatrick.'

'So when do I get to question your man Byrne?'

'Everything you've said about Father Byrne is speculation.'

'I don't think so, sir.'

James Donaldson frowned. It was there again, 'sir', as a kind of insult.

'The woman never even mentions his name in these letters.'

'Come on, how many priests did she know at UCD?'

Donaldson's tight lips grew even tighter.

'She was pregnant, Sergeant. Sadly we know that was true. As for the rest, a woman in that sort of trouble might come up with any kind of story. Shame does strange things, particularly to women. She may not even have known who the father of the child was. It wouldn't be the first time a woman has fantasised about a good man being the father of an illegitimate child. Monsignor Fitzpatrick has no doubt about Father Byrne's integrity. He is a fine man and a fine priest. He knows him. The man lived in his house!'

Stefan stared at the inspector. He had already heard this. Hadn't another policeman said the same thing to Susan's father? But he doubted it could have been said with such conviction. He struggled to keep the word 'bollocks' in his mouth, but there wasn't another word that would do.

'I didn't pick the questions, sir. I just need to ask them. And the man I need to ask is Father Byrne, sir. He's the only witness there is now.'

'I understand. That's exactly what I've said to the monsignor.'

'Does than mean Father Byrne is coming back to Ireland?'

'Not in the foreseeable future.'

'Then shouldn't I be going to him in Danzig?'

'I hardly think we'll be sending you to the Baltic, Sergeant Gillespie.' Donaldson laughed. Reluctant as he had been to enter into this, it was done. It hadn't been so hard after all. Detective sergeants could be controlled.

'Monsignor Fitzpatrick will speak to Father Byrne. He can telephone him if necessary. I suggest you draw up a list of questions and we can send them straight off. If the letter is sent via London the air mail system will have it in Danzig in less than twenty-four hours. Let's deal with this speculation head on, Sergeant. Let's get it out of the way and clear the air.'

It was not often that real determination showed in Inspector Donaldson's face, but Stefan recognised it when he saw it. There would be no argument. If the inspector had, even for a second, wondered about the relationship between Father Francis Byrne and Susan Field, Monsignor Fitzpatrick had demonstrated, with infectious infallibility, that there really was nothing to wonder about. The list of written questions was an empty gesture. It meant that the investigation had already reached a dead end.

There was a mug of tea waiting on Stefan's desk when he returned. Dessie MacMahon didn't have to be in Donaldson's office to work out what was happening. The inspector knew there was a priest in it now all right; he was as agitated as hell. Hadn't he been to Mass twice that day already? But it wasn't the first thing Dessie said when Stefan returned.

'*She* was in to see you.'

Stefan ignored the smile that went with it; Dessie didn't miss a thing.

'When?'

'An hour ago maybe. She waited a bit, then she had to go.'

For once Stefan was glad Hannah hadn't stayed. Everything she might have anticipated about the way Francis Byrne was going to be treated had just happened. If anything it was worse. Not only had Donaldson decided that Susan Field never did have an affair with the priest, the man would be questioned by post. Stefan had two bodies, two murders, and nowhere to go. He reached across the desk for a file. It wasn't there. He had been looking at it when the summons from Inspector Donaldson came. He looked round, puzzled, then saw some sheets of paper on the floor. He bent and picked them up. As he put them back he peered at the desk again. Things were not where he had left them. His desk was the exact opposite of the tip that was Dessie's. He knew where everything was; except now it wasn't, not quite.

'Here's an odd thing, Sarge.' Dessie leant back. 'Billy Donnelly.'

'What about him?'

'Six months for getting his cock out in a jacks.'

'You said. That's not so odd, is it?'

182

Stefan was still looking down, frowning.

'Have you been looking for something over here, Dessie?'

'You think I don't know better than that?'

'Why are these papers all over the floor? Everything's in the wrong –' He smiled; it was simple enough. 'Did you leave Hannah here on her own?'

'I've got the report on Billy.' Dessie got up, ignoring Stefan's question. 'Here. "The defendant approached the detective and said, isn't that a fine big one. It'll give you the horn." Jesus wept!' He was laughing.

'She's gone through everything.'

'You know who it was, Sarge?' Dessie still wasn't listening.

'Who what was?'

'The detective in the jacks.'

'What do I care who was in the bloody jacks?'

'It was Jimmy Lynch, keeping the Free State's toilets safe.'

It was about as far from Special Branch work as you could get.

Billy Donnelly wasn't feeling great. He could take his drink but he'd drunk himself senseless through most of that afternoon. He couldn't remember what he'd said to his barman when they opened the pub, but Derek Blaney had walked out and said he wasn't coming back. He would, but he'd leave it a couple of days to make his point. The dreary, familiar campery in the bar that night had made Billy want to take the lot of them by the scruff of the neck and kick the shite out of them till they said something, anything different. He felt he'd been listening to the same empty conversations all his life and what lay ahead was just the same thing, over and over, night after night after night. And he was right. But he had drunk himself into a stupor and out the other side now. He was sober and wished he wasn't. The knock on the door was the last thing he needed, but he had no anger left to hurl at the unwanted visitor. He opened the door. Stefan Gillespie stood there.

Billy didn't bother to protest. He hadn't got the energy. He walked back to the bar and sat down. He left Stefan to close the door as he came in.

'I thought we were done.'

'I didn't.' Stefan sat down opposite him.

'Tell me about the letter.'

'There wasn't a letter.'

'Tell me about Jimmy Lynch then.'

'He's a gobshite, the same kind of gobshite you are.'

'He put you inside.'

'That's right.'

'Eighteen months hard labour. You were out in six.'

'I was lucky.'

'No one's that lucky. Jimmy put you in there and Jimmy got you out.'

'That what he said?'

'What did he want?'

'I thought he was just doing his job, locking up queers.'

'Then maybe I should take a leaf out of Jimmy's book. I'll put in a report that you approached me in a public urinal. I'll have Dessie MacMahon back me up on it. It'll be the usual thing, gross indecency. It'll be your third time.'

Billy didn't answer. He was remembering those six months.

'Three years at least, maybe more with the wrong judge.' Stefan waited for it to sink in.

'That's hard labour too. You're not getting any younger.'

'You're not Jimmy Lynch, Mr Gillespie.'

'I won't break your arms first if that's what you mean. But I will put you away if I have to.'

'What the hell does it matter to you? Vincent's dead, isn't he?'

'What was in the letter Vincent sent you?'

There was nowhere for Billy Donnelly to go; he had to talk now.

He sat back, remembering that night.

'All right the Blueshirts didn't just turn up. They wanted Vincent.'

'I'd worked that out.'

'There was a feller he'd been with. He'd written Vincent some letters. The sort of things people write and wish to God they never had. Vincent was mad about him. From up the arse to true fucking love! Jesus! He wasn't just anybody, this feller, either. I don't know what happened but he wanted the letters back. The Blueshirts came to get them. All Vincent had to do was hand them over, but he couldn't see it was your man who sent the bastards in the first place. He thought he was protecting the feller, hiding his fecking billiedoos. So he ran. He stuck the letters in a bloody envelope and sent them to me! They wouldn't look in the same place twice! That's what he wrote.'

'So did he come back here that night?'

'No. The letters came, a couple of days later, but he never did.'

'Where are they now?'

Billy Donnelly still didn't want to say it.

'You know, don't you, Billy?'

'I gave them to Sergeant Lynch. I don't know how he found out they were here, but he did. I'd kept them. I did think

Vincent would come back. I should have just put them on the fire, but I couldn't. They didn't mean a thing to the man who wrote them but they meant everything to him. Jimmy Lynch turned up about a year later, asking about Vincent, about the letters. It didn't matter what I said; he knew. So he put me away. I took six months of it. For what? Vincent was dead all that time. But then, I still thought he –'

'Was Jimmy Lynch there that night, with the Blueshirts?'

'No, he was fucking IRA before he was a Broy Harrier, wasn't he? I don't know who they were.'

'What about the man who wrote the letters?'

'There wasn't a name. All I know is what Vincent told me. He was some sort of teacher, not a school teacher . . . it was the university. And the bastard was a priest.'

# 11. Adelaide Road

The train from Baltinglass arrived at Kingsbridge just after ten the next morning. It was barely a week till Christmas now. Tom had come to Dublin with his grandmother and grandfather and Stefan had a day off. It was a day to gaze at the windows of the shops in Grafton Street and O'Connell Street, to look at Christmas trees and Christmas lights, to buy the small presents they would put round the tree in the sitting room at Kilranelagh. A day to eat dinner in the restaurant in Clery's and have tea at Bewley's Café. And there would be a long time to spend looking in one window in particular, just to the left of the clock outside Clery's, where the tricycle still sat, surrounded by glitter and tinsel, toy soldiers and dolls, tin drums and teddy bears.

Stefan and Tom were in Bewley's when Dessie MacMahon found them that afternoon. Pretending they had something else to do, David and Helena were out Christmas shopping for Tom and Stefan; Tom and his father had been Christmas shopping for them too. It had involved another slow walk past Clery's window, and a last look at the tricycle, which Tom had, with impressive resolution, persuaded himself Santy might not be able to bring all the way to Baltinglass. Dessie came over to the table with a cup and saucer and sat down. He poured himself some tea from the pot. It was thick, black and tepid, but nothing was undrinkable with enough sugar in it.

'*She's* been on the phone. That's three times today.'

He eyed the coconut macaroon in the middle of the table.

'You can have it if you want it, Dessie,' said Tom.

'Well, if it's going begging.' He didn't wait to be asked twice.

'I think she's a bit pissed off with you. Jesus, that tea's disgusting!'

'I can't do anything now, Dessie. I'll phone her later.'

'Well, she's at the synagogue in Adelaide Road with Mr Field. Funeral arrangements and all that. That's where she was going anyway.'

He got out a cigarette and lit it.

'She was on about seeing you.'

The grin on Dessie's face was irritating Stefan now.

'Did she have something to say?'

'I should think that one's always got something to say.' He winked at Tom. Tom laughed, though he hadn't got any idea what he was laughing at.

Stefan hadn't thought about Hannah all day, but now she was in his head. He wanted to see her, and he wanted to see her as himself, not as Detective Sergeant Gillespie. This was who he was, sitting here with his son. The rest was only what he did. They still knew almost nothing about each other. And he was sure she must want to see him too. That's why she kept phoning. There were two hours before he had to meet his mother and father at Kingsbridge Station. He looked at the bill on the plate beside him and fished in his pocket for some shillings and a half crown. When he got up to leave with Tom, Dessie stayed where he was. He called over the waitress.

'Can you freshen this pot up, darling? It's stewed to buggery.'

The tram to Adelaide Road was another part of Tom's day in Dublin; sitting upstairs, looking at the streets and the people, was its own entertainment. As they walked past the terraced houses to the synagogue it started to rain. Hannah was waiting on the steps of the big red and white brick building.

'This is Tom. Tom, this is Hannah.'

'Hello.' Tom looked slightly sheepish; he wasn't used to new people.

Hannah smiled, sensing his awkwardness.

'It's lovely to meet you, Tom. Are you having a good day?'

'Yes. We've been to Clery's.'

'Looking at toys? Well, you would be just now, wouldn't you?'

Tom's expression was very serious. 'Were you at Clery's at all?'

'Yes, lots. I can't remember the last time though.'

'Did you ever see the bike?'

'I don't think I did, no.'

'It's in the window, right by the clock. It's a tricycle.'

'Will I have a look next time I'm up there?'

Tom thought she should. She glanced at Stefan and winked. She already knew about the tricycle. Her eyes seemed very bright as Stefan looked at her. Tom's nervousness had suddenly gone and he was smiling. He liked her. The rain was falling harder now. Hannah took Tom's hand.

'Come on, you'll both be soaked,' she laughed. 'We all will!'

She hurried up the steps with Tom. Stefan followed, running. The rain was beating down. As they entered, he instinctively reached to take his hat off. Hannah touched his arm, smiling, pushing it back on his head.

'It's the other way round. Just leave it on!'

Tom looked at the dark interior. It was full of unfamiliar things, but it was enough like a church to feel familiar all the same. It smelt like one too.

'Is it a church, Daddy?'

'Yes, a Jewish church.'

Tom watched as several children walked past, wet from the rain.

'I'm sorry, I forgot you were having the day off.' Hannah spoke more quietly. 'I hope I didn't mess it up. You should have ignored me!'

'It's fine.' He felt she seemed slightly more awkward now. Perhaps it was just being in the synagogue, perhaps it was the sense that they were still somehow standing on the bridge between what was personal and what was professional in their relationship. More children hurried past them. Tom was looking at the dark interior more closely now, the rows of pews and the high gallery above, but his eyes kept coming back to the children, his own age and older, now closely packed in front of the Torah Ark, by a branched candelabrum, laughing as the elderly rabbi told then the Hanukkah story.

'You can go and listen,' said Hannah gently.

Tom looked up at Stefan doubtfully.

'Come on.' She took his hand again and walked him towards the other children. Stefan followed. He could see Tom's doubts had already gone.

'This is Hanukkah,' she continued. 'It's about a bad, bad king and the people who kicked him out and sent him packing. We light candles to remember that.' She caught the rabbi's eye, and pushed Tom gently forward.

'And what's your name?' asked the rabbi.

Tom looked back at his father for reassurance. Stefan nodded.

'It's Tom, Father.'

The other children giggled. Tom didn't understand why, but it felt welcoming and good-humoured enough, so he just smiled back at them.

'All right, Tom. First the battle, then the miracle. Well, if God's going to take the trouble to give us a miracle he expects us to put some work in too. That's the battle. I think it's fair, don't you? Now, we have a wicked king, a very wicked king, more wicked than you could ever imagine. Antiochus was his name.' The others hissed and booed. 'And we have a hero, Judah the Maccabee, fighting the evil king, to save Jerusalem. He was a brave man and his soldiers were brave, but there were only a few of them, and at first Antiochus chased them all into the hills with his great army.'

'Like Michael Dwyer and Sam MacAllister,' said Tom. 'They hid in the mountains behind our farm, when they were fighting the redcoats.'

'Yes, it was just like that, Tom. And like Michael Dwyer, Judah and his men had no weapons, no food, no shelter. In Jerusalem the wicked king's soldiers were eating the people out of house and home and putting up statues of the Greek gods in the Temple of the Lord.' More hisses and boos; Tom joined in. 'Everyone thought the war was over and Antiochus had won!'

Hannah and Stefan had walked a little way back towards the doors.

'He's like you,' she said quietly.

'Is that a good thing?'

'I wouldn't say it's so bad.'

They were silent for several seconds. She seemed reluctant to speak.

'You wanted to talk to me, Hannah?'

'I wanted to know if there was any more news?'

'There's nothing new.' The question had been surprisingly vague. It was the same question she asked every day. After three phone calls he had assumed she had something to tell him. And he wasn't really sure she had forgotten about his day off. He knew there was something else going on.

'I know you're still not telling me everything, Stefan. I'm trying to understand that, but I'm also waiting for more. I think you owe me more.'

He was surprised, almost hurt. It sounded like she was using the fact that they had slept together as a lever. But as he looked into her deep eyes, the honesty and the openness told him instantly that she wasn't. It was simply that she believed he owed her the truth, whatever that meant. And the part of him that wasn't a policeman said she was right. But there was still something else, something different about her unfamiliar awkwardness.

'Is something wrong?' he asked, trying to read her face.

'The thing is, I have to go. That's why I needed to talk to you.'

She tried to throw the words away, as if they weren't that important, but her face told a different story. She didn't like what she was saying.

'Go where?'

'I have to leave Ireland.'

It was the last thing he expected to hear. There was no reason why Hannah shouldn't leave Ireland, but it was out of step with everything that had happened since they met. All her attention had been on Susan Field.

'You mean you're going back to Palestine?'

'Eventually, yes. I need to go to England. I have some work to do.'

It felt like a brush-off. She was only telling him part of it. He realised he hadn't ever asked what she did. And she hadn't told him. He realised how little he knew about her again. He knew about the death of her friend. He knew something about her childhood, from Susan's letters and an hour in a pub. He knew there was a man in Palestine, Benny; a farm where they grew oranges. It wasn't much. Perhaps she'd never intended him to know much.

'Back to the oranges?' he smiled, trying to make a joke of it.

'What?'

'Doesn't your fiancé grow oranges?'

She moved closer to him. This wasn't easy for her. She wanted to tell him that he mattered to her. She wanted him to understand that there were reasons she had to go. But she couldn't explain the reasons. Not now.

'I'm sorry. I was never going to be home very long.'

'I wish I'd known that.'

The sound of laughing children filled the synagogue.

He knew she had more to say. And he knew she wouldn't say it.

'I want to know what happens, Stefan.'

'Yes, naturally. If you tell me where you are –'

'If you find anything, my father will be able to contact me.'

Now she wouldn't even give him an address.

'I'm not going because I want to, Stefan.'

'When do you go?'

She took a moment to answer.

'The day after tomorrow.'

'And that's that?'

'No,' she said, shaking her head. 'Could we see each other tonight?'

He took a deep breath and nodded; he was still surprised.

'Thank you,' she said, taking his hand.

He looked at her, not at all sure what to make of her behaviour, then all of a sudden he was conscious of the time and the train and his mother and father waiting at Kingsbridge Station. There wasn't time to say any more.

'I've got to get Tom to the station. My parents will be there.'

'I'll be at Neary's tonight, Stefan.' She let go of his hand.

They walked back towards the children, now gathered tightly round the menorah. The rabbi held the lighted shammus candle that sat between the eight others, four on each side, as he said the blessing. The Hebrew words were as unfamiliar to Stefan as to Tom, though Stefan had heard similar words spoken over Susan Field's body. For Tom they were no less impenetrable than the Latin he heard at Mass; he happily assumed it was the same language he heard every Sunday. As the rabbi spoke he translated the words for Tom. 'Barukh atah Adonai, Eloheinu.' Blessed are you, Lord God. 'Melekh ha'olam.' King of the universe. 'She'asah nisim la'avoteinu bayamim haheim baziman hazeh. Amein.' Who wrought miracles for our fathers at

194

this season long ago. Amen. He gave the shammus to the youngest children in turn, then to Tom, guiding his hand to the fifth candle; the others would remain unlit today. As the rabbi took the shammus and put it in the centre of the menorah, Tom crossed himself and bowed his head. The other children giggled good-naturedly again; he didn't notice. Stefan rested his hand on his son's shoulder. He knew who Tom's silent prayer was for.

Hannah and Stefan sat in Neary's again that night. It was only the second time they had been together like this. He knew it would be the last time too. She didn't want to talk about leaving Ireland, or about where she was going, and he didn't ask her. They were both conscious that there were things they weren't saying and couldn't say. Then quite unexpectedly, she asked him about Maeve. He was surprised that it made things easier. He told Hannah about the camping trip in the mountains and the night by the lakes at Glendalough. How he woke in the morning to find he was in the tent on his own with his two-year-old son. He knew what Maeve was doing. She was swimming in the lake. They had swum together the evening before. But when he went outside he couldn't see her. It was midday before the body was found. He would never know whether it was the cold of the water, or cramp, or whether she had just swum too far. She had drowned. It was as sudden and as meaningless as that. He told the story of Maeve's death well. He had told it too many times not to. Sometimes, even now, it felt as if it was a story, someone else's story. He was barely aware that for most of the evening he spoke and she didn't; she was more relaxed when she was listening. Several times she did begin to tell him something about

Palestine and her failings as an orange grower, but then she laughed and stopped abruptly, as if she had thought better of it. She seemed to need to keep Ireland and Palestine apart. Neither of them wanted to talk about the future either, even about the next day. But it didn't matter; what mattered was that they were together tonight. That was all they had now. When they left the pub, she put her arm through his. And he didn't ask her if she was going home.

*

The next day Stefan Gillespie sat in the upstairs drawing room of a flat-fronted Georgian house at thirty-two Fitzwilliam Place. He hadn't forgotten the conversation with Lieutenant Cavendish on the train to Baltinglass. He hadn't forgotten that Dessie MacMahon watched Cavendish and another man searching Hugo Keller's house two days after the abortionist left Ireland, or that Dessie had followed them to Fitzwilliam Place. Now that he had hit a dead end with Frances Byrne it was time to see what he could get out of the Military Intelligence operation no one else knew about, not even Dessie. The interest G2 had in Hugo Keller made sense from what Cavendish had told him, but Detective Sergeant Jimmy Lynch was something else, and it was Jimmy Lynch he kept bumping into in one way or another in this investigation. Lynch didn't only connect to Keller, now he connected to Vincent Walsh.

A fire blazed in the grate and there was a Christmas tree in the window, hung with what were unmistakably the home-made decorations of young children. When Lieutenant Cavendish brought in a tray of tea, Stefan heard children's voices and the pit-a-pat of feet running up to the next floor.

Neither Cavendish nor the older man was in uniform. They had seemed only slightly surprised to find him on the doorstep. Cavendish did ask how he had found them but Stefan didn't reply. It felt like a good idea to suggest it was something cleverer than Dessie MacMahon following them from Merrion Square. He had assumed he would find a military office; instead he was in Captain Gearóid de Paor's home. It reminded him of what he had already worked out about the G2 operation; whatever it was, it wasn't officially sanctioned. That was his leverage. The lieutenant sprawled on a horsehair sofa that hadn't seen much horsehair in a long time. Stefan shifted uncomfortably in an armchair with a broken spring. The older man, de Paor, sat by the fire with a cigarette that he didn't seem to smoke; he was tall and dark, with a neatly trimmed moustache. He had been writing Christmas cards as Stefan walked into the room. He listened to what the detective told him as if he couldn't quite understand what it had to do with him, but the amiable smile didn't fool Stefan. He watched the man's eyes; they were less amiable. If there was anything useful to be found, it would be extracted and filed.

'Intriguing stuff, but I'm not sure what we can offer you, Sergeant.'

'You can tell me more about Hugo Keller, sir.'

'What do you want to know?'

'I wouldn't mind starting with where he is.'

'We can't do any better than you there. Germany's as far as we've got. He's of no real interest to us now he's out of the country anyway.'

'If Susan Field didn't come out of his clinic alive, that's murder.'

'I suppose it would be.'

'You don't seem very bothered, Captain.'

'If he's responsible for the woman's death then he should pay the price. Whether he is or not, I haven't got the faintest idea. That's your show. Two bodies makes it all rather more complicated of course. Not much of a connection between the man and the woman from what you're saying. But when all's said and done, it's got nothing to do with Military Intelligence.'

'Maybe not, but it's got something to do with Special Branch.'

The two officers looked at him. Cavendish stopped sprawling.

'Detective Sergeant Lynch went to considerable trouble to get hold of some letters that belonged to Vincent Walsh,' continued Stefan. 'Jimmy was happy to perjure himself and put a friend of Walsh's in Mountjoy in the process. That was more than a year after Walsh disappeared. Now he's turning Dublin upside down for Keller's memoirs, or whatever it is he keeps in his little book. I assume that's why you two were searching Merrion Square. Jimmy's not so dumb he wouldn't have found it if it was there by the way. I keep bumping into Jimmy, that's the thing. I don't know why.'

'I can't help you there,' smiled de Paor.

'No one's helping me very much anywhere. As far as my inspector's concerned, exactly the opposite. So I have to help myself.'

'That's admirable, Sergeant. I still don't see –'

'I'd like to find Hugo Keller.'

'Easier said than done now, I imagine.'

'So what's in it, Captain? The book.' Stefan wasn't going to let go.

De Paor lit another cigarette that he wouldn't smoke.

He looked across at Lieutenant Cavendish, who shrugged. The captain said nothing.

'Look, Keller's door is where my investigation into Susan Field's death stops,' continued Stefan. 'It's a dead end. But it's a very busy one. It's got Special Branch pulling Keller out of a Garda cell and dumping a woman they don't know at a Magdalene Laundry. It's got the director of the National Museum driving Dublin's favourite abortionist to Dún Laoghaire after a Nazi shindig at the Shelbourne. It's got detectives beating up all sorts of people, including other detectives. And it's got Military Intelligence breaking into crime scenes and following Special Branch men all round Dublin, not to mention me. Now whatever Jimmy Lynch is up to, you don't really expect me to believe you've got orders to spy on Special Branch, do you? I think you're doing it off your own bat. Or have I got it all wrong?'

The captain threw his cigarette into the fire and stood up.

'Do you think there's going to be a war, Sergeant?'

'Are we expecting the English back?'

'In Europe, I mean.'

'Not according to Herr Hitler. Isn't that the last thing he wants?'

'Your family's German, Mr Gillespie.'

Stefan was surprised. It was clear they had checked up on him.

'It's always useful to know who people are, Sergeant.'

'I see. Well, my grandmother was German.'

'You follow these things?'

'Up to a point, Captain.'

'So is it the last thing Herr Hitler wants?'

'I'd say that depends who he's talking to,' smiled Stefan.

Cavendish laughed. 'Spot on!'

'And what do you think about the Nazis?' continued the captain. Stefan was conscious he was the one who was being asked questions now. 'Do you have an opinion?'

'My mother still gets Christmas cards from her cousins. For the last two years they've come with swastikas on them. She doesn't put them up. I'm not looking for Hugo Keller because he's a Nazi. That's his business.'

'Everywhere there are Germans, there's a Nazi Party,' said de Paor, now turning to look out towards the street. 'We've got our own here, as you know, run by Herr Doktor Adolf Mahr, when he's not doing a thoroughly admirable job on the archaeology front, as director of the National Museum. You were at their Weinachsfest bash, of course, at the Shelbourne.'

'I didn't get an invitation though.'

'Maybe next year.'

'I'm not sure I couldn't find something better to do.'

'Everyone likes the flags and the uniforms, don't they, Mr Gillespie? We've a bit of a soft spot for all that ourselves, trench coats and Sam Browne belts. But there's a little bit more to it as far as the Nazi Party is concerned. Every German who's living in Ireland, working, studying, is expected to belong to the Party. Choice is not an option. There's the Hitler Youth too, just like the Boy Scouts they say, lots of hiking and cooking sausages on an open fire. But you don't join the Party for the craic. I'm not so sure the craic would be that good. There are jobs to be done. You have to earn your keep.'

'And what was Keller, the Party abortionist?' asked Stefan.

'When you take away the cultural evenings and the women's baking circle, it's all about information. The first thing is information about Germans in Ireland. If they're not in the Party, why aren't they in the Party? If they're against the Party, who are they, who do they spend their time with, who are their friends, what family have they got back in the fatherland? Then there's all the stuff about us. Who's who? Who thinks Adolf Hitler is the cat's pyjamas? Who thinks he's a loudmouthed gobshite? Who thinks the new Germany's heaven on earth? Who thinks it's the road to hell? Who wants the government closer to Germany? Who wants to keep quiet ties across the channel? Where are the socialists and communists? If the time came, who'd plant the bombs below while they dropped them from the sky?'

'You mean O'Duffy and his Blueshirts? They're finished surely?'

'Kaput as our friends would have it. No, the Blueshirts are old hat. They never counted for much anyway, did they? It's the IRA that's cosying up to the Nazis now. De Valera may have forgotten that England's difficulty is Ireland's opportunity, but they certainly haven't. Dev may have dumped the IRA but some of the friends he left behind have got their eyes on the war no one thinks will happen. Mahr's probably got a longer list of those fellers than we have. Not that you'd want to be heard saying it in polite society.'

'So you're spying on the spies,' said Stefan.

'I'm sure Herr Mahr would be shocked, genuinely shocked, to hear you use the word spy. I've had dinner with him several times. He's a man with a great love for Ireland. And a real admiration for Dev too. They all think there's something coming down the road though, any Nazi you speak to, and by the time the brandy bottle's been round the table a few times you get a whiff of it. And somewhere what's coming means England getting its just deserts. Mahr is doing what he's meant to do, collecting information and sending it home. And I'm sure he feels he has got the interests of both Germany and his newly adopted home at heart.'

'And Keller was a part of all this?'

'Keller's a different kettle of fish, Sergeant. I doubt he's any more of a Nazi than he needs to be. Information is a business for him. He's earned a good living here providing certain services the state prohibits. Along the way he's collected a lot of information, about all sorts of people who've availed of those services. Abortion's the main thing, but there are others, from the simple provision of contraceptive devices to treating sexual diseases you might be reluctant to refer to your own doctor. Herr Keller didn't come cheap, so a lot of the people he dealt with matter. But that's not all. A lot of people owed him favours. Blackmail breeds blackmail and what you can't get that way you can pay for. There's a market for everything.'

'So he was selling information to Special Branch too?'

'Let's just say there was some you-scratch-my-back in play.'

'It's all a bit beyond Jimmy Lynch, isn't it, Captain de Paor?'

'I'm sure it is. You need to get the tail and the dog in the right order of wagging however. Keller wasn't working for Lynch, Lynch was working for Keller.'

'And no one in Special Branch knows?'

It was Cavendish who shook his head and answered.

'I'm sure Keller fed him enough information to keep it all sweet. So if anyone asked Lynch about Keller he could say he was his pet informant.'

Stefan took this in. It raised a lot more questions about Jimmy Lynch.

'So how far would he have gone to protect Hugo Keller?'

'It wouldn't be the first time he's buried someone in the mountains,' continued the lieutenant. 'He pulled the trigger in the execution of two RIC men in Cork in 1920. During the Civil War, he shot a Free State soldier outside Portlaoise. Those are the ones for publication. Part of Detective Sergeant Lynch's proud war record. But there are others. There was a lad outside Mullingar, who was supposed to have told the police about an IRA ambush; that was mistaken identity. And a seventy-year-old farmer in Kildare who had a row with him in a pub. I don't think he says much about those two now. They just disappeared. The bodies were never found.'

Stefan shrugged. 'So if something did go wrong in Keller's clinic?'

Cavendish finished the thought in his head about Susan Field.

'Well, he wouldn't do better than DS Lynch to get rid of a body.'

As he walked down the steps to Fitzwilliam Place Stefan was no nearer finding Hugo Keller. And if he did find him, somewhere in Germany, no one was going to send him back to Ireland to answer any questions; certainly not the German police. But if Keller wasn't in Ireland someone was, someone who had been working for Hugo Keller as a paid informant, and someone who also knew about the letters Vincent Walsh was carrying the night he died. There didn't seem to be any connection between Keller and Vincent Walsh, but there was a connection between Jimmy

Lynch and Keller, and between Jimmy Lynch and Walsh. If the investigation into Susan Field's death stopped at the door to Hugo Keller's clinic, the next door along led straight into Garda Special Branch at Dublin Castle. However, it wasn't much more promising than the first. If no one would let him speak to a priest, what were the chances of investigating a detective in Special Branch for corruption and maybe murder? The Branch was a law unto itself within the Gardaí. It was full of ex-IRA men now, whose methods reflected that, and whose strongest loyalties were to each other. You took your life in your hands taking on men like that. There was plenty of room out there in the Dublin Mountains.

## 12. Weaver's Square

The tricycle left the window of Clery's the day before Christmas Eve. It found its way to Baltinglass on the train, via Kingsbridge and Naas, and Declan Lawlor's horse and cart brought it up the hill to Kilranelagh. On the morning of Christmas Eve, Stefan and David and Tom cut a pine tree in the woods below the farm. That afternoon the chosen goose was eaten enthusiastically by Stefan, David and Helena and, less enthusiastically than he had expected, by Tom, who had chosen it after all. At least he made sure the bird did not go unmourned. After dinner, keeping Christmas as they always had, to the German calendar, there were the presents, and the tricycle from the newspaper cutting by Tom Gillespie's bed was finally a real thing. He was still riding it round the farmyard in the dark when David and Helena left for the midnight Eucharist in the Church of Ireland church by the abbey, and it was dragged into the kitchen with him when he finally came inside.

Father and son sat by the range with the fire door open, and Stefan started to read the book David and Helena had given Tom, *Mary Poppins*, but by the time Mary had arrived with her carpetbag, Tom was asleep. Stefan carried him upstairs. Then he sat staring into the fire for a long time, long after David and Helena were home and asleep. There was a bottle of Powers on the table beside him. When he finally went upstairs to bed himself the bottle was half empty. And it was already Christmas morning. Christmas was still not easy, it shone a light on the empty place at the table. And what had happened with Hannah didn't make it easier.

*

The presbytery that housed the curate and the parish priest stood where the ground started to rise up behind Baltinglass towards Baltinglass Hill. It was built slightly higher than the church it served and looked down on Weaver's Square and the eastern end of the town. It was a squat, inelegant building, put together in a way that seemed to say nobody had cared very much what it looked like. There were lace curtains at all the windows, though it was not overlooked. Stefan stood in the bare front room. There was a dining table and a desk. A print of the Sacred Heart sat above a fireplace where there was no fire burning. It was a long time since one had been lit from the look of the dust on the kindling and newspaper ties in the grate. There were half a dozen cards on the mantelpiece but there were no other Christmas decorations. A grandfather clock ticked loudly. It felt like it was the only sound in the house. On the table were newspapers, *The Irish Independent*, *The Wicklow People*, *The Carlow Nationalist*, *The Irish Catholic*, all dated before Christmas and all unread. Fanned out in a careful display, next to the papers, were several Catholic Truth Society booklets; 'Stand and Deliver: a Call to Social Action', 'The Soviet War against God', 'Tolerance: Too Much of a Good Thing?' Stefan recalled a display of the same pamphlets at Monsignor Fitzpatrick's house in Earlsfort Terrace. The door opened. Father Carey entered, brusque and businesslike as always. He shut the door. There had been a summons, delivered via Mary Lawlor when she brought Tom home from Mass on Christmas Day. It was Stephen's Day now and Stefan was here as requested. He had assumed it would be about Tom starting school in January. That was all agreed though; what did the bloody man want now?

'It didn't seem right to speak to you yesterday, Sergeant, on Christmas Day. But something has come to my attention, so utterly fantastical that my first instinct was to dismiss the thing entirely. Yet it appears to be true.'

'I'm not with you at all, Father.'

'I'm right in thinking Tom was in Dublin with you before Christmas?'

'Yes. He came up for a day with his grandparents.'

'And were they party to this? I would hope not.' The look of sanctimonious shock would have made Stefan laugh under different circumstances, but the aura of satisfaction that hung about the priest told him that there was nothing funny going on. He still made no connection though.

'Party to what?'

'You took a Catholic boy into a Jewish place of worship?'

For a moment he was puzzled that Father Carey had this information at all. What was Tom's Christmas outing and the bit of police work that had intruded into it to do with him? Stefan's job and the farm at Kilranelagh rarely touched. It was nothing he worked at; it wasn't a separation he sought. It was just how it was. But the two worlds had touched, for a few moments, that afternoon in Dublin. He'd barely thought about it since, even if he had thought about Hannah Rosen. It was only as the curate brought the worlds into collision

207

that the implications of those minutes in Adelaide Road hit home. Tom would have talked about it, of course he would. Why wouldn't he? It was something new, something exotic, something he had enjoyed. The rabbi had made him laugh. Stefan finally understood why there was satisfaction behind the look of holy pain on Father Carey's angular face.

He saw a winter's day, fourteen years ago. He was fifteen. A crowd of men and women and children, forty or fifty, stood in front of the ruined abbey in Baltinglass, as his grandfather's coffin was carried into the little Church of Ireland church beside it. Snow had fallen the night before. Thin ice was breaking up on the Slaney below the abbey. Among the crowd were some of his grandfather's closest friends. Three men came forward to walk into the church behind the other mourners. The rest would bow their heads in the cemetery beside the church, as the coffin was lowered into the ground; some would wipe away tears; but they would not walk through the door of the church that their own Church said was not a real church at all.

'He lit a candle there, that's what I'm told!'

'There were children lighting candles. He lights a candle whenever he goes into the church, to say a prayer for his mother. He wouldn't know –'

'Are you telling me he was praying there now?'

'The priest was telling them a story from the Bible. He was listening.'

'You told him the man was a priest, did you?'

'All right, the rabbi. I didn't tell him anything. We're talking about minutes, a few minutes. I didn't think. I'm sorry.' It was hard not to wonder whether he would have thought if it hadn't been Hannah he had been meeting. There had been no real reason to be there with Tom. It could have waited.

'You stood there and let this happen?'

'It was a candle holder, like the one we put in the window at Christmas, and children lighting candles, like we do at home. That's all.'

He had to say something, but he realised that nothing he said would satisfy the curate. Every word was a trap Father Carey was waiting to spring.

'I will have to speak to Tom.'

'I'll explain it to him.'

'That can hardly be enough. He has to know that it was wrong for him to be there, let alone participate in what was going on. Even a child must be made aware when a sin has been committed, even unwittingly, and ask for the forgiveness that always comes. I'm sure the boy understands that.'

Stefan's hackles were rising at the thought of what Carey would put Tom through to make sure he really did understand that forgiveness. But the traps were all around him now; any protest would spring another one.

'This is a serious matter, Sergeant. Righting this shocking error of judgement is one thing, but comprehending how you could make it is much harder. Even from a Protestant point of view, your behaviour must appear extraordinary. I have to ask, are you in the habit of associating with Jews?'

'I'm a guard, Father, I don't choose who I meet.' He was evading the issue and he felt ashamed of himself, even as he did so. Hannah was looking at him. He saw the expression on her face. He shouldn't even have answered the question. By answering it, he had given the priest the right to ask it.

'You know that a Roman Catholic should not enter any place of worship that isn't Catholic. But a Jewish synagogue is disturbing in a very particular way. I have to make some allowances for ignorance on your part, and I do.' There seemed no choice except to allow Carey to make those allowances. 'The Church is under attack. Christianity itself is under attack. I know we're not immune from the menace of communism and atheism in our quiet West Wicklow backwater, but I feel as if you have brought the agents of all that among us, because the Jews are its agents, make no mistake. You exposed an innocent child to that, your own child. Don't you understand?'

Stefan understood very well. These were not the curate's words. The voice and intonation were almost Robert Fitzpatrick's. Stefan could have no doubt Father Carey had heard him speak. He spoke the monsignor's words as if he had been waiting to say them for a long time. He was a prophet now. And there was nothing Stefan could say in reply. Anthony Carey had his burning bow and Stefan was the one who had given him the poisonous arrows. The priest shook his head and stepped down from the mountain.

'The question is where we go from here, Sergeant Gillespie.'

'I'm sorry about what happened. But you're making more of this –'

'Did you tell him it was a place of people who turned their backs on Christ, who handed Him to the Romans for execution, who rejected God?'

'I said it was where Jewish people prayed.'

'The boy told Mrs Lawlor's son that Jesus was a Jew.'

'Should I have said he wasn't?'

'You're a man of many talents. Now you're a theologian too.'

210

'It's hardly theology.'

'No, it's not. But on top of everything, I'm afraid it is too much.'

'Just tell me what you want me to say –'

'I have had every consideration for your feelings, Sergeant, and for the boy's. I have been patient. I have put the fact that you are Tom's father before other concerns. Too much so! He has another Father, a Father you are distancing him from, whether it is your intention or not. I have felt it for a long time. I have nothing against your mother and father personally, but they are not the right people to raise the boy in the faith you committed him to when you married. And even if you were here, you are not the father his dead mother would have wanted for him, I am sure of that now.'

'How dare you say that! You know nothing at all about his mother.'

This was more than temper; anger was in his heart and it was pounding in his chest. His hands were clenched very tight.

'I wonder what she thinks as she looks down now,' said the curate.

'You have no right to even begin to wonder what Maeve might think. My God, if she *was* looking down on us here, your ears would be burning.'

'I have expressed my concerns to Father MacGuire.'

'Where is Father MacGuire?'

'He always has his week off after Christmas. He's not here just now.'

'I bet he isn't,' replied Stefan. The parish priest wouldn't like this. It was no accident he wasn't there. But it would make no difference. He was an old man. Even when he disagreed with his curate, he no longer argued.

211

'I've spoken to the bishop. And to your brother-in-law in Portlaoise.'

'Dermot? What the hell's Dermot got to do with anything?'

'They have three children, Tom's cousins. They'd happily take him.'

Stefan stared. He hadn't seen where this was going at all. He thought it was still just another opportunity for Father Carey to throw his weight around. But as soon as the words were said, he knew it had been obvious.

'No, under no circumstances. I'm not even going to discuss it.'

'We will discuss it, and I'm sure you'll agree what's best for Tom –'

'I said no.'

'I can't leave it there.'

'Jesus, there's a fucking Christmas card on the mantel-piece, from Dermot and Kathleen. "Happy Christmas, all the best for the New Year, hope to see you soon!" Not a word, not a fucking word. See you soon!'

'I think if you reflect on the situation –'

'I won't be reflecting on anything.'

'Then I need to make myself clearer. Mixed marriages are a bane to the Church. They are against God's law and against natural law. The Church shows her displeasure, even when she gives dispensation, refusing the Holy Sacrifice during the marriage. My own view is that too much leeway is given in approving them at all, even with a commitment to bring children up as Catholics. But the commitment is there, irrespective of your wife's death.'

'And I am carrying that out.'

'Not as far as I'm concerned. Not as far as the bishop is concerned.'

'What do you want me to do? Give up my job?'

'It's not about you being here. The boy's home is entirely unconducive to the health of a young and impressionable Catholic soul. There is no shortage of evidence to demonstrate your inability to bring him up in the faith he was born into. But the sight of Tom praying in a synagogue is beyond anything the Church can accept. His place is with his cousins, with his mother's brother. For his sake, and your own, I would advise you not to fight this. The courts are no place for families. And the end result will be the same, I promise you. As for the damage to your career –'

'Are you threatening me now?'

'I'm telling you what will happen, Gillespie.'

'I promised Maeve –'

'There is no more to say, Sergeant. You need time to calm down. When you have, we'll talk about this again and put the arrangements in place. It doesn't mean you won't see your son. But when you do, he'll be part of a family, his family. In time you'll understand that the Church's interests and your son's are the same. Those interests should be yours too.'

Stefan stood very still, looking at the satisfaction that Anthony Carey made no real attempt to hide. The curate stood taller than he had, straighter.

'You've always wanted this, haven't you?'

'It's about what's right.' The priest shook his head, frowning, almost as if he really did regret what he was doing. 'It's not about what I want.'

'That's shite and you know it.'

Carey pursed his lips; he wasn't finished yet.

'From my little talk with Tom's playmate, Harry Lawlor, I gather that your visit to the synagogue was all about seeing

213

a lady, am I right there?' He smiled a man-of-the-world smile; his sanctimoniousness turning into a sneer as he fixed his eyes on Stefan. 'All in a day's work for a policeman, eh? I wonder, what would your Maeve have thought about that?'

As Stefan's fist hit the curate's face it was Maeve's name that propelled it rather than the taunt itself. Carey had taken her name and thrown it into a mire of shabby and spiteful innuendo. He spoke as if he knew her, as if there was some part of her precious memory that belonged to him. He staggered back against the desk, but he didn't fall. He was hurt, there was no doubt, yet he could still find a smile. He wiped his mouth and looked down at the blood on the back of his hand. It was Stefan Gillespie's final mistake.

*

Christmas was over. Stefan was back in the detectives' office at Pearse Street. The letter from Father Francis Byrne in Danzig had arrived on Inspector Donaldson's desk with a glowing affidavit from Monsignor Fitzpatrick. It seemed completely at odds with the barely controlled anger the monsignor had shown when Stefan had asked him about the priest little more than ten days ago. Donaldson had made the arrangements, clearly in consultation with Robert Fitzpatrick. The questions Stefan wanted asked had been asked in such general terms that the answers, not worth much in a letter anyway, were worth nothing at all; some questions had clearly not even been put to him. Father Byrne was shocked and saddened to hear of Susan Field's death, naturally. She had been one of his brightest and best students. It was a tragic and irreplaceable loss to her family.

He had not known her well outside the confines of the lecture room, but he had certainly liked her and remembered her fondly. He was puzzled where the idea of any close or particular friendship came from. He wasn't fully able to understand the circumstances of her death, of course, but it was all very shocking, and he prayed she was at peace. By the way he didn't know Doctor Hugo Keller.

That was where it ended.

Monsignor Fitzpatrick spent several more pages of his own letter eulogising Father Francis Byrne's almost saintly integrity. He went on to express his indignation that the Gardaí would presume to ask questions based on the fantasies of a woman who was evidently disturbed. He didn't quite say Susan Field had brought it all upon herself, but he didn't need to.

It was as pointless as Inspector Donaldson could have wished. But what Stefan saw clearly was that Francis Byrne had too little to say about the woman he'd had a passionate love affair with, and Robert Fitzpatrick had too much to say about the man he'd felt such aversion to so very recently.

'Jesus, Stevie.' Dessie McMahon sighed, watching as Stefan re-read the letter.

'I know,' replied Stefan. 'Don't start again.' He didn't want to talk about what Dessie was trying to talk about. He didn't want to think about it.

'I mean what the feck?'

'What the feck indeed,' he shrugged. Dessie wasn't going to stop.

'Would he ever just forget about it?'

'Father Carey's not a turning-the-other-cheek kind of priest.'

'Did you ever meet one that was?'

The telephone rang. Dessie MacMahon picked it up.

'It's Inspector Donaldson. He wants you in there, now.'

When Stefan Gillespie walked into Inspector Donaldson's office, the first person he saw was Detective Sergeant Lynch. It wasn't the Jimmy Lynch he'd last met turning over his room. This one had had a bath and was wearing a suit that nearly fitted him and a white shirt that was even ironed.

'We need to sort these bodies out.' It was Inspector Donaldson who spoke. 'Sit down, Gillespie. You know Detective Sergeant Lynch of course.'

The two sergeants nodded. Stefan already sensed something was wrong. There was no smirk or smile on Lynch's face. He looked serious, alert, attentive; you could almost have mistaken him for a real detective.

'The woman first,' announced the inspector. 'We know she was pregnant. Sadly you've seen the evidence of that yourself. Sergeant Lynch has established that she probably did procure a miscarriage from Keller.'

'Was that before or after I established it, sir?'

Donaldson ignored him. 'As is the way with these things, there were complications. And it seems very likely that she died at Merrion Square.'

Lynch looked grim, as saddened by the awful events as the inspector.

'And how did Sergeant Lynch establish that?' enquired Stefan.

'Sheila Hogan,' said the inspector. 'Keller told her what happened.'

'She was at it with your man, you know that.' Lynch offered up this additional information as if it provided a complete explanation in itself.

216

'With a dead woman in his clinic, he had to do something,' continued Inspector Donaldson. 'The assumption is he put the body in his car and took it out to the mountains and buried her. Unfortunately, I don't imagine it's the first time that sort of thing has happened with these backstreet abortionists.'

'Is that what Sheila Hogan said too? It's not what she said to me.' Stefan's words were addressed to Donaldson, but he was looking at Lynch.

'She didn't know the details, Stevie,' said the Special Branch detective grimly. 'I'm filling in the gaps, but I got what I could out of her.'

'I know. That's why she was in the Mater Hospital.'

'That will do!' snapped the inspector.

'Is there some reason you've decided to help us with this now, Jimmy?'

Lynch said nothing to Stefan; he didn't need to give explanations.

'I think we'll concentrate on the case please, Gillespie.' Donaldson glared at his sergeant. 'I haven't been idle on this myself. Mr Keller has questions to answer. We didn't know that before, neither did Sergeant Lynch. If we had he wouldn't have been allowed to leave the country of course. We have good reason to believe he is somewhere in Germany.'

'Since he was driven to the mail boat by our local Nazi chief, Herr Mahr, after Detective Sergeant Lynch dropped him at the Shelbourne for a Weihnachtsfest do, I'd say it's not a bad guess. Are we all agreed on that?'

'Let me make something clear, Sergeant. There are a number of reasons why this case is being handed over to Special Branch –'

Lynch just watched, smiling confidently.

'Like hell it is!'

'Shut up, Gillespie!'

James Donaldson's fist thumped on the desk.

'Enquiries about Hugo Keller's whereabouts will obviously have to be directed to the German police. That's not a job for us. It isn't our business to ask exactly why Mr Keller had a relationship with Special Branch in the first place, but we have to accept that in their area of activity, which is the security of the state after all, they encounter their own share of unsavoury informants, in the same way you do as a detective. That doesn't alter the fact that this man Keller is responsible for the death of a young woman and, naturally, every effort will be made to find him and bring him to justice.'

'My arse!' proclaimed Stefan.

Jimmy Lynch laughed. Inspector Donaldson didn't.

'Enough! You'll hand any information you have to Sergeant Lynch.'

'That's one down, sir. What about Vincent Walsh?'

'Don't waste your time, Stevie.' Lynch stretched back in his chair.

'Is that a Special Branch case too, Jimmy?'

'No, I'm just saying the boy had been up there a long time.'

'You knew him then?'

'Poofs aren't my speciality.'

'No?'

Stefan looked at the Special Branch man for a long moment. There was no point arguing with Inspector Donaldson now. There was no point even starting on the way the inspector had pushed aside the need to question

Francis Byrne. And there was no point letting Detective Sergeant Lynch know what Billy Donnelly had told him about Vincent Walsh's letters. If Lynch thought it was all done and dusted, it was better to let him think it. Stefan needed to know what it meant; then he might have something to use.

'The discovery of these two bodies so close to each other seems to be a coincidence. There's nothing to connect them.' Inspector Donaldson put his hands together on his desk; he had dealt with it. However much he disliked Special Branch, Lynch would take it away. That would be that.

But Stefan wasn't done.

'Except that they were both shot in the head by a captive bolt pistol.'

James Donaldson nodded complacently; he wasn't unprepared.

'It's an imaginative theory on Doctor Wayland-Smith's part. I know he likes to play the detective, but I understand that what's actually there is simply damage to the skulls, along with all sorts of damage to other bones, all exacerbated by the landslip. I think he's rather cooled off on the idea.'

As Stefan walked back to his office, Jimmy Lynch caught up with him.

'I've never liked you much, Stevie, but you've surprised me.'

'What's the matter now?'

'I tell you, I've a list of priests I'd like to knock the crap out of, that's as long as your arm. I never quite had the balls. Could you do a few for me?'

'Good news travels fast.'

'Donald Duck doesn't know yet?'

'No, but I'm sure he will.'

'Me too, Stevie, me too.'

Lynch carried on downstairs, whistling cheerfully. Stefan watched the swagger as he went. If he was really looking at a murderer he was looking at one who was being paid by An Garda Síochána to cover up his own crimes.

Stefan walked slowly back into the detectives' office to find Dessie MacMahon looking more forlorn than when he'd left him half an hour ago.

'You're wanted at Garda HQ. It's the Commissioner.'

They turned to see a slightly wild-eyed Inspector Donaldson standing in the doorway. Only minutes ago, Stefan had left him congratulating himself on getting rid of an uncomfortable case and bringing his detectives under control. The call from the Garda Commissioner had come only seconds later. The news about Stefan's Christmas had reached him at last.

'You ignorant, fucking, Protestant bollocks, Gillespie!'

\*

Through the windows of the Garda Commissioner's office Stefan could see the bare winter trees of the Phoenix Park. Across the desk in front of him sat the Commissioner, Ned Broy, turning the pages of a slim file of letters. His round face was deceptively benign; the severely cropped hair and the small, piercing eyes told more. They didn't really know each other. Broy had been head of the Detective Branch when Stefan joined in 1932. Not long afterwards he had moved into the top job when the new president, Éamon de Valera, had sacked General Eoin O'Duffy, the hostile commissioner he had inherited from the previous government. In response O'Duffy put his Blueshirts on the streets and threatened to march on Dublin. No one was quite sure what the Gardaí would do if it came to a coup. Ned Broy's answer was to draft scores of ex-IRA men into Special Branch. They were immediately dubbed the Broy Harriers after a pack of Wicklow foxhounds. Their job was to take on the Blueshirts if they had to, but no one had any doubt they would take on their new comrades in the Garda Síochána if it came to the crunch. It didn't. That was history now, but in Ireland history never quite goes away. Stefan was reflecting on the conversation at Pearse Street. Jimmy Lynch was one of the Broy Harriers. He was Ned Broy's man.

There was a knock on the door. An elderly priest came in. Father Michael McCauley was the Garda Chaplain. Broy gestured to him to sit.

'You'll know Father McCauley, Sergeant?'

'Not really, sir.'

'I'm here to pray for you, Sergeant.' The priest gave a wry smile.

'You know you broke this curate's nose?' said the Commissioner.

'I didn't know, sir.'

'I have that from his bishop. I have quite a lot from his bishop.'

'I've got no excuse, sir.'

'I wouldn't say that. I got your father into the station at Baltinglass this morning. I spoke to him on the telephone. I knew him in the DMP.'

Stefan looked at Broy with considerable surprise. He was unaware of any past connection between his father and the

Commissioner, but when his father left the Dublin Metropolitan Police, before the War of Independence, Ned Broy had been both a detective and an IRA spy. David Gillespie had always said he resigned because he wouldn't take sides. But it was true that he had never elaborated on his choice; maybe it hadn't been a choice at all. It had never occurred to Stefan that it might have been because of what he knew.

'It was a long time ago, but I have reason to remember him.' The past hung over them for a moment. It was all the Commissioner was going to say. 'The point is I know what it was about.'

'Does that help, sir?'

'No. It still means it was the stupidest thing you could have done.'

'He was goading me. I think he almost wanted me to do it.'

'That wouldn't surprise me. And you gave him what he wanted.'

Stefan nodded; he knew that all too well himself.

Broy turned to the chaplain. 'Do you know this Father Carey?'

'I've never met him, but I've asked around now. He has a history of this kind of thing. In his last parish there were complaints about him refusing to sanction mixed marriages, even when dispensation had been given, and there was some insulting behaviour towards the Church of Ireland minister. There was also a child taken away from her father in similar circumstances to Sergeant Gillespie's. In the end the man converted to keep his daughter. It caused such bad feeling that Carey was moved on. But even though I've never met the man, he has written to me, about you, Sergeant Gillespie.'

'What for?' Stefan was puzzled.

'He wanted my opinion on your suitability as a father, in the light of your wife's death, and bearing in mind that you weren't a Catholic. I told him it wasn't my business to have any opinion on your abilities as a father, but that the Garda Síochána had a very high opinion of you as a policeman. He wrote again asking me to put what he called "professional pressure" on you to convert to Catholicism. I have to say I didn't bother to reply to that.'

'You've made a pig's ear of it, Sergeant,' interrupted Broy.

Stefan didn't need telling.

'Look, sir, when I was married I agreed our children would be brought up as Catholics. I took it seriously and I've stuck to it – so have my parents. There's hardly a Sunday Tom misses Mass. And it's not even what my wife would have wanted. I persuaded her we should marry in a Catholic church. I knew what it would do to her family if we didn't. Now, whatever I do it's never enough. It's not like I'm ramming anything down Tom's throat, I don't even believe –' He stopped, feeling he was making things worse.

'There you go again, Sergeant. If you're going to be an atheist you need to be a Catholic atheist, not a Protestant one!' The chaplain smiled.

'There's a pile of shite here any self-respecting bishop would have thrown back at the man.' Ned Broy gestured at the file on his desk. 'You can feel the spit coming off the page. Jesus, you'd think you were running the Hellfire Club down in Baltinglass. He's got lists of books in your father's sitting room we should all be out there burning. There's even the year you spent at Trinity to show what an evil-thinking bollocks you are. God only knows what kind of low-life Protestant bastards you were associating with! It goes on. I don't know how many nights you've had a few too many in Sheridan's in Baltinglass with Sergeant Kavanagh. It can't be that many. You don't live there! But you're a drunk as well. I know Kavanagh as it happens. Now he is a drunk! This gobshite's got it in for you and he's got his bishop behind him now. But what was this jaunt to the fecking synagogue?'

'It was ten minutes, that's all. I was just following up on some information in a case.' He stopped, unsure. It wasn't exactly the truth. 'It was a stupid thing to do. I should have left it. I wasn't thinking . . .'

'You picked the wrong curate,' said Father McCauley, shaking his head. 'I can't say your boy standing in the Adelaide Road Synagogue would keep me awake. I know Rabbi Herz. I wouldn't be sorry to see some more priests who knew the Old Testament like he does. But Father Carey belongs to a different school; the nest of Christ-killers and communists school; the Monsignor Fitzpatrick crowd. Do you know who I'm talking about?'

Stefan knew all too well. He was slightly uncomfortable. The Commissioner was looking through the file on the desk again. This was a personal matter, but that didn't mean Ned Broy hadn't had something to do with putting the lid on his investigation. There was the way any serious questioning of Father Byrne had been pushed aside, and the way everything was now in the hands of Special Branch. Broy continued reading. Father McCauley spoke again.

'Where do they want your son to go? It's Tom, isn't it?'

'My brother-in-law's, in Portlaoise.'

'That's not so far.'

'He's not even five. I wouldn't dream of it.'

'If it came to a court case, I'm not sure what the conse-quences would be,' replied the chaplain. 'There are a lot of people in the Church who don't like this sort of thing, I assure you, but there are risks in taking a bishop on. And it's not as if you're with the boy all the time. You're working in Dublin. Is it really so different, seeing him in Laois and seeing him in Wicklow?'

'It's not his home. It would be different to him.'

'To him or to you?'

'I know my son.'

'You need to think hard, Sergeant, very hard. It's not easy advice –'

'I don't need to think at all, Father.'

'I wish you would. I will do what I can on your behalf. I know the bishop. But they are serious about this, that's all I can say, very serious.'

'Thanks, Derek.' The Commissioner closed the file.

The chaplain got up. He smiled at Stefan and then left.

'It's good advice, Gillespie,' said Broy. 'Perhaps it's the only advice. I can't help you with that side of things. I wish I could. I've got enough on my plate with your assault on the fecking curate. I can't ignore it, can I?'

Stefan said nothing.

'The bishop's full of threats about a prosecution for assault. It's bollocks. I can probably sit on that one. But he wants me to kick you out.'

Stefan nodded. Why would he have expected anything else?

'There are a variety of disciplinary charges involved. I don't know where we'd end up if we went down that road. So we won't bother. I'm going for the chaplain's approach. That means I won't fight everything.'

'So I'm out?'

'No, we go along with it, but only so far. I have the power to suspend you, without any recourse to formal disciplinary procedures. I don't need to ask anyone or explain it to anyone. I'll write to the bishop and express my horror at what you've done, and say I'm suspending you forthwith. I can make that sound as near to a dismissal as makes no difference. You go away. We all shut up and forget about it. And in six months' time I reinstate you.'

'When would my suspension –'

'For now, just make Inspector Donaldson a happy man. Go home.'

'I'm in the middle of a case.'

'Not any more. You know what forthwith means. Fuck off, now!'

As Stefan Gillespie walked through the Phoenix Park it was colder. There was ice in the air. Uppermost in his mind was what waited for him in Baltinglass. The threat that was hanging over the house and over Tom was a real one. He had pushed it aside because he couldn't believe it, but the chaplain's words were in his head now. Other people did believe it. Tom couldn't know, whatever else happened. His parents would have to share the burden though. So far he'd only told them of another row with the curate, but they already knew it was more serious than anything that had happened before. Now his father had spoken to the Commissioner too. He still had his job after a fashion; if he shut up and kept his head down. That was the real message from the Commissioner and the Garda Chaplain. But how far was Ned Broy really sticking his neck out? They were telling him to do what the Church

226

wanted and pretend it was a way out. People always said the Irish had three curses: the English, the drink and the Church. The English had faded away; the drink was your own choice in the end; but the priests were always there. And once he took the first step, once he accepted that they could decide what happened to his son, there'd be no turning back. He couldn't do it, not to Tom, not to himself, not to Maeve. If losing his son was the price for keeping his job, then the job wasn't worth having.

He didn't bother to go back to Pearse Street. They could have Susan Field and Vincent Walsh. They could have Hugo Keller and Jimmy Lynch. It didn't matter. The only thing left from that was Hannah Rosen. He wondered where she was. But there was no point needing a woman he would never even see again. He walked on faster. Kingsbridge was just beyond the park gates. He reached Albert Quay and crossed the Liffey to the station. Fifteen minutes later the train was taking him back home to West Wicklow.

*

The upstairs room looked out over Main Street in Baltinglass. The solicitor's office was untidy, cluttered with papers and files and books. But it was a bright room. The big windows let in the pale midwinter light and the dust that hung in the air showed how rarely the place was cleaned. A man in his sixties stood at the window looking out. He leant on a walking stick. In Dublin, thirteen years earlier, during the War of Independence, the Black and Tans had thrown him from the first floor of a solicitor's practice in Leeson Street. His legs had been broken in too many places to ever mend properly. Ever since, he had been more comfortable standing up than sitting down. Through the window came the noise of cattle being driven through the town to the market place. Emmet Brady had listened to Stefan without interruption. Now he paced slowly in front of the window, while Stefan sat on a chair in front of the desk the solicitor only used to pile papers on.

'There is a simple solution of course, Stefan. You could convert.'

'Is that all there is?'

'It would certainly be the end of it.'

He watched Brady limping slowly up and down. The old man was thinking hard, but what he was thinking wasn't what Stefan wanted to hear.

'Are you telling me they can do this, Mr Brady?'

'No, of course I'm not.'

'But –'

'But it doesn't mean I'm telling you they can't.'

'It's one or the other surely?'

'You know the law better than that. A wife would be another option.'

'What?' Despite everything Stefan laughed.

Brady stopped, grimacing as pain shot down his leg, then paced again.

'You're not unattractive. Admittedly your employment prospects are slightly uncertain right now, but then you've a bit of land coming to you up at Kilranelagh one day. A good Catholic girl would do the job nicely. Maybe it's time you put off the black armband, metaphorically speaking.'

'I hope the fact that you think it's funny is a good sign, Mr Brady.'

'I don't think it's funny at all. But why not convert?'

228

'I can't convert to something I don't believe in.'

'You mean you'd rather not lie.'

'I shouldn't have to lie.' Stefan turned in the chair, angry again.

'You shouldn't, I agree, but what if Father Carey and the bishop take this all the way to the Four Courts? What if the Church drags you into a courtroom and persuades a judge that the interests of your son would be best served if he lived with his uncle and aunt. I'm not saying they can or will.'

'But it's possible,' said Stefan quietly.

'Stick with the question. Wouldn't a lie be better?'

'I suppose it ought to be.' He said the words with a frown. It wasn't easy to know why he felt he couldn't even contemplate that. Why should it matter so much, if one simple lie could take the vindictive curate off his back? Emmet Brady had stopped again, rubbing his leg as he watched him.

'You did promise the boy would be brought up as a Catholic.'

'And he is.'

'And you're a fit man to do that?'

'I'm his father.'

'How many of us have ever really been fit for that?' The solicitor smiled, setting off again, pacing up and down in front of the window.

Stefan shifted uneasily in the chair, following Brady's movements as he walked back and forward. The constant motion was irritating him.

'Let's look at you, Stefan. You're a guard who's on suspension for assaulting a priest. That's quite some place to start, wouldn't you say?'

'What's being a guard's worth? I'd probably be better out of it.'

'No, that won't do.' The old man halted abruptly, shaking his head. 'You have to stick with the job, at all costs. You'll be back in what –'

'Six months. That's what the Commissioner said.'

'A man with a job is better than a man without one. A Garda sergeant with a blot on his record is better than a man who looks like he was kicked out. Hitting Father Carey is the biggest thing they have against you. The rest adds up, but on its own it wouldn't amount to much. No one's going to take you to the High Court brandishing a copy of *The Communist Manifesto* and a King James Bible! Walking into a synagogue with Tom for a couple of minutes might be high on Father Carey's list of abominations, but it wouldn't normally cut much ice elsewhere. Although taking the woman you had to talk to so urgently on Garda matters to your bed, is something else.'

Stefan's lips tightened. It wasn't Brady's business or anyone else's.

'Is the curate right about that?' insisted the old man.

'If that's how you want to put it.' Stefan shrugged.

'It's not about how I want to put it, it's how a barrister in the Four Courts would put it, when he describes you taking your four-year-old son into the synagogue, so that you could make arrangements for a sex session with your Jewish mistress. That's what he might say. How does it sound?'

Stefan knew the courts; he could hear the words.

'I see, and it's even worse if she's Jewish, is it?'

'You need have no doubt that there are judges who would think exactly that. It's a side of our Free State no one would want to admit to, but this isn't about what's right, Stefan. It's about what you might have to deal with.'

The implications were sinking in. The man he had come to for help was making it sound worse than the Commissioner or the Garda Chaplain.

'How does Carey know?' The solicitor started to pace again.

'He doesn't. A good guess, that's all.'

'Come on, you said he'd written to the Garda Chaplain about you, even before this. He told him to feck off, but it doesn't mean our curate hasn't been busy elsewhere. Who else has he talked to? Who else knew?'

'One other guard. Dessie wouldn't –'

'For God's sake, man, I hope you're a better detective than that! You've lived in a Garda barracks before. Do you really think there's a single guard at Pearse Street who didn't know what you were up to?'

Stefan couldn't help laughing. Who had he been kidding?

'So who would Father Carey have talked to?'

'Maybe my inspector. Inspector Donaldson. He's a real Holy Joe. You know, Mass every day, novenas, the Knights of St Columbanus, the lot.'

'Well, aren't you the lucky one? So are there any more?'

'Any more what?'

'Any more women you've been fucking. Any affairs? Have you got a string of mistresses? Do you spend your evenings in a whorehouse? They need to find all the reasons they can to prove you're not a decent man to bring up a Catholic child. If they go for it they won't hold anything back.'

'There's been no one else, not since Maeve died.'

'All right, next question. Do you believe in God, Mr Gillespie?'

'What?'

'If I was their barrister, I'd ask. You can always lie.'

'This is crazy.'

'You bet it is! Come on! Do you believe in God, Mr Gillespie?'

'I was brought up to believe. I believe in what Christianity –'

'Do you believe in God? Yes or no.'

'I don't, but I –'

'There are no buts in the witness box. If I were you, I'd say yes. If you don't, the next question will be how can this court believe a word you say? Didn't you just swear to tell the truth, the whole truth and nothing but the truth, so help you God? Why did you do that if you don't believe in God?'

Stefan couldn't sit there any more. He stood up, angry, confused.

'So are you saying they can take Tom away, or not?'

'No.' Emmet Brady stopped again. He smiled. 'I'm not saying that.'

'So what do I do?'

'How far are you accommodating Father Carey now?'

'Well, Tom starts at Kilranelagh Cross National School next week.' Stefan found he was walking up and down beside the old man. 'That's what Carey wanted before. We'll make sure he never misses Mass on Sunday. I'll teach him his catechism and his rosary. My mother and father will never say a word about God or religion in the house. We'll all keep our mouths shut.'

'It's personal with Carey. He's made it very obvious, Stefan.'

'I know that.'

The solicitor stood by the window. He turned briefly, looking out. Stefan stood behind him, saying nothing. It was quiet outside now. The noise of the cattle in the street below had gone. A car drove past.

'So would you be happy taking on the Church, Mr Brady?'

Emmet Brady turned back towards him with a combative grin.

'Why not, it's my fucking Church, isn't it?'

\*

A week later Stefan drove his father's John Deere tractor the mile or so along the road into the mountains, to the low stone building next to the chapel at Kilranelagh Cross. It was Tom's first day at school. He sat on the trailer behind Stefan, by the pile of turf they were taking to the school, to keep the fires burning in the two classrooms. The crossroads below the big, long mountain called Keadeen was a bleak place on a January morning. There was nothing much there; the chapel and the school, a farm and a holy well, and further on along the road a shop with a bar in the back room. But Scoil Naomh Téagáin, St Tegan's School, was noisy with children starting back after Christmas now, and Tom's nervousness was quickly swept away as he ran off into the classroom with his friend Harry Lawlor. He knew nothing about what was happening around him, only that he was suddenly going to school. Stefan and David and Helena all believed, in different ways, that the threat to Tom would pass; because to believe anything else was still impossible.

By the time Stefan had unloaded his turf into the shed

at the back of the school, classes had begun. Driving back to the road he could see the desks in Tom's classroom through the window. He saw Tom looking out, hearing the familiar noise, and waving. Then he saw Anthony Carey, stepping over the stone wall that divided the school from the chapel. The curate raised his hand in greeting; Stefan did the same. But Father Carey's smile wasn't a smile of reconciliation. It was a statement: don't let yourself think this is the end. He had no intention of losing face. It wasn't over.

Stefan didn't go straight back to the farm. He took the road to Baltinglass, to collect cattle feed for his father. On the way he stopped at the post office to post the letter he had written to Hannah Rosen. He didn't know where she was, but he addressed it to her father's house as she'd asked him to. It would find her eventually. She wouldn't like what he had to tell her. She had trusted him. He wanted to believe it was more than trust. But there was nothing he could do now. The investigation into the deaths of Susan Field and Vincent Walsh was over. The files were sitting in a Special Branch office somewhere in Dublin Castle, and he had no reason to believe they would ever be opened again. It was beyond his control, but he still couldn't help feeling he had let her down. He knew how much it would matter to her. He wondered if it mattered as much to her as it did to him that they would never see each other again. He couldn't know. And even if it did, it didn't change anything. The case was finished. It was no use pretending otherwise.

# PART TWO
# Free City

*Mr Seán Lester, the League of Nations High Commissioner of Danzig, was publicly insulted yesterday by Herr Greiser, President of the Senate, who threatened that Mr Lester might be forced to leave the city. Mud was thrown at the Commissioner's car by a crowd of people as he drove through the city. Feeling in Danzig is running very high. The Diet was dissolved at the beginning of February, and new elections have been fixed for April 7th. At the last elections in May, 1933, the Nazis gained 38 seats out of 72, and thus had a small majority. They now aim at eliminating the Opposition altogether. Mr Lester, who has the task of holding the balance between the rivals, has apparently been suspected of partiality.*

*The Irish Times*

# 13. Oliva Cathedral

*Danzig, April 1935*

Hannah Rosen arrived in Trieste on the train from Milan. After Venice it followed the Adriatic south, running beside the sea all through a long afternoon as it finally approached the port. It was April and it was already hot. She knew people here. In the Via del Monte, where the city started to wind up the hillside overlooking the Gulf of Trieste, was the headquarters of the Jewish Agency. It was there for the thousands of men, women and children who came every year to take the boats to Jaffa and Haifa to start a new life. Less than twenty years ago, Trieste had been the main port of the Austro-Hungarian Empire; it was still the funnel into the Mediterranean for most of Central Europe. Few of the Jews who travelled to Trieste had much in common with the young socialists and communists who staffed the Jewish Agency office; they were simply people who believed that keeping your head down wasn't going to be enough. They were running from what was to come, and they were no more than a drop in Europe's Jewish ocean.

Hannah's job was over. In Leeds, in London, in Manchester, in Bournemouth, in Lyons, Paris, Amsterdam,

Milan – she had done what she had been sent to do. They weren't large sums of money. No one ever said that now it was for guns, not tractors, but people had stepped back. Not everyone was so sure about guns. Yet the money still had to be moved, in cheques, money orders, bonds; it still had to reach its destination in ways the British government and the Palestine Mandate Police could not trace.

Leaving the Stazione Centrale, she didn't head for the centre of Trieste and the Via del Monte. She turned left and walked the few hundred yards to the harbour. At the offices of the Adriatica Line she rebooked her next day's passage to Haifa on the SS *Marco Polo* for a fortnight's time. Then she turned her back on the Adriatic Sea and returned to the railway station. Just before seven that evening she was sitting in a compartment on the sleeper to Vienna, heading for the Free City of Danzig, at the other end of Europe, via Vienna, Prague and Warsaw, a route that would avoid her going through Germany. It was the only precaution she felt she needed to take.

From Trieste she shared her sleeper with a woman who spoke a little English. Hannah's German wasn't good, and it was coloured in ways she had been unaware of by the Yiddish her grandparents had spoken. She was surprised how easily it identified her. The woman was from Vienna, middle-aged, well-dressed and Jewish, and perceptive enough to know immediately that Hannah was Jewish too, despite the name she was travelling under, Anna Harvey. The conversation slipped from English into German and back again, but once the woman was in full flight she just kept talking; all Hannah had to do was listen to her, or at least pretend to. The woman didn't make any real distinctions between England and Ireland, and if there were any she wasn't interested in them. From Vienna it looked like the same place. She did think the English should keep out of European politics though. They had the rest of the world to make trouble in. As for the Nazis, she told Hannah everyone made too much of a commotion about them. The Germans had always beaten up Jews; in Vienna anti-Semitism was a fact of political life. It came and went, loud and soft, and in between people got on with their lives. Adolf Hitler was an Austrian, that's all you needed to know. It was second nature to him to use anti-Semitism to get to power, but now that the reality of government had dawned, things would calm down; people would have to get on with their lives. It would be business as usual. It always was. As for the Jews who made too much fuss about all that, they didn't help anybody – socialists, communists, liberals, Zionists, they should shut up. Now it was all very loud; soon it would be quieter again. If you shut up it always was.

The next day, on the train from Vienna to Warsaw, she sat in the dining car some of the way with an elderly couple from Czechoslovakia, though as Germans born in the Sudetenland they didn't consider their country to be a country at all; they belonged in Germany. They didn't like politics; politics was what was wrong with Europe. They certainly didn't like everything Adolf Hitler did. He was too vulgar by half. He had saved Germany from socialism, that was undeniable, but the old man wasn't sure he was good for business. They were delighted to discover Hannah was Irish. They had visited Ireland thirty years ago when the man had gone to England on business. As they talked about Dublin before Hannah was born it was like listening to her father and mother. They made her smile, a sweet

239

couple, still very much in love in their seventies. At one point, the old man took his wife's hand, telling the story of how they'd met, and he held it tenderly for half an hour. They were good company at first, and that part of the journey went quickly. Then in Katowice, in Poland, a Jewish man in the dark clothes of orthodoxy asked if he could borrow the old man's Austrian newspaper. It was passed across with a polite smile, and the conversation about Ireland continued. The Jew returned the newspaper when he got off at Częstochowa. The old man shook his head sadly. The Jews had a lot to answer for. Politics was what was wrong with Europe and the Jews were the ones who controlled politics, the way they controlled everything. Hadn't they started the war that destroyed Austria and brought Germany to its knees? Hadn't they turned Russia into an atheistic wasteland? They were everywhere. You couldn't move for them in Poland. She was lucky to live in Ireland, in a country without Jews. No, they didn't like everything Adolf Hitler did, but he was right about the Jews. As they left the train at Warsaw, the old lady kissed Hannah and told her how much she reminded her of her daughter.

Two days after she had left Trieste, the train from Warsaw crossed the border into the Free City of Danzig. Hannah was almost at the end of her journey. There had been three months of silence from Ireland as far as Susan Field was concerned. She knew from her father that Brian Field had been to Pearse Street to see Inspector Donaldson several times. There were no developments. The police in Germany had been contacted about the whereabouts of Hugo Keller, with no results. As Keller was an Austrian citizen they assumed he must be in Austria. No one knew whether the police in Vienna had been contacted. None of it was surprising, and Hannah didn't need to be there to hear what went unspoken. The choices Susan Field had made were not the choices any decent woman would even contemplate. She was an unsolved murder, but the Gardaí weren't looking for a solution, any more than they had looked for an explanation when she first disappeared.

At Christmas Hannah did believe Stefan Gillespie really would find out what had happened to her friend. Perhaps he would have done, despite the doors that were slammed in his face. But he had his own problems. She didn't know everything, but she was aware that he had been close to losing his job. He had written once, early in January. She knew he was sitting on a hillside in West Wicklow, fighting to stop his son being taken away, because of what he thought or what he didn't think, because of who he was, and who his parents and grandparents were. He was probably very new to that. She wasn't. It came as easily and familiarly as breathing. Stefan had been in her mind a lot since she'd left Ireland. During those three months in Europe she had come close to contacting him several times. Sometimes she told herself it was only because Susan's death was still there, still unresolved, but there were other reasons, and they had as much to do with what was unresolved in her own life as with her friend's murder. However, she had made decisions about her life that she couldn't change. It was too late now. She would be back in Palestine soon. She didn't know when she would return to Europe or to Ireland. Perhaps she never would. But there was still the debt of love she owed her friend. It wasn't enough that Susan's death was forgotten. She knew where Francis Byrne was; Stefan Gillespie had told her that much. And if no one could find Hugo Keller, she would at least find the priest.

It was late when Hannah arrived in Danzig. The train had few passengers. When she had crossed the border, the flags were the flags of the Free City, a bright, cheerful red with a crown and two white crosses. The policeman who gave her passport a cursory glance wore the same insignia on his uniform. She had travelled on in the darkness, too tired to do anything other than stare at her reflection in the glass of the carriage, yet not tired enough to sleep. She had no expectations of the city. Danzig had its problems, she knew that, but it wasn't Germany. Yet it was still a journey no one would want her to make. It would irritate Benny; it was all too personal. But in the end he would understand, at least he would do what he did when she annoyed him – say nothing. Sometimes a show of anger from him would have made her feel less patronised. But all that was for another day now.

When she stepped off the train at Danzig Hauptbahn, the flag of the Free City was nowhere to be seen. This wasn't Germany; it was supposed to be another country, but every platform was draped with swastikas. And as she walked out to the station forecourt, the men standing around the Imbiss stall, eating bratwurst and drinking beer, wore the brown uniform of the Nazi SA. They were the first stormtroopers she had seen outside a newsreel.

*

The dining room of the Hotel Danziger Hof was noisy with breakfast. It had been almost empty when Hannah Rosen entered, but almost immediately it started to fill up. There was a crowd at the door now, waiting for tables. She sat by a window, looking out at the Hohe Tor, the High Gate, a great blockhouse of bricks pierced by an arch, once the main gate through the city's encircling fortifications. The walls had been demolished to make room for the modern city, though as modern cities went Danzig wore its antiquity with pride. Once it had been an independent city-state, and it had maintained that independent spirit through the centuries of war that sucked it in and out of the kingdoms of Poland and Prussia. A hundred and fifty years ago the city had fought to remain part of a Poland that guaranteed both its autonomy and its Germanness, in the face of a Prussian juggernaut that had no use for any kind of Germanness other than its own. But that was long forgotten. Beyond the window of the Danziger Hof, in front of the Hohe Tor, was the statue of a man on a horse, wearing a spiked helmet; Kaiser Wilhelm, the first emperor of the unified Germany that had incorporated Danzig into its territory for barely fifty years before the First World War, finally sweeping away its cantankerous independence in a great tide of all-embracing Germanness. Now the Free City of Danzig stood on its own again, a tiny statelet, barely the size of Wicklow, locked in by Poland in the west and south and by German East Prussia to the east. The Free City was the creation of a fledgling League of Nations whose high democratic ideals sat uneasily with the city's new purpose: to punish Germany for a world war and to pacify Poland. At the heart of the Free City, the League's High Commissioner fought with the only weapons available to him, little more than good-humour and patience, to defend a democracy almost everyone in the city-state seemed to despise. The last thing German Danzig wanted was to be free again. It was typical of the city's bloody-mindedness that having regained its ancient independence, most of its inhabitants dreamt only of disappearing back into the all-consuming sea of Germany once more.

'The Free State of Danzig was involuntarily severed from Germany on January 10th, 1920 by the Treaty of Versailles.' Hannah read from the guide book she had found in her room. She had brought it with her for the map, but she was grateful that it gave her something to do now. 'In the face of all force the city has defended its German character through the ages; its very architecture speaks of German character, German art and German will.' A tour of historical Danzig was the last thing on Hannah's mind, but *The Important Sights of Danzig*, along with the view of the Kaiser's statue and the Hohe Tor, at least kept her eyes from the busy dining room she wished she had walked straight past when she came down from her room. She was uneasy. She would drink her coffee as quickly as she could. She would eat whatever came. Or if it took much longer she would just leave anyway.

The tables were almost entirely full of men, businessmen, salesmen, politicians, journalists. In a few days Danzig would vote for a new parliament. The expectation was that the ruling Nazi Party would win, very comfortably, the overall majority it needed to change the constitution, dispose of the opposition, kick out the League's High Commissioner, and make this the last election the city would ever see. The road to reunification with Germany would follow; Hitler had already set a pattern for the abolition of democracy by democratic means. Danzig would be next.

Dotted everywhere among the dark business suits, contributing loud, excitable, argumentative voices to the buzz of conversation, were the uniforms of Nazism, of the Danzig Party and visiting SA and SS dignitaries from

Germany. Hannah hadn't expected to be thrown so completely into this world. The Nazis had power in Danzig, but there was still a constitution that was meant to stop them abusing it – at least that's what the English newspapers said. Yet walking the short distance from the station to Dominikswall and the Danziger Hof the night before it didn't feel like that. The dark streets were lined with the red, white and black of the crooked cross. In Elisabethwall she stopped to ask for directions. When she turned to walk on she saw she was standing in front of a shop selling children's clothes. The windows were broken. A Star of David was daubed on the door; and the words 'Die Juden sind unser Unglück'. The Jews are our misfortune.

She had slept very little that night. She had thought about Stefan. Now she wished he was with her. She told herself it was because he knew what to say, because he would know what was true and what wasn't, but it was also because she felt he would make her stronger. She hadn't considered Danzig being another Germany now. She should have done. She read the papers. Sometimes she could be too single-minded to think things through; her mother always said that. But when her mother said it there was usually something to laugh about. Now she was having breakfast in a room full of Nazis. She felt people were looking at her, and they were. There were other women in the dining room, but she was the only one on her own, fair game for businessmen and reps with nothing better to do. Normally it wouldn't have bothered her, but now she was starting to feel she couldn't breathe. A tall SS man was trying to catch her eye. He had been looking at her since he came in.

She got up abruptly, just as the waiter arrived with a basket of bread and pastries, beaming his regrets about

245

how busy it was. He fussed over her, full of kind, concerned apologies, telling her the bread was still warm from the oven, but only drawing more attention to her with his paean to the pastries. She smiled awkwardly, mumbling something about being late, and left. As she passed the SS man caught her eye again; this time he winked.

Irritated by the sense of panic that had started to envelop her, she focused firmly on the concierge's instructions. She walked quickly away from the hotel. Boys from the Hitler Youth were giving out election leaflets on the pavement. In Kohlenmarkt a column of teenage girls in brown dresses, two-by-two, moved across the square, singing a German folk song, so beautiful that she stopped and stared, almost forgetting where she was. The girl at the front carried a swastika pennant. Hannah could see a Number 2 tram, waiting. She ran to catch it. She felt more relaxed now, grateful for the rattling of the tram. Movement had become important to her in the last few months. A train, a boat, even a few moments on a tram. Everything was easier when she was moving. The tram ran along Stadtgraben, past the station. On the left, the green wooded hills of the Hagelsberg rose up above the city. She thought that in a different time she might have liked this place. Her grandfather had come from Lithuania; it wasn't so far away across the Baltic. She tried to remember the stories he had told her; the journey that brought him out of Russia to Ireland, through Germany and Holland and England. Hadn't the boat stopped here? She was sure it had. The journey started on a boat, she knew that. She looked down at the map. The tram was moving out of the city, through the Langfuhr suburbs to Oliva and Zoppot. A line of linden trees stretched ahead. She would see the Baltic Sea soon. But none of that mattered. What mattered was that she would see Father Francis Byrne.

All of a sudden the people sitting around her on the tram got up and moved to one side, crowding at the windows and looking out. She didn't get up, but she looked. She had been too absorbed in her thoughts to notice the groups of people along the road, watching, waiting, holding swastikas. She could see flags waving now. People were cheering. The passengers on the tram started applauding as they gazed out through the windows. She could see a line of black cars coming the other way, heading into the city. There was an open Mercedes-Benz. A big man in an elaborately belted and bemedalled uniform sat in the back, smiling and waving at the crowds. She recognised Herman Goering from news-papers and newsreels, even in the seconds it took the car to pass. The hotel manager had told her as she checked in; he was flying from Berlin to speak at an election rally. The tram passengers were shouting. 'Germany! Danzig back to Germany!' In the Danziger Hof she felt panic; what she felt now was the cold sweat of fear.

She left the tram at Oliva and walked through the quiet park that led to the cathedral. Behind her was the Baltic Sea and the resort of Zoppot. Ahead the hills rose up again, thickly forested, dark even in the spring sunlight. The path led her through landscaped gardens and neat groves of trees. It was a place of carefully tended calm. There were no flags, no uniforms. The city seemed a long way away here. Two gardeners greeted her as she passed. Though the greeting was German they spoke in Polish as she walked past.

She asked for Father Byrne at the office opposite the cathedral. The secretary spoke some English and was keen

247

to use it. Father Byrne was doing confessions in English now, but he would be finished any time. When the woman discovered Hannah was from Ireland she struggled to find the English words to tell her how pleased he would be to see her, then gave up and told her in German anyway. Hannah needed all the ignorance of German she could muster to curb the woman's enthusiasm and persuade her not to come with her across the square to find the priest. She hurried out quickly.

She stood for a moment, looking up at the two red-brick towers, topped with copper spires, blue-green against a sky that was very clear now. The sun was warm in the sheltered square in front of the cathedral. She felt she wanted to stay a little longer in the light of this place she didn't know, unsure what finally arriving meant. She steeled herself and walked on.

As she entered the cathedral she expected it to be dark. Instead it was full of light. There was colour everywhere. Stretching along either side of the narrow chancel were dozens of carved and painted altars. It was silent and empty and its beauty briefly stilled the noises in her head. There was a deep smell of old wood and centuries of incense. The only great churches she had been into were St Patrick's in Dublin and Westminster Abbey in London. They were history lessons in stone. This was a softer place. She could feel the faith that made all its ornateness something simple and reassuring. The almost random confusion of colour and light was a perfection no one had ever set out to create, but there it was. It was everything a synagogue wasn't. Judaism was a faith that rested in words. It had no truck with all this, decoration piled on decoration. Yet it wasn't so different. She didn't often think of the psalms she had heard sung every Saturday of her life as a child, but they spoke of the wild places of the spirit, and in that wilderness they imposed order and peace. These were the words, the same words somehow, in brick and stone. There was a calm here that almost seemed to drain away her purpose. But suddenly that intrusive calm was gone. She saw the priest.

He emerged from one of the wooden confessionals and unhooked a small sign from the door. 'Father Byrne English Confessions.' He walked through a line of pews and genuflected in front of the high altar, then moved towards the main door where she was standing. He smiled as he approached. 'Guten morgen.' 'Good morning, Father,' she answered. He caught her accent easily in those few words. And he was pleased to hear it. He wasn't very tall. His hair was fair, almost blond. Hannah remembered Susan saying it made him look younger than he was, even though it had started to recede. It was a boy's hair. She'd said his eyes were very bright. They didn't look so bright to Hannah. Far from looking younger than he was, he looked older.

'You're a long way from home.'

'Are you Father Byrne?'

There was an intensity in the way she was looking at him that made him very uncomfortable almost straight away. But he smiled pleasantly.

'I am. Is it a holiday then?'

'I came to see you.' There was no lightness in her voice. He didn't know what to make of her. It was as if there was an accusation in her eyes.

'Well, I'm glad you did. I just wondered why you were in Danzig.'

'I was a friend of Susan Field's.' She spoke the words softly.

He looked at her with an expression of almost pained bewilderment. It was as if he had to think hard to understand what she meant before he could answer. Hannah said nothing. She just waited. The next words had to be his.

'I'm sorry.' He seemed even older as he said the words. It wasn't much. She could see he knew it wasn't enough. 'I heard, of course. It's a terrible loss.'

Hannah's presence really was an accusation; she could see that he felt that. Her eyes didn't move from his. She could see how much he wanted to look away too. They stood there, looking at one another, for only a few seconds, but the priest seemed frozen. Something was happening behind his eyes, something painful was forcing itself into his head, from the dark corner where he had pushed it. But he said nothing.

'I want to know why she's dead. You must know something!' She blurted out the words. 'I want to know what happened to her.'

'What *happened*.' He repeated her words slowly, not a question, not a statement, but as if they were in a language he didn't know very well.

'Nine months ago she went to Merrion Square for an abortion –'

'Please, I'm sure you know where you are!' he whispered, leaning in towards her, his eyes darting nervously now, as if he was being watched.

'I do, and I know who *you* are.'

'What do you mean?'

'I know you were the father of her child and I know you made the arrangements with the doctor, Mr Keller. Susan wrote to me about you.'

He was calmer now. He had never seen her before, but he had realised who she was. He didn't know her, yet he felt as if he did. He had heard too much about her from Susan not to. There was only one person she could be.

'You're Hannah.'

'Yes.'

'You could only be Hannah.' There was a smile on his lips. It surprised her, not because it was a smile, but because it was tender. There was a memory, and somewhere, in a way she didn't understand, it mattered to him. As they walked out of the cathedral he put the sign he was carrying down on a table by the door. 'Father Byrne Confessions in English.'

'I know you've lied to the Guards, in your letter. They know that too.'

It wasn't quite the truth. The only policeman who knew was milking cows in West Wicklow. The priest didn't reply. His face was expressionless, but in his silence she could still feel his pain, even though she couldn't get hold of what it was. They were in the gardens now, among the linden trees and the close, neat box hedges in front of the Bishop's Palace. He had said hardly anything, but already he wasn't what she had expected. He was quieter. There was nothing about him that felt like the man Susan had described, talking endlessly, passionately, excitedly through a whole night as they walked the streets of Dublin. He finally spoke again, slowly at first.

'I didn't know she was dead. It was only when the Gardaí contacted me that I found out. I didn't know what to think. It seemed hard to believe.'

'But not very hard to lie, to pretend you hardly knew her.'

'I'm not proud of that. But I couldn't change anything.'

'And that makes it all right?'

He shook his head, looking down at the ground.

'I'd already told lies. I didn't know how to undo those. There were a lot of things I couldn't face. I kept lying.'

She almost felt sorry for him as he looked up, but not for long.

'You know where they found her?'

'Yes.' He didn't want to think about that; it was in his voice.

'He's left Ireland now, the man Keller, the doctor. He's been gone for months. They don't know where he is.' She wasn't asking questions now, simply stating the bleak, unhelpful facts to herself. 'So no one can ask him. No one wanted to ask him though. People even helped him leave Ireland.'

As she watched Francis Byrne she could see something else in his face now; it looked like fear. It hadn't been there before; that was something else, more like self-pity. But suddenly he seemed oddly far away, as if what he was feeling had nothing to do with her or with anything she was saying.

'I'm sorry,' he said again bleakly.

Hannah persisted, pulling him back to what mattered.

'What happened the day she went for the abortion?'

'I don't know. I wasn't with her.'

'But you knew she was going?'

'We hadn't seen each other for nearly a fortnight. I was about to leave Ireland to go to Germany. It's what we'd agreed. We both needed to start again. Once we knew it was over, Susan was the one who – she was very firm about what we had to do – even about – she said the end was the end.'

Hannah heard Susan's voice in those last words; that at least was true.

'Didn't you try to find out if she was all right?'

'We'd made our decision. It's what she wanted.'

'You could have asked Mr Keller.'

'Do you think I felt easy about dealing with a man like that?'

'No, it must have been unpleasant for you, Father.'

'That's not what I meant. Not at all.'

The self-pity was back. It was enough of what he meant.

'I don't know what happened. I can't even begin to imagine – obviously something went wrong with the operation. I didn't have any idea.'

'You did send her there. You paid for it. She told me.'

'Yes. It was wrong. All of it.'

'Perhaps it was God's judgement on her, is that it?' she snapped.

'Do you think I didn't care about her?'

'I don't know. I know she cared a great deal about you once.'

'Look, Hannah, I don't know what she said about me.'

'Why does that matter now?'

He didn't reply, but it did; it still mattered. She was uncomfortable with him. He felt unexpectedly a part of Susan, in a way that confused her. She didn't know what was true now. She didn't know if she believed any of it.

'There was a time I did try to talk to Susan, about another way, about leaving the priesthood. It wasn't a long conversation. She said she didn't want me to do that. I think we weren't very good for each other really. She felt that more than I did at the end. We'd both made a mistake. Susan

253

said she didn't want me to destroy my life for that. We went our separate ways.'

'What about her life?'

'If I hadn't cared about her life, do you think I'd have gone through with it? There was a child, a child we – it was what she wanted. I owed her that, even if the price was a sin.'

'I don't care about your sins. I only care about my friend!' There were tears of anger in her eyes.

Her voice was softer suddenly, almost pleading.

'There must be something else you can tell me!'

'I did love her. I don't know what she felt about me. I never did.' It felt like the truth, but it was his truth, selfish, secret, self-absorbed.

Hannah wanted to turn on him and scream. She couldn't give a fuck about his feelings, but the words startled her. No, he never did know. She saw something she hadn't seen before, something she had never caught in Susan's letters. The words were in her head again and she could hear Susan's voice saying them; the words tumbling over each other as they did when she spoke. Susan had always used the word love too easily. There was attraction, friendship, fun; there was intellectual fire; there was the joy of a passionate secret; there was sex. She used to laugh at Hannah because she held on to the word love and kept it close, as if it was too precious to use. As Hannah looked at he priest now he seemed weaker, smaller. She wondered if he ever had been quite the man Susan wanted him to be, the man she wrote about when she first met him. Did he really know nothing? After all this time, was it just that he simply didn't know?

'I need someone to tell me why my friend is dead,'

Hannah said, her voice more measured again 'You're the only person there is. Can't you understand?'

'I don't know. I only know I wish she wasn't dead. I wish she wasn't.' He whispered the words over and over again, like a prayer. 'I wish she wasn't.'

As he spoke, the first of the Angelus bells tolled. Father Francis Byrne crossed himself. It was as if he had put on a new face quite suddenly; the vulnerability was gone. He seemed stronger. She knew he would say no more now. He had told her enough of the truth for her to almost lose her way in it. But it still wasn't the whole truth. She knew that. She shook her head.

'I won't let her be forgotten. I won't stop!'

She spoke quietly, fixing his gaze as she had when she first saw him in the cathedral. Then she turned away, walking faster and faster. The sound of the Angelus bell filled her head. Perhaps it had stopped, but as she hurried out through the park, back towards the road, she could still hear it ringing.

Francis Byrne watched her walk away. He heard the bell too, in his own head. It was a daily sound of reassurance and faith in his life. Now it hurt. The strength Hannah had just seen in his eyes was an illusion. As he whispered the familiar words to himself they seemed less familiar, less comfortable, less reassuring, as if they no longer quite belonged on his lips. 'Angelus Domini nuntiavit Mariae.' The angel of the Lord declared unto Mary. 'Et concepit de Spiritu Sanctu.' And she conceived of the Holy Spirit.

*

Hannah sat in the restaurant in Frauengasse for a long time that night. She wasn't hungry, but she didn't want to go back to her room at the Danziger Hof. She needed to do something. She felt a long way from the people she cared about, the people who cared about her. But she wasn't sure being with them would help. Her mother and father thought she was in England. That was a simple enough lie. Other lies weren't so easy. Her mother probably knew some of them, but she would never say anything. Sarah Rosen had always believed that life's difficulties would go away if only you spent long enough not talking about them. Hannah's father never spoke when things went wrong for different reasons; he didn't notice. She loved them; him for his fond blindness, her for her indefatigable hope in a natural law that said things got better if you left them alone and didn't pick at the bones. As a Jew it was an approach to life that set hope defiantly in the face of experience.

Hannah had always envied Susan's family its furious passions and even more furious arguments. In the Fields' house everyone talked about everything; every slight, every mood, every love, every hate. Sometimes it seemed as if the smaller the problem the more noise it generated, as the whole family, mother, father, grandparents, children, dissected and criticised each other's opinions and moods. They lurched from laughter to tears and back again with chaotic intensity; they were rude, dismissive, sarcastic, intolerant and unforgiving, sometimes for as long as a whole afternoon. They told each other everything and if there were no secrets or conflicts or emotional disasters to be revealed, they'd make some up anyway. Hannah's house was, by contrast, a place of small gestures of fondness rather than fierce statements of love and despair. They never said exactly what they felt. And yet it had all changed for Susan. Her mother died, her sisters left Ireland, and after a while her father's voice was only heard in the synagogue. With all the open hearts that had surrounded her as a child, she found no one to talk to in the face of what became the last as well as the first real crisis of her adult life. Perhaps Hannah and Susan weren't so different. Or perhaps there were times you were alone, simply alone, and that was it. Hannah felt that now.

In Palestine Benny was waiting for her to come back. And it was back, not home. Whatever she sometimes wanted to believe, Ireland was still home. It had seemed like a good idea for her to spend these months in Europe. There was the money to collect and send on its circuitous way through Europe to Palestine, to buy arms for the Haganah. There was a system in place and no shortage of helping hands along the way. It wasn't dangerous. Hannah was a courier, no more than that. But she knew why Benny had pushed her forward. It gave her the chance to spend some time with her family in Ireland. He knew she needed to try to find out what had happened to Susan Field too. He wanted her to get it out of her system. Not just Susan. Ireland. He understood that she had to come to terms with her friend's death, but he didn't understand everything it had stirred up. Finding out about Susan was complicated. It was not only a reason to go home; it was also an excuse.

When she first left Ireland for Palestine, Hannah was determined she wouldn't live anywhere she was ill-at-ease. She had felt the darkness in Europe drawing in. She wanted Ireland to be immune from that but it wasn't. Yet Jewish Palestine hadn't become the place she wanted it to be. She was ill-at-ease there sometimes as well. She had poured her passion into it, and if that flagged she had Benny now; he had enough passion for both of them when it came to

Israel. But it wasn't enough. She had left her home behind, with the full consciousness that she wanted to escape the kind of mild and unemotional ordinariness of her mother and father's marriage, yet she was going to marry a man she felt friendship and admiration for, rather than love and passion. All around them there were extraordinary things happening. And there was nothing ordinary about Benny Jacobson. Life was too important for ordinariness as far as he was concerned. They were creating a new Israel. But when the door closed on that, and they were alone, she wasn't sure she knew him. When they stopped talking breathlessly about the future of a nation, she wasn't sure they had anything else to talk about. Perhaps he had used up all his passion. He never argued with her; he never lost his temper. How could she tell her parents she was afraid of a life that was only distinguished from theirs by the sunshine?

Hannah and Susan had never lied to one another in their letters, but there was a truth that neither of them recognised in the other. Susan read about Hannah's relationship with Benny, already a second-generation Jewish immigrant in Palestine, with envy. When Hannah first read about Susan's secret love affair, she was sometimes envious too, simply because it was full of the passion she told herself didn't matter. That envy faded on Hannah's part as she became more and more anxious about her friend's hopeless relationship. But both of them were lost in different ways; perhaps they had both sensed it in each other. If they had, it was too late to say anything now.

The waiter poured her another glass of wine. As she drank it she felt the events of the day blurring with all the other things that were in her head. The person she needed to talk to was Stefan. He would have got more out of Francis Byrne, much more. Her journey was ending and she still hadn't achieved what she had set out to achieve. There were still no answers. She was angry, with herself as much as with anyone else. As she left the restaurant and walked back to the hotel through the narrow, ancient streets, the swastikas fluttered above her all the way. They seemed to hang at every window, flapping and cracking threateningly in the wind blowing from the Baltic.

In Langgasse an open truck drove past. In the back were young Nazis in uniform, electioneering; making sure that any opposition that dared to appear on the streets was beaten to a pulp. After two months there was no one really left to beat. Shouts and wolf-whistles were flung in her direction from the truck as she turned into Kohlenmarkt. The lights of the Hotel Danziger Hof shone brightly ahead. The square was full of people. Coming towards her was a brass band, flying the obligatory red, white and black and playing 'The Watch on the Rhine'. The crowds around her were applauding and singing. 'Zum Rhein, zum Rhein, zum deutschen Rhein, wer will des Stromes Hüter sein?' The Rhine, the Rhine, our German Rhine, who will stand watchman on the Rhine? She took no notice of the cars outside the hotel or of the uniformed Danzig policemen at the door. She had no reason to. Even if she had noticed the man in the leather coat talking to them she wouldn't have known he was a Danzig Gestapo officer. Suddenly a car door opened in front of her. She almost collided with the man who leapt out. 'Jesus, look where you're going!' He was young, twenty-five. He looked at her hard, but there was a smile on his lips. He saw she was a little drunk.

'Fräulein Rosen?'

'Yes,' she said automatically, unthinkingly in English.

He grabbed her wrist. Now she was aware of another man behind her, holding her other arm. She struggled and started to call out. 'What are you doing? Let go of me!' The second man put his hand over her mouth and then she was inside the car, the two men on either side of her. She was still being held tightly; her mouth was still covered. There was no room to struggle. The driver put the car into gear and pulled away. It had taken only seconds. No one had heard her over the sound of the brass band. Most of the people in the square hadn't even noticed. Those who had were too used to seeing people pushed into cars by the Schutzpolizei or the Gestapo, or being thrown off the back of moving trucks by Nazi stormtroopers, to feel there was anything unusual going on. There was, after all, an election to win. It was just the rough and tumble of democracy. Inside the car the grip on Hannah Rosen's arms was unyielding. The hand over her mouth pushed her head back even more painfully into the seat. There was no point fighting.

# 14. Danzig-Langfuhr

The De Havilland Dragon Rapide rattled down the runway at Baldonnel and pulled up into the sky south of Dublin. Below Stefan Gillespie were the hills that stretched down into Wicklow. It was a clear April morning, a little after nine o'clock. It was the first time he had been in an aeroplane. He was surprised how unsurprising it was. There was a sense of exhilaration when the bi-plane lifted off and he first gazed down at the countryside below, trying to recognise where he was as they headed east towards the sea. He looked at the fields pegged out with sheep and cattle, sloping up into the Dublin Mountains. He followed a road as it wound through the fields and the bare hillsides into thick, dark woodland. Somewhere underneath him were the slopes of Kilmashogue, where the bodies of Vincent Walsh and Susan Field had been buried. He had been a long way from that. He knew from Dessie MacMahon that the investigations had stopped. But unexpectedly it wasn't over; that was why he was here. It was why he was flying to London, to take the Deutsche Luft Hansa plane from Croydon Aerodrome to Berlin and Danzig.

Very quickly the mountains were gone. The plane hummed with the steady drone of the propellers. They were over the sea. Stefan sat at the back of the plane. Only two other seats were occupied. The other passengers were Irish civil servants, travelling to a League of Nations meeting in Geneva. At Baldonnel they had plied him with questions. He had been pushed on to the flight by someone who knew someone, so there had to be something interesting about him. He made sure there wasn't. They soon found his polite monosyllables irritating and the role he had come up with – a cattle dealer looking for new markets in Germany – decidedly down-the-country. He sat far enough back to make conversation impossible on the noisy two-hour journey to Croydon. The grey sea spread out below them, the waves catching the spring sunlight. There was a boat sailing to England. He looked down as the plane passed over it, and watched it until it had disappeared.

The months had passed quickly at Kilranelagh as winter moved into spring in the mountains. Stefan had plunged himself into work at the farm with an energy that absorbed his days and left him tired enough to sleep at night. The smell of stone and earth and animals was something to hold on to, and the longer the days were out in the fields the less time there was to talk about the threat that still hung over him and his parents, and over his son. Tom's fifth birthday had come and gone now and he still knew nothing about the curate's plan to send him to live with his uncle and aunt. Stefan had made it clear over and over again that he would never agree. There had been a brief exchange of letters between his solicitor, Emmet Brady, and the bishop in Carlow, then nothing. Tom was happy at school and happier still because, for reasons he didn't understand, his father was at home. Father Carey was polite whenever Stefan saw him and had not referred to the matter since February now. David and Helena had read into that silence a truth Stefan was far less sure about. They thought it was done. For more than a month now none of them had discussed the threat as they had through the long winter evenings after Tom had gone to bed. But there were still nights when Stefan couldn't sleep, however hard he worked. The curate's bitter determination was still a shadow over him. He would lie awake, turning Emmet Brady's cautious words around in his head for the hundredth time. He heard himself in the Four Courts, trying to persuade a judge not to take Tom away. And sometimes, as he imagined the judge telling him he was unfit to be a father to his son, he thought about the answer that was there, always unspoken, the answer even his mother and father must know had to be in his head. If it wasn't finished, if it wasn't forgotten, if the threat was as real as the old solicitor claimed it was, then one day the only option might be the journey to Dún Laoghaire, and the boat across the Irish Sea he had just been looking down at. But all that was for another day, however, a day he still hoped would never come. Now he was casting his mind back to the events of the previous morning and the reason he was on a plane to London.

The unfamiliar car had pulled into the farmyard at Kilranelagh early. He had never met Hannah Rosen's father, but unexpectedly Adam Rosen was there, bringing back everything that had happened at the end of the previous year. Stefan had not forgotten Hannah, but he had pushed her to the corners of his mind. There seemed no point doing anything else. The other man introduced himself as Robert Briscoe. Stefan knew who he was. A Member of Parliament in Dublin and a close friend of Éamon de Valera's; an old IRA man who had fought against the British and then against the Free State in the Civil War. He was also a leader of Ireland's Jewish community. He was a surprising guest. The two men offered no explanation for why they were there. Briscoe spent no more than five minutes congratulating David Gillespie on the quality of his cattle, and Helena on the biscuits he smelled when he walked into the kitchen, but by the time he and Adam Rosen were installed in the sitting room, with a cup of tea and a plate of those biscuits, still hot from the oven, it felt as if he had been speaking to old friends for an hour. He had a politician's skills and, as Stefan's father remarked later, a politician's handshake; a little too hard and a little too sincere. But despite all the good humour, neither David nor Helena had any doubt that when the sitting room door shut, the visitors weren't there to discuss the weather.

'It's about Hannah.' Adam Rosen spoke urgently once they were alone.

'Isn't she back in Palestine now?'

'I wish she was.' Hannah's father hadn't said much while Robert Briscoe was making conversation about cattle and cooking, but now it was obvious he was worried.

'She's in trouble, Mr Gillespie.' It was Robert Briscoe who continued.

'What do you mean?' asked Stefan

'She's in Danzig. You'll know why she's there I think.'

It was all in front of him; the priest, Father Francis Byrne.

'I can make a good guess.'

'I'm sure you know a lot more than either of us, Mr Gillespie.'

Stefan frowned. At first he was simply puzzled, not because Hannah had gone to find Francis Byrne, but because of the time that had passed. It was months since he had last seen her, he had assumed she had left Europe completely.

264

'I thought she went back to Palestine ages ago.'

'She's been on the Continent.' Adam Rosen answered awkwardly. It was an odd turn of phrase. It sounded as if his daughter had been on a long holiday. 'She didn't tell anyone she was going to try and find this priest.'

'But she arrived in Danzig two days ago,' continued Briscoe.

In December, Hannah had told Stefan she was going to England. That was nearly four months ago now. If she had intended to go to Danzig, why had it taken so long? He could feel the two men were skirting around something, something that made the simple fact of Hannah's arrival in Danzig dangerous in some way. He was conscious of Briscoe's hard eyes watching him, in the silence that hung over the dark sitting room, weighing him up.

Adam Rosen was Robert Briscoe's friend, and his friend's daughter needed help. Hannah had put herself at risk, and not only herself. Now someone had to bring her back. It was Brian Field who had suggested Stefan Gillespie. He was a policeman. He spoke good German. And he probably cared about Hannah. There had been something between her and the guard, at least that's what her father thought. That was good. It was a lever, and where trust was an issue, perhaps it was something to put some trust in too.

'The situation is complicated, Mr Gillespie,' said Briscoe.

Stefan smiled. 'That doesn't surprise me, with Hannah.'

'We can't do anything openly in Danzig.'

'I'm not sure I understand.' Whatever Robert Briscoe and Adam Rosen were uncertain about Stefan knew that it must go deeper than Francis Byrne.

Briscoe looked at Adam Rosen again. Hannah's father nodded. They had made the decision that Stefan Gillespie could be trusted, that he had to be trusted. It was the only way.

'She was staying with some friends in Italy,' said Hannah's father. 'She was meant to be sailing to Haifa three days ago, from Trieste. We do know she got as far as Trieste, but the boat sailed without her. She cancelled the booking. And then she took a train to Danzig the same night.'

'She waited a long time,' said Stefan, 'but you know why she went?'

'I know about Susan Field and the priest –'

'Francis Byrne. He was certainly in Danzig in December.'

'We can't make contact with her.' Adam Rosen's anxiety was clear. It seemed out of proportion, but it was clear.

'Is that really such a big problem?'

'Of course it bloody is,' snapped Briscoe.

'I don't suppose she's going to make herself very popular in ecclesiastical circles in Danzig,' said Stefan, 'but Father Byrne has already denied any kind of relationship with Susan Field. There's a statement to that effect collecting dust in Dublin Castle. I don't believe it any more than Hannah does, but that's the Garda line here, and that's all he's going to say if she finds him. I doubt she's going to beat the truth out of him, whatever it is.'

Hannah's father shook his head. That wasn't what this was about.

'It's not that simple.' Briscoe was still watching Stefan intently. 'Hannah needs to leave Danzig before anything happens. She's not safe.'

'If you're worried, perhaps you should contact the police?'

'The police?' smiled the politician. 'You really don't understand –'

'Then maybe you'd better explain, Mr Briscoe.'

'First of all, she wasn't travelling under her own name.'

'A false passport?' It was a strange beginning.

'For all practical purposes, yes.'

'Why?'

The question went unanswered. 'We have found out where she's staying. Adam tried phoning the hotel. She hasn't checked out, but they haven't seen her since the morning after she arrived. She's disappeared.'

'I see. But if she's missing, then surely the police –'

'She's a Jew, Mr Gillespie,' interrupted Adam Rosen, irritated, almost angry.

'She's an Irish citizen. Besides, Danzig's not Germany.'

'Not yet.' Robert Briscoe shrugged. 'Not quite yet.'

There were several long seconds of silence. Stefan's tone was harder. It was his turn to show irritation.

'Are you going to tell me what's going on, or not?'

Briscoe nodded.

'Do you know what the Haganah is?' He put his cup down. There was a change of mood. He was more brusque.

Stefan shook his head.

'The nearest thing would be the Volunteers here, under the British. It's a Jewish self-defence force in Palestine. When the Arabs started attacking Jews about ten years ago it became clear the British weren't going to do much about it. It wasn't just that they didn't want to take on the Arabs. There are people in the Mandate administration giving arms to the Arabs at the same time as they're preventing the Jews getting any. The Haganah was formed to defend homes and farms, that was all, to begin with but it couldn't really stay like that. It all changed one day in 1929. When sixty Jews were killed in Hebron.'

Stefan remembered. He'd read about it and forgotten

about it. There was a lot of slaughter everywhere after all.

'That was five years ago. Maybe the Mandate Police didn't know it would be a massacre on that scale, but they knew enough to keep out of the way. While people were having their heads hacked off, they were nowhere to be seen. Of course, the Mandate Police aren't exactly the British bobby on the beat. It collects up all sorts, including a few friends we know of old, Black and Tans who needed a job when they were kicked out of Ireland. The Empire's always got dirty work for that sort somewhere. It's got dirtier for everyone in Palestine now, Jews and Arabs. There's a feeling that something bloody is on the way again. That means the Haganah has to be better armed. You know Hannah quite well. Perhaps you know who Benny Jacobson is?'

'I know he's Hannah's fiancé.'

'He's a Haganah commander too. And she's a Haganah courier. She's been collecting money in Europe for the last three months, to buy weapons.'

Stefan felt as if the months that had passed since he saw Hannah were shrinking away in front of him. What Briscoe had said surprised him, yet it made sense of her finally. It made sense of the moments when she was talking to him about Palestine and then, quite suddenly, she remembered to stop. Now he understood why it was so complicated for her. He also understood why she was at risk.

'And who knows that? Who knows what she's been doing?'

'The Mandate Police must have a pretty good idea. That means British Special Branch too. If the British Consul and the British police get involved in Danzig, if Hannah's arrested, I've no idea what sort of information they'd pass on if it suited them. I wouldn't trust what they'd do, out of spite or sheer bloody stupidity.'

'Danzig's still a long way from Palestine, Mr Briscoe.'

'It's not a long way from Berlin. The SS and the Gestapo have people in Danzig. They wouldn't care very much about her embarrassing a priest, but they care about other things. Hannah knows a lot of names. The Nazis like names, long lists of names. Long lists of Jewish names are even better.'

'She must know that.'

'As you said, Danzig isn't Germany. I imagine she felt the same.'

'She doesn't know as much as she thinks.' It was Hannah's father who spoke again. There was almost a smile. Whatever else Hannah was, she was his daughter. He was remembering her as that now, strong-willed and wilful.

'You speak good German, Mr Gillespie,' continued Robert Briscoe.

'Yes.' He already knew why they were there.

'Will you go and find her?'

'I wouldn't know where to start, Mr Briscoe.'

'You're a policeman.'

'I'm not at the moment.'

'I think you're the policeman Hannah needs. Someone who's not connected to her, someone who's not Jewish, someone she cares about –'

The politician smiled. He already knew Stefan cared about Hannah too.

'I would pay you well of course, Mr Gillespie,' said Adam Rosen.

'It's not a question of money, Mr Rosen.'

'Hannah trusts you. Find her and bring her back, please.'

'It could take me three or four days to get there.'

There was silence. In that silence, his decision was made. If it hadn't been for him Hannah wouldn't be in Danzig. She wouldn't be in danger. She was there because the Gardaí had failed her, most of all because he had failed her.

Robert Briscoe took an envelope from his pocket.

'There's a government charter to Croydon Aerodrome tomorrow morning. I can get you on it.' He handed Stefan a plane ticket. Stefan looked, not quite sure what it was. 'That's for the midday Deutsche Luft Hansa from Croydon to Berlin. The Berlin–Danzig flight leaves at 7:20 in the evening. You'll be there by 10:30 tomorrow night. You already have a room at Hannah's hotel.'

Clearly the TD hadn't considered the idea that Stefan wouldn't go. But if the look on Briscoe's face was all about what had to be done, Adam Rosen's face was full of his fears for his daughter. And Stefan understood that too.

'Please find her and get her out as soon as you can, Mr Gillespie.'

*

*Dear Tom, I'm at Tempelhof Airport. That's in Berlin. You never saw so many aeroplanes. The picture on the front of this card is like one I came in from London. It's a Junkers. My second plane and I'm waiting for another! One day we'll go up in one. I'll see you as soon as I get back. Love, Daddy.*

There was a long wait at Tempelhof for the flight to Danzig. Stefan had walked round and round the airport for over an hour now. The swastikas that lined the walls and hung from the high ceilings were occasionally interspersed with

270

the flag of the Olympic Games. Everywhere there were photographs of the stadiums that were going up in Berlin for the following year, and everywhere there was the message that the Games were Germany's opportunity to show its great miracle to the world. He couldn't walk for more than five minutes without a brown-uniformed arm thrusting a tin at him and demanding money. It was twelve years since Stefan had been in Germany with his mother and father. They didn't go now. The last family contacts were fading away and there was very little left except a few Christmas cards and the occasional black-bordered letter that told of a death. News of births and weddings had stopped altogether; as the family ways were finally parting, it was only death that was worth the price of the stamp.

He thought about the cousins he had walked the Bavarian mountains with, so long ago it seemed. Some of them would be wearing Nazi uniforms now; their children would be rattling those Nazi Party tins. He ate a meal he didn't really want and drank two Berliner Weisse beers. After two more he told the next Nazi who thrust a tin at him what he could do with it, not to mention the loose change inside. So it was no bad thing that the Junkers 52 that would be flying him to Danzig was on the tarmac, ready for boarding. The angry Nazi youth had returned with several of his comrades-in-armbands. And they were looking for him.

The sun was setting as the three-engined Junkers took off, and as it turned over the great sprawl of Berlin he could see very little. The cloud was low and heavy until the plane broke through it. He sat back in his seat and closed his eyes. It was another two-hour flight, the third of the day. As a man who had never been in an aeroplane until that

271

morning he had already had enough. He opened his eyes. Across the aisle a man in a dark suit who had just a little too much aftershave on smiled and nodded at him. His head was bald two-thirds of the way back; close-cropped hair started just before the crown. He looked at Stefan with the kind of easy assurance that meant there would be no sleep. The man would talk, even if he didn't. In the lapel of his jacket was a Nazi buttonhole, just like the one Stefan had been given by the German Santa Claus at the Shelbourne Hotel. 'Deutschland Erwache.' Germany Awake. He recalled that was the day he had first met Hannah Rosen.

'Business?'

It was an amiable question, but Stefan hadn't really thought about the need to explain what he was doing, even in idle conversation like this. He had disposed of two curious Irish diplomats with the whiff of cow dung. It seemed something closer to the truth, if not quite the truth, begged fewer questions now. It was too much elaboration that made lies sound like lies. As a policeman he knew that.

'Business in Danzig?'

'A friend of mine's on holiday there. I was in Berlin so I thought I'd catch up with her.'

It sounded ill-thought-out and unconvincing. Not that there was any reason why that should matter to a stranger he'd know for two hours on an aircraft, but it irritated him that he hadn't thought about this before. The uncertainty of his reply, far from puzzling the man, seemed to amuse him.

'I should probably ask no more questions, eh?' It wasn't a wink, but it was a smile of the you-sly-dog variety. Stefan couldn't help laughing, both at the ease with which the assumption had been made, and also at the fact that perhaps, somewhere he hadn't quite allowed himself to get to, it wasn't so far from the truth. He had no idea what to expect in Danzig, but he still hoped that finding Hannah wouldn't be difficult. Getting her to leave might be something else, but would it be such a bad thing if that took longer than Adam Rosen and Robert Briscoe anticipated? He hadn't forgotten those two nights with Hannah. The faint smile served to confirm the assumptions of the man across the aisle. It was a feeling of comradeship, sly dog to sly dog, that Stefan was not keen to pursue for the next two hours. However, travelling companions were like relatives, you couldn't choose them. It was some consolation that they were with you for hours and not a lifetime.

'She's in Zoppot?' asked the German.

'No, in the city.'

'The city's something to see, of course, very old, very German, but go to Zoppot. It's too early for bathing, but the casino will keep you occupied.'

Stefan tried to look as if he really did have an interest in gambling.

'But you're visiting us at an exciting moment. These are great times.'

'Really?' He tried to look as if he had an interest in those great times.

'The elections.' The man delivered the word with a knowing look.

'Oh yes, I was reading about them.' Stefan gestured at the newspaper on the seat next to him. It was an exaggeration to say he had actually read it. He had made an effort to wade through the propaganda, but he'd given up.

'It's been hard work, what with the Poles and the League of Nations, interfering in everything. But we'll sweep away the opposition this time.'

'I'm afraid I'm not too well up on all that.'

'Where are you from? You're hard to place.'

'I'm an Irishman.'

The man looked at him suspiciously, for no reason Stefan understood.

'Ah, that explains it. I'm usually very good on accents.'

'My mother's family was originally from Stuttgart.'

'We have an Irishman at our helm, so to speak. In Danzig. Herr Lester.' The contempt was ill-disguised. 'The League of Nations Commissioner.'

'I've heard of him.' Stefan had talked about him only the day before. If there was trouble, real trouble, Robert Briscoe had said he was to go to Seán Lester as a last resort.

'He's a man who likes to be in the news. For what, who knows? Who cares?' The German laughed, quite loudly. Stefan sensed that that laughter would have been accompanied by a gob of spit if he hadn't been sitting on a plane. Briscoe was right. Danzig's Nazis didn't like their High Commissioner. The man stretched across the aisle towards him. 'Arthur Greiser.' They shook.

'Stefan Gillespie.'

'You don't know our Mr Lester then?' There was a hint of suspicion in Greiser's face again. He wasn't trying to hide his dislike for Seán Lester.

'We're a small country, Herr Greiser, but not that small.'

'Danzig is smaller. We know everyone. Warts and all! Such warts too!'

He turned abruptly and shouted along the aisle of the plane. 'Schnapps!' He looked back. 'You'll have a drink?'

Stefan didn't want any more to drink, but he already knew Greiser would insist. He wasn't a difficult man to read. It was easier to say yes.

'We've left Germany now,' reflected Greiser, looking out at the dark. 'We're over what was Germany before the end of the war, and what will be Germany again. We're supposed to call it the Polish Corridor. German towns with Polish names. As for our Danzig Free State, it will be free again only when it is part of Germany. We all know it. The world knows it. Even the Poles must know. But you're Irish. I don't need to tell you. You know all about fighting for freedom, my friend?' He raised his glass. 'To freedom!'

As Stefan raised his glass, Greiser's was already empty. He called out. 'Another schnapps!'

The steward returned with the bottle. The German took it off him.

'We have a guest to entertain!'

'Jawohl, Herr Senatspräsident!' The answer was delivered with a heel click, and Stefan was now aware that this was a man of some importance.

'Where are you staying, Herr Gillespie?'

'The Danziger Hof.'

'Not bad. We have better. Busy but discreet, very discreet.'

He smirked and Stefan returned the man-of-the-world smile that was required. Greiser leant across and topped up Stefan's glass. He filled his own and drained it again. The bottle would be going back to the Luft Hansa steward empty.

'If there's anything I can do during your stay, Herr Gillespie, I'd be delighted. Mention my name at your hotel, in a restaurant, wherever. My name is enough.' He puffed himself up as he spoke the last words. He poured himself a third schnapps and then settled back in his seat again.

'We have things in common after all. A common struggle, and even, one is not encouraged to say it too loudly just now, a common enemy.' Arthur Greiser tapped his nose, then carried on, unconcerned whether his travelling companion was interested in what he was saying or not. 'Germany had no choice about leaving the League of Nations. It's a farce. Run by the English and paid for by the Americans. Look at Lester, our so-called High Commissioner. Everyone knows he's too close to the English. Can't have made him too popular in Ireland, eh? We'll see the back of him after the elections. He's going to find Danzig just a little too hot. And when we call on him with his train ticket to Geneva, he will be well advised to take it.'

Herr Greiser shook his head and chuckled, clearly expecting Stefan to understand. He didn't, but he smiled politely anyway. The Free City's Senate President poured another schnapps; he had forgotten about his guest's glass now. These weren't the first glasses of schnapps he'd had that day. Moments later Stefan was relieved to see the balding head thrown back in the seat. There was a faint snore too. The schnapps bottle was about to fall from Greiser's hand. Stefan started to reach over but another hand was there first. The steward caught the bottle as he moved through the plane, with a deft assurance that made it look as if he had been waiting there for it to fall.

The plane had flown over the lights of the Free City for only minutes, out of the darkness of surrounding fields and forests. As the Junkers turned to descend, Stefan Gillespie saw where the lights of Danzig and its harbour ended abruptly. He knew that beyond it was the Baltic Sea, now just a deeper blackness in the blackness of the night. Danzig-Langfuhr Aerodrome was little more than a collection of hangars in a field. The other passengers headed for the small brick terminal building, but the Senate President's big Mercedes–Benz was standing on the tarmac as they stepped out of the plane. A small shield on the radiator grille showed the crown and two white crosses on red of the Free City of Danzig, but the pennants that flew from each wing were swastikas. Arthur Greiser thrust his arm through Stefan's and pulled him into the black limousine while the chauffeur held the door open for them.

The effects of the schnapps were evident on Greiser's breath and in his behaviour. Stefan, for this short journey at least, was a new friend, a best friend. There would be no taxi for the Senate President's friend! Arthur Greiser's arrival home had brought the election back to the front of his mind. It was only days away now. He filled the first half of the drive to the city with scatological references to the socialists and Jews who would be swept away by the election, and the sham democracy that would be swept away by the election, and the Poles and their fucking priests who would be swept away by the election, and the need for any further elections that would be swept away by the election. And when everything that had to be swept away had been swept away, there would be a golden future. It would bring the city of Danzig back into the arms of the fatherland, which was sometimes the motherland, depending on whether Greiser's feelings were martial or sentimental.

By the time they reached the outskirts of the city, the Senatspräsident was, thankfully, asleep again. The chauffeur, who seemed almost as pleased about that as Stefan, delivered him to the door of the Hotel Danziger Hof.

Greiser was right about one thing; his name, or in this case his car, with the sight of him snoring in the back seat, was enough. It was enough to bring the hotel manager out of his office to promise Stefan the best room he had available, and his personal attention at any time of the day or night. His expression changed when Stefan asked if Frau Anna Harvey was there. That was the name Hannah had been using, Mrs Anna Harvey, of Blackrock, Dublin. The manager looked puzzled, then angry, then puzzled again, as if he couldn't relate the man who had got out of the Senate President's car to the question he had just been asked. No, she wasn't there. She certainly wasn't there. In fact Frau Harvey had walked out of the hotel after only one night, one night when she'd booked a room for two, without a word to anyone. She had left her belongings in the room. And she hadn't paid her bill.

Stefan stood in the luggage store behind the concierge's desk at the Hotel Danziger Hof. Hannah Rosen's small case, bearing a label with the name Mrs Anna Harvey, contained very little. There was not much more than a change of clothes and some underwear; a bag with soap, a flannel, toothpaste; make-up and a bottle of Chanel No. 11; a bracelet, a brush. He had seen her take off that bracelet and put it beside his bed. There were strands of her dark hair in the brush. He smelt the scent of her perfume. The porter who showed him the case had spoken to her before she left the hotel, the morning after she'd arrived. It was two days ago now. She had asked him for directions to the cathedral in Oliva. That was all. The man seemed slightly nervous, as if he had something more to say. When Stefan turned to leave he pushed a banknote into the porter's hand. It was a five dollar bill. Adam Rosen had given him a roll of dollars at Baldonnel that morning. It was a lot more than the man expected. It was enough. He stepped in front of Stefan and pushed the door back into the lobby firmly shut. Stefan waited.

'The police were here that night looking for her.'

'Do you know why?'

'They said she hadn't registered her passport.'

'You don't think that was it though?'

'They don't send the Gestapo to check your passport.'

# 15. Zoppot Pier

Stefan took the same tram through the suburbs of Danzig that Hannah had taken. He walked through the same gardens to the cathedral. It had been impossible to sleep. He had lain in the bedroom at the Danziger Hof, staring out of the window, waiting for the dawn. The idea that Hannah was in danger had become real in Ireland, but not as real as it was here. He knew a lot more about her now. He understood her sudden departure before Christmas. There had been a part of her she kept shut away; he had sensed that. He thought it had all been personal, but at least he knew it was about something else now. And for anyone who had grown up in Ireland in the last twenty years, none of it was so remarkable. When he was child, it was all around him. Guns were smuggled and money was collected and people were hidden in barns and attics. As a boy, while his father was still a policeman in Dublin, he could sense which of his friends' fathers were Volunteers and Sinn Feiners and IRA men. David Gillespie tried hard to keep his family outside what was happening, but Stefan knew instinctively what it was good not to see and even better not to talk about. What Hannah Rosen was doing in Palestine didn't feel so far away. But if he had thought

Robert Briscoe was exaggerating the danger, to put pressure on him to help, he didn't think so now. He knew Germany would feel very different from the place he'd visited as a child. He'd read enough after all. But it was much more. The hours at Tempelhof had unsettled him. There was danger, directionless perhaps, but there all around him, hanging in the air. And it was here too in Danzig. He felt its breath as Arthur Greiser welcomed him to the Free City.

A Mass was ending at the cathedral when he arrived. The sun was shining. There were people everywhere. Through the open doors of the Cathedral of the Holy Trinity and the Blessed Virgin he heard the organ. He recognised a Bach Chorale. His mother used to play it on the piano at Kilranelagh. 'Es ist das Heil uns kommen her.' It is salvation brings us here. He walked slowly through the crowd, taking his bearings. He had already decided that the less attention he drew to himself the better. It wouldn't take him long to find the priest, but he would rely on his own resources; he wouldn't walk in and leave his calling card. There was no question now; Hannah was missing. All he knew was that she had set off to find Father Francis Byrne at the cathedral in Oliva. That was where he had to start.

As he looked through the crowd towards the cathedral doors he was suddenly staring at someone he knew. He recognised him immediately. The face was thinner. There wasn't the same sense of immaculate, careful dress. If anything he looked scruffy. But Stefan hadn't forgotten the man who had smiled at him so contemptuously in the hallway of the house in Merrion Square. He hadn't seen him since the day he arrested him, but the image was fixed in his head. It was Hugo Keller. And as he stared, he was aware that Keller would almost certainly recognise him. He stepped back into the shadow of a tree. People were standing in groups, talking. Keller seemed to be waiting for someone. The Austrian turned back towards the cathedral; a priest was coming out. And as the two men met, Stefan had no doubt who Keller had been waiting for. He had never seen the priest before, but he was there now; thirty-five perhaps, not very tall, with fair hair just starting to recede. Stefan couldn't begin to explain what the abortionist was doing here with Father Francis Byrne, but he knew he needed to be careful. He knew Danzig was a place where anything that couldn't be explained was probably dangerous.

The Mass-goers were drifting away from the cathedral square. Keller and Byrne walked towards the gardens, deep in conversation. The priest was agitated. He didn't speak loudly, but Stefan could feel he was holding his voice in check, along with his emotions. The two men were close to him now. He turned his back and walked in the opposite direction. Then he stopped abruptly and looked round, across the square and through the trees. They were heading for the park. There were other people going that way too, back to Oliva and Zoppot and the trams into the city. Stefan waited. Once the two men were in the park the trees would be thick enough to hide him. He would be able to follow them without being seen. He wouldn't approach them together. He still needed to start with Father Byrne. As he watched their backs ahead of him he could see that they had stopped talking now. It was not a happy silence. They were both angry, but as the conversation resumed Stefan could tell that it was Hugo Keller who was controlling it.

The priest and the abortionist emerged on to the main road through Oliva. Stefan stayed back among the trees at the park gates. He watched them approach the tram stop. A Number 2 tram was pulling up, heading back into Danzig. He was unsure what to do. If he got on the tram Keller might see him. He stepped out on to the road uncertainly. He might have to risk it. At the tram stop Byrne took an envelope from his pocket. He thrust it furiously into Keller's hand, then spun round and walked rapidly away towards Zoppot. Keller watched him go, a satisfied smile on his face. He put the envelope in his pocket. And as the doors of the tram opened he got on.

Stefan didn't want to lose Keller after all this. He knew the Austrian's presence here was no coincidence, but he had to follow one or the other. And it still had to be the priest. It was the priest Hannah had come to see. He was the one who had sent Susan Field to Merrion Square. And he would know where to find Hugo Keller again, that was obvious. Stefan let the tram pull away, then crossed over behind it and followed Byrne. The priest was still agitated, maybe even more agitated now. He was walking fast, but there was no purpose in it. There was something about the way he moved that told Stefan he wasn't going anywhere in particular, however fast he might be moving. He was just walking because he didn't want to stand still.

It was a long walk too. The pace slowed a little but the priest kept going, as if the only thing in his mind was keeping his back to the cathedral. Eventually they were walking down a steep hill towards the seafront at Zoppot, towards the spa buildings and the cafés and the hotels. It was only when he reached the sea that Francis Byrne stopped, quite suddenly, because there was no further to go. A railing separated the promenade from the beach, and beyond that there was only the Bay of Danzig and the Baltic Sea.

Trying to get his bearings, Stefan focused on the high red roofs of the Hotel Casino, the biggest building along the busy promenade; it was directly behind the priest. He recognised it from the brochure he had picked up in his room at the Danziger Hof. It was where Arthur Greiser had recommended he went when the artistic treasures of Danzig palled. 'Afternoon tea-dances, roulette and baccarat; the largest and most elegant hotel in Eastern Europe. Have you ever sat on a bar stool and watched the sun rise over the sea? You can enjoy such a spectacle in the Casino Bar, the prettiest cocktail bar in Europe.' Stefan couldn't imagine many hotel guests sitting in the bar all night waiting for the sun to rise, but the Senate President would probably have been up for it. All around there were holidaymakers now, cheerfully braving the cold wind that blew in off the sea. It had been warm in the sheltered cathedral square, but on the front the wind still bit hard in April.

Francis Byrne stood for a moment, gazing down at the sweep of white sand and grey water. Immediately below him a group of children, laughing and squabbling, were building a sandcastle. He turned away and continued along the promenade to the wide wooden pier that stretched out into the calm Baltic waters. It wasn't so busy here. Couples walked slowly, arm in arm; children ran; old men stood at regular intervals with fishing rods. The priest stopped to light a cigarette. Stefan was close to him now. Francis Byrne's hands were shaking as he cupped them round a match; twice a match went out. Stefan watched. Agitation was good. People talked when they were agitated and they didn't think about what they were saying. Stefan took the lighter from his pocket and held it up to Byrne's face, blocking the sea breeze with his back so that the priest could finally light the cigarette.

'Vielen Dank.'

'I didn't expect to find Keller here, Father,' Stefan replied in English.

The priest stiffened, his hands stayed cupped to his face.

'This is one of the longest piers in Europe, seven hundred yards. Sea air, sea views, and the end of the pier is highly recommended for its lack of dust. The brochure says the only thing there isn't is monotony. Let's see.'

The priest still didn't move.

'Will we take a constitutional, Father? I think so.'

Francis Byrne did as he was told. They started to walk slowly along the pier.

'Who are you?' he asked.

'Detective Sergeant Gillespie. I'm a Garda officer.' Byrne didn't respond. 'I've been wanting to talk to you since last year, about Susan Field's death. You'll remember you wrote a letter to my inspector, to say you didn't know Susan very well, and how sorry you were to hear she'd died. I had a lot more questions at the time, but they were never asked. You did say you'd never heard of Hugo Keller. You know him now though.'

'Are you with Hannah?' The hand holding the cigarette was shaking.

It was Stefan's turn not to respond. He didn't need to.

'I told her what I could,' said the priest quietly, looking out to sea.

Even in those uncertain, fearful words Stefan knew that whatever Francis Byrne had told Hannah Rosen, it was not the truth, certainly not all of it, but none of that mattered.

'Do you know where Hannah is, Father?'

The priest was too preoccupied with himself to hear the question.

'I wanted to tell her everything. I tried to. I can't lie any more!'

He stopped and turned to face Stefan. There was a plea for help in his eyes, and they were growing wet with tears. Getting someone to confess was usually the hard part for Stefan, yet it looked like getting Byrne to stop was going to be the problem now. It was what had happened yesterday and the day before that Stefan needed to know about, not the past; but Hannah had broken the lock on the cupboard where Francis Byrne kept his secrets and Stefan's arrival had just kicked the door open. However hard he tried to bring the priest back to Hannah and Danzig, it was the past that was pouring out now.

It was fast and confused. He told Stefan he hadn't gone to Merrion Square with Susan that day. It was only when something went wrong that Keller had phoned him and told him he had to come. It was serious. She was bleeding badly; she was barely conscious. She was asking for him. Someone had to take her to hospital. There was a car. The driver said he was a guard. They only had to drive across the square to Holles Street but the guard drove to the Convent of the Good Shepherd instead. The Mother Superior took one look at Susan and said she couldn't help. They needed to get her to a proper hospital. The Coombe was nearest, but on the way the guard stopped the car. Susan wasn't moving. It was too late. She was dead. The guard told him to go home. No one could help her. The only thing he could do was pray for her. And he had done what the guard said. He left her there. As Father Byrne closed his eyes, his lips moved silently. He was praying, for himself. Stefan didn't need divine guidance to know who the unknown guard was: Jimmy Lynch.

As Father Byrne spoke, staring out at the Baltic Sea, Stefan simply listened. He knew he wouldn't get any more out of him till this was over. The priest hadn't looked at Stefan as he told the story; only once, at the end, did he turn and hold the detective's gaze, shaking his head, somehow still in disbelief. Then he turned back to stare silently at the grey sea. Stefan had the feeling he was wondering if he couldn't find an answer and an end to it all out there. He doubted Byrne had the guts for that, but he didn't much care if he had or not. There was more self-pity in Francis Byrne than Stefan had the stomach for. He had been on Kilmashogue when the earth spewed up Susan Field's body. That was something to feel pity for. All this was a waste of time. He grabbed the priest's arm and pulled him back round again, hard.

'Where did Hannah go?' Stefan demanded.

Byrne looked at him blankly.

'When she left you, where did she go?'

'I . . . I don't know.'

'The police were looking for her. Why?'

'I don't know anything about the police. Why would I?'

There was a brief hesitation. It didn't sit with all that gushing truth.

'Who did you speak to?'

'She came here, and we talked, and she went away. That's all.'

'What were you saying to Hugo Keller this morning?'

'Nothing. Nothing that concerns Hannah or you.'

The defences were going up again, but Stefan already knew that when Hannah left him the priest had contacted

Keller. It wouldn't have been difficult to find where she was staying, and the first thing the police would have discovered was that the name Hugo Keller had given them wasn't the one on the Danziger Hof register, or on her passport. She was supposed to be Mrs Anna Harvey, not Hannah Rosen.

'You're still lying, Father. You told him she was in Danzig.'

'All right. I panicked. I didn't know what else to do.'

'What did he say?'

'He said not to worry. It didn't matter. He said he'd sort it out.'

'With a little bit of help from the Gestapo.'

'No, of course not. He said she wasn't important.'

'But you're important, aren't you? Important to Keller. I don't know why exactly, but I do know what his speciality is. He's blackmailing you.'

Byrne didn't answer, but the answer was in his eyes.

'It wouldn't be so hard would it, not with your track record? An affair, an abortion, a dead woman. It's not going to get you a job in the Curia.'

There was grim silence now. Perhaps the hold Hugo Keller had over the priest was stronger than the fear inside, stronger than guilt, stronger than what, once, he felt for Susan Field. But Stefan had to push. He had to know what he was dealing with.

'Would you know what a captive bolt pistol is, Father?'

It felt like the words barely registered; they meant nothing.

'They use it to stun animals, before they slaughter them.'

The priest looked puzzled. Stefan watched his face.

'Susan Field took a bolt in the head from one before she was buried.'

If anything Byrne had said was real, so was his disbelief. 'But she was dead! The guard said she was dead!'

'I'd say the guard who drove the car from Merrion Square that night was a man called Jimmy Lynch, Father. He's a guard all right, a detective sergeant. He was taking back-handers from your friend Keller. But I don't think he'd have killed Susan Field without Hugo's say so. That's the man you handed Hannah Rosen to, to sort things out. Now no one's seen her since.'

*

A day earlier, around the time Stefan Gillespie was boarding the midday Deutsche Luft Hansa flight from Croydon to Berlin, Hannah Rosen was standing in the library of a big apartment in the Danzig suburb of Langfuhr. Through the window most of the view was taken up by a large building of red brick and stone with a highly decorated, crenellated frontage that echoed the Hanseatic houses of the old town. It was the city's university, the Technische Hochschule. Behind it were the wooded hills she had seen from the tram on her way to Oliva. Half an hour earlier the men who had pulled her into a car in front of the Danziger Hof had unlocked the door of the small bedroom that had been her cell. They led her through the apartment to a library. It was empty. They left her there with a cup of coffee and a roll.

That morning she had heard the sound of shouting and cheering outside, even in the locked room. Now she watched through the library window. The ever-present swastikas hung along the front of the university building; hundreds of students stood in front of it with flags and banners.

Somewhere a man was speaking, but she could make out none of the words, only the ebb and flow of roaring and chanting from the crowd. She felt their wild enthusiasm. They were laughing and applauding. Without the flags, and with the words unheard, they seemed almost like people she knew. They looked like people she knew. She turned round, startled, as the door opened.

A man entered. He wasn't one of the people who had snatched her off the street. They were around her own age, not much older than the students outside. This man was in his sixties. He looked at her hard. His face was stern, but there was nothing about him that felt threatening to her.

'Why am I here?'

She spoke in German. He replied in English.

'Just be glad you are. There are worse places to be.'

'What do you want?'

'They were waiting for you, at the hotel.'

'Who was?'

'The Gestapo, Fräulein Rosen, Frau Harvey. I don't suppose you knew we had the luxury of our own Gestapo here in the Free City, did you?'

She said nothing. He was right. There was a lot she hadn't known.

'My information is that when your room was searched, they found two passports. One Irish, in the name you registered in at the hotel. The police believe that's false. The other issued by the British Mandate in Palestine.'

'I could be of no interest to the Gestapo,' she said defensively.

'Nevertheless, they are interested. That's all that matters.'

A great roar erupted again beyond the window. The old

man walked past her. He stood looking out at the rally. It was coming to an end now.

'When I was a student, we protested about the books they wouldn't let us read. That was our passion, freedom. Now my students pull books out of the university library to burn. That's their passion, hatred.' He turned back into the room. The noise outside had suddenly stilled. The rally was over.

'You will stay here today, Fräulein. Tomorrow Leon and Johannes will go up into the hills with you. The borders are policed very aggressively at the moment, but they'll take you across into Poland through the forests. Leon will get you to the train that runs from Gdynia to Bromberg, that's Bydgoszcz now, in Poland. You can get to Warsaw from there without re-entering Danzig. You have a ticket to Trieste, via Warsaw and Vienna. You'll have a week or so in Trieste before your boat leaves for Palestine. It's pleasant at this time of year. A lot pleasanter than our Free City anyway.'

'You're very well-informed.'

'And you're very lucky. You were very stupid to come here.'

'I had a reason to come.' The words didn't convince her the way they would have done two days earlier. They didn't convince the old man either.

'There are a few decent men left inside the Schutzpolizei. When they can, they pass on information, especially about people the Nazis want to pick up. Perhaps you can imagine the risk someone would take doing that.'

Hannah nodded. She knew people had taken risks for her.

'We heard about you by chance. The Gestapo put a call

out for you. Some kind of passport irregularity. No one knew who you were, but the information came to a friend of mine. And as this irregularity involved a passport issued in Palestine he contacted me. I didn't know who you were either, but it felt like you and the Gestapo might not get on very well.'

'They had no reason to know who I was.'

'Well, somebody knew you were Fräulein Rosen, not Frau Harvey. Somebody knew something. Who have you been speaking to in Danzig?'

'The only person I've talked to is a priest, an Irish priest in Oliva.'

'You came here to see a priest?'

'Yes.'

'Why?'

'Because nobody else would do it.'

'It must have been very important in that case.'

'My best friend was killed. He was one of the last people to see her alive. I think that's important. But I'm about the only person who does.'

'That all sounds very worthy. And you think you've got the right to put other people's lives at risk because of your very important personal life, do you? All sorts of people, all over the place, now here in Danzig as well.'

'This has got nothing to do with anybody else.'

'You don't think so?' He shook his head. 'I had to find out who you were. I did, this morning. A Jew with a British Mandate passport and a ticket from Trieste to Haifa? I telephoned the Jewish Agency in Trieste. Not an easy conversation, given the Danzig exchange's propensity for listening in to overseas calls, but with a lot of guesswork and a little Hebrew to hide what I was saying, I got there.

You're working for the Haganah. Whatever you've been doing in Europe, I don't doubt you've met dozens of people. All names the Nazis would like to have. Don't think they wouldn't ship you off to Berlin if they believed you had anything useful to tell them. Nobody in the world would even realise, because nobody knows you're here, isn't that right? Your friends in Trieste are pretty pissed off with you, Hannah.'

'I'm sorry. I wasn't even going to be here two days.'

'I don't know what you did to draw attention to yourself, but the sooner you're out of Danzig the better, for your sake and everyone else's. I'm not a Zionist myself. Fighting fascism here in Europe is more important than making the desert bloom. It's a disease. You can't run away from it.'

'It's not about running away.'

'No, probably not. I used to believe that. There are a lot of things I'm not sure about any more. I'm an old man who didn't expect to spend his old age gazing into the darkness I thought we'd left behind a long time ago.' He looked at her and smiled more warmly; his irritation had gone. 'I'm sorry about your friend. But that's the way the world is now. I've got friends who didn't die a natural death too. Before long we'll all have friends like that.'

'Doesn't that matter?'

'Of course it matters, but the personal life doesn't. Not now. No one has a personal life any more. That's gone. All we have is our survival.' He touched her arm. 'Good luck, Hannah,' he said softly; then he walked out.

She stood in the room, alone again. She felt all the more alone because of those last, bleak words. She walked slowly back to the window. The students had gone. The swastikas still flew on the front of the Technische Hochschule. Behind it the dark hills rose up. That was where she had to go tomorrow. The man was right. She shouldn't have come to Danzig. But though she understood what he said, she refused to believe it – it was the personal that mattered most of all now, now more than anything else.

*

Stefan sat in the bar at the Danziger Hof with a beer that he thought might help. It didn't. He knew he'd got most of the truth out of Francis Byrne, except for one thing. Whatever was going on between the priest and Hugo Keller wasn't about Hannah Rosen, or Susan Field, even if Susan Field's death was what gave the abortionist the leverage to blackmail him. Father Byrne mattered, that was very clear; he mattered a lot. He was an important asset, and whatever he was doing for Keller, Hannah had been a threat. If she had been arrested it was because the abortionist was protecting his asset. Stefan sensed that he stood on the edge of something darker than he understood. He had seen the fear in Francis Byrne's eyes. But he didn't really care what it was about; the two men deserved each other. All he cared about was that he wasn't finding Hannah. Hugo Keller had to be his next stop.

He had forced Keller's address in Langfuhr out of Francis Byrne at the end, but this would be a very different proposition from a guilt-ridden priest. Keller would be doing what he did, buying and selling information. He would have connections, and if Dublin was any measure he would have connections with the police. Stefan knew he might have to push the Austrian hard. Keller would have to believe he would suffer serious physical damage unless he told him what he knew about Hannah's whereabouts. He would probably have to hurt him. But he couldn't take it too far. If she had been arrested he might need Keller's help. Instincts he trusted told him the abortionist would respond to two things: real pain and real money. Stefan had to get the balance right. He had some money; more could be wired from Adam Rosen. The only other route was the diplomatic fuss Robert Briscoe could get out of the Irish government. Keller wouldn't like the threat of the public eye on him, neither would the Danzig police. But he had to find her before anything else could happen. And the darkness he had sensed in Francis Byrne was gnawing at him. As he drained his glass and got up, he realised it was already too late to call on Keller. Two men were approaching across the bar. In the doorway the hotel manager looked on with a smile of sour satisfaction. One of the men was a uniformed Schutzpolizei. The other sweated in a belted leather coat that was too big for him. Stefan could already identify the Danzig Gestapo.

# 16. Mattenbuden Bridge

Weidengasse was a long wide street across the river from the old town, with a tramline running its length and a tram depot at the far end. It was dominated by a sprawling, drab, four-storeyed building full of windows, its facade regularly broken by square turrets. In Imperial Germany this was Danzig's cavalry barracks, the Reiterkaserne, but it was a long time since the last regiment of Death's Head Hussars clattered out on to the cobbles to take the road to the front line, where men and horses would die together in the mud, blown apart by mortars and cannon. It was mostly empty now, a place of echoing corridors and bare, damp, unfurnished rooms. However, at one end of the building, on the corner of Reitergasse, was the District III Police Station, serving the old docks, the warehouses of the Speicherinsel and the streets of apartments south of the Mottlau River. With the election in full swing police cells throughout the Free City were crammed with disruptive opposition supporters and the Reiterkaserne, with its easily adapted cellars and a plentiful supply of vacant barrack rooms, offered the capacity for extra accommodation. The Free City's Gestapo men found it particularly useful.

No one at Police Headquarters in Karrenwall much

minded what happened to the anti-social elements who wanted to vote for someone, almost anyone, other than the Nazis, but the building was still too close to the League of Nations Commissioner and to a Senate where there were a few politicians unpatriotic enough to ask awkward questions. The election was only two days away now and people were still trying to put up posters and hold meetings in the face of the Nazi juggernaut. There were still socialists, communists, liberals, Jews, Poles and other scum conspiring to exercise their right to vote. But it was a lot easier for an indignant Police President to deny his disdain for the constitution if people weren't being beaten up in the next office to his. There was plenty of space for all that in Weidengasse after all. And if there was some serious business to be done, to save Danzig from its political and racial degenerates, the Reiterkaserne's long corridors led to places where nobody would even hear the screams.

Stefan had been driven from the Stockturm across the city, through the oldest part of Danzig, into Langgasse and the Lange Markt, down to the Mottlau River and through the island docks and warehouses to Langgarten and Weidengasse. The uniformed Schutzpolizei officer drove, concentrating on blasting his horn and cursing pedestrians. The Gestapo man was still sweating, but he had become more affable once they were in the car and he was no longer on stage. Occasionally he pointed out places of interest, almost at random, as if they were on a tour. The crenellated facades of the eighteenth-century houses in Langgasse; the Neptune Fountain; the Ratsweinkeller under the Town Hall, which he thoroughly recommended for the quality of its beer and the size of its dumplings; the great medieval crane along the Lange Brücke as they crossed the river and left the old town.

In Weidengasse Stefan was put in a cell with seven other men. They included a newspaper editor whose paper had just been shut down for the third time since February, a fourteen-year-old boy who had put up an election poster outside the parliament building, and a pickpocket who claimed he was a Party member and didn't see why he should be locked up with a bunch of degenerate politicos. After two hours, Stefan was taken up to an interview room. He stepped round an old woman cleaning blood off the wall and the stairs. Someone had been unlucky enough to trip and knock his head against the wall on the way down. They were very unlucky stairs.

In a bare room that reminded him uncomfortably of Pearse Street Garda station the tour guide was joined by another Gestapo man. He announced himself as Kriminaloberassistent Rothe. The first thing they did was to tell Stefan what he wanted to know. They asked him why he was asking questions about Anna Harvey. What exactly was his relationship with her? Did he know where she was? They asked him if he knew where she was too many times. It didn't tell him where she was, but he felt sure the police didn't have her. And if she'd avoided the police, who else would be looking for her? The Gestapo men didn't seem at all clear what else they wanted from him. They had been told to find out if he knew where the woman was and that was it. He could sense, as a profes- sional among professionals, that they were now looking for questions to ask to justify a report that would say nothing.

'So, who is she, Hannah Rosen or Anna Harvey?'

'I know her as Anna Harvey, that's all, Mrs Harvey. Maybe

Rosen was her maiden name. I don't think she's been married very long. Look, we're not old friends. I'm not up on her bloody family history.'

'Did she change her first name too?'

'I don't know. My name's Stefan, but most people call me Stevie.'

The questions came almost exclusively from the crop-haired Rothe now.

'Did you know she was Jewish?'

'Yes, I suppose so. I hadn't really thought about it.'

'Did you know she'd been living in Palestine?'

'That must be where she got her suntan.'

The tour guide grinned. Rothe didn't.

'Why are you in Danzig, Herr Gillespie?'

By now it was clear he wasn't there for a Gestapo thrashing. He didn't have the information they wanted. He knew when something mattered and when it didn't. He was a policeman. This wasn't important to them. He remembered the conversation with Arthur Greiser. He could take a chance.

'Look, if I knew where the bitch was, I'd tell you. What's she done?'

'It's not your business.'

'It's not her husband after her then?'

He had their attention. They thought he was opening up. Maybe they'd get something out of him after all. The tour guide offered him a cigarette.

'What do you mean?' asked Rothe.

'I had some business in Berlin. We arranged to meet up, you know. A bit of fun, no strings. I don't know what she was doing in Danzig, but it seemed as good a place as any. I liked the sound of Zoppot too. And if you're going to fuck a man's wife, well, the further away the better.'

'She was waiting for you here, is that what you're saying?'

'Yes.'

'Did she know anyone in Danzig?'

'No idea. I've only been seeing her a couple of months. Mostly in England. It's a night here, a night there. That's how these things go.'

'But it seems she didn't wait.' Rothe wasn't entirely convinced yet.

'Her husband's been a bit suspicious. Maybe she changed her mind.'

The tour guide grinned. The Kriminaloberassistent was less amused.

'You fuck a lot of Jewesses?'

'It's not illegal, is it?'

'It will be,' he barked, looking at Stefan with disgust.

'It's just a fuck. What's his problem?' He winked at the tour guide. That was when the slap came. It was only a slap, but it was hard enough.

'Jesus!'

'Filthy bastard.' Rothe was in the mood for more.

'I don't know what she did to you, but it looks like she's dumped me now, the bitch.' Stefan shrugged as if to say it was a pain in the arse but only a woman. 'Doesn't look like I'll make it to Zoppot after all. Pity after what Herr Greiser told me on the plane.' He laughed a sly-dog, boys-will-be-boys laugh that was a fair stab at the Senate President's style. 'What did he say? A place not to be missed or a great place to get pissed?' He sniggered. And now he really had their attention. 'We'd had a couple. You know Greiser!'

He stopped. No need to overdo it.

The tour guide chuckled. Rothe was frowning. He regretted the slap.

'You know the Senatspräsident?' he asked.

'We were on the plane from Berlin. He dropped me at the hotel.'

It wasn't exactly an answer but it was the detail that mattered. The tour guide looked at the Kriminal-oberassistent. He expected him to know more about the movements of senior Party officials than he did. As long as he didn't step on anyone's toes he couldn't care less. He definitely didn't want to tread on Greiser's. The nod from Rothe was barely perceptible. Yes, he did know Greiser had been in Berlin. The silence was uneasy now. The tour guide lit a cigarette. It was all over as far as he was concerned. Klaus Rothe had decided it was over too, but he still had some face to save.

'How much longer do you intend to stay in Danzig, Herr Gillespie?'

'I might try the casino after all. A little bit of culture goes a long way.'

'You think Frau Harvey, Fräulein Rosen, has left the city then?'

'If her old man got the scent she wouldn't want to cross him. Too much dough. Well, he's a Jew. Still, if you can't screw them one way, you can screw them another.'

The tour guide liked the joke. Rothe didn't. Sexual inter-course with a Jewess was the abomination of abominations. He couldn't approve of what Stefan was doing, but at least he was doing it with the proper degree of contempt. If he'd been a local he would have taught him a lesson about racial purity he wouldn't forget in a hurry. But this was a waste

301

of time. He had better things to do. He looked at his watch. The rally would have started. Josef Goebbels, the Reich Propaganda Minister, had just flown in from Berlin to wind up the faithful for the election. He didn't want to miss it.

As the two Gestapo men walked to the front desk with Stefan, a door from an office opened ahead of them. He recognised Hugo Keller again. He was in the suit he'd been wearing in Merrion Square, but it hung on him like something from a second-hand clothes stall. He was thinner, greyer. His skin was pale. He wasn't the same man now that Stefan was close to him. He laughed as he stepped into the corridor, calling back into the room, 'I'm counting up those fucking drinks you owe me. Make sure you can afford it!'

The moment he saw the Kriminaloberassistent his face was more serious.

'Were you coming to see me, Hugo?' asked the Gestapo officer.

'I just needed some money, Herr Rothe.' His voice was deferential.

'Whatever you need, you ask me. I thought that was clear.'

'You were busy, Kriminaloberassistent.'

'Then you should have waited till I wasn't. You only talk to me.' There was irritation in his voice and behind that there was contempt.

Hugo Keller may have been about to say more, but he wasn't looking at the Gestapo man now, he was looking straight at Stefan Gillespie. The surprise on Keller's face was entirely genuine. And he didn't know what to do about it. Stefan could read the thought process in the abortionist's eyes. He needed time. He needed to know what this was about. The two men looked at each other warily. Then, quite unexpectedly, Rothe laughed.

'Perhaps you know our friend here, Hugo. He's an Irishman.'

Keller was recovering his composure. He smiled at Stefan.

'I don't think so, Kriminaloberassistent.'

Stefan's eyes widened.

'There were a few people I didn't get round to meeting,' continued Keller, his gaze fixed firmly on Stefan. The two Gestapo men were unaware of the intensity of that gaze, but Stefan understood what it was telling him: 'Shut up!' He couldn't make any sense of it, yet he had no choice but to be grateful for the lifeline he had been thrown. Hugo Keller could have driven a coach and horses through the story he had just given to Klaus Rothe.

'I lived in Dublin for several years, Mr –' Keller spoke in English.

'Gillespie. I'm in Dublin myself.'

'Have we met then? I didn't think –'

'No.' It seemed to be what Keller wanted him to say.

'Where are you staying?'

'The Danziger Hof.'

'He speaks good German, Hugo. Don't give us all that English crap.'

'We must have a drink, Mr Gillespie.' Keller still spoke in English.

'A word, Hugo, now please!' The Kriminaloberassistent turned back along the corridor, walking slowly; the Austrian followed him obediently.

The tour guide walked on with Stefan to the front desk. Moments later he was in Weidengasse, walking back to the river and the old town, wondering why Hugo Keller had saved him from the beating the Gestapo officers only needed an excuse to deliver. It was all the more odd because despite the fear that had risen in his throat when he saw the Austrian in the police station, he had sensed that Keller's fear went deeper than his own. Yet even though he was obviously working for the Gestapo, he had lied to them.

As Stefan turned into Langgarten, towards the Mottlau and the stone tower that Danzigers called the Milk Can, he heard his name being shouted.

'Mr Gillespie!' He stopped and waited as Keller hurried towards him.

'Let's have that drink.'

'Why?'

'One reason would be that Kriminaloberassistent Rothe told me to.'

'So that we could talk about old times in Dublin?'

'So that I could tell him whether I think you're lying about anything.'

'But we're both lying, aren't we?'

Stefan smiled. There was no answering smile.

'You've got no idea what you're sticking your nose into, Sergeant. But if you end up back in a Gestapo cell again, you just might not come out.'

The bar was dark and full of smoke. There was the smell of tobacco and beer and somewhere the sourness of the cured sausages that hung behind the counter. Steps led down to the cellar from Mattenbuden, the street that ran along the edge of the New Mottlau, looking across at the warehouses and granaries of the Speicherinsel and beyond that to the city. Barges were moored at the water's edge and the cellar bar belonged to the city's old docks. As Stefan

Gillespie and Hugo Keller entered, the languages of the Baltic were there along with German and Polish. Stefan didn't need to recognise the snatches of Latvian, Lithuanian, Swedish and Estonian to know that this was a lot further from the police station in Weidengasse than the distance they had walked. It wasn't German Danzig and most of the customers weren't Danzigers. Keller had ordered in German, but oddly it was the fact that they were speaking in a language other than German that made them invisible. The waiter seemed to know the Austrian and as they talked he brought regular refills for the schnapps Keller was drinking with his beer. The abortionist hadn't struck Stefan as a drinker in Dublin but that had changed. He was conscious again how drained the man was, how much older he looked. It was a very long way from the Shelbourne Hotel.

Stefan was unsure what he could say and what he couldn't. There were things he knew about Hannah now that he wouldn't dream of telling Keller, yet it was pointless repeating the lies he had told in Weidengasse. He had to offer some reason for being in Danzig. It felt like anything they both knew already had to be safe, though this didn't seem like the time to accuse the abortionist of telling Jimmy Lynch to kill Susan Field. He had to use as much of the truth as he could. Half truths worked better than lies.

'Hannah's father got wind she was coming to Danzig to find the priest, Father Byrne. She's still got it in her head somebody has to pay for Susan Field's death. Let's not pretend you don't know who Susan Field was, Hugo.'

Keller shrugged. It didn't really matter what Stefan knew about that, not here.

'Byrne was the only candidate. In your absence. And as

her old man didn't want her in a Danzig gaol for attempted murder, he paid me to bring her back before she got into trouble. I haven't done very well so far.'

'No, it's a pity you didn't get here earlier, Sergeant.'

Keller downed a schnapps.

'What the hell did you set the Gestapo on her for?' said Stefan.

'I just wanted the police to put her on a train and get her out of Danzig.' The abortionist's lips tightened. Stefan sensed that it hadn't worked out the way it was meant to. 'She made trouble for me in Dublin. I wasn't going to let her do it again. I didn't know the Gestapo would get involved.'

'Why not? I'm sure the Nazis are very particular about the reputations of Catholic priests, at least the ones they're getting information out of.'

'This isn't the place to show how clever you are, Mr Gillespie. If you think you know what's going on with Father Byrne, forget about it. You'd be better keeping your mouth shut. I am protecting you. Remember that.'

Stefan nodded; for whatever reason it was true.

'I want to know where Hannah is. That's why I'm here.'

'They didn't pick her up. They haven't got her.'

'And I suppose you'd know.' He looked at Keller with distaste.

'Yes, I'd know. I don't know why she was using a false passport though. That's why the Gestapo are looking for her. I gave the police one name, and when they went to the hotel the bitch was using another one.'

'Does she know you're blackmailing the priest?'

'I don't care what Hannah Rosen knows. I've got a job to do in Danzig. I can't let anything get in the way. I didn't

306

ask to come here. They sent me. Because of the priest.' The words were simple enough, but they sounded bleak.

'The only thing that matters to me is Hannah.'

'Look, I talked to the Schutzpolizei about her, that's all. They don't know anything about anything. All they had to do was deport her. But Kriminaloberassistent Rothe got hold of it, because of the passports. They found two fucking passports. Rothe's the man I work for. The last thing I can afford is the priest going off the rails. Byrne's not easy to control as it is. He's a clever man, but underneath it he's a coward. He's weak. But he's got a conscience and it's not going to help me or him or anybody if he finds it. I can't let that happen. I had to get Hannah Rosen away from him. He's not far off a breakdown.'

Stefan didn't say how much closer to a breakdown Francis Byrne was now. He didn't care. Hugo Keller was saying more than he intended to. The schnapps helped, but it was his own anxiety that was making him talk. There was never anyone to talk to in the job he did. There were always too many lies to remember to make it safe.

'Are you going to tell me what you know about Hannah?'

'They went to the hotel to pick her up. She didn't go back there. They couldn't find her.'

'And that's it?' Stefan watched Keller's face.

'That's it. If I were you I'd be pleased that's it.'

'And they're still looking for her?'

'So she must have got out, right? Maybe somebody helped her.'

'Like who?' Stefan asked.

'Look, Sergeant, I don't why Hannah Rosen had a false passport, but I've been doing this for a very long time. Tourists don't have two passports in different names, even tourists with dead friends. I don't know who she is, or what she is, but someone does. In fact, you wouldn't want the Gestapo to question you about that for real, would you? They're not exactly the Garda Síochána.'

The Austrian was reminding him who was doing the favours.

'All right. But where did she go? Could she have got out of Danzig?'

'It's not that hard if you know what to do. If they had her I would know. I'd know because they'd be questioning me too. They'd want to know what damage she'd done. It wouldn't take much to send Klaus Rothe off the deep end. She's made for it. You've got to understand these people believe all this stuff, about Jewish conspiracies and Jews trying to destroy Germany and take over the world. It's not a game for them. One false passport and a Jewish woman from Palestine and there's a Zionist spy. Not only that, she's got some hold on a man who's a valuable informant. It doesn't have to make sense. When they doubt, they doubt everybody. And that means me too.'

As Keller spoke the last words there was real fear in his eyes again.

'So all this is about Francis Byrne?'

'There are two ways to stay safe, Sergeant. Either you've got to know everything or nothing at all. You've managed to persuade the Gestapo the only thing you were doing with Hannah Rosen was screwing her. That's no mean achievement. Go back to your hotel. Get the train out in the morning.'

'And Hannah?'

'I give you my word, she wasn't arrested.'

'I'm sorry,' Stefan laughed, 'did you just give me your word?'

The Austrian smiled; he still had a sense of humour.

'I've kept my mouth shut about who you are, and about the lies you've told the Gestapo. I might have my own reasons for that, but you need to know the shit you'd be in if I changed my mind. I don't have to help you.'

'Then why are you?'

'Does it matter?'

'No, I suppose not.'

Keller said nothing for a moment. He wasn't looking at Stefan now. He was gazing into the mid distance, as if he was remembering something, or regretting something. The waiter brought another schnapps. He drank it.

'I have a lot of friends in Ireland.' He smiled, and very briefly he looked more like the man Stefan had seen at the house in Merrion Square.

'Is friends the right word?' said Stefan.

'People I can rely on. I'd like to go back. I still think of it as home.'

'And I thought you were home now.'

'Germany? You're joking!'

'They must owe you a pension by now.'

The sarcasm washed over Hugo Keller; he was entirely serious.

'I don't want enemies in Ireland. I've done you a favour, Sergeant. I hope you'll remember it when you get home.'

It was an uncomfortable feeling for Stefan Gillespie, but it was true.

'Why would you worry about me, Hugo? Like you said, you've got friends. No one's waiting to arrest you. Whatever happened in Merrion Square no one even wants to talk to you.'

That seemed to please Keller. For a moment he smiled; but he couldn't keep the present at bay.

'There's nothing to stay here for. Not just Danzig, Germany, Austria.'

He lowered his voice, shaking his head as he spoke.

'If you want to know what's coming, Mr Gillespie, you only have to listen. But nobody is. Nobody wants to hear. You're close enough to it in Danzig though. Use your ears. Walk through the streets and fucking listen.'

He drained his glass of beer and stood up. 'If Miss Rosen isn't here, be grateful for it. Just forget what you know and what you think you know and fuck off.' He walked out.

When Stefan left the bar, the street outside was quiet. The water of the New Mottlau lapped gently against the barges moored on the Speicherinsel side. He didn't know how much faith to put in anything Hugo Keller had said. What he did know, because it was in every line of the Austrian's now thin and sallow face, was that fear was driving everything he did. Hannah was a part of that fear; anything that threatened him was a part of that fear. If the Gestapo had arrested her, Keller would have known. It wasn't much, but it was something. He took his bearings, trying to work out where he was as he walked towards the Mattenbuden Bridge. It would take him over the canal to the Granary Island. The island was a maze of old, crumbling warehouses, but if he kept to the lane called Münchengasse it would bring him across the island to the Cow Bridge and the Mottlau River itself. Hundegasse would lead him to the other end of the old town, and back to the Danziger Hof.

As he stepped off the bridge into Münchengasse the high, gabled fronts of its medieval granaries rose up on either side of the narrow lane. They were shuttered and barred; there were no lights anywhere. He could hear a rumbling sound from the other side of the city. It came and went. It was the Goebbels rally. He could make out the sound of people cheering and shouting; it was like a distant football match. He was conscious of footsteps behind him. He looked round. The footsteps stopped. He could see no one, but he was sure there had been movement in the dark street. And innocent footsteps didn't stop that quickly. He walked on. There were lights ahead, along the Lange Brücke on the other side of the Mottlau; he could hear the traffic now. And still the ominous roar of voices rose and fell over the Free City. The footsteps were behind him again. He looked back, not stopping this time. There was a man following him. As he turned his head the man's footsteps slowed. When he turned back towards the river there were headlights. A car had pulled into the narrow street in front of him. It was moving quite slowly. Then it stopped. The headlights went off. The doors opened and two men got out. They stood where they were, just waiting.

He had seconds to make a decision. The best bet seemed to be the man behind him. If he could get past him he had a chance. In the Granary Island's maze of alleyways he didn't have to know where he was going; he only had to get lost. He turned and ran. He could hear the two men from the car chasing him. Ahead he saw the third man waiting – a youth – barely out of his teens. The boy was terrified, but he stepped forward to block Stefan's way. Stefan flung out his hand to push him off. The youth threw himself across the street, bringing Stefan crashing down on to the cobbles on top of him. As he pulled himself up the boy clung to his coat, then to his leg, holding him back. Stefan kicked him away, but stronger arms held him from behind. He tried to hit out. He felt another arm round his throat. A hand holding a white cloth clamped itself over his face. He could hear the roaring voices on the night air. 'Back to Germany! Danzig, back to Germany!' There was the sweet, sharp smell of chloroform. And then he blacked out.

# 17. The Forest Opera

As Stefan Gillespie came to he was in complete darkness and the darkness was in motion. He was dizzy. He tried to move but he could push his legs only a few inches before they came up against some kind of wall. There was a smell of oil and leather and something sweet. The disorientation was clearing; he recognised the sweetness. It was chloroform, quite faint now, but enough to bring what had just happened into focus. He was in the boot of a car, doubled up and barely able to move, but not tied. He could make no sense of why he was there. If the Gestapo wanted to teach him a lesson, surely a few broken ribs would have done. This was something else. He didn't know the Nazis but he had grown up in a civil war. When they came for you, whichever side it was, they didn't need to take you away for a thrashing; they only took you away when they intended to kill you.

Occasionally he heard faint voices over the sound of the engine. Nothing he could make out, but he thought there were two of them in the car. He couldn't tell how long they'd been driving. The jolting was worse now. The car had to be off the road on some kind of track. His thoughts were all of Tom now. It couldn't end here. He had to do something. He reached out with his left hand. He could feel something on the floor. He stretched his fingers along it. It was a wrench or a tyre lever. He gripped it. When the boot opened he might have his opportunity. If he feigned unconsciousness they'd pull him out. There would be a moment, maybe the only one, to take them off guard and run. The car stopped. He heard dogs barking. The doors opened. The sound of feet. They were at the back of the car now. As the boot lifted he saw darkness and trees. That was good. If he could get into the trees he would have some chance at least. Torchlight shone down on to his face. He closed his eyes.

'He's still out.'

Someone else was approaching. Stefan was gathering his strength. As soon as he was upright he would have to use every bit of that strength.

'Wake him up.'

His hand tightened on the tyre lever. He was ready to hit out. But the touch on his face was unexpectedly gentle. There was a scent he recognised.

'Come on then sleepy head!'

He opened his eyes. In the torchlight, Hannah was smiling at him.

*

They were somewhere above the Free City, in the forests that climbed the hills overlooking Langfuhr and Oliva. There was a small clearing here, and an old hunting lodge. It was a single-storey building with some kennels and an enclosure of cast-iron railings at one side. Tiles had fallen from the roof; windows were broken; ivy crawled up the crumbling brickwork. But inside the lodge a fire burned in the grate and there was a basket of cut timber. Animal traps hung from the walls. There was an oak table in front of the fire. And there was a bottle of Machandel vodka on it. Hannah Rosen and Stefan Gillespie sat on a bench opposite one of the men who had pulled her off the street outside the Danziger Hof. An hour ago the same man had clamped a chloroform-soaked handkerchief over Stefan's face on the Speicherinsel. He was in his mid-twenties, thin, with fair, curling hair. He called himself Leon, here anyway. Two grey Weimaraner dogs stretched out in front of the fire.

The fact that Hugo Keller was in Danzig had surprised and shocked Hannah. She wanted explanations, but as Stefan gave them they only silenced her. She had achieved nothing. She had put her own life and the lives of others at risk, and she hadn't even got the truth out of Francis Byrne. She heard the words of the old man in the library again. He was right. She had almost delivered herself to the Gestapo, walking blindly into a situation she didn't understand, in a place she had no business to be. Stefan had been in a Gestapo cell because of her. He didn't tell her he was lucky he wasn't still there, but she knew it anyway. She thought about the boy he had brought with him to the synagogue in Adelaide Road, who talked about the tricycle in the window at Clery's. She had felt a lot in the last few days, anger, frustration, loneliness, shock, fear; now as she sat beside Stefan she felt sick inside. She needed to touch him, but she couldn't. She was glad he was there; she had wanted him there. But she was irritated by the number of people who had every right to make a list of her mistakes and throw it at her now.

Hugo Keller troubled Leon; the whole thing troubled him.

'So you bump into this Keller, in the police station in Weidengasse, where you've just been interrogated by the Gestapo, about Hannah. He's a man you arrested in Dublin last year, who was spirited out of Ireland by influential friends, including some Irish policemen and the Nazi Gauleiter, Adolf Mahr. You find out he's working for the Gestapo in Danzig now, and he's blackmailing this priest, Byrne, at the cathedral. Then the two of you go out for a drink together.' He looked at Stefan hard. 'Does that sound odd?'

'It wasn't easy to say no to a drink. He'd just lied about knowing me. If he'd told them who I was they'd have taken me straight back to the cell.'

'That's what doesn't fit. Why would he do that?'

'He's a frightened man, I know that. He's been brought to Danzig because of Father Byrne, because he's the one who's got a hold over him. I don't know why the priest is so significant, but that's what it's about.'

Leon was silent, thinking through what Stefan had told him. It was beginning to make some kind of sense.

'Generally everyone in Danzig's got a good idea who the informers are, but this man Keller's an outsider. I don't know him. I doubt anyone knows him. The priest isn't good news,' he reflected. 'Not at all. There's not much opposition left in our Free City. Socialists, communists, liberals, Catholics, Jews, we've all been battered into silence over the last few years. We've got an election now, but don't let that fool you. The Nazis have probably held a thousand election rallies this year. Compare that with a dozen from the opposition, and most of those were broken up by the brown shirts and the police. Tomorrow they'll be outside every polling station. They already know who's going to vote against them. And you'll need guts to do it. Some of the only guts left are in Oliva Cathedral. I'm a Jew, Herr Gillespie. I haven't got much to thank the Catholic Church for, but while Edward O'Rourke is bishop of Danzig there's someone still standing up to the Nazis here, someone they can't just knock down. People trust him.'

Stefan nodded. It explained the relationship between Byrne and Keller. 'Well, they might want to think twice about that with Father Byrne on the bishop's payroll.'

'Not all the opposition is out in the open,' said Leon. 'A list of everyone the bishop talks to would be worth a lot. Especially if the Nazis win this election big time. That's when the arrests will really start, on a scale we've never seen.'

Stefan remembered the sense of darkness he had felt earlier, knowing nothing about any of this. Keller was doing what he did best, but Stefan still felt there was something else, something more urgent than mere information. Hannah reached across and took his hand.

The two dogs suddenly leapt up, growling, and raced to the door. Leon stood and moved to the window. He could see nothing in the darkness, but the dogs had heard something. He pointed to another door, at the back of the room.

'If I say go, walk out that way, into the woods, and keep walking.'

He opened the front door. The Weimaraners disappeared into the night, barking furiously. Leon followed them outside. Over the noise of the dogs Stefan and Hannah heard an engine. Stefan got up and went to the window. He could see white headlights through the trees. A pickup emerged into the clearing. The dogs bounded towards it. Leon turned away and walked back inside.

'It's all right,' he smiled, relieved. 'We'll be going soon.'

He poured a glass of vodka and drank it.

'How long will it take?' asked Hannah.

'It depends which way he goes.'

A man Hannah knew as Johannes walked in, smiling, wearing a student's cap. He had been the driver of the car outside the Danziger Hof. He had been the other man in the car that brought Stefan to the hunting lodge. He was younger than Leon, barely in his twenties. Where Leon was tense and nervous, Johannes was cheerful and relaxed. Behind him was an older man, bearded, dressed in green loden. He had a pipe between his teeth that had gone out some time before. The Weimaraners pattered beside him, sniffing at the leather bag over his shoulder. He clicked his fingers at the dogs. They went back to the fire and curled up in front of it. Leon's expression had changed as the man walked in. It wasn't who he expected.

'Who's this, Johannes?'

The older man smiled, taking out a box of matches to relight his pipe.

'How's it going?'

'Peter's broken his leg,' explained Johannes. 'This is Karl. He's a friend of Peter's. It's fine. He knows the forests backwards.'

'I'm sorry, Karl.' Leon looked at him uneasily. 'I don't know you.'

The bearded man carried on lighting his pipe.

'He's the same price as Peter,' said Johannes with a shrug.

'It's not about the bloody price. We don't know him!'

'Peter sent him instead. He said Karl knows what he's doing.'

'It's not up to Peter to decide –'

'Look, it's no skin off my nose, son.' Karl drew on his pipe, grinning amiably. 'I had to come up and feed Peter's dogs anyway. I could do with the cash, but if you don't want a guide, that's your business. I've done it before. You wouldn't be the first ones I've helped get across into Poland.'

Leon still wasn't happy; he'd been backed into a corner.

'We've got to get them out, Leon,' said Johannes, shrugging.

'I know that.'

'Well, I'm here if you want me. I'll feed the dogs.' Karl whistled quietly to the Weimaraners and went outside. They trotted out after him.

'It's not a decision you should have made, Johannes.'

'We've always trusted Peter.'

'There are people you pay and people you trust.'

Stefan exchanged a look with Hannah.

'Is there a problem, Leon?' she asked.

'No. It's just not the way we do things. But we'll have to get on with it. It's too late to worry about it now. The sooner we go the better. Ten minutes, right? You two get some air. I've just got a few things to sort out.'

It was clear Leon wanted to speak to Johannes on his own. Stefan smiled, knowing there was a bollocking to be delivered. He glanced across at Hannah. She nodded. As they walked out into the night the forester was heading back in, filling his pipe. He stopped to relight it once again.

'Boys! You wouldn't think their mothers would let them out, would you?' He carried on into the lodge, whistling cheerfully to himself again.

They walked on in silence. Hannah held Stefan's hand.

'I still don't know how you got here.'

'Someone told your father what you were doing. He'd found out where you were. He came to see me, with Robert Briscoe. I assume you know him?'

'Yes. But how did my father –'

'Maybe you've got better friends than you know.'

'Probably,' she said very quietly.

'He wanted me to get you out of here before you did anything stupid.'

'Talking to Francis Byrne didn't feel like it was stupid.'

'Maybe it wouldn't have been if he'd been in the Isle of Man. I know what you've been doing for the last three months. At least I know who you've been doing it for. And I just thought you were growing oranges.'

'If they'd leave us alone to grow oranges I wouldn't be doing it.'

They were still walking, deeper into the trees, away from the lodge.

'I'm sorry, Stefan. I'm sorry you got involved –'

He shrugged. 'I know why you left Ireland the way you did anyway.'

'I had to go. And I think it was time to go.'

'What does that mean?'

'Because if I'd stayed any longer, I might not have wanted to.'

'Maybe it was worth a session with the Gestapo after all,' he smiled.

'What?'

'To hear you say that.'

'Do you think it didn't matter?'

'I didn't want to think that.'

For a moment they looked at each other. He took her in his arms and kissed her. All of a sudden he was very tired. He didn't want to talk any more; nor did she. There was a deep silence in the woods that surrounded them. As they kissed again they moved backward slightly and Stefan stumbled. Hannah laughed. He turned to look down at what he had stumbled over. It was the carcass of a dead Weimaraner. He saw the body of the other dog, closer to the clearing. He walked across to it, unconsciously silencing his footsteps. He didn't need to know what the danger was to feel it. Hannah was still staring down at the first dog, aware of the unidentified threat in the darkness too. Stefan crouched down. There was a pool of vomit by the second dog's mouth and there were several pieces of undigested meat.

'They've been poisoned,' he whispered.

'He just went out to feed them. How could –'

Stefan put his finger to her lips. She didn't understand, but suddenly he did. He stood perfectly still. His hand moved down to hold her arm. They waited. The silence seemed as deep as it had moments earlier when they were kissing. There was the sound of an owl some way off. Then another one, much closer, more urgent, and the noise of wings and branches as it took off, unseen, disturbed and irritated, into the night sky.

'We've got to tell them!' She hissed the words. She knew what he was listening for now. He shook his head. He sensed it might already be too late. There was a sound, a short snap; dead wood under a foot. Then something that could have been feet moving through leaves. He crept forward slowly, closer to the clearing where the lodge stood. There was movement. Out from the trees, into the moon-light, stepped three men in the brown uniform of the SA. Stefan and Hannah saw Karl emerge from the lodge, sucking on his pipe. He walked straight towards the three men. He carried on past them into the woods, as if he didn't see them. More stormtroopers were coming out from the dark

321

trees now. They seemed less worried about the noise as they started to fan out around the front of the lodge. Two of them were holding guns.

Hannah took a pistol from her pocket.

Stefan was surprised. He didn't know she was armed.

He shook his head, pushing the gun back into her coat. 'Too many!'

She hesitated. Her instincts were to help the two men in the lodge.

'Walk very slowly. As quietly as you can.'

For a moment she just stared, still looking towards the lodge. He pulled her away from the edge of the clearing, further into the trees. There was a shout, then a gunshot. More shouts. More gunshots from the direction of the lodge. A scream. Hannah stopped, looking back, too shocked to move.

'Keep going!'

As they walked, they heard more shots. Then the bullets stopped.

There was laughter now, outside the lodge. The light from several torches was sweeping around the clearing, into the forest. Stefan and Hannah were still not far away. They had to go carefully. They couldn't make a noise. An order barked out. 'Shut the fuck up, you bastards!' The stormtroopers were heading into the trees. The light of the torches went before them. 'There's two more somewhere!' The moon disappeared behind a cloud. Then Hannah tripped. The cry was barely anything; she stifled it in her throat. But it was still a sound. The torches swept round towards them. As she scrambled up, Stefan dragged her forward. It was too late for silence.

Now they were just running. The moon appeared and disappeared through cloud, giving enough light to see for a few seconds before it was gone, and they were plunging blindly into the undergrowth again, crashing through branches. They had no idea where they were going. They stumbled and tripped, pulling each other up as they ran. But each time the moon reappeared, and they saw a gap through the trees to aim for, their pursuers saw them, and the torches focused in. The Nazis had their own problems with the inconstant moon, blundering and falling as they spread out behind the fugitives. But they were enjoying the hunt. They followed with a mix of curses and laughter. Stefan and Hannah smashed their way through branches and bushes, over a stream, through a clearing, back into thick forest.

Somehow they kept together. There was more cloud and less moonlight suddenly, but their eyes had adjusted to the darkness. The torchlight was too far away to catch their backs now. They halted, gasping for breath. The trees were thicker and more regimented here. They were on the edge of a forestry plantation. A narrow path seemed to open up to the right. The stormtroopers were calling out to each other behind them. Then the voices were still. They were listening, listening for movement from their quarry.

Stefan and Hannah plunged into the narrow gully between the walls of trees. It was darker than ever, but the path meant they were making less noise. They ran faster. Suddenly the ground below their feet was no longer there. They were falling. It wasn't far, but in the split second before they hit the forest floor below, it was all they could do not to cry out. Somehow they didn't. The ground knocked the breath out of their bodies. For a minute they lay still. Stefan reached out and found Hannah, lying next to him. She sat up. They filled their lungs with air as quietly as they could. The stormtroopers were near again, still crashing noisily through the undergrowth, still cursing and laughing. Two voices were very close. 'Listen you arsehole!' 'I am fucking listening!' 'Hans, where are you?' 'Here!' There was another voice, further away. 'Where's here?' 'I can't hear the fuckers, can you?' 'They're somewhere. Flush the bastards out!' There was more crashing about, more cursing. But it was quieter now. The SA men were going the wrong way.

They didn't move. They waited in silence for what felt like a long time, till they could hear nothing, till they were sure their pursuers had gone.

'You all right, Hannah?'

'I think so.'

As they stood up the cloud broke. The moon shone through. They had fallen down a low bank on to a broader track. There were piles of felled timber. The road wound away in both directions. They heard a voice again. It seemed much further off, behind them. They had to go the other way.

They began to walk, saying nothing. They kept to one side of the track, close to the line of trees, ready at the slightest sound to disappear into them again. The moon was still coming and going, but the track was wide enough for them to see without light now. They had been walking for half an hour when the road divided. There was nothing to tell them which way to go; they had no idea where they were in the first place. There was nowhere they were trying to get, except away. Hannah shrugged. Stefan's guess was as good as hers. They took the left fork, for no good reason, and walked on for another mile. Then they heard something. They stopped. It was nothing that made them freeze with fear. There were no voices, at least not straight away. It was a deeper, richer sound, not identifiable but already strange. They moved on cautiously towards the noise. It was as they turned a sharp bend in the track, and it sloped rapidly and steeply downhill, that the sound took on real form. It was music. It was the sound of an orchestra in the night. The thick ranks of evergreens stopped. There was a fence and a gate. Beyond it the track wound through pale silver birches. The music was growing louder and clearer. There was a dim haze of light in the distance.

'What is it?

Stefan listened for a moment, and then he laughed.

'I'd say Wagner. Die Meistersinger von Nürnberg.'

'Whyever not?' Hannah was laughing too. It was the release of fear.

He took her hand again. Now they could hear voices, singing. The lights were brighter, just a few at first, where the track emerged on to a small, metalled road. The air was full of music, and as the road turned again and the trees thinned, they could see the raked seats of the Forest Theatre. Nothing felt safer than being where there were people, lots of people. They walked towards the theatre and stood watching, where the trees came right up to the auditorium. They could even see part of the stage, where Hans Sachs was singing to the citizens of Nuremberg about the glory of Germany.

Then Stefan looked behind him again. He could hear something other than the music. There were different lights now, headlights, coming out of the forest. Hannah felt his grip tighten on her hand. She followed his eyes. They recognised the vehicle as it pulled on to the road. It was the pickup that had brought Johannes and Karl to the hunting lodge. It stopped. Three SA men leapt down. As the truck drove on they recognised the bearded man who was driving it. The three stormtroopers were walking towards the auditorium. Ahead the truck had stopped again and more brown shirts jumped off. Hannah and Stefan could see the rifles they carried. They were trapped. If they stayed where they were they would be found; if they tried to run they would be seen. The only option was the auditorium itself. They looked at each other, taking in their clothes and their dishevelled hair. Hannah shrugged. They both knew that the only chance was the crowd of opera-goers. They brushed off what dirt they could and slipped quietly into the theatre. They sat at the end of the first row they could find with empty seats. The final words of Hans Sachs rang out. 'Ehrt eure deutschen Meister.' Pay homage to your German masters. 'Zerging' in Dunst das heil'ge röm'sche Reich, uns bliebe gleich die heil'ge deutsche Kunst!' If the Holy Roman Empire turns to dust, Holy German Art will still be ours!

With the last note of the opera the audience rose as one in an eruption of applause and cheering. Stefan and Hannah rose with them. Their applause was not for the perform-ance; it was for the fact that they were alive. But as the lights went up and they looked around they became all too aware just how many uniforms, Nazi uniforms, there were in the audience.

The applause was dying down. The orchestra started to play again. It wasn't anything they knew and they moved into the aisle as everyone else began to move, or almost everyone. The crowd was pressing too close for anyone to really notice their appearance. But scattered amongst the audience were a handful of people who didn't move. As Stefan and Hannah shuffled towards the exit an old man stood at the end of a row of seats, unmoving, blocking people's way, and singing. 'Kennst du die Stadt am Bernstein Strand.' The city on the amber strand. 'Umgrünt von ew'ger Wälder Band.' Where green, eternal forests stand. People pushed past him, muttering and swearing. But there were other voices now, and another song. A group of SA men had climbed on to the stage, singing the Horst Wessel Song. There was renewed applause. And now everyone had stopped; everyone was singing with them, drowning out the anthem of the Free City. The orchestra changed tunes. 'Zum letzten Mal wird Sturmalarm geblasen!' The final call to arms rings out! 'Zum Kampfe steh'n wir alle schon bereit!' We'll put our enemies to rout! 'Bald flattern Hitlerfahnned über alle Strassen.' Hitler's banners fill every town. 'Die Knechtschaft dauert nur noch kurze Zeit!' Our time of slavery is done! People were glaring at Stefan and Hannah, not because of their appearance, but because they were not singing. Hannah seemed grimly unfazed. Stefan looked at the man next to him and produced a smile that was as inane as he could manage. 'Sorry, we're Irish!' The man frowned, not quite hearing, and then laughed. Other people laughed and smiled, as if this explained everything. But as they moved out of the auditorium towards the exit there were Schutzpolizei and more SA men ahead of them. The foyer was still packed with people, chatting and laughing, gathering up coats and hats. It wouldn't be full for much longer. Soon the opera-goers would all be gone.

'They can't know what we look like, Stefan.'

'No, if we stick close to all the other people who look like they've just run through a forest at night to get here, we shouldn't have any problems.'

'The crowd's still all we've got.'

He nodded. It was. Then he heard two voices, just behind him. The words were English and the voices were unmistakably Irish.

'At least it's stirring stuff.' It was a man who spoke. He was middle-aged, balding, with sharp features and dark, thick brows. He sounded like someone who was trying to make the best of something he hadn't much enjoyed.

'I like my stirring stuff shorter and a bit less Wagner, Seán,' replied the woman with cheerful indifference. It was obvious she was his wife.

'And a bit more Mozart?' he laughed.

'It wasn't even a good production,' she continued. 'Wagner can be sung in registers other than loud. You really were over the top at the interval, darling. One of the best productions you've seen! Danzig's made you such a convincing liar. I'm never going to be able to believe a word you say again.'

'I'm unpopular enough here as it is, Elsie. If I can't enthuse about the bloody Forest Opera –'

'Why worry? Herr Greiser and Herr Forster both cut you dead.'

'Well be fair, darling, they did cut each other dead too,' the man continued. 'If the Senate President and the Nazi Gauleiter won't speak to each other except on instructions from Berlin, why should they bother with the poor old League of Nations High Commissioner? Besides, did you really want a conversation with them anyway, Elsie?'

'Certainly not. Gobshites the pair of them.'

'Now, now, no political opinions please. It's undiplomatic.'
She laughed as they moved forward towards the exit.

'Smile and say yes,' said Stefan, putting his arm through Hannah's.

'What?' She narrowly avoided bumping straight into the woman.

'Mr Lester? I'm Stefan Gillespie.' He stretched out his hand. Seán Lester looked slightly puzzled as he registered the dishevelled appearance of the stranger, and the fixed grin on the equally dishevelled woman's face.

'We're over here from Dublin. This is Miss Rosen, Hannah.'

Mrs Lester reached across and shook Stefan's hand, unfazed.

'I'm Elsie Lester. Shake the man's hand, darling.' She took Hannah's.

'Hannah Rosen.'

'Did you enjoy the opera?'

'We missed quite a lot of it.'

'That was very sensible of you.'

Lester had now shaken hands with Stefan; he still hadn't spoken.

'I'll give you a very short version, Mr Lester. Do you have a car?'

'Yes, I do.'

'We need a lift into Danzig very badly,' continued Stefan, 'avoiding the police officers and stormtroopers who may or may not be watching the exits. If they are, they're looking for us, for reasons I haven't got time to explain at the moment. We're both keen not to be arrested, that's the thing.'

'I'm not with you, Mr Gillespie. Have you done something wrong?'

'I don't think we've broken any laws.'

'Mr Gillespie, my position –'

'It's not easy to go into the details here, sir.' The crowd was thinning out noticeably now. 'Robert Briscoe said that if I – if we – did get into any tight spots – and I suppose we have done – you might be able to help.'

'He did, did he?'

'Oh, and how is Bob?' exclaimed Mrs Lester. 'It's ages since I've seen him. And do you know Lilly as well?' She looked at Hannah.

Stefan was lost, but Hannah was on board at last.

'I know Mrs Briscoe, of course. She's a friend of my mother's.'

'Wonderful! I did see her last time I was in Dublin –'

'Mr Gillespie,' interrupted Lester, 'if the police need to speak to you, the easiest things really would be just to talk to them and clear things up. I can't imagine you have anything to be concerned about – as Irish citizens –'

'Don't be so stuffy, Seán,' scolded Mrs Lester. She put her arm through Hannah's. 'We'd be delighted to give you a lift, why wouldn't we be? Perhaps you'll pop in for a drink, and possibly a bath.' The two women headed towards the exit. Seán Lester put on his hat.

'We'd better do as Elsie says then. Bob Briscoe's got a damned cheek. I haven't spoken to the man in years. Just smile and talk about Wagner.'

'I'm not really that well up on Wagner.'

'You're in good company here, I can assure you. The Party requires them to worship Wagner, not actually to like his music. I'm rather fond of the old bastard myself, but Elsie's great love is Mozart, especially the Magic Flute. Her view is that if the Magic Flute is the human spirit at its

330

most profound, masquerading as nonsense, the Ring Cycle is nonsense masquerading as something immensely profound. I'm not sure she hasn't got a point.'

They walked past the policemen and the stormtroopers, who looked at each other uncertainly. The High Commissioner's car was waiting. It flew the red pennant of the Free State. The chauffeur held open the door. As Stefan and Lester followed Hannah and Mrs Lester to the car, two Gestapo men were close behind. One of them moved forward. The other barked an order and the first one stopped abruptly. Seán Lester turned, waiting for Stefan to get into the car. He smiled amiably and raised his hat. 'A splendid evening, didn't you think?' He spoke in English. Stefan sat in the car. Lester got in next to him. The chauffeur closed the door. Then the car pulled away. There was nothing the Gestapo officers could do. Elsie Lester was laughing now.

'That was the highlight of the evening. I could murder a whiskey!'

# 18. Silberhütte

The house in Silberhütte, where the League of Nations High Commissioner and his family lived, looked like a French chateau, though in pursuing that ideal the architect had concentrated on size at the expense of charm. A year after moving in Elsie Lester still hadn't been into every room; she had eventually decided there must be more interesting things to do. The house was surrounded by its own small park, which was like a green moat keeping the city at bay. It was the only building in sight not swathed in swastikas. The police who stood at the gates were there because a lot of people in Danzig didn't like that. In the drawing room Seán Lester was pouring four whiskeys. Hannah Rosen and Stefan Gillespie, still grubby and dishevelled, sat by the fire with Elsie. The butler who had brought in the bottle and the glasses hovered and fussed behind the High Commissioner.

'That really is all. If it's a two-bottle session, I'll wake you up.'

The butler smiled patiently. He had heard the joke before. But he left.

'He wants to know who you are.' Lester handed round the drinks.

'I suppose we don't look like your usual run of visitors,' said Stefan.

'Oh no, it's not that, he wants to know who everyone is. He's a spy.'

Hannah and Stefan laughed.

'I'm entirely serious. He reports everything that happens to the SS.'

'Can't you get rid of him?'

'I could, but then I wouldn't have any control over what I let them know and what I keep to myself. I decided it was better to have a spy I could trust, if you see what I mean. If I was forever changing the staff I'd have no idea who was spying on me and who wasn't. This suits everyone.'

'He's quite a good butler as well.' Elsie held up her glass for a refill.

'He won't be listening at the door, but I think the less you tell me the better. I don't know what you're doing or whose nose you've got up, but the less compromised I am the easier it is to lend a hand. Ignorance is better than insight at times. You see we really are through the looking-glass here.'

'Now you've ruined a good story, Seán!'

'But at least they're safe, Elsie.'

Hannah started to cry, very softly. It was as much the release of tension as anything. She could have no doubt that if they'd been caught in the forest they would be dead. Elsie moved over and put her arm round her.

'I'm sorry. I don't mean to – the men who were killed –'

'I don't even know who they were,' said Stefan quietly. It had been his decision not to try to help Leon and Johannes. It was the right one, even though Hannah had a gun. That didn't make it easier. He drained his glass.

The High Commissioner got up. He took the bottle of whiskey and filled all the glasses again, a lot fuller than he had filled them the first time.

'Two men who were trying to help me,' said Hannah, 'the Nazis killed them. I think they'd have killed us too.' Her tears had stopped now, but her face was grey and drawn. It was hard for her not to feel that she was responsible for what had happened to Leon and Johannes at the lodge. Stefan was less sure. He hadn't been in Danzig long, yet he already had a sense of the risks people took, fighting the Nazis. Tonight hadn't been about Hannah or him. He couldn't sense any connection. They'd been in the wrong place at the wrong time. They would certainly have died in the forests above Danzig if the SA men had caught up with them, but Stefan still felt as if they were just part of someone else's mess that had to be cleaned up and tidied away.

'We were lucky,' Stefan said. There was nothing more to add.

The High Commissioner simply nodded. He knew how lucky.

'You'll both stay here tonight.' Elsie Lester got up. 'Right, now for that bath! And bring your drink, my dear. A whiskey and a hot tub won't solve everything, but by God it helps.' Hannah smiled, getting up too. She headed out, following Mrs Lester. The High Commissioner, still holding the bottle, reached out and topped up Stefan's glass. 'I think it might be a two-bottle job after all, Mr Gillespie.' Then he walked across the room to a desk. He picked up the telephone and dialled.

'I'm calling the police.'

Stefan was surprised and momentarily alarmed.

'You're not the first people to see a bunch of our finest Nazi thugs murdering the opposition, but it hasn't quite been accepted as government policy yet. You need to call their bluff sometimes. The police can't be after you for anything officially, which doesn't mean the police aren't involved in doing a lot of dirty work for the Nazis, because they damned well are.'

He spoke into the phone in halting German.

'I need to speak to Oberleutnant Lange. It's the High Commissioner.'

He turned back to Stefan. 'But there's enough daylight left to keep the dark at bay. At least till after the election. God only knows what will happen then. It could be that Elsie and I will be joining you on the next train out. And you really do need to get out. I'm sure you understand that. The fact that Miss Rosen is a Jew changes the way they think here now, even about foreigners. Quite apart from all the things I don't want you to tell me about.'

He spoke into the phone again, this time in English.

'Reinhold, how are you? I'm sorry it's so late, but I've got a pair of rather dim Irish citizens, friends of friends of Elsie's, you know the kind of thing. They've had some run-in with the police, a misunderstanding that's all. Elsie seems to think they're utterly beyond sorting it out themselves and they've got into a bit of a state about it all. If I can reassure them the Gestapo aren't out scouring the city for them, it would be splendid. Yes, I'm sure they've much better things to scour the city for. Hang on, I've got the details.' Lester pointed at the whiskey bottle. Stefan picked it up and walked across to fill his glass. The High Commissioner winked. 'They are Stefan Gillespie and Hannah Rosen. Staying at the Danziger Hof.' He laughed, sharing a joke. 'There may well be something improper going on. I've never heard that was any great obstacle to staying at the Danziger Hof before!'

*

The next morning Stefan and Hannah were late down to breakfast. The bedrooms they had been given were next to each other, but they had used only one. They had said very little; holding each other was enough. It wasn't an easy sleep for either of them, but it was rest. And they were safe.

When the High Commissioner had spoken to Oberleutnant Lange of the Free State Police the night before, the policeman could find no problem on the books relating to either Hannah Rosen or Stefan Gillespie. There had been some query about Fräulein Rosen's passport, but it all seemed to be in order, even if it wasn't the passport she arrived in the Free City with. None of which meant it wasn't time for Hannah and Stefan to leave Danzig.

They had seen no one except a maid and the butler. The noise of the city was faint through the windows looking out on to the garden, but it was insistent. The butler hovered as he had hovered the night before, reappearing with more eggs and bacon and coffee when no more was needed, and talking about the election. He carefully avoided any political opinions but he exuded a sense of excitement and self-satisfaction that was a political opinion in itself. It was the big election; today everything wrong would be put right.

The door opened and Seán Lester came in, followed by a tall man in a dark suit and clerical collar. The butler stiffened to attention. Stefan stood up. Hannah did the

336

same, not quite sure why she did. Lester scowled, irritated to see the butler hovering in the room, as ever, watching them.

'You can leave all that.'

The butler picked up a plate of fried eggs and left, with a resentful scowl. The High Commissioner waited until the door had shut firmly behind him before he spoke. He was concerned and agitated this morning.

'This is Count Edward O'Rourke, our bishop.'

The bishop nodded, not agitated, but as grim-faced as Lester. Stefan regarded the two men, remembering what he knew about Danzig now. They seemed an unlikely bulwark against Adolf Hitler. Seán Lester looked like a bank manager in a small Irish town; Edward O'Rourke looked like the town's parish priest, round faced, with a house-keeper who fed him too well.

'It's a mess, a very unpleasant one.' Lester shook his head. 'From the sound of it I don't suppose it's really your mess, Gillespie, but it seems to come on your coat-tails. The priest Miss Rosen was here to talk to, Father –'

The High Commissioner stopped, looking at O'Rourke.

'Father Byrne is dead.' The bishop's voice was oddly matter-of-fact. 'The police pulled his body out of the Mottlau River early this morning. He is in the mortuary. The cause of death was drowning apparently. The police inspector at Weidengasse hasn't said as much but the question of suicide is hanging in the air. That's the implication anyway. I'm not sure I can rule it out, either, not after the conversation I had with Father Byrne yesterday.'

He looked from Hannah to Stefan. Neither of them was sure whether it was a look of compassion or accusation. After several seconds his gaze returned to Hannah.

'I know the details of his relationship with your friend, Miss Field. I knew nothing about it before yesterday. There were a lot of things I didn't know about.' He was silent for a moment. He wasn't thinking about Francis Byrne and Susan Field, but Francis Byrne and Hugo Keller. He shook his head. 'I don't know how much longer Francis could have held it all in, but your appearance started to break down the wall. And Mr Gillespie's arrival a little later,' he turned to Stefan, 'well, you are a policeman, aren't you? I imagine your approach was harder. You also knew more about him, more about what happened to Miss Field. Perhaps more than he could cope with.'

Stefan felt Hannah's eyes on him, questioning, as O'Rourke spoke. He hadn't told her what he knew about how Susan had died yet. He hadn't had time. And he needed the right time too. But all she saw was that he had still been holding something back, even now, even here, after everything else.

'The relationship between your friend and Francis belongs to them alone now I think, Miss Rosen, except to say that you should not underestimate the feelings he had for her, or what he suffered because of the weakness he showed in abandoning her. It was weak; it was selfish. His death doesn't alter that. The fact that she died in the way she did was cruel enough; the idea that she had been killed, murdered – that was more than he could face.'

There was no reason for either Hannah or Stefan to feel much for Francis Byrne. Stefan knew enough to believe he had it coming. Hannah still knew less, but knew that if the priest wasn't responsible for Susan's death himself his lies had protected whoever was, whether inadvertently or not. Yet as they listened to O'Rourke's quiet voice it didn't seem that neat.

'How long had he been an informer?' said Lester.

'Long enough,' replied the bishop. He looked at Stefan again. 'How this man Keller found him here, I don't know. But I do know the Nazis and their obsession with gathering information. From Dublin to Danzig isn't so surprising. And once he'd found Francis he knew what to do with all the weakness and selfishness, the fear and guilt. He threatened to expose him and destroy him. Sadly Francis didn't have the faith in me he should have done. Perhaps that was my fault. I was too concerned with great events to see a man in need before my eyes. He was Keller's spy. I'm sure you have worked that out yourself. There are people who have trusted me, confided in me, whose names will be in the hands of the Gestapo and the SS.'

He was silent, knowing all too well what that could mean.

'You see I can't stand in the pulpit and tell people not to vote for the bastards, even if everyone knows that's what I think. They'd want me sacked and the Church would sack me. It's too busy making sure it's not on the wrong side to make sure it's on the right side. I think of Martin Luther a lot these days. Simply to stand here is perhaps all I can do. Father Byrne was a victim of his own weakness, but he was also a victim of the darkness that's all around us now. Yet he found his way back at the end. You may not think that matters, but I'm a priest. I see it differently. Perhaps he wouldn't have found his way without you two. Angels come in many guises, we're told.'

As he finished he was looking at Hannah again, and she had no doubt that what she saw now was compassion. He stepped forward, taking out a letter.

'This was in his room, Miss Rosen. He meant to send it to you. It's addressed to your hotel.' He turned back to Stefan. 'I think Father Byrne went to see this man Keller. I imagine to tell him he would no longer be blackmailed. I want to know what happened. It may be that he drowned. It may be that he killed himself. If it was something else, then I probably won't be able to do anything anyway. Earthly justice won't be on offer. But I have another angel to serve, the recording angel. Since there isn't a policeman I can trust, your opinion will have to do instead. Will you look at the body?'

*

The River Vistula rises in the Carpathian Mountains, over a thousand kilometres south of the Free City. It flows through the plains of Poland, past Kraków and Warsaw, and eventually issues into the Bay of Danzig and the Baltic Sea through a delta of sluggish channels and lagoons. For almost a thousand years it has been the great artery of Poland in every sense. When Poland disappeared from the map of Europe, as it did from time to time, for Poles their country was somehow still alive in the great river. In Danzig the Vistula was the Weichsel. The city ended where a branch of the Vistula, the Mottlau River, flowed out of the port and into the silted and moribund channel that was called the Dead Vistula, Die Tote Weichsel. It was here, by the seaplane station on the shore of the Dead Vistula, that the morning flight from Stockholm so narrowly missed the floating body of Father Francis Byrne. A priest who rediscovers his religion can be dangerous, not least to himself.

The body was not at the mortuary. When the bishop phoned the police station in Weidengasse, close to where Father Byrne had been found, he was told it had already been moved. Now the bishop's car drove Stefan Gillespie and Count O'Rourke out through the gates of the High Commissioner's residence on to Silberhütte, into Holzmarkt and Kohlenmarkt. Outside a polling station, a gang of brown-shirted SA men stood, almost blocking the entrance, checking the people going in to vote. The car continued past the Danziger Hof and into An der Reitbahn. It was only now, as he passed the building with the great dome and the Russian-looking spires, that Stefan realised it was the city's synagogue, sitting with unintended defiance at the heart of Danzig. It wasn't mentioned in the guide book he had looked through that first night at the hotel; it wasn't even on the map. In front of the synagogue a group of boys in Hitler Youth uniforms held up election placards and flags. Several of them were stretching out a banner. It became legible as the bishop's car passed. 'Die Juden sind unser Unglück.' The Jews are our misfortune. O'Rourke didn't notice. He'd seen it too many times. In Vorstädtischer Graben they passed another polling station and another SA gang noting the names of the voters. It was unlikely very many of Danzig's Jews would be pushing their way past the brown shirts to cast their votes.

As Stefan looked out at the city, Edward O'Rourke seemed to be doing the same thing, but his eyes didn't see very much. He was weighing the consequences of what had happened. Then, quite abruptly, as they crossed the river, he started to talk about Francis Byrne. He didn't look round. Stefan wasn't really sure the words were addressed to him at all.

'I met Francis at the Eucharistic Congress in Dublin. They assigned him to me as a guide. He had good German and an interest in genealogy. My family fled Ireland after the battle of the Boyne. They ended up in Russia, fighting for the czars. It was the family business. My father intended me for a general but the way things have turned out in Russia I probably made a wise decision to turn my hand to something else. Francis ended up spending more time arguing about the future of the Church than looking into my family tree. We disagreed about a lot but he was very bright. I liked him. When I left, I offered him a job, if he ever wanted one. I didn't hear from him for nearly three years, and then unexpectedly he appeared in Danzig. He wasn't the same man though. Somehow all his vitality had gone; along with all his curiosity, all his passion. But I didn't see how troubled he was. There is a high price to pay for that now. It was only when he came to me yesterday . . .'

O'Rourke stopped as suddenly as he had started, and he said no more. They drove across the river on to the Speicherinsel. In Milchkannengasse they pulled up outside Grund & Co, funeral directors.

A considerable amount of the undertaker's art had already been expended on Father Francis Byrne. His face was an unnatural, almost clownish pink. His hair had been oiled and combed back in such neat, stiff lines that it looked like a wig. He was wearing a dark suit and clerical collar that had certainly not accompanied him into the dark waters of the Mottlau. The coffin he lay in was lined with white silk, which only accentuated the pinkness of his flesh. He looked like a mannequin from the windows of Freymann's department store. Herr Grund scurried behind the bishop with a combination of fawning obsequiousness and ill-disguised fear. It was a privilege to have such an eminent personage on his premises, but the corpse had been brought by the Gestapo. O'Rourke bent over the body of the priest. He made the sign of the cross on his forehead and prayed silently. As he straightened up he turned to the undertaker. 'Leave us alone, please.' The words were said quietly and graciously. The undertaker hesitated. The bishop's stern eyes said what his words had not. 'Now piss off.' The undertaker bowed, walking deferentially backwards before leaving the room.

'Well?'

'Apart from the fact that he's made-up like a –' Stefan stopped.

'Like a madam in a whorehouse.' O'Rourke took a handkerchief from his pocket and applied it firmly to Byrne's face, wiping away the pink cream that had been spread and plastered into the skin. Stefan had seen policemen more squeamish with the dead. As he scraped around the eyes the skin was dark and bruised underneath. There were cuts on the cheeks as well. He pulled the upper lip away. There were black gaps where teeth had been.

'Look under his shirt.'

Stefan unbuttoned the jacket. He pulled away the shirt and collar. There were more bruises, cuts, weals. He pressed down on to the rib cage.

'Broken ribs.'

They looked round as someone entered the room. There was a click of heels. Stefan immediately recognised his Gestapo interrogator, Klaus Rothe.

'Kriminaloberassistent Rothe, Your Excellency.'

He stepped forward, holding out a report. As the bishop eyed him carefully the Gestapo officer looked sideways at Stefan, frowning. He was the last person he could have expected to find with the Bishop of Danzig.

'The Kriminalkommissar extends his sympathies.'

'And this is?'

'The report into the accident, Your Excellency.'

'I understand Father Byrne drowned.'

'Correct.'

'There was no crime then?'

'Correct.'

'So why is the Gestapo involved?'

It was hard for Rothe to suppress a smile as he gave what he felt was a very neat reply. 'We take the death of a priest seriously, Your Excellency.'

'And before he drowned, what do you think happened?'

'Impossible to say, Your Excellency. There were no witnesses.'

'I'm sure. And you are certain about drowning?'

'Unfortunately, yes. There was a full medical examination.'

'Take a look, Kriminaloberassistent.' The bishop moved away from the coffin and gestured for the Gestapo man to step forward. He didn't. 'No other theories? He couldn't have beaten himself to death by any chance?'

'I'm afraid I don't understand, Your Excellency.'

'I'm sure you understand perfectly.' Edward O'Rourke turned back to the coffin. He made the sign of the cross. As he left the room he screwed up the report he had just been given by Rothe and dropped it on the floor.

The Gestapo man was staring at Stefan again, about to speak.

'I'm with him.' Stefan followed the bishop out into the corridor.

*

'Why didn't you tell me?' Hannah had been waiting for Stefan in his room. 'You knew about the pistol in December.'

344

'I didn't tell you because it was evidence we were holding back. You don't throw these things around. It was part of another investigation as well. There were two bodies. The captive bolt pistol was the only thing Susan and Vincent Walsh had in common. I needed to know what that meant first.'

'It meant she didn't die, she was murdered. You knew that and you didn't say it.' She threw the letter from Father Byrne on the bed. 'It didn't take him long to work it out. It was a gun. It doesn't matter what kind of gun, so somebody shot her. Was it Keller? Why would Keller shoot her?'

'No. It wasn't him.'

She looked at Stefan, shaking her head.

'But you know who it was. You know and you haven't told me!'

'I think I know.'

'Isn't that enough!'

'It's not enough to prove anything. It's a lot less now Francis Byrne's dead.'

'Who did it?' She wanted the truth now. He would have to tell her.

'It was a guard.'

First she was surprised; then there was a question. He could see it.

'It's not why I didn't tell you. It was only when I talked to Byrne —'

'Who is he?' She wasn't going to listen to any more evasion.

'You've met him. He took you to the convent. Sergeant Lynch.'

She stopped, remembering the December day she went to Merrion Square to see Hugo Keller; the interview room at Pearse Street; Mother Eustacia; DS Lynch. It felt a long time ago.

'Did Father Byrne know that?'

'He knew the man driving the car was a guard, that's all. When the guard told him Susan was dead he believed it. And he ran. He left Jimmy to deal with the body. He was a guard, wasn't he? It could have been true. Maybe she was dead. If she wasn't, he shot her in the head to make sure –'

'He killed her. Like an animal!'

'Yes.'

'Why?'

'He worked for Keller. When there was a mess, he cleaned it up.'

'So it was Hugo Keller who told him to do it?'

'He could have done. I don't know. '

'I think you *need* to know, Detective Sergeant Gillespie,' Hannah said, her voice trembling. 'And so do I. If you won't find out, I shall.'

She walked across the room and picked up her coat.

'You know where he is, Stefan, don't you?'

'It's not that simple,' he said.

'Why not?'

'Francis Byrne was going to have it all out with Hugo Keller. I don't know whether he got there or not, Hannah, but I've seen what they did to him. Keller's got a lot more police pals here than he had in Dublin, not to mention the SS. It's not just one Special Branch man taking kickbacks. Every Gestapo officer in Danzig is Jimmy Lynch with bells on. And they don't do it for the money, they do it all for love. Keller's too dangerous.'

She was standing by the door, pulling on her coat.

'Recording angels have been in my family a long time.'

He knew he wouldn't stop her. She'd find where Hugo Keller was, one way or another.

'All right, we'll go. But I'll take the gun.' He held out his hand.

Stefan and Hannah got off the tram by the railway station in Langfuhr. There were new street signs as they crossed the main road, the recently renamed Adolf-Hitler-Strasse. They turned into Eschenweg. That was the address Francis Byrne had given Stefan. It was quieter here. Small apartment blocks lined the suburban street at first, with the ever-present swastikas hanging from almost every window. At the far end of the street there were several bigger, older houses with red-tiled roofs and tidy gardens. The last house, on the corner with Mirchauer Weg, was a lot less tidy. Trees and uncut bushes screened it from the road. There was no gate; it lay among the weeds that sprawled across the garden, rotting where it had been thrown a long time ago. The house reflected the garden. The paintwork was peeling; a length of gutter had come away from a wall and hung down almost to the ground; the broken shards of roof tiles crunched underfoot as Stefan and Hannah walked up the steps to the front door. Even from the outside it reminded Stefan of the empty, dilapidated rooms upstairs at Keller's house in Merrion Square. He stood at the top of the steps, still unhappy about what they were doing.

The door was slightly ajar. Hannah stepped past him and pressed the bell. It rang loudly. There was no movement inside the house. They waited. She pressed the bell again. There was still no response. Stefan pushed open the door and walked in. Hannah followed him. There was no carpet; the floor was thick with dust. But on a table there was a new telephone. Next to it was stacked a neat pile of unopened letters. He stopped by the table, looking through the letters. One of them had a Saorstat Éireann stamp on it. He put it in his pocket, unseen by Hannah who was continuing along the hallway.

There were two large rooms on either side. One was furnished with a sofa, an armchair and an unmade bed; the other was empty. Stefan was behind Hannah again as they passed the stairs and entered the kitchen. They didn't see the broken furniture or the smashed crockery or the blood on the blue and white delft tiles of the big stove in the corner. They only saw the figure of the man stretched out on the floor. His hands and feet were tightly bound. He was almost naked. His bruised, wealed body was black with congealing blood. It was the right address. They had found Hugo Keller.

# 19. The Westerplatte

He wasn't dead. Stefan found a knife on the kitchen floor and cut away the ropes. They sat him against the wall. He opened his eyes and looked at them, as if coming out of a deep sleep that he didn't want to leave. He was struggling to find the place and the time he had been brought back to.

'I know you.' He was looking at Stefan. He turned to Hannah. He was sure he knew her too, but he couldn't quite remember. He coughed. His face contorted. He had found where he was now and it was a place of pain.

'They've gone?' he asked.

'Yes.'

He looked at Hannah again; he remembered her now. 'The priest told me you were here.' There was a smile on his lips for a second. 'It wouldn't have been so bad, would it, an Irish gaol? Well, better than this, eh?'

'We'll get an ambulance.' Stefan glanced at Hannah. She nodded.

'It's too late.' Keller's eyes seemed clearer. 'It's Hannah, yes?'

'We can worry about that later. Stefan can phone –'

'I'm enough of a doctor to know, my dear.' He coughed

again and a spasm of pain rocked his body. Blood trickled from his mouth. 'They've done enough. They killed Father Byrne. It was my fault. I was the one they didn't trust. I'd found out. They knew I'd found out. He didn't even know what they were going to do. He didn't know anything.'

'I'll phone now,' said Stefan getting up.

'No!' Somewhere Hugo Keller found the strength to bark it out like an order. 'There's no point. I know. Do you think they'd send a doctor anyway?' He clutched at Hannah's coat. 'He didn't even know. The priest didn't know what they really wanted! Neither did I. I'd only just found out why he was so important. It wasn't only information. He was a way in. That's why he mattered so much.' There was unexpected determination in his voice. But then he stopped, his head dropping, his breath slowing. He struggled to look up at Stefan. 'When he's dead they're going to blame the Jews. That's what it's for.' He closed his eyes. Now the place he was in seemed to be fading. 'I didn't want to know. I wanted to find a way home. I just wanted a way back to Ireland!'

'What are you talking about?' asked Hannah.

Keller stared, as if he had forgotten who she was again. 'Blame the Jews for what?'

'They're going to kill him,' whispered the Austrian.

Hannah looked at him blankly. 'Kill who?'

'Count O'Rourke.' Hugo Keller grimaced in pain, choking out the words. 'They're going to kill the bishop. If the election doesn't go the way –' His eyelids drooped shut. There was a rasping in his chest. Phlegm and blood oozed from his mouth. His eyes half-opened again. He was still looking at Hannah, but the present was slipping away. 'Your friend shouldn't have died. There was time. I told the guard to take her to the hospital! But he didn't. I thought

350

she'd just died. I didn't know. I didn't know he'd killed her. I don't know why. He was working for the priest.'

Stefan and Hannah stared at him; this contradicted everything.

'But Father Byrne didn't know anything, he didn't know she was dead,' said Stefan. Could the priest have fooled him that much?

Even in Keller's pain there was irritation.

'Not the flunky, you gobshite! The monsignor.'

The words meant nothing to Hannah. Stefan understood though.

'What monsignor?' said Hannah.

Hugo Keller seemed to be staring straight ahead, straight into her eyes, but he didn't see her.

'Who are you talking about?' Hannah was almost shouting.

'He's dead, Hannah,' said Stefan, taking her arm.

She moved back a little, still gazing down at Hugo Keller.

'What did he mean, Stefan?'

'We need to go.' He pulled her up.

'I don't understand who was he talking about.'

'It can wait. I'll explain. We're not safe here.'

As they turned round, two men were standing in the doorway, watching them. The first was Kriminaloberassistent Klaus Rothe. The other was the bearded man who had come to feed the dogs at the hunting lodge above Oliva. Rothe was surprised, but not so surprised that the long barrel of a Mauser machine pistol wasn't already pointing at Stefan and Hannah.

'We came to clear up one pile of shit and now we've got three.' He walked forward. 'That's your Jewess then. You're right, she's worth a fuck. If I had more time I might try her out first. But we've got an election to win.'

'She's the one from the lodge,' said the man they knew as Karl.

'Now you know why Jews have big noses. They stick them in where they're not wanted. But then Jews aren't wanted anywhere, are they?'

Stefan stood very still. There weren't many options he could see.

'We've got no idea what went on here. We don't care. This is about something that happened in Ireland, that's all. We were too late anyway. He was already dead.'

'It looks to me like you killed him, Herr Gillespie.'

The Gestapo man was pleased. It made the mess easier to clean up. He had Hugo Keller's murderers in front of him. He only had to shoot them and the job was done. Stefan didn't have to fill in the gaps to be able to read that thought. Talking wasn't going to get them out of this, but talking could buy them seconds.

'All we want to do is leave Danzig.'

'I'm sure. Unfortunately, you'll be shot while resisting arrest.'

Stefan glanced at Hannah. Her face was almost expressionless, but the tension in her body was enough to tell him that she wouldn't stand there and be shot. They didn't have much of a chance, but Hannah was ready to move. He nodded, hoping it was a signal she would understand. He was ready too.

'You don't need to do this, Kriminaloberassistent,' he pleaded.

'No, but it suits me to do it. And apart from anything else, you pissed me off, Irishman, in Weidengasse, in the mortuary.' He stepped closer.

The big pine table that stood in the middle of the kitchen

was between Stefan and Rothe. Stefan put his hands on the end of the table, leaning down and shaking his head, with an expression that made him seem utterly defeated.

'I'm sorry, Hannah.' He looked up. 'There's nothing we can do. Nuair a bhrúim an tábla, ionsaigh an ceann eile.' He spoke to her in Irish.

She smiled sadly and shrugged. 'Tá mé réidh.'

'Words of fond farewell, that's nice,' said Rothe, smiling.

All at once Stefan pushed the table forward, with every bit of force he could find, driving it across the floor into the Gestapo man's legs. It was a heavy table and it hit Klaus Rothe hard. It was still moving as he fell under it. At the same moment Hannah rushed forward and flung herself on top of Karl, knocking him to the ground. Rothe rolled out from under the table and leapt to his feet very fast. He was still holding the Mauser and he was grinning. It was a good try. He didn't expect the pistol in Stefan's hand, Hannah's PKK. His surprise didn't last any longer than it took Stefan to fire.

The Kriminaloberassistent was dead. In the doorway Hannah and Karl were still struggling. The bearded man lashed out and pushed her away. He scrambled to his feet and ran. Stefan hadn't moved. He still had the PKK pointed at Rothe. Hannah got up and stepped over the body. 'He's dead. The other one isn't!' Stefan didn't understand for a moment. It didn't seem to matter. They were alive. She grabbed the pistol and raced to the door. 'What are you doing?' He ran after her into the hall. There was the sound of a car.

As Hannah reached the steps the black Mercedes was already heading down the drive, picking up speed. Stefan was there beside her now. 'You won't stop him.' She stood quite still, holding the PKK in both her hands. The car was at the gate when she fired a single shot. The Mercedes carried on, straight on, out into the middle of Eschenweg, not turning to the right or the left. Then it halted; the man slumped over the wheel was dead too.

Stefan stared at Hannah. It was a shot he could never have made.

'You've done that before.'

'It was never a human being, just a target.' She was still staring at the car. Then she turned, handing the PKK back to him, as if she didn't want to touch it now.

'What do we do, Stefan?'

'We find anything that moves that's leaving Danzig. If we needed to get out before, I'd say we've more than over-stayed our welcome now.'

'And Bishop O'Rourke?'

'There is that,' he smiled wryly. They were in this now, whether they wanted to be or not. They couldn't just walk away with what they knew.

'We can't let it happen, can we?'

He shook his head. 'No, we can't. Keller's got a phone.'

'The phones aren't safe, Stefan, none of them are.'

They needed to act. Stefan's mind was racing.

'Seán Lester's the only one who can stop this.'

Hannah took his hand, pulling him down the steps.

'I'll go to the cathedral. You go to the High Commission.'

They ran down the steps and back out into Eschenweg, past the Mercedes in the middle of the road and the dead man slumped over the wheel, past the houses with red roofs and tidy gardens, past the apartment blocks where the swastikas hung from the windows, into Adolf-Hitler-Strasse. Hannah went one way and took the tram to Oliva;

354

Stefan took the tram the other way, back into the city. There wasn't really any choice.

*

At the mouth of the Tote Weichsel, where the river dissolved into the Baltic, there was a narrow spit of sand that became thinner and thinner until it disappeared into the sea itself. This was the Westerplatte. In high summer the beaches here were far less crowded than Zoppot's. Here, scattered among the trees, were the concrete bunkers that represented Poland's only military presence in Danzig. A hundred soldiers sat there for no very good reason, except that they could. When the League of Nations established the Free City it was a tiny concession to mollify Polish anger that the city they still claimed as part of Poland wasn't Polish. The League saw the Polish flag flying over this windswept spit of sand as a gesture so modest as to be unimportant. The Poles saw the flag over the Westerplatte as proof that one day the city they called Gdańsk would be Polish, whatever language was spoken in its streets. For the Germans of Danzig it had been an irrelevance to some and an irritation to others; an itch rather than a sore. But as the years went on and Hitler's voice grew shriller in the city, the Polish fort and the Polish flag that flew over the Westerplatte had become an insult. It was a sore now. And if it could sometimes be ignored it could never be forgotten.

Stefan Gillespie sat in Seán Lester's car, looking out at the Baltic. Behind them, among the trees, was the red and white Polish flag. On a day like this the Westerplatte was a wild place. The beaches were empty and there was only the low hum of the wind off the sea. They were a long way from the streets swathed in swastikas and the trucks of stormtroopers cheering for a democratic end to democracy. The High Commissioner had driven the car himself. He had no reason to believe his chauffeur was a spy but trust wasn't something that could be taken for granted in the Free City any more. And here, today at least, there would be nobody to see them.

They had been silent for a while now. Lester was trying to make sense of what Stefan had told him. Some of it made no sense at all, but then he had only fragments of information. Where it did make sense it frightened him.

Another car drove towards them. The High Commissioner watched it approaching, still thoughtful. He got out of his own car and Stefan followed. The constant hum of the wind was louder. As the second car pulled up Stefan could see that the driver wore the uniform of the Schutzpolizei.

'Oberleutnant Lange is the nearest thing to a policeman I can trust.'

'You don't sound very sure,' said Stefan.

'Trust can be bought and sold like everything else. Diplomacy isn't really geared up for this. I remember some advice given to me by a British diplomat before I left Geneva: When deciding what to wear in the morning, bear in mind the day may bring unforeseen demands. Women should always keep a hat and gloves in the office for emergencies and men should keep a black tie in the desk for unexpected mourning. I don't keep one in mine. Reinhold Lange is my best chance of not having to go home to get one.'

Oberleutnant Lange got out of his car and walked towards Stefan and the High Commissioner. Seán Lester shook the policeman's hand warmly.

'This is Herr Gillespie. I spoke to you about him before.'

'You're the detective sergeant?'

'Yes, sir.'

'And you're here on some kind of holiday?'

'Not exactly a holiday.'

'I can see Irish understatement puts even English under-statement into the shade,' said Lange. He looked at Lester. 'Do you know if the bishop is all right?'

'He's been told anyway. Fräulein Rosen went straight to the cathedral. And I have spoken to him now as well. The question is, who's going to protect him?'

'The Langfuhr police have picked up the car and the dead driver. Not easy to miss really. The car was in the middle of the road. They also found the two men inside the house, Kriminaloberassistent Rothe and Herr Keller. But the investigation has been officially handed over to the Gestapo now. So there is a solid wall up around it, which tells its own story of course. I can't get any more information.'

'Are they looking for Herr Gillespie and Fräulein Rosen?'

'I don't know that either. But I'd say probably not. They don't know who else was at Keller's house. There may be some descriptions, but that's going to take time. I think we can work on the assumption that it just looks like a Gestapo operation that went wrong. What is clear is that this man Keller was working for the Gestapo and the SS. That's all I have. I think you know that already, Herr Gillespie?' Stefan nodded. Lange continued. 'That's why they've shut it down as far as the Schutzpolizei are concerned. It's political. But nothing seems to be happening, which is odd when there's a dead Gestapo man. However, maybe not so odd if there's something more important to cover up. I do take this threat against the bishop seriously.'

'You do know something then?' asked Lester.

'Last night there were some SA men up in the forests above Oliva.'

Stefan and Lester exchanged glances. It wasn't news to them.

'Yes, I think you know something about that too, Sergeant. This is just rumour as far as I'm concerned. It's the kind of information I'm not allowed to do anything with these days. It's political,' he smiled. 'No crime has been reported and no bodies have been found, but I think two men were killed. What's going around is that they were killed for a reason. I mean other than the usual reason, that the Nazis didn't much like their opinions.'

'And there's a connection to Bishop O'Rourke?' said Lester.

'Scapegoats,' replied the policeman. 'It's a well-established Nazi trick in Germany. You shoot someone you don't like, say a businessman who doesn't want to pay his dues to the Party, then you dump the body of someone else you don't like at the scene of the crime, say a communist or a socialist, and announce he was the killer, shot while trying to escape. You've not only got your murderer, you can arrest all his friends as well. Anyway the rumour is that the two men who were shot in the forest are going to reappear and assassinate someone. The rumour doesn't say who's going to be killed but it seems to tie in with what Keller told you, Herr Gillespie. I don't suppose it's a coincidence that a priest who apparently committed suicide yesterday was one of Herr Keller's informants. Is that correct?'

'It's not correct that he committed suicide,' answered Stefan.

'I use the term loosely. We get a lot of suicide in Danzig these days.'

Seán Lester was frowning. The gaps were filling in.

'Why now? The elections are almost over. If Edward O'Rourke –'

'You've been here too long, High Commissioner. You're starting to believe what the Nazis tell you. They're not so sure they're going to win this election. Oh, they'll keep their majority and we'll still have that arsehole Greiser as our president, but they may not get the numbers to change the constitution and kick the League of Nations out. And if that happens, whatever Greiser and Gauleiter Forster and the rest of them say, they're going to lose a lot of face. They've promised Hitler a Danzig without you, without opposition parties, without elections, and with the Jews stripped of everything they own, including any rights they've got left under the constitution. If they can't deliver all that, a dead bishop might solve the problem for them.'

'The only people who could want Edward O'Rourke dead are the Nazis.'

'I don't know who exactly the scapegoats are,' continued Lange, 'socialists, communists, Zionists. It doesn't much matter as long as they're Jewish. Who cares if the last person in Danzig they'd want to see dead is Bishop O'Rourke? They'll be guilty. And the Nazis will be right. They'll have a Communist-Jewish conspiracy. So when they turn on the Jews, and whatever's left of the opposition, they'll be doing it to protect not just German Danzig but Catholic Danzig too. There'll be blood on the streets and the police, God help us, will lead the charge. The only option left to you and the League would be to bring in Polish troops to restore order. But Hitler won't accept that, so he'll have to take over Danzig. The Poles will either put up with it or face a war with Germany in which they are the aggressors.'

Seán Lester said nothing. Now it all made sense. And the sense it made was far more frightening than the death of a man he regarded as a friend.

'I'd say this is the SS. Not from the top, but it's got SS all over it,' said Lange.

'Is it coming from Berlin?' asked the High Commissioner.

'Not necessarily. They need to force Hitler's hand. I don't know, but I wouldn't think it's what he wants right now. But if the Free City collapses into chaos, he'll have to do it anyway. He'd look too weak if he didn't.'

'Will the police protect the bishop, Reinhold?'

'They'll do what they're told. It all depends who's giving the orders.'

The High Commissioner said nothing. He gazed across the Westerplatte towards the Baltic Sea. He turned back. His voice was lighter all of a sudden. He looked from Stefan Gillespie to Oberleutnant Lange, but his whimsical words didn't disguise how seriously he took this, and how much it mattered.

'My mother always used to say that the best way to deal with something unpleasant is to open all the windows and let God's clean air in. She had a habit of doing it on the coldest days, and the threat of that had a powerful effect on family rows when I was young, at least in the winter.'

Neither Stefan nor Oberleutnant Lange understood.

Lester looked out to sea again. 'There's quite a breeze today.'

*

Behind the great oak desk of the Senatspräsident there was a small plaque that bore the arms of the Free City, the crown and the two white crosses. Above it a swastika flag stretched almost to the ceiling. Next to it was a framed photograph of Adolf Hitler, signed at the bottom. Arthur Greiser could have taken the plaque off the wall long ago, but its diminutive size made a point. Sitting opposite him were Seán Lester and Stefan Gillespie. The president had been surprised by Lester's visit. He avoided the High Commissioner as far as possible, and their meetings usually took place when he had been summoned to Lester's office to hear a catalogue of complaints that he had no intention of taking any notice of. He had assumed, for a moment at least, that this rare visit by Lester was some kind of recognition of the imminent and sweeping victory of the Nazi Party after the day's elections. Even the irritating and pedantic Irishman had to recognise that the rules would change once the Party had a two-thirds majority in the senate. The constitution forced on Danzig by the League of Nations could be torn up for all practical purposes. If the High Commissioner adjusted to the new situation in the right way, they might wait a while before kicking him out, but if he wanted to be difficult his days in the Free City were numbered.

However it was quickly evident that Seán Lester had not come to kowtow. He demanded a private conversation, with no one else present, except for the man Greiser remembered meeting on the plane from Berlin. Greiser might have been pleased to see Stefan Gillespie again, especially when he was looking forward to the mother and father of all celebrations that night, in the bar under the Town Hall in the Lange Markt, the Ratskeller. Now, out of nowhere, Lester was in his office, spouting some incoherent nonsense about a plot to kill the Bishop of Danzig. It was a desperate attempt to rain on his parade, but it could hardly be taken seriously. He barely took in the details. He despised Lester. He didn't know why the High Commissioner had brought this other Irishman with him, but it didn't matter. He had better things to do. Lester was a stooge for the English; always polite, always smiling, always lying. But he would keep his temper. The League's days were almost over anyway. He would enjoy kicking Sean Lester out of Danzig. He couldn't help thinking that whatever anyone said to the contrary there was a bit too much of the English about the Irish.

'You don't expect me to believe this, High Commissioner?'

'I think you would be very wise to, Herr Senatspräsident.'

'It's preposterous. It's absurd. What evidence do you have?'

'If you contact the Gestapo you'll find they are investigating three deaths in Langfuhr. That was this morning. Obviously I can't tell you who else is involved in the plan to assassinate the bishop, but one of the dead men is a Gestapo officer, Kriminaloberassistent Rothe. He *was* involved. I suppose that might be a good place to start. The bishop is aware of the situation of course, but if I were in your shoes I wouldn't spend any time sitting on my backside.' Lester spoke in a quiet voice, as if he was following the diplomatic niceties that usually marked his conversations with Greiser.

'I have put up with your interference in the day to day running of the city for long enough,' growled the Senate President, 'your contempt for its elected government, your disdain for the principles of the Party. I'm sure you know that you won't be playing that tune after the count tonight. This is beyond patience, High Commissioner, with or without the election. Even your colleagues in Geneva will find these allegations outrageous. Do you think you can walk in here and accuse us all of murder? I'm speechless!'

Stefan smiled. Greiser didn't seem to be speechless.

The High Commissioner shook his head.

'What happens if you don't get your majority today, Herr Greiser?'

'Now you're grasping at straws. The victory is already ours.'

'Not everyone in the Party has your faith.'

'Are you going to attack the Party too?'

'Ninety per cent, that's right, isn't it? That's what you promised Herr Hitler. Who takes the blame if it doesn't come off? You or the Gauleiter? I'm sure Herr Forster will claim a victory if there's one going. If there isn't he'll put it down to you. And he's the one with the Führer's ear, I think.'

'The Party will claim the victory. Individuals only serve the Party.'

'Forster's the Party leader. You're only head of government. I'm not up on Party etiquette but won't the first phone call from Berlin go to him?'

Greiser didn't like it. The conflict between him and the man who was his Party boss in Danzig was common knowledge but no one talked about it to his face. Lester seemed to have abandoned all the diplomacy he usually worked so hard at; first the insane allegations and now the snide comments. Dignity mattered a great deal to Arthur Greiser. Lester was sneering at him.

'We have treated each other with courtesy in the past, Herr Lester, whatever our differences. I have never heard you speak to me like this.'

'This is not a conversation either of us will need to

remember, Herr Senatspräsident, but let me make something clear. I do have a little understanding of how the Nazi Party works. You don't call yourselves a Führer Party for nothing. It's never been policy that matters, or ideas; only action counts. And that's not about what the Führer tells you to do, it's about what you think he wants you to do. It's called working towards the Führer, yes? Doing what Hitler can't because of political expediency, or the cowardice of the people around him, or because sometimes it's just better to lie through your teeth. So if you can't take the Free City democratically, why not have the streets running with blood instead? If you can create enough mayhem and slaughter, Germany will have to invade to save Danzig and keep the peace. That's what assassinating Bishop O'Rourke is about. And if you really don't know, I don't think it should take you very long to work out the consequences.'

'This is madness. I shall be reporting every word of this –'

'No, unless you find a way to stop it, I shall. I will be sending a report to the League in Geneva and to every head of government I can. I will also send it to the Vatican. I will speak to as many people as possible by phone as soon as I leave this office. I will make it public that I have passed this information on to you and you have refused to act. You don't have the power to stop me, yet. Try and you'll make matters worse. I will also ensure that the details reach the press. It can still make waves outside Germany.'

There was silence in the room. Greiser had no doubt now the High Commissioner meant everything he said. There was a definite shift of gear.

'And this man is your witness, is that what I'm supposed to believe?'

Greiser was looking at Stefan now. It was the first time he had registered his presence since he had entered the room with Seán Lester.

'Some of the information has come from Herr Gillespie. But I don't need a witness. Call it propaganda if you like. That's something you can understand. If anything happens to Edward O'Rourke any attempt to claim somebody else killed him is simply going to prove what I've said is true.'

'You're threatening me?'

'There's no threat if he's safe. But, yes, if you like it's a threat.'

'How do you think you can keep your job here after that?'

'I'm a lot less interested in keeping my job than you are. I might get a bollocking in Geneva. The worst that could happen is that I end up back in Ireland with a lot more time to spend fishing. That's not necessarily how it turns out when you make a mistake that embarrasses the Führer, is it?'

Greiser's fury was deeper than ever but he was running out of words.

'Working towards the Führer is all well and good when it works.'

'Are these mad allegations an accusation against me as well?'

'I don't know. Probably not. But not everyone would believe that.'

Greiser and Lester gazed at each other. It was the man in the uniform, surrounded by his flags and photographs, who was most uncomfortable now. The next words were meant to sound like a sneer, but they were a question.

'So who are these hypothetical renegades?'

'Do you need to know them to stop them?'

'You're supposed to have evidence, aren't you?' Greiser scowled at Stefan again. 'Who are they? If these people exist, who the fuck are they?'

'I only know the dead ones. But Hugo Keller was taking orders from the Gestapo and the SS.'

Lester glanced round at Stefan and nodded.

'So, should I question everyone in the SS?'

'If you can't control the SS, Herr Senatspräsident, a phone call to Himmler –' Lester smiled.

'If I need to talk to Reichsführer Himmler, I can assure you I will!'

'No, I meant I might call him. If his men are out of control here –'

Arthur Greiser had been glancing at the silver tray on his desk for some time. There was a decanter of golden brandy, a sparkling brandy glass. The idea of Heinrich Himmler's response to what he now believed the High Commissioner was thoroughly capable of doing was the tipping point. He reached across the desk and poured himself a brandy. By the time Stefan Gillespie and Seán Lester left shortly afterwards the Senate President was pouring a second. He knew he would be quietly congratulated by the hierarchy in Berlin for preventing a foreign policy disaster in Danzig, but the same people who congratulated him would always remember what he had stopped; they would never forgive him.

Stefan and the High Commissioner sat in the café opposite the senate building in Neugarten. Seán Lester finished a black coffee and called for another one. He had said very little since they walked out of Greiser's office. He felt as if he had done almost nothing, yet there was almost nothing else he could do. He had made his decision. Now he had to trust Senatspräsident Greiser. He had to trust that open windows and clean air would work. The Party was a hornets' nest of fear and deceit; sometimes, if you didn't get stung, you could play those things off against each other. He hoped he'd kicked that nest hard enough. As Lester drank the second cup of coffee Stefan saw that the High Commissioner's hands were shaking, very slightly. He looked older than his years. Stefan could sense the weight of this place on him. Lester took a sip of water from a glass the waiter had put down. He smiled a wry smile that didn't quite hide how drained he was.

'I think under the circumstances he took it very well.'

They got up and headed for the door. Three boys in Hitler Youth uniforms, fifteen or sixteen, were coming in carrying handfuls of election leaflets. They recognised the High Commissioner. Their hands shot up in the air. 'Heil Hitler!' Seán Lester smiled amiably at them. One of them smiled back, holding the door open. As Lester walked past, the boy spat in his face.

# 20. The Dead Vistula

By the time Stefan Gillespie arrived at the cathedral, the Schutzpolizei were there too. They were patrolling the park and a truckload of officers stood around the cathedral doors, smoking. Arthur Greiser had done what he could to put a positive spin on the matter. The police had been told they were there because of a threat to the bishop from unspecified anti-social elements, code for communists, socialists and the opposition in general. That wouldn't convince anyone but the Party faithful. As it was, the Schutzpolizei assumed they were just there to intimidate the opposition as usual. But orders and threats had filtered down through the Gestapo, the SS and the SA to ensure that anyone who knew anything no longer knew anything, and that nothing that had been planned had ever been planned after all. The death of Kriminaloberassistent Rothe was proving unexpectedly useful. Most of those involved in the plot assumed he had been shot by the Party, to make the point that Arthur Greiser meant business. It was how things were done.

Stefan didn't know any of that. But if it had felt like it was all over, sitting in the Senate President's office with Seán Lester, it didn't seem that simple as he walked past the police guns into the cathedral that evening. He still had a job to do. He still had to get Hannah out of Danzig.

The cathedral was crowded for vespers. Over the slow reverberation of the great organ the choir sang the Magnificat. He recognised Mozart's music, though he had last heard it when he sang in St Patrick's at barely eleven years old. There were some things that stayed inside you. 'Magnificat anima mea Dominum.' My soul doth magnify the Lord. 'Et exultavit spiritus meus in Deo salutari meo.' And my spirit hath rejoiced in God my Saviour. 'Suscepit Israel puerum suum recordatus misericordiae suae.' He remembering his mercy hath holpen his servant Israel. Stefan looked at the Nazi uniforms scattered through the congregation around him. Beside him two men in brown shirts gazed towards the high altar, their lips moving silently, almost in unison, as rosary beads slipped through their fingers. It was not usual for the Bishop of Danzig to lead vespers, but he was here as he had been at every Mass throughout that election day. If all he could do was to stand he would stand; nothing that had happened would change his mind about doing so, not even the threat of an assassin's bullet. When he stepped forward to speak the final prayer and bless his people there were many who spoke the words with him. 'A cunctis nos, quaesumus, Domine, defende perculis.' Defend us we beseech thee, O Lord, from all dangers. It was a prayer the Nazis in the cathedral heard only as familiar ritual. There were others in the congregation that evening who heard it very differently.

The cathedral cleared slowly. The men in uniform were the first to leave with their families, hurrying back into the city for the end of the election and the celebrations that would follow. The overwhelming feeling that this was their day, the day that would change everything, shone in their faces. It was what they had prayed for, standing beside those who were praying for anything but that change. Other people were slower to go, stopping to talk to friends, sitting quietly in the pews, lighting candles, standing in the quiet evening light beyond the cathedral doors. They were more reluctant to take the trams home to Oliva, Zoppot, Langfuhr, Brösen, Weichselmünde and Danzig itself, where they too would pour into the red, white and black streets to celebrate what they had prayed would not happen.

Stefan sat at the end of a pew until the cathedral was almost empty. He looked up to see a nun approaching him. She spoke to him in English.

'Please follow me. The bishop is waiting.'

She walked to one side of the nave and opened a small door. It led out to a cloister. There was still sunlight on the tree at its centre but they were walking in deep shadow. Stefan's feet sounded on the stone floor. Her footsteps were silent. He remembered the moment when Hannah Rosen had slapped the Mother Superior at the Convent of the Good Shepherd. It seemed a long time ago now, and it seemed as if every decision along the way had been someone else's. Whether it was the wall around the death of Susan Field, the threat that still hung over his son, his suspension from the Gardaí, even coming to Danzig, he felt as if he had been dragged along by events he had no control over. Perhaps he'd only kidded himself it had ever been different since Maeve died. What had he done in that time? When had his decisions or his actions made anything at all happen? Hannah was the reason he was here, the only reason. He'd thought that was his decision but it wasn't. He'd been dragged to Danzig too, to find her. And that would be over soon. They had to leave. And when it was all over they wouldn't really talk about what they felt. He had found her again. Now she was only something else to lose.

An archway on the other side of the cloister led to a cold, stone passage. There was a row of ancient, oak doors. The nun stopped at one of them and knocked. There was a voice from inside. She opened the door and waited for Stefan to go in. He was in a bare, white-walled room. It contained little more than a bed, a small writing table and a bookcase. It was lit by a lamp on the table. The only natural light came from an iron grille high up on a wall. It reminded him of a police cell. On the bed the vestments Edward O'Rourke had been wearing at vespers had been dumped in an untidy heap. The bishop emerged through a door at the side of the cell, doing up his shirt.

'Lester tells me I'm quite likely to survive.'

'He seems confident enough now, sir.'

'I suppose that's something.' He sat down on the bed, pushing aside the vestments to put on his shoes and socks. He looked at Stefan and smiled.

'Thank you, Mr Gillespie.'

Stefan nodded awkwardly.

'I'm not as nonchalant about death as I'm supposed to be in my profession, I assure you, but there are other things to think about, and other deaths too, real ones. Several people have died in all this, is that right?'

'Yes.' He assumed O'Rourke knew no more than that.

'I shall pray for them all, including the ones who were involved in the plot to kill me. It doesn't come easily, but it goes with the job. You saw the two Jewish men who were

371

murdered? Miss Rosen explained a little. It makes sense of course. If the lie is big enough, isn't that what they say? The desire to believe the Jews are responsible for every evil you care to mention is a madness even decent people seem unable to resist. The Church has a lot to answer for, but it's more than that I'm afraid. Have you read Hitler's book?'

'No.'

'People tell me the Jewish question is peripheral to what he believes. It's all about a strong Germany and a good life for everyone. But that's the self-deceit that's required to stomach the man. They want to believe he doesn't know what he's saying. Read his book. His hatred of the Jews is everything. It's all there is. It's the rest that is peripheral, even Germany.' As he stood, he pulled up his braces. He reached for a black jacket and put it on.

'Let's find Miss Rosen.'

Stefan followed the bishop back into the cold corridor.

'The palace is being renovated at the moment. The intention is to turn part of it into a museum. Not that there's much involved in that; it's already a museum. I've never warmed to the idea of living in a museum. The sisters are letting me use a room in the convent's guest wing. People come and go, so sometimes I'm in one cell, sometimes another. But it's really all I need. And do you know the best thing about it? Nobody knows where I am.'

They walked along another corridor lined with doors, upstairs, along another corridor, downstairs to another one that looked identical to the first.

'Can I ask you something about Father Byrne, Your Excellency?'

'I don't promise to be able to answer.'

372

'He worked very closely with a priest in Ireland, Robert Fitzpatrick.'

'I know who Monsignor Fitzpatrick is.'

'Did he talk about him?'

'Why do you ask?'

'I'm asking because I'm a policeman.'

'I met the monsignor only once, in Dublin in 1932, at the Eucharistic Congress. I can't say I liked him. I like his ideas even less. God must have a reason for allowing such people before his altar. I think it's to make sure we don't forget who delivered Christ to the Romans for crucifixion. It doesn't matter in the least that they were Jews; what matters is that they were priests. But much as I dislike the man's views, why would they interest the police?'

'Monsignor Fitzpatrick helped to provide us with a statement from Father Byrne. In it Father Byrne lied about his relationship with Susan Field, whose death is the subject of a police investigation. But then you know that.'

O'Rourke simply nodded.

'I'm not suggesting the monsignor is in any way involved in what happened, of course, but I think he has information that could help us, that he may have been reluctant to give, because of his friendship with Father Byrne.' He was being careful with his words. However different Edward O'Rourke was from Robert Fitzpatrick he knew that the Church still looked after its own.

'I think friendship would be overstating it, Sergeant Gillespie.'

'They really had fallen out then?'

'You seem to know that already. I'm not an easy man to interrogate. I'll tell you what I know, because I think Francis would have wanted me to. Monsignor Fitzpatrick represents a vision of the Church that isn't very far from the ranting of Adolf Hitler as far as I'm concerned. We're all at the mercy of a Jewish-Communist-Capitalist-Masonic-Atheist conspiracy that has as its only aim the destruction of Christian civilisation. You'd think that kind of insanity would get pretty short shrift in the Church these days, but I'm afraid not. Having identified a phantom enemy, too many of my colleagues want to believe that our enemy's enemy is our friend. They see democracy itself as the root of the problem and quietly, very quietly they whisper that Hitler may save us from it. They want a pope who will stand above it all and won't point out the darkness. They want a man who will only ask what's best for the Church when he should ask what Christ would do. The monsignor represents the noisier end of all that. Father Byrne was his protégé when I first met him. I thought he was worth more, as a man and as a priest. I couldn't change his opinions. He was as fanatical as Fitzpatrick. It was the woman he fell in love with who took away the poison. Whatever sins he committed by loving her, I think she saved him from worse ones.' He gave a wry smile. 'None of that is of any use to you of course, Sergeant.'

'No.'

'I know Monsignor Fitzpatrick put Francis in touch with the man Keller. He did tell me that.'

'Knowing he was an abortionist?'

'So it seems.' The bishop stopped at a door.

'But why?'

'You must ask him. In the light of what you think happened that's your job, whether anyone else likes it or not. We all have our jobs, Stefan.'

He smiled again in a way that made Stefan feel that the

bishop didn't much like his own job very much, but that somehow that wasn't the point. He knocked gently on the door then turned and walked away. The door opened. It was Hannah. She was laughing with relief, seeing him there now. Even though she knew he was all right she needed to see him. She needed to touch him. She pulled him into the room. It was another simple cell; the same bed, table, chair. He took her in his arms and kissed her. And he left the thought that it would soon be over between them somewhere else.

*

They spent the last night back at the Hotel Danziger Hof. It would be a noisy night in the hotel and in the Kohlenmarkt outside. The bar and the restaurant were already full of Nazi uniforms, black and brown; wives and girlfriends hung on the arms of the uniforms. Trays of beer and sekt circulated in the lobby for anyone who wanted them. It was obvious they had been circulating for some time, and since somewhere the people of Danzig would be picking up the tab for all this the waiters were as drunk as everyone else. As Hannah and Stefan stood at the reception desk two glasses of sekt were thrust into their hands. An SS officer clapped them both on the shoulders and laughed. Words were unnecessary. It was the man who had winked at Hannah that first morning. He winked again. As the hotel manager handed them the key he smiled a satisfied and supercilious smile that said, unmistakably, 'That'll show you, you arseholes.' He still didn't know who they were, but he knew they were trouble-makers and foreigners, and she was a Jewess. Still, it wouldn't be very long now before he didn't have to put up with Jews in his hotel.

They walked towards the staircase. Unless they wanted to join the celebrations the bedroom was the safest place. As they reached the bottom of the stairs the band in the dining room stopped playing abruptly. A ripple of excitement spread through the lobby. There was a crackle of static, very loud. People laughed and then started to grab for every drink in sight. Bottles of sekt were popping all around. There was cheering and applause. The static was coming from speakers that had been fixed to pillars all round the Danziger Hof. Then, as the manager tuned the dial on the radio behind the reception desk, there was music. A military band played. The music faded. 'Gauleiter Forster will now read the results of the Danzig election.' Hands shot up in salute. 'Heil Hitler!' And then there was an expectant silence.

Stefan and Hannah stood by the stairs, listening with everyone else. There was the rustling of papers and what sounded like a hesitant cough. The voice of the leader of Danzig's Nazis, the protégé of Hitler, Albert Forster, was quiet and deliberate. It felt like a man who was weighing every word. 'The full count of the votes cast in the election to Danzig's Volkstag gives yet another victory to the National Socialist German Workers' Party, another victory for German Danzig, another step on the road to reunification with the fatherland, and another step towards –' There was silence. Forster's voice had become quieter as he spoke. It was hesitancy. This was not a man weighing words to find the right way to celebrate the landslide they all expected – it was a man who didn't know what to say. 'Towards victory! Sieg Heil!' All around Hannah and Stefan people raised their arms again and echoed the cry of victory. But they had all heard the hesitation. There were too many victories in there somehow to believe in victory. Where was the full count they wanted to hear? Where was the ninety per cent of the votes that would sweep away the opposition and the decadent constitution of the League of Nations and the interfering Poles and the High Commissioner and let them do whatever they wished? They weren't expecting steps; they wanted leaps.

The radio was still silent except for a crackle of static. The station wasn't ready for such a short speech. It was quiet in the Danziger Hof too. The idea that the result was not the triumph that had been proclaimed beforehand was in every mind, but no one wanted to be the first to say it. Abruptly there was music again as a needle fell heavily on to a record. It was Beethoven's Ninth Symphony. In the ballroom the band took it as a cue. For a few moments Beethoven vied with 'The Sun Has Got His Hat On'; then the radio was switched off. The buzz of conversation started up at the same time, concerned and surprised and puzzled under the safe, muffling music. Hannah and Stefan turned back to the staircase. A waiter was beside them, with an ice bucket and a bottle of champagne. He smiled a conspiratorial smile.

'So what happened?' asked Stefan.

'Fifty-nine per cent.' The waiter's whisper was conspiratorial too; he grinned happily. 'That's not much more than they got in the last election.'

'Why don't I take that?' Stefan picked up the bottle of champagne.

'Help yourself. It's their money.'

Stefan and Hannah continued up the stairs. She put her arm through his as she had that night in Grafton Street, but there was something more intimate about it now;

377

perhaps it was because all either of them wanted to do was sleep. Downstairs the sense that everything had not gone to plan was already disappearing. Triumph was required and triumph would be delivered. Their faith was in their Führer and their day was coming. The dance floor was full; the corks were popping; everyone was singing. There was no syncopation; the rhythm was a fast, flat march. It was swaggering, insistent, joyless, brutal, mindless, remorseless, irresistible. It would carry on long into the night. 'He's been tanning niggers out in Timbuktu, now he's coming back to do the same to you. So jump into your sunbath, hip-hip-hip-hooray, the sun has got his hat on and he's coming out today!'

*

They left the next morning, on the seaplane to Kalmar and Stockholm. As there was now no one in Danzig or Berlin who had ever known anything about a plot to kill Bishop Edward O'Rourke, there was no one with any interest in either Hannah Rosen or Stefan Gillespie. But Seán Lester thought it was still better for them not to travel home through Germany. There were always lists and there were always Nazis with their own view of what working towards the Führer meant. At around the same time as they moved out on to the Dead Vistula from the seaplane station, Father Francis Byrne was being interred in the cathedral cemetery at Oliva. The bodies of Johannes Berent and Leon Kamnitzer, now surplus to requirements, were never found. They had been dumped somewhere in the forests above Danzig. Hugo Keller would find an unmarked grave in Langfuhr. The man called Karl was buried in the cemetery in Oliva too, close to Francis Byrne, after a requiem Mass at the cathedral. His family was given no explanation about where he died or why he had a bullet hole through the back of his head. Kriminaloberassistent Rothe was buried with full Party honours, and after the funeral, to mark his passing, a journalist from the Social Democrat *Danziger Volstimme* very carelessly fell under a tram and died. It was the least Rothe's friends could do. The Nazis still ruled Danzig, but Lester was there too, so was O'Rourke; and somehow enough people had braved the thugs at the polling stations to keep the Free City alive for a few more years.

Now, as the Dornier Delphin lifted up from the muddy waters of the Dead Vistula and banked over Danzig, the sun was shining. Hannah and Stefan looked down. It seemed peaceful enough. But there was no peace of course, and there would be no peace to come. In less than five years Seán Lester would be gone, along with the city's obstreperous Russian-Irish bishop. The first shots of the Second World War would be fired at the Polish fort on the Westerplatte by a German battleship in the Tote Weichsel. Most of Danzig's Jews would have left by then; the Great Synagogue would be razed to the ground so no sign of its existence remained. Some of the Free City's Jews would find safety, but many would simply be rounded up by the Nazis later, somewhere else in Europe, and sent to the ghettos and death camps. In less than ten years the German city of Danzig would be reduced to smouldering rubble by the guns and bombs of the Red Army. A quarter of its population would die in the battle for the city and in the forced marches and deportations that followed. No one would be very interested in mourning them. It was their war after all. And when the city was built again, German brick by German brick, it would be as the Polish city of Gdańsk; it would only look like the German city of Danzig that once stood in exactly the same place. And the language that had filled its streets and buildings for five hundred years would disappear, along with the people who had once lived there. In all the rebuilding, though, no one would ever bother to rebuild the synagogue.

# PART THREE
# Free Will

*Freemasonry, the Jews and Communism were among the subjects discussed by the Rev. D. Fahey, C.S.Sp., D.D., in the course of a paper entitled 'Will Ireland Remain Faithful to Christ the King?' which he read before delegates to the Catholic Young Men's Society Convention, at the Gresham Hotel . . . Wherever, in any country, he said, men had thrown themselves into the stream, of which the agents of Communism controlled the current, the end was slavery under Jewish finance, with the obliteration of the Christian family and the Catholic idea of native land . . . These truths must be borne in mind in connection with the rapid increase in numbers, power and wealth of the Jews in Dublin.* The Irish Times

# 21. Glenmalure

*Wicklow, April 1935*

The field behind the house at Kilranelagh was full of sheep. On one side, penned tightly and bleating noisily, were the grubby, thick-woolled ewes waiting to be sheared; on the other were the newly shorn, bewildered by their sudden weightlessness, their gleaming white coats flecked here and there with blood. It was the day after Stefan Gillespie's return from Danzig, but nothing, not even Tom's excitement, could stand in the way of the shearing. The Farrell brothers would be there from the break of day, when the sheep were brought in from the fields, until the last one was clipped, late that afternoon. Stefan and his father carried ewe after struggling ewe from the pens to the thudding Lister engine that drove the shearing heads. The smell of diesel mixed with the smell of the animals. Their clothes reeked of sticky lanolin and sheep shit. Now the sun was almost overhead. Half the flock had been clipped and they would soon stop for dinner. Stefan looked up to wipe the sweat from his eyes. He saw the bent figure of Emmet Brady walking through the field towards him, leaning on his stick. It was four months since they had first talked about Tom. The threat from Father Carey and the Church had been brooding over the farm all that time. It was never quite forgotten, but for a time the business of life had pushed it away.

Stefan and the solicitor walked away from the noise of the shearing, saying nothing. David Gillespie watched them as he carried on his work.

'I'm sorry, I'm not a very welcome guest, Stefan,' said Brady finally.

'I thought after all this time –'

'They won't let it go. You have the choice you had before, to go along with it and send Tom to his uncle and aunt's, or they'll take it to court. I think they'll move quite quickly now. And they have their reasons for that.'

'What do you mean?'

'They'll want to ensure it goes before a particular judge. No one ought to be able to guarantee that, of course, but let's just say it will happen.'

'And why's that so important?'

'The man is Alexander Phelan. I've looked very hard at what's been happening in the last few years, in cases like this. Phelan sat on one in 1934. A woman had custody of her children taken away from her. She was a Protestant. The Catholic husband was in hospital and dying. There'd been a falling out and the husband accused the woman of interfering in the children's religious upbringing. Not much evidence, other than his word, but Phelan refused to accept her assurances that she would continue to bring the children up as Catholics. He said he was duty bound to secure the fulfilment of any agreement that was made before a mixed marriage, because of the special position of the Catholic Church in the state. And because, and these are the words he used, "the state itself pays homage to that Church".'

They walked on in silence again, looking up towards Baltinglass Hill.

'When we first talked after Christmas, I gave you the bleakest picture, Stefan, but I believed that with the right barrister we could fight this. The more I've seen of what's going on the less sure I am. It's even bleaker now.'

'It still feels like this should be impossible, Mr Brady –'

'It should be. But you need to think hard before taking this on.'

'Are we back to me accepting it and being grateful I still see him?'

'I only know you have to tread carefully.'

The old man stopped.

'There is another option.'

Stefan shook his head in weary disbelief.

'You mean convert? Are we back to that?'

'No, I mean leave the jurisdiction.'

Stefan turned back to the shearing, watching as his father struggled with a recalcitrant ewe. Then he looked round again, up to Baltinglass Hill.

'That's the best our Free State can offer us? Leaving the country?'

'Don't tell me you haven't thought about it.'

As he turned to face Brady once more he didn't need to answer.

'If it's the decision you're going to make in the end, make it now. They can't pursue you for something that won't stand up in a court in England, but if we go to trial and lose, taking Tom out of the country when he's a ward of court is a different matter. You could end up in gaol yourself.'

The green John Deere tractor was chugging up the field towards them. Helena drove and Tom perched on the trailer behind her, with a basket of sandwiches and cans of hot, sweet tea. Tess the sheepdog ran alongside, barking.

'Dinner! It's the dinner!' Tom's voice was shrill and happy above all the other noise.

That evening Stefan and his father were milking in the dark parlour that smelt of fresh hay and the warm breath of cows and the smoke from David Gillespie's pipe and the urine and disinfectant swirling in the open concrete drain. Stefan sat on one stool, his fingers squeezing milk into the galvanised bucket beneath an udder. On the other side of the cow, out of sight, his father's fingers pulled at the teats of another one. For a moment the only sounds were the rhythmic spurting of milk into the buckets and the mouths of the cows pulling the hay from the hay racks.

'Did Mr Rosen pay you well?'

'What?'

'I'd say there was more to it than putting your woman on a boat.'

'Maybe a bit more.'

'Your mother was listening to the German news on the radio.'

'You'd think she'd know better. They didn't mention me then?'

They couldn't see each other, but he felt the look of disapproval on his father's face. Stefan didn't want hard conversations; he wanted to think.

'I'm not asking you to tell me what happened in Danzig, Stefan.'

'I've told you, Pa, not much. It's over. It doesn't matter now.'

'Other things aren't over, are they?'

'Is this a conversation Ma told you to have?'

'That's the way she is. We've all been avoiding it, haven't we?'

Stefan didn't answer. After a few seconds his father continued.

'Lawyers are going to cost money.'

'I know.'

'What we've got is yours and Tom's. I hope you know that too.'

'Perhaps it won't come to that.'

'It's going to come to something, Stefan.'

'I've a bit set aside.'

He was still sidestepping. David Gillespie couldn't see the shrug, but he knew it was there.

'Emmet Brady's not so sure you can win, is he?'

'Is that Ma's question?'

'The question's do we give the money to the lawyers, or do you take it and start again, somewhere else? Wasn't Mr Brady saying the same thing? It doesn't mean there mightn't be a day you could come back home again.'

It was the first time the words had been spoken. For David, however hard they were, they were easier without seeing his son's face. Everyone knew how rarely anyone came home, even when somewhere else was only hours across the Irish Sea. There was only the sound of milk spurting into buckets again.

'There's a way to go yet, Pa.'

'You think so?' David was surprised by his son's quiet self-control. 'If Mr Brady's not convinced, I don't know who else can help us.'

'Sometimes it's not who you know, it's what you know,' said Stefan. It felt like the shrug was still there.

'Should I know what that means?' There was a note of irritation in David's voice. Riddles weren't answers. These were difficult things to say.

'No,' Stefan snapped in return, 'and you wouldn't want to.'

At almost the same instant father and son got up from the milking stools and walked to the battered churn behind them. They poured the milk from the buckets in silence. Stefan knew what it had cost his father to speak those words, and what it had cost his mother to tell him to speak them. But it wasn't time for answers. They said no more till the milking was done and the cows were back in the fields.

When the two men walked into the kitchen the only recognition that the conversation in the milking parlour had happened was the look Helena gave David, and the slightly puzzled shrug he gave her in return. Explanations would have to wait, but she knew the questions no one wanted to ask still had no answers. Stefan and David stood next to each other at the sink, washing their hands. Tom sat at the kitchen table, unaware of anything except for the radio and a woman's voice reading a story that had taken him somewhere else altogether. Stefan listened too: 'A faint glimmer floated down from the hills. That was Seamus, holding a candle and riding Long-Ears. The storm lantern the turf-cutter used danced across the bog like a will-o'-the wisp, and the big steady glow of the kitchen lamp advanced on the road and Eileen knew her mother carried it. All the lights came together at the crossroads. "Hee-haw," sang out Long-Ears, and Eileen knew she was found.' As David Gillespie opened a bottle of beer and poured out two glasses,

Stefan sat down at the table beside Tom, watching him happily absorbed in the story, and wishing he could just be where his son was now, far away from everything.

*

The following morning Stefan Gillespie set off early on the bicycle it had taken him the best part of the previous evening to repair, after its years in the loft of forgotten things behind the pigsty. His father was milking the cows. It would be a long ride into the mountains. The air was still cold but it was a clear, almost cloudless day; it would be hot as he climbed up to Glenmalure. The last time he had made this journey on a bicycle he was probably sixteen or seventeen, with Terry Lynch and Richard Kavanagh and Billy Harrison and Niall Quinn. None of them really kept in touch now. Terry was in America, somewhere in New York. Richard was still farming in Englishtown, just down the road, but there was never much to talk about other than the way the grass was growing and the price of cattle. Billy was in Yorkshire, a travelling salesman the last he'd heard, with an English wife and three children. Niall was in Baltinglass now, back from Dublin and trying to make something of the auctioneer's firm his father had drunk into the ground.

There was time to remember a lot as he cycled past the track up to the cemetery under Kilranelagh Hill where Maeve was buried, then through Balinroan and on past Tom's school at Kilranelagh Cross; by the long, crumbling wall of the crumbling Humewood Estate and on to Rathdangan and Rathcoyle; up on to the Military Road where it rose more steeply now, towards Aghavannah, and then suddenly, as the road turned sharply, he was riding down the steep slope into the valley of the Avonbeg River, beside the ruins of the English army barracks at Drumgoff. For a moment the reasons that had brought him into the mountains didn't matter as he looked down. He knew this place. It was in his blood. He needed it to be in his son's blood as well.

Hannah was in Dublin with her father. He hadn't seen her since the train took them into Dublin from Dún Laoghaire. The journey from Sweden to Ireland had taken four days; by train to Gothenberg, by boat to Hull, then train and boat again. They were four days the two of them would not have again. It was hard to accept that. But it didn't quite drive out the sense of exhilaration he felt as he sped down the wooded hillside into Glenmalure. He was doing a job no one wanted him to do – except for Hannah Rosen. It wasn't only about her though. It wasn't duty or some great sense of right and wrong, or a responsibility to the law or the Gardaí or some higher purpose he hadn't found a word for. He wasn't there to speak for the dead. They didn't care. He was carrying no fine motives up into Glenmalure. He wanted someone to pay for something. But it was more than that. There was an unspoken hope in this journey into the mountains. There were no scruples in that hope. He wasn't looking for the truth; he was looking for a weapon.

He stopped at the Glenmalure Inn for a glass of lemonade. They told him they knew Mrs Donahue well. She lived in the cottage by the ford below Ballinagoneer and they kept her letters for her. She'd a few chickens up there and she'd had new slates on the roof last month. It was Joe Crosbie from Greenan who done it so she'd have to have a bit put away with the prices he'd charge, not that it was anybody's business but her own. She'd never said she was a widow, but there was a feller from Dublin bought the house two years ago and she had it from him. She didn't have much to do with anyone, but then if you were up at the top of the glen there wasn't anyone to have much to do with anyway. Once a week she came down to the crossroads and took the bus into Rathdrum. On the way back she'd have a Guinness or two and wait for a lift from Eddie McMurrough. She wasn't a bad looker, taking all things into account. It wasn't only out of the kindness of his heart Eddie took her on past the farm at Ballinaskea and all the way home.

The road into Glenmalure stopped below Ballinagoneer, not long after the ford over the Avonbeg. There were only the mountains beyond. It was a long, narrow valley, with the hills climbing up more and more steeply. Even in summer it could be dark. The fields that were strung out along the valley were small, hard-won, stony things; they didn't stretch far before the valley walls rose up at angles only the sheep could walk. Glenmalure had always been a bleak place. Down the centuries it had been a place of refuge too, as rebellion after rebellion against the English failed. It was a place of refuge for Mrs Donahue now. Stefan knew from the letter he had found at Hugo Keller's house in Langfuhr that she was waiting in Glenmalure. Now he would have to tell her that the man she was waiting for was dead.

He crossed the ford and cycled through the woods until the track was too rough to pedal any further. He pushed the bike for another quarter of a mile. On one side of the track, among the trees, there were broken walls, overgrown with moss. It was a long time since anyone had lived here, but as the trees thinned out and the sunlight broke through on to the road there was a small cottage. It was neat and white-washed. There was washing on the line and half a dozen speckled hens were picking about for food in front of the house. As he leant the bicycle against the wall, a woman came out, smiling. He recognised the nurse, Sheila Hogan, immediately. She recognised him.

'How's it going, Sheila?'

'You'll want some tea.' There was no smile now.

'I wouldn't mind.'

She walked back in without another word. He sat down on a bench by the door. The wood was warm from the sun. It would be better said outside.

When she came out with the tea he took her letter to Hugo Keller from his pocket and gave it to her. She sat down on the bench, holding it tightly.

'Where did you get it?' she asked.

'I was in Danzig.'

'You saw him.'

He nodded.

'I haven't heard from him in a while.'

She stared down at the letter. She knew what he was going to say.

'I'm sorry, but he's dead, Sheila.'

She looked around her, at the garden and the mountains.

'What happened?'

'You know what he did. His luck ran out. It was bound to one day.'

'Someone killed him?'

'Yes.'

She stared across at the hens.

'He didn't like what he was doing there.'

'I'd say it was a bit late for him to start being choosey. How many years was he at it, blackmailing people and selling information? It was never a recipe for a quiet old age. He could get away with a lot here –'

'He didn't want to go to Danzig. It was because of the priest –'

'It doesn't much matter now, does it?'

'All he wanted was to come back here. He wanted to stop. That's why he bought this place. But they wouldn't let go. They wouldn't let him stop. He didn't want to leave Ireland in the first place. If you hadn't –'

'The man's dead, let's leave it there. I'm not here for the wake.'

'Then what are you here for, Mr Gillespie?'

'The notebook.'

'Jesus, are you still on about that?'

'We found the woman.'

'Who?'

'Susan Field. You don't remember?'

'I remember I wasn't there when she came to Merrion Square.'

'But he'd have told you she died.'

She said nothing for several seconds, then nodded.

'Someone shot her. Did you know that, Sheila?'

'No. Hugo didn't know either,' she said, clearly surprised.

'No, I don't think he did. But I'm not really bothered about what he knew now. What matters is who he knew. It was a Special Branch man shot her, Detective Sergeant Jimmy Lynch. You know who he is, don't you?'

'I should do. He put me in hospital.'

'And is that why you're up here as Mrs Donahue?'

'What do you think?'

'I don't know. Wasn't Jimmy working for Keller?'

'He was working for himself.'

'And when Hugo went, he wanted the book – for himself.'

She said nothing again. The habit of silence was an old one.

'So what's in this book, Sheila?'

'Nothing that matters now.'

'Why not?'

'It was his insurance policy. That's what he called it. If anything went wrong. He put everything down in it. What he knew, what he sold, what he kept for himself. It was what he kept for himself that mattered most. He said it was his ticket to stay in Ireland. There were so many people he knew about, important people. He'd had enough. He just wanted to come up here and forget it all. When he went back to Germany he didn't know they'd force him to keep working for them. It was only to lie low, till he came home again.'

'You make blackmail sound like the Vincent de Paul, Sheila. It would have been a little nest egg too, to dip into when the winters were hard.'

'You're probably right. Maybe he'd never really have stopped.'

'Is it here then?'

She didn't respond.

'It's no use to you now.'

'And what use is it to you?'

'I don't know yet, but if it's not me isn't it Jimmy, sooner or later?'

'People are stupid, you know that?' She spoke the words bitterly. 'They do stupid things. They steal and lie and cheat and fuck. That's all they do. That's all they are. Why shouldn't someone get something out of it? If it hadn't been him it would have been someone else. Didn't they deserve it anyway, most of them? He always said when he got to the pearly gates they wouldn't let him in, but he'd find a way. He'd just keep his eyes open and sooner or later he'd have something on God himself!' She shook her head and looked up at the mountains again. There were no tears.

'You've kept it for him long enough. He's not coming for it now.'

He couldn't pretend to feel much for Hugo Keller, but he understood what loss was; and somewhere in those last words Sheila Hogan sensed that. She touched the final letter she had written to Hugo Keller, a letter he had never read. Stefan Gillespie had brought with him the last breath of the man she loved, and she was oddly grateful that he had. She had waited. She had believed, as Keller had believed, that he would come back here and find her. And now he wouldn't. She got up and walked to the vegetable garden. There was a spade sticking into a bed where she had been earthing up potatoes. She pulled it out and went across to an apple tree by the stone wall. It was full of white blossom. She pushed the spade hard into the ground and started to dig.

He stopped at the ford across the Avonbeg and sat by the river. He opened the Jacob's biscuit tin Sheila Hogan had dug up under the apple tree; there was a picture of a gold-finch feeding on yellow gorse flowers. It was a small, dark green notebook. The handwriting was tiny and meticulous. It filled every lined page though it took no notice of the lines. At first he thought it was in some kind of code but it was no more than a truncated shorthand of abbreviations and numbers. The abbreviations were names, sometimes addresses. The numbers were dates, sometimes sums of money. Sometimes there was a page of notes following a name, but they were written in the same shorthand, missing out vowels, often stopping a word half way through. Sometimes there were lists of dozens of names on a page, with no more than an address and a series of letters after them that classified them in some way. Keller's shorthand was German of course. It had an elliptical quality that would make it tedious to decipher, but it wouldn't be so hard.

At the back of the book, in a small cardboard wallet, there were several pieces of folded paper. The first was a letter. He knew the woman's name Hugo Keller had written at the top, even in its shortened form, and the name underneath it. She was the wife of a government minister and he was a senior diplomat. There was little more than the address of a hotel in London, but there didn't need to be any more. The next sheet of paper was a list of names. There were politicians, businessmen, senior clerics, several senior Garda officers. There was no explanation but at the end of the list was the name Becky Cooper and the sum of money Keller had paid her. Stefan knew her name well enough; she ran a brothel in Dublin. By two of the names there were abbreviations and dates. The word 'Syph.' wasn't hard to expand on. Keller had treated two of the men on Becky's list for syphilis. Next there were four letters folded together. 'My Dearest Vincent.' He had found them.

They weren't long, but they were filled with vivid, almost unstoppable sexual desire, interspersed with strangely banal details about work. The third letter ended with an expression of growing excitement about the upcoming Eucharistic Congress. 'Only a month away and there is so much to do! It's wonderful! Your Loving Friend, Robert.' There had been little to connect the two bodies on the mountainside at Kilmashogue. There was the earth in which their bones were buried. There was the single hole from a captive bolt pistol in each of their skulls. And there was Detective Sergeant Jimmy Lynch, who sold these letters to Hugo Keller and drove the car that collected Susan Field from Keller's clinic. That made Lynch the only link between Vincent Walsh and Susan Field. Now there was something else. Monsignor Robert Fitzpatrick had been Vincent's lover. He was also the man who had sent Jimmy Lynch to twenty-five Merrion Square to take Susan Field away. Fitzpatrick was someone else the Special Branch sergeant worked for. That day in Earlsfort Terrace, when Stefan had questioned the monsignor, the priest had shown only bitterness and resentment towards Francis Byrne, the follower and protégé who had abandoned him. But it seemed like he wasn't so bitter or resentful that he couldn't find an abortionist for the young priest in his hour of need and a bent garda sergeant to sort the mess out for him afterwards.

*

Stefan met Dessie MacMahon in Neary's in Chatham Street the next day. It wasn't long after opening. Dessie sat in the corner by the back door that led out to the Gaiety Theatre, wreathed in smoke. The only other people in there were actors coming and going for rehearsal. The two policemen hadn't seen each other in three months but Dessie asked no questions. If there was something Stefan wanted to tell him he would tell him. This was business, and it was serious business. That was clear enough from the phone call.

'How's it going, Dessie?'

'Ah, you know how it is yourself.'

'Detective Sergeant McGuinness?'

'He's no trouble.' It wasn't a compliment.

'Inspector Donaldson?'

'Well, he doesn't like the fact that Charlie McGuinness takes a drink, but once the Angelus bell rings and he goes to Mass and Charlie's off to the pub, we've a nice quiet station so. All in all he likes that bit well enough.'

'What's happened about the bodies at Kilmashogue?'

'I told you, we've a nice quiet station now.'

'I was in Danzig,' said Stefan quietly.

Dessie nodded as if that was about as interesting as a trip to Clontarf.

'I saw the priest there, Francis Byrne. I saw Hugo Keller too.'

'Still in touch with your woman, then?' reflected Dessie, unsurprised.

'Yes.'

'And I thought you were milking cows.'

'You can only milk so many. They're both dead, Byrne and Keller.'

Detective Garda MacMahon finally raised an eyebrow.

'Danzig's not a place you'd go on holiday from what the papers say.'

'It isn't,' replied Stefan. 'But nothing new this end? You haven't heard Jimmy Lynch has got to the bottom of it so?'

'If he has he's kept it to himself,' said Dessie.

'He wouldn't have to look far. I think he killed Vincent

Walsh and Susan Field. And if he didn't kill them he made dammed sure they were dead.'

'Jesus!' Dessie looked round. No one was listening. 'What the feck for?'

'At the moment I'd say it was for Monsignor Robert Fitzpatrick.' He took Keller's small notebook from his pocket. He opened it and handed one of Fitzpatrick's letters to Vincent Walsh across the table.

Dessie's eyes widened as he read.

'I need you to watch my back,' said Stefan simply.

'They won't let you do anything with this.'

'That depends what I can put together before anyone notices me. I've got a bit of time. Fitzpatrick won't go running to the Commissioner, not with what I know about him, but he's quite likely to go running to Jimmy Lynch. And Jimmy might take matters into his own hands. I need to know where he is.'

'You want me to follow a Special Branch sergeant?'

'No, I couldn't ask you to do that,' said Stefan, laughing.

'No, you couldn't.' Dessie took out an unopened pack of Sweet Afton. 'That could get me into some real shite!'

*

When Sister Brigid opened the door of the house in Earlsfort Terrace she knew she recognised Stefan Gillespie. She wasn't quite sure where she'd seen him, but so many people came to her brother's meetings nowadays. They were so full that she couldn't expect to remember half the people.

'Hello, Sister, I was hoping to talk to the monsignor.'

'He's not here just now, can I help at all?'

'Are you expecting him back? It is important.'

'He won't be long,' she smiled. 'Well, you can wait if you like.'

'Thank you.'

'Come in and have a cup of tea.'

He followed her into the hall and down the stairs to the basement, into a kitchen that was dark and old-fashioned but scrupulously neat. There was the smell of baking and a kettle was already steaming on the black range.

'I get so little time to bake now. There's so much work. But this afternoon I thought, blow it! I haven't baked a scone in a month and Robert loves scones. Well, I tell him he loves them but I'm the one who does really. You need someone to make cakes for though. There's no pleasure just making them for yourself. If you wait till they cool you can have one as well.' She poured hot water into the teapot as she talked and while it was standing she opened the oven door and took out a tray of fruit scones. She put them out on a rack, one by one, in tidy rows. When she had finished she looked pleased with the results. She went to the teapot and poured a cup out. 'Help yourself to milk and sugar, it's on the table. I didn't ask your name?'

'It's Gillespie. Detective Sergeant Gillespie.'

'Oh, yes. I do remember you, Sergeant.' Then she frowned. 'It was before Christmas, wasn't it? Robert was really very upset. He didn't tell me what you were discussing with him, but I know he didn't like it. Perhaps I shouldn't have asked you in. I don't know if the monsignor would want –'

'I need to see him. It isn't something that can wait.'

'When you were here before, it was about Francis, Father Byrne, I do remember that. You wanted to know where he was. But he's dead now. We heard last week.'

'I know.'

'He drowned.' She shook her head. 'We hoped he would come back.'

There was something about the way she spoke that suggested more intensity than just a train across Europe and a Holyhead boat.

'Come back?'

'He lost his way.' She smiled sadly and crossed herself. 'But where he is now, he will never lose his way again. When we ask forgiveness, we are forgiven.' She turned her head. Stefan could see that she was close to tears.

'I'm sorry, Sister.'

'Francis meant a lot to both of us. He lived in this house for many years. He was very special to my brother. He always felt that Francis would be beside him in his work and that one day, when the time came, it would be Francis who carried it on. When he turned away from everything Robert had taught him –' She started to re-arrange the scones on the rack. 'I don't know why you're here, Mr Gillespie. I don't know what you can have to say.'

Stefan looked round as the door opened behind him. The monsignor was there. And there was no question that he remembered exactly who Stefan was.

'What are you doing here?'

Stefan stood up slowly, his eyes fixed on the priest.

'I need to talk to you, Monsignor.'

Robert Fitzpatrick's face showed a mixture of anger and indignation, but Stefan saw uncertainty too, somewhere behind all that.

'I don't believe we have anything to talk about, Sergeant.'

'Perhaps we could go upstairs. There are still questions –'

The monsignor was more agitated now. He walked forward.

'He's dead! Don't you know Father Byrne is dead?'

Brigid stepped forward and took her brother's hand. He was immediately calmer.

'I did tell him. I'm sorry, Robert. I didn't know who he was.'

'It doesn't matter, Brigid. I think you can get out, Sergeant.'

But Stefan had no intention of getting out. His eyes hadn't left Robert Fitzpatrick's since he turned to see him in the kitchen. He had all the cards he needed.

'I do know he's dead, Monsignor. I saw him in Danzig. I was with Bishop O'Rourke, at the undertakers, after they pulled his body out of the river.'

The priest and the nun stared at him. Fitzpatrick frowned as if he couldn't relate these ideas: the garda sergeant, Danzig, Francis Byrne. Brigid closed her eyes and bowed her head. As she looked up her lips were moving silently; her fingers were clasping the beads on the rosary at her waist.

They stood in Fitzpatrick's study. It was a room at the back of the house, behind the office and the bookshop. It looked out on a small, high-walled garden. There was a flowering cherry, full of white and pink blossom. The priest stood with his back to the window. He didn't ask Stefan to sit down.

'As I understand it you were suspended from the Gardaí earlier this year. I don't know whether you've been re-instated, but if you have, the best thing you can do is walk out of this house now, or I'll make damned sure you're kicked out completely. Don't think I haven't got the ability to do it either.' The threat was cautious and considered. He was trying to weigh Stefan up as he spoke. He didn't know what to make of him. The idea that the policeman he had been in Danzig, talking to Francis Byrne, was still as startling as it was unexpected.

'Let's forget the lies about Father Byrne, shall we? He did have an affair with Susan Field. He did pay for an abortion for her at Hugo Keller's clinic. You not only knew Keller, you put Francis Byrne in touch with him. I'm not asking you, I'm telling you what I know. And when the abortion went wrong and Susan had to be taken to hospital, you sent someone to sort it all out.'

'Is that what Francis said?'

There was quiet calculation in the priest's eyes. This conversation meant nothing after all. These were just words, and the man they were talking about was dead.

'It's also what Mr Keller said,' replied Stefan. Fitzpatrick couldn't know Keller was dead. He had no links to what had happened in Danzig.

'Mr Keller is still in Germany?' The monsignor was less sure now.

'He's in Danzig at the moment,' said Stefan. That much was true.

'And he'll be coming back to testify to all this?' smiled the priest. If Keller wasn't in Ireland it didn't matter.

'You don't deny you knew Hugo Keller, Monsignor.'

'He was a friend, at least an acquaintance, of Adolf Mahr's, the director of the National Museum. I'm sure I met him a few times, at dinners or receptions. I have close ties with the German community, especially the German Catholic community. If what you say about his involvement in abortions is true I am deeply shocked. We can't always know where the bad apples are in a barrel. As far as Father Byrne is concerned I was satisfied with the answers he gave to your questions in December. It was my impression your senior officers were too. Unsubstantiated and scurrilous allegations about a priest who died tragically won't endear you to anybody.'

The monsignor was used to being believed. He had no reason to think that lying would change that. This policeman knew a lot, but in the end it counted for nothing, not against his word. The man wasn't important enough to matter. He was a problem though and he would have to be dealt with. Stefan could feel the confidence growing in the eyes that now fixed his. He had caught the priest off guard, but it hadn't taken him long to regain his composure. Fitzpatrick already thought it was over. However, it wasn't.

'The guard you sent didn't take Susan Field to hospital,' continued Stefan, ignoring the denials he had just heard. 'He took her to the Convent of the Good Shepherd. They couldn't do anything. She'd already lost too much blood. I'm not sure what happened next. Either she died or the guard killed her. And if he didn't actually kill her, he went to some lengths to make sure she was dead. I don't know what his instructions were, but I know you sent him.'

'I don't understand what you're talking about. This means nothing to me, nothing.'

He spoke quietly. It wasn't so much about confidence now. Stefan's words troubled him in some way, but it wasn't the right way. He still felt he was untouchable, but there was something else. He looked puzzled. The indignation was gone and it was hard to read what was in his face now.

'I don't think my superior officers are going to be

satisfied with what Father Byrne told us in his letter,' said Stefan, 'however much they want to be. You wrote most of it for him anyway. But that's only the beginning. There was another body next to Miss Field's. You'll remember him.'

Monsignor Fitzpatrick looked confused. 'What other body?'

'The one you longed to feel throbbing next to yours – Vincent Walsh's. That's what it said in your letter, didn't it? I've seen them, the letters. Obviously Vincent's body won't have been throbbing next to anyone else's for a long time now. Not since someone shot him in the head with a captive bolt pistol, which is, oddly, what happened to Susan Field as well.'

The priest stared blankly.

'Vincent.'

It was all he said but he made no pretence that he didn't know who Stefan was talking about. He moved towards the desk, very slowly. He stood for a moment, leaning on it. He repeated the name quietly. 'Vincent.' It was barely a whisper. He seemed unaware that Stefan was still there. He sank into the chair. Stefan hadn't known what to expect, but it wasn't this. And it wasn't right. He couldn't believe that the man in front of him knew anything at all about Vincent Walsh's death. But there was still Detective Sergeant Lynch; Lynch and the love letters, Lynch and Keller, Lynch and the car that came for Susan Field.

'Tell me about Jimmy Lynch, Monsignor.'

'What?' Robert Fitzpatrick looked up again.

'Detective Sergeant Lynch.'

'I don't know any Detective Sergeant Lynch.' Fitzpatrick was a beaten man. It was hard for Stefan to believe he was dragging this lie out of himself, but it couldn't be the truth.

'You sent him to help Father Byrne. You sent him to get Susan Field.'

'I didn't send anyone,' he said. 'When Francis called, he said he needed a car. I told him we'd see to it. So we sent a taxi, just a taxi. I don't know anything about a guard.'

They were automatic words, like automatic writing. He was somewhere else, and the fact that he was somewhere else testified to the truth of the words. And suddenly Stefan was looking at another face. It was the face of Hugo Keller, dying in the kitchen of the house in Eschenweg. Keller talked about the guard driving the car, the guard who took Susan Field away, the guard the monsignor sent. He didn't know who that guard was – Hugo Keller, the man who knew everything about everybody. But Jimmy Lynch had been selling him information for years. He was bought and paid for. Stefan had been so fixed on the one connection he had that linked Vincent Walsh and Susan Field that Hugo Keller's nameless guard had automatically become Detective Sergeant Lynch. But now, suddenly, it wasn't him at all.

As Stefan came out into the hall of Fitzpatrick's house again, Sister Brigid was climbing the stairs from the kitchen, carrying a tray with a cup of tea and a plate of scones and jam. She pursed her lips disapprovingly at him.

'I'm sure you've upset him again.'

'Yes.' He didn't feel like apologising, but he did. 'I'm sorry.'

'Did Francis look peaceful when you saw him, Mr Gillespie?'

There wasn't any point telling her he looked the way people do when they've been beaten to death, and that peacefulness isn't really in it.

'He looked peaceful enough, Sister.'

'I think in a way he has come back to us.' She smiled sadly and walked to the door into the study. She knocked. There was no answer. As Stefan stepped out into Earlsfort Terrace, Brigid opened the door. Monsignor Robert Fitzpatrick was sobbing, his head buried in his hands on the desk. She put down the tea and the scones and folded her brother in her arms.

The man who followed Stefan Gillespie from Earlsfort Terrace across into Stephen's Green would not make the mistake of being seen. He wasn't good at everything he did, but he was good at that. He could keep his distance; he had the instincts that told him when to disappear; he could always see his man again in a crowd. It didn't much matter if he lost him anyway, he wouldn't be difficult to find. If not today tomorrow, but today would be best, before he made more trouble. It was still early. It wouldn't be dark till after nine, but when night came he'd know where Sergeant Gillespie was. That would be the time to do it.

# 22. Dorset Street

Twenty-four hours earlier Stefan had known who killed Vincent Walsh and Susan Field. If Detective Sergeant Jimmy Lynch could be bought by Hugo Keller to collect information, he could be bought by Robert Fitzpatrick to clean up after him. A priest with such a high profile, who was in the habit of having sex with men like Vincent Walsh and writing them letters describing it, was always going to need help with his dirty laundry. The image of the moral crusader didn't sit very well with arranging abortions for priestly protégés who got themselves into trouble either. That's how Stefan had put it all together. The only question had been how far Lynch was following Fitzpatrick's instructions and how far he'd been, in the way of the Nazis the monsignor saw as the Church's salvation, working towards his Führer. Now, as he sat over a bony kipper and stewed tea in Bewley's Café he could see how much of it didn't fit after all, and how much he had ignored to get an answer.

Hugo Keller had told him and he hadn't heard. It was a guard, not Detective Sergeant Lynch, a guard. There were the Blueshirts too, the ones who had come for Vincent that night after the Eucharistic Mass, the night he was murdered. They couldn't have had anything to do with Jimmy Lynch.

He was exactly the kind of anti-Treaty IRA man the Blueshirts had been created to fight. Besides, Billy Donnelly had sat on those letters for a year before Lynch even joined the Guards. And however Lynch found out about them he didn't take them to help Robert Fitzpatrick, he took them to sell to Hugo Keller. There were always too many holes. The fact that Jimmy Lynch was bent didn't make him a killer, though he'd killed easily enough in the IRA. The fact that Robert Fitzpatrick hated Jews and admired Adolf Hitler didn't make him a killer either. Perhaps Stefan had wanted it to be the monsignor. He wanted it because of everything Fitzpatrick believed. He wanted it because the curate in Baltinglass was a little Fitzpatrick too. And there was Hannah. Perhaps he wanted to give her the answers she needed just a little too much. He had missed something. Now he had to go back and find what he'd missed. If anyone would let him. But if he couldn't, the book was still in his pocket, Hugo Keller's insurance policy, and tucked into it at the back were the letters to Vincent Walsh. It was his insurance policy now. If there were no more answers to find, Stefan had his weapon, and he would use it.

He was tired of thinking as he followed the familiar wall of Trinity College along Nassau Street, but the back bedroom on the top floor of Annie O'Neill's Private Hotel in Westland Row wasn't anything to hurry back to. The trains would have stopped now, but by five in the morning they'd be rattling over the bridge again and shaking the windows. It was cheap and Annie knew the Gardaí. Her husband had been in the Dublin Metropolitan Police when he disappeared in 1921. She always said he'd been shot by Michael Collins personally, which was no small honour, but everyone knew he'd left her for a woman who had a butcher's in Clonmel. There were always bottles in the sideboard in the dining room at Annie's and if you wanted to sit up all night with one of them you paid her what you thought you'd drunk, and if you couldn't remember she wouldn't overcharge you. The sheets weren't as clean as you'd like but at least they got washed now and again, and because she was used to guards staying when they were up from the country, she didn't care what time of the day or night you came and went. If you wanted rashers at five o'clock in the morning you'd find her in the kitchen cooking them. She said she could never sleep once the trains started up. When she was younger you could get more than rashers if you had a problem sleeping. Stefan smiled. At least Annie made him laugh. And one drink before he went to bed wasn't such a bad idea after all that tea.

In Lincoln Place there was a terrace of empty buildings. There were boarded-up shop fronts below and rows of black, broken windows above. The previous year one of the buildings had collapsed. There were piles of rubble where demolition had started and abruptly stopped, and on either side of the gap scaffolding held up the walls of adjacent buildings. A corrugated iron fence had shut off the collapsed building at first but the steel sheets had been robbed and the rubble and broken walls were open to the street. The man had followed Stefan Gillespie back to Annie O'Neill's earlier. He had followed him again that evening and waited, first outside Neary's and then in Grafton Street, never staying still for long, never being in one place too many times, always at a good distance. And when Stefan was clearly heading back to Westland Row he didn't follow him at all. He made his own way straight to Lincoln Place and waited. All that mattered was that there was no one there to see him. And it was late enough now. It was quiet. It would be all right.

He came at Stefan from behind, out of the darkness of the rubble of the ruined building. One arm was round Stefan's head, pulling his neck back, stopping his breath. The other was round his chest, pinning his arms to his sides. He was being dragged into the darkness, over the piles of bricks and broken glass and roof tiles and rubbish. It was so sudden and so unexpected that it took only seconds before he was behind half walls and heaped debris, unable to breathe, unable to make any sound except the choking in his throat. He was trying to kick, but the man was very strong. And as he was pulled back, further and further from the street, the man's elbow closed tighter on his neck. His lungs were bursting. Then the grip loosened. The man spun him round and pushed him against a wall. He held him with one hand and punched him in the stomach with the other, again and again.

Stefan dropped to the ground. He tried to move but he couldn't. He looked up. The man was standing over him. He couldn't see properly. It wasn't just the darkness. He had been almost unconscious. Now he began to make out the shape looming above him. Then it was clearer, even in the dim light. It was Detective Garda Seán Óg Moran, Jimmy Lynch's errand boy. He was holding a pistol in his hand. Stefan struggled to get up. Moran kicked him back. Then he knelt down. One knee was on Stefan's chest. One hand pinned his neck again. The other hand held the gun. Stefan knew what it was: the captive bolt pistol. He was going to disappear too. Maybe he'd lie in a shallow grave in the mountains, just like Vincent Walsh and Susan Field.

Tom would never even know what had happened to him. It was the image of Tom that filled his head. He tensed his hands. They were the only part of his body that had any strength left. And they were free. His fingers were touching something hard and cold close by. It was a piece of lead pipe.

As the big man cocked the pistol and bent closer Stefan swung his arm up, finding every bit of strength he had left. The lead hit Moran on the side of the head. He cried out and fell sideways. There was silence for a moment. Stefan knew that moment might be all he had. His blood was flowing; he was breathing deeply. He pulled himself up, leaning against the wall. Seán Óg was pushing himself up too, still dazed. He was still holding the gun, but it was no use to him at a distance. Stefan stepped forward, steadier now. He swung the pipe again, holding it with both hands now, driving it into the detective's ribs. Moran fell again. The gun dropped. He was in pain, agonising pain. But he was still trying to lift himself. Stefan swung the pipe against the back of his head. Seán Óg collapsed for the third time. And he didn't try to get up. For a few seconds Stefan stood over him with the pipe. He wanted to keep hitting him. He wanted to kill him. There was a little light now. The cloud was clearing. As he looked down he saw the pistol glinting in a puddle of oily water. He picked it up. Then he climbed over the piles of bricks and rubble and walked back into Lincoln Place.

\*

Stefan winced with pain as the Mother Superior of the Convent of the Good Shepherd dabbed iodine on to his chest and back. It was the next morning and he sat shirtless

412

in Mother Eustacia's office. He hadn't asked for her help, but the blood still seeping from the wounds inflicted on him by Detective Garda Moran was spotting his shirt. She looked at the bruising on his throat and neck. She drew her own conclusions, but said nothing. It would be an exaggeration to say she was pleased to see Stefan; she remembered his last visit and she remembered the dark-haired woman he'd come to collect.

'You shouldn't have left this.'

'It looks worse than it is.'

'I'd say it's worse than it looks.'

She walked to a cupboard and put the bottle away. As he dressed himself she sat behind her desk and put her clasped hands on the table. The good-shepherding was over. She looked at him with an air of cautious disapproval. 'I need to ask you some questions, Reverend Mother.'

'So I understand.'

'It's about a woman who was brought here.'

'A lot of women come here.'

'It was last year. The twenty-sixth of July. She was brought here quite late that night, in a car, by two men. One of them was a guard.' She was not going to be communicative, that was obvious enough; to say the other one was a priest wouldn't help. She might know about that or she might not know, but it was Garda Seán Óg Moran he needed to find out about now.

'I think you know that's not unusual.'

'He wouldn't have been in uniform.'

She said nothing.

'It was an abortion. Something went wrong. They couldn't stop her bleeding. She should have gone to a proper hospital, but the men came here with her.'

'These things happen. It wouldn't be the first time.'

'I think you saw her.'

'If I did I would have told them to take her straight to the Coombe.'

'That's what you did.'

'Then there don't seem to be any more questions, Sergeant.'

'She died.'

'Unfortunately that also happens.'

'Do you remember her? Her name was Susan Field.'

'Why do you want to know about this?'

'She didn't die because she couldn't get to a hospital in time. She died because the guard didn't bother to take her there. Either he let her die or he killed her.'

She was silent again. He knew she remembered that night.

'We found her body buried in the Dublin Mountains.'

'Unpleasant as that is, it doesn't mean she was killed.'

'I know she was killed. That's my job.'

'And my job is to provide a place of refuge.'

Stefan's opinion of that place of refuge was written on his face.

'People want their sewers to run under the streets, Sergeant, out of sight and out of smell. Isn't that part of your job too? You're a policeman. When I pray for the women in my charge it's not because the people who send them here don't need praying for too. But I leave that to others.' The contempt in her voice was not for the women who were locked away behind the convent walls.

He looked at her hard. In those last words there was almost contact, not sympathy, but something.

'You don't seem very surprised by any of this.'

'It's a long time since what men do to women has surprised me.'

'Did you know the men who brought her here?'

She hesitated, but she had made her decision.

'I saw the guard. He carried her in. The other man stayed outside in the car.'

It made sense. Moran was a big man. It wouldn't have been difficult. She was giving him what she knew now. If she didn't know the man in the car was a priest it wasn't going to help to tell her, let alone tell her about the other priest, the one in Earlsfort Terrace, who had arranged it all and wanted it covered up.

'You knew the guard?'

'I think he'd brought women here before.'

'Not in that state.'

She shook her head.

'But that wasn't why I recognised him. I remembered him from a pilgrimage to Lourdes, with some of the sisters. It was about five years ago now. General O'Duffy was taking a Garda pilgrimage at the same time. He was the Commissioner then. We were all on the same train through France. When we got to Lourdes he sent some of his lads to carry our luggage to the hostel. It was the guard who brought my suitcase. I didn't know his name.'

'You could testify that he was here that night?'

'No, I'm not in the business of testifying, Sergeant Gillespie.'

'But you just said —'

'You have your job to do in the sewers, and I have mine. That's all.'

When Stefan left the office, Mother Eustacia got up and pulled a thick foolscap book from a bookshelf. She took it back to her desk. It was a diary for 1934, a daybook with a page for every day of the year, where she noted everything that happened in the Convent of the Good Shepherd. She opened it at the twenty-sixth of July. It was the Feast of St Anne, the mother of the Blessed Virgin Mary. She carefully tore out the page and screwed it up. Then, without looking down, her hand reached for her rosary.

*

There were several pubs close to Dublin Castle that almost belonged to Special Branch. The same pubs the men of the Dublin Metropolitan Police's G Division had drunk in fifteen years earlier when they were hunting some of the men who stood at the same bars now. Since you could never quite tell in those days whether the Special Branch man on the corner stool was collecting information for the British or passing information about the men he was drinking with on to Michael Collins, assassinations in pubs could be counter-productive. It was safer all round to kill British intelligence officers when they were at home. The pubs all had different functions then and it was the same now. There were pubs for getting drunk in, pubs for meeting informants in, and pubs where your inspector was unlikely to find you. Farrelly's in Crane Lane had a small snug at the back, with a door to the jacks and a yard that led to an exit into Essex Street. Detective Sergeant Jimmy Lynch was in the snug when Stefan Gillispie arrived. He was eating a plate of rashers and drinking a mug of tea. He seemed amused to see Stefan again. It had been a long time.

'How's the farming going, Stevie?'

Stefan sat down. He knew Lynch's grin wouldn't last.

'Can I get you something?'

'I'm grand, thank you, Jimmy.'

'You'll be back on the job before long, I'd say.'

'Maybe. We'll have to see.'

'A man of mystery, eh?'

'Was Seán Óg in this morning?'

'Are you looking for him?'

'I will be at some point.'

'No. He done himself a bit of damage. Says he's broken a rib.' Lynch was looking at Stefan more cautiously. It wasn't an idle visit. He needed to know what it meant.

'He did me a bit of damage too. Nothing broken. I won't show you.'

'When was this?' The Special Branch man was uneasy. He didn't know why there should have been any contact between Moran and Stefan. Beating up another detective on his instructions was one thing; that was work. Seán Óg sometimes needed reining in, but still, it was only a fight.

'Last night, Jimmy. He was trying to kill me at the time.'

'He goes at it after a few –' Lynch laughed, but he didn't like this.

Stefan took the captive bolt pistol from his pocket and put it on the table. Lynch looked at it. He knew what it was, but that was all he knew.

'You've pigs to kill down on the farm then,' he grinned.

'Remember Susan Field?' continued Stefan, watching the detective closely. 'You took over the investigation into her death, last time we talked. I hear you didn't get far. The State Pathologist thought she'd been shot in the head with a captive bolt pistol. You said you didn't. But that's the gun. You might remember Vincent Walsh. He was buried in a little plot next to Susan's on Kilmashogue. You'd know him best for the letters Monsignor Robert Fitzpatrick wrote to him, the ones you sold to Hugo Keller. Wayland-Smith said he'd been shot in the head with a captive bolt pistol too. And that's the gun that shot them both.'

'What makes you think that?' Lynch was choosing his words carefully now. He didn't understand and he didn't know where this was going. But if he was thrown by the mention of the letters it didn't show.

'Seán Óg tried to put a hole in my head with it last night.'

Detective Sergeant Lynch was not often surprised; he prided himself on being too well informed for that. But he was certainly surprised now.

'I see. So what are you going to do, Stevie?' he asked.

'I don't have any witnesses, that's the trouble.'

'If that's true then all you've got is a gun from a slaughterhouse.' Lynch spoke slowly. He didn't know why Stefan was showing him a weaker hand.

'You'll have to do something, Jimmy. It's pushing it, even for Special Branch. You've got a guard who's murdered two people. It could have been three. What are you going to do, leave him where he is until the next time?'

Lynch's lips tightened. There was conviction in Stefan's words. He couldn't just dismiss them.

'He did kill them, Jimmy.'

'You know that?'

'I know it.'

'Let's say he did. Do you know why?'

'Not really. I don't know why he'd be covering up buggery and abortion, but that's all I've got now. Till yesterday I thought you did it.'

'Thanks.'

'Because of Hugo Keller. He was doing the abortion.'

'But not the buggering.'

'No.' He had to admire Lynch for his expressionless face. He had thrown Keller into the conversation again to see what response he got. It was nothing, almost nothing. But Keller was the Special Branch sergeant's weakness. How much did Stefan really know and how much was bluff?

'How did you know about Fitzpatrick's letters, Jimmy?'

'Is it letters or murder, what are you on now?'

As bluffs go, it wasn't one of Jimmy Lynch's best. Stefan smiled and ignored it.

'You found out from Seán Óg somehow, that's what I think. Wouldn't that be it?'

The detective didn't answer, but it was answer enough.

'When Broy brought you into Special Branch, Seán was already a guard. I'd forgotten that. He wasn't an obvious candidate for the Broy Harriers, was he? He was a pro-Treaty, Fine Gael man. You got him in.'

'We took different sides in the Civil War. So? Aren't we meant to put all that behind us now? Besides, we went through a lot together before that, fighting the Tans.'

'Camaraderie, that's nice to see, Jimmy. Was he ever a Blueshirt?'

'If he was he'd keep pretty quiet about it now.'

'I heard he went on a Garda pilgrimage with General O'Duffy.'

'A lot of guards did that. It's how you got promoted then.'

'Well, if any of them try to kill me I'll add them to the list. In the meantime, if you looked at the back of Seánie's wardrobe I'd be interested to see what colour the shirts

419

are, because I'd say he was there when that gang of Blueshirts went to Billy Donnelly's to get the letters, Monsignor Fitzpatrick's dirty letters. And when they didn't get them, someone sent him back to kill poor old Vinnie, to keep him quiet. What do you think, Sergeant?'

Lynch held Stefan's gaze but he was uneasy now. 'You'd have to ask Garda Moran, not me.'

'Come on, he told you about the letters. He must have done. And you worked out who might have them. Maybe you're not such a bad detective after all, when you put your mind to it. You traced them back to Billy Donnelly, and you put him in the Joy until he delivered them.'

'I thought this was about Seán Óg trying to kill you.'

'I'm short on evidence, I told you.'

'So?'

'I've got a lot more on you than I have on him. I've talked to your friend Keller.'

'Yes? Where is the old bastard now?' He made it sound like he wanted to send a postcard and all he needed was his change of address.

'He's not easy to get hold of,' replied Stefan. Again Hugo Keller alive somewhere was more useful than he was dead in Danzig. 'But I've got chapter and verse on what you sold him down the years. I've seen the book. Remember that book you wanted so much? I know why now. He kept very meticulous notes. I even know how much he paid you. I know which bits he passed on to our esteemed director of the National Museum and the Nazi Party na hÉireann too, and which ones he kept for a little private blackmail.'

Detective Sergeant Lynch's body tensed. He'd just run out of banter. This was all too close to home.

'That's a lot of bollocks.'

Stefan smiled. If all Jimmy Lynch could do was bluster, he had him.

'Right. And when I take it all to the Commissioner, it'll be your bollocks.'

*

The green door between Coyne's cycle repair shop and Verecchia's ice cream parlour in Dorset Street opened straight on to a flight of stairs. It led to a flat on the second floor of 47a that was a Special Branch safe house. Seán Óg Moran knew it well enough. He had a key. Sometimes he'd met an informant there with Jimmy. Sometimes there was a man his sergeant wanted questioned, who had to be kept there till he coughed up. Sometimes there was an informant who needed to lie low. There might even be an IRA man on the double-cross who had to hole up. He didn't ask too much. Jimmy never liked that. And it was Jimmy who'd got him his job. He owed a lot to Jimmy. If his sergeant wanted him to know something, well, he'd tell him.

Seán Óg's ribs were hurting like hell. The doctor had bound him up but there wasn't much else he could do. He had to take it easy; it would take time. He wasn't worried about Stefan Gillespie. No one had seen him. What was the word of a guard already on suspension against a Special Branch man's anyway? Special Branch looked after their own. He might have to come up with some explanation. He'd just say Gillespie had a grudge against him. They bumped into each other and got into a fight. That's as much as he'd need. Jimmy didn't have any time for the Protestant gobshite either. Seán Óg had been drinking steadily since the previous night. It was partly pain and

421

partly because he didn't know what else to do when things went wrong.

As he walked into the bare kitchen there was only a lamp on. Jimmy Lynch was sitting at the table. There was a bottle of Powers and several glasses. The room smelt as it always did – of stale air, cigarette smoke and greasy newspaper from the chipper. He didn't notice Stefan Gillespie at first.

'Jesus this rib's giving me some gyp.'

'We've got a problem, haven't we, Seánie?'

Moran saw Stefan, sitting in an armchair. 'What's he doing here?'

'Sit down.'

The big guard did as he was told. Lynch pushed a glass at him.

'What's he said?' Seán Óg reached for the bottle and a glass.

'This is yours, I think,' said Stefan as he got up and joined them at the table. He put the Accles and Shelvoke captive bolt pistol down in front of Moran.

The guard turned to Lynch uncertainly, then smiled.

'We got in a fight, that's all, Jimmy. We can work it out.'

'You think so?' There was nothing warm in the reply.

'Who's going to believe him?' Seán spoke as if Stefan wasn't there.

'Me. I believe him. You were going to fucking kill him.'

Moran was puzzled. He didn't expect Jimmy to talk to him like that.

'And then there's two people with holes in their heads that you buried out in the mountains at Kilmashogue. The little queer and the woman you picked up from Hugo Keller's clinic. Why, Seán? What did they do to you?'

'We can put it right. We always did. In the old days.'

'This isn't a fucking Tan or some RIC informant! It's not a war!'

'That's not true, Jimmy. There's more than one kind of war.'

'What's that supposed to mean?'

'There's the war against God.'

Lynch stared at him. It came from nowhere. It meant nothing to him. But Stefan already knew where it came from. It was shorthand, but he had heard it before. Seán Moran looked at Stefan directly for the first time. He spoke softly now, as if he was explaining something entirely reasonable.

'I'm sorry, Mr Gillespie, but what you tried to do to the monsignor, you couldn't be allowed to do that. Why couldn't you leave him alone? He's been chosen and you're trying to hurt him. If you understood the danger –'

Lynch was staring at them as if they had suddenly started talking to each other in another language. Stefan nodded as the big guard spoke.

'I do understand, Seán. I've heard the monsignor speak.'

'Then you know –'

'Well, I know what he believes.'

'I'm sorry. I wasn't meant to kill you then.' He smiled at Stefan, as if the thing had been resolved now. If Stefan knew about that, he must believe too. He must be all right.

'What the hell are you two on about?' interrupted Lynch.

'It's not so different from the Tans and the English, Jimmy.' Seán Óg turned towards his friend again. 'It's just the same. You remember what you told me when we shot those fellers in the war? Jesus, I still wake up sometimes

423

and I hear that lad in Finglas, screaming for his mother when you put the gun to his head. You don't choose them, you said. You don't want to kill them. You do it because there's something bigger, too big to let feelings get in the way. It was Ireland then, but this is the whole world. Jews and communists, plotting to destroy God's Church. The monsignor's the one fighting the evil at work in the world, you see, the evil even the Church can't see.'

He was articulate in a way that was unlike him. He spoke with calm assurance. He knew about this and, detective sergeant or not, Lynch didn't.

'Am I the only one here thinks he's in a madhouse?' asked Jimmy.

'I'm sure you can make Detective Sergeant Lynch understand, Seán.'

Stefan's eyes fixed on Lynch, telling him to shut his mouth and let Seán Óg talk. And the big guard did. Whether it was the familiarity of the safe house or the alcohol he'd been drinking all day, Garda Moran seemed to feel Sergeant Gillespie understood what had happened now. He was talking in a way he had never talked before. He'd thought about all this. He wanted other people to know. He had been carrying it for a long time. He didn't kill easily and now that it was in the open he had to explain it. Detective Sergeant Lynch wasn't in a madhouse but he was closer to a confessional than he knew.

'The queer lad was going to blackmail Monsignor Fitzpatrick. We had to protect him.'

'And what about Susan Field?' said Stefan.

'I didn't like it, but she was going to die anyway.'

Lynch reached for the Powers. Seán Óg pushed his glass across.

'Fill her up, Jimmy.'

'If you'd got her to the hospital –' Stefan felt he was close.

'It could have all come out then. And that wasn't right. It would have got in the way of the fight. Besides, after what she did to Father Byrne –'

'What was that?'

'She took him away,' said the big guard, shaking his head. 'Away from the light, Sergeant Gillespie. Away from the Mystical Body of Christ. That's where the struggle is. And Father Byrne betrayed it. It broke Monsignor Fitzpatrick's heart. But she did it, the woman. Sister Brigid said it was the sin that could never be forgiven. That's in the Bible. The woman knew what she was doing to him, you see, because she was a Jew, don't forget that. I did what I could though. I took her to the nuns, but they couldn't help her. It was too late. The abortion was piling sin on sin, you could see it in her body. That's why she was bleeding so much. There wasn't another way. I had to do it. And Sister Brigid said she would have died anyway. She knew.'

It was very silent. Jimmy Lynch just stared at his old friend. But now Stefan knew. He knew why it had all meant nothing to Robert Fitzpatrick.

'And was it Sister Brigid told you to kill Vincent Walsh?'

Moran nodded as if to say, why wouldn't she? He drained his glass of whiskey and reached out to pour one more.

'I hadn't seen her for years you know. When I was in the industrial school in Clontarf the monsignor was the parish priest. She kept house for him, just the way she does now. My best friend was Enda Dunne then. We'd go and do the garden for them. I don't say we did much really, probably made more mess than anything, but she'd give us a few coppers, and they'd a big orchard at the back. We

425

could take what we wanted. And sometimes we'd stay over. She'd read to us, stories like. She was the only one ever read a story to me. It was a little room at the top of the house. The best bed I ever slept in. If I'm home there's never a night I don't read to my kids. You know what's daft? They can read better than me. They pretend they can't but they show me up.' He laughed but as he spoke the words he said them with pride.

'You've known Sister Brigid a long time then, Seán?' said Stefan.

'We lost touch during the fighting. I think she guessed I was in the IRA, and she didn't approve. So, I don't know, about five years ago I saw the monsignor saying Mass at the Pro-Cathedral one Sunday, and there she was. She knew me straight away. I was a just a guard then, uniforms. That was before you turned up and got me into Special Branch, Jimmy. We go back a long way too, don't we? Sister Brigid said I should come and hear the monsignor at Earlsfort Terrace. I tell you, I never knew what was going on in the world. It frightened the life out of me. I wouldn't understand it all of course. She says one day Robert, that's the monsignor, one day he'll be a saint. But if you could vote for saints, I tell you she's the one I'd vote for.'

He stopped as if, having said what he had to say, it was over. He got up, smiling at Stefan like an old friend, even as he winced with pain. 'One to remember you by, Sarge.' He winked at Jimmy Lynch and then he left.

They said nothing for a long moment, listening to Seán Óg Moran's feet going down the stairs. The door slammed as he walked out to Dorset Street. Lynch poured the last of the whiskey from the bottle. He passed a glass to Stefan.

426

'Jesus Christ.'

Stefan could only nod in agreement.

*

Detective Sergeant Gillespie did most of the talking. Jimmy Lynch said very little. That was partly because he knew very little and partly because he was terrified of what Stefan was going to say about him. He knew Hugo Keller was dead now, but he felt as if his ghost was going to manifest itself at any moment in the Garda Commissioner's office and point the finger at him. He had nothing to worry about in the end. Stefan stuck to the matter in hand, the murders of Vincent Walsh and Susan Field and the murderer, Garda Seán Óg Moran. There were things Stefan didn't want to say in front of Detective Sergeant Lynch, and Lynch knew that, but it didn't mean they wouldn't be said eventually. He still didn't know how much Keller had told Stefan. Meanwhile the Garda Commissioner, who had spent most of the time standing at the window of his office looking at the trees of the Phoenix Park, was well aware of the gaps in Sergeant Gillespie's story. He wasn't sure he wanted more than he was getting. He might be happy to leave it at that. A guard killing on the instructions of a nun who happened to be the sister of one of the country's most prominent churchmen was more than enough to be going on with.

'I want every file you've got on this, both of you. Whatever notes there are, whatever paperwork, either at Pearse Street or Dublin Castle, I want it here. I want no copies left for anyone else to find. You tell no one.'

Ned Broy dismissed Jimmy Lynch first, though the Special Branch man seemed reluctant to go. It wasn't that he'd discovered a sudden liking for Stefan Gillespie but just now he didn't want to be separated from him, at least not when that meant leaving him on his own with the Commissioner.

'Get it done, Lynch!'

The door shut and a worried Detective Sergeant Lynch departed.

'I'll have to talk to the Minister of Justice. I'm not setting out to cover this up, but I know the first thing he'll say, "Why the fuck did you have to tell me?" I'll be frank, Sergeant, I don't know what we'll do. Whatever you're not telling me is probably best left alone. I don't need to know any more about Sergeant Lynch. The information from Mr Keller didn't only go one way.'

'I thought Jimmy was working for him.'

'He was. So he knows who's who. That makes him useful.'

'I wouldn't trust him further than I could throw him myself.'

'I can throw him a long way, and he'll find that out.' Broy smiled. 'But you can always do something with a man who'd sell his best friends for a few quid. If you know you can't trust a man, at least you know something.'

By the time Inspector Donaldson heard that Detective Sergeant Gillespie was in the building, every trace of material relating to the deaths of Vincent Walsh and Susan Field that hadn't been taken by Jimmy Lynch the previous year had been packed into cardboard boxes to be carried out of Pearse Street Garda station by Stefan Gillespie and Dessie MacMahon. There was a car from Garda HQ parked by the entrance. A uniformed guard took the boxes and packed them into the boot. As he slammed the boot shut and walked to the driver's seat, Inspector Donaldson appeared, flustered and red-faced.

'What are you doing here, Gillespie?'

'Orders, sir.'

'What's he taken, MacMahon? He's taken something!'

'Files, sir.' Dessie took out a Sweet Afton and put it between his lips. This seemed promising.

'What files?'

'Detective Sergeant Gillespie told me not to say.'

'You're still under suspension, Gillespie! You can't walk into my station and – I'll have you kicked so far the Commissioner –'

The back door of the car swung open.

'Jesus, Stefan, what are we waiting for now? Get in!'

The inspector stared. Then he snapped to attention and saluted.

'Sir!'

Stefan got into the car and shut the door. As the car drove off Inspector Donaldson was still saluting. Dessie was lighting his cigarette.

'Drop the sergeant at Annie O'Neill's in Westland Row.'

The Commissioner's driver nodded. Broy leant back into his seat.

'That's the lid on it as far as you're concerned, Gillespie.'

'Yes, sir.'

'And no more fecking freelancing.'

'No, sir.'

'I was never a by guess and by God sort of detective. Neither are you. So the holes in your story don't tell me what a clever feller you are, they tell me you're keeping something to yourself. You'll have your own reasons.'

Ned Broy's face was impassive; his words were matter-of-fact. But Stefan had every cause to believe that despite the Commissioner's disregard for guesswork, he was pretty good at it. He had guessed more than he said.

'I don't know what you mean, sir.'

'You wouldn't. But whatever you intend to do with what you've got hold of now, just make sure none of it finds its way back to me. I won't save you twice.'

*

The next morning Stefan Gillespie met Lieutenant John Cavendish upstairs in Bewley's. Cavendish was in uniform. Where his stock-in-trade before had been that he didn't really know what he was doing, now he was more business-like. Stefan pushed the Jacob's biscuit tin across the table. He had to do something with it. He had been tempted to throw Keller's book into the fire. But it was more important than he wanted it to be. It had to go somewhere.

'You'll want this.'

Cavendish opened the tin and took out the notebook. He nodded.

'Where did you get it?'

'It doesn't matter.' Stefan didn't know whether Eddie McMurrough was still driving his tractor up past the Avonbeg ford to Sheila Hogan's cottage, but he thought he probably was. Wicklow farmers were persistent. There was no reason why she shouldn't be left alone to find some kind of life.

'What did you make of it, Sergeant?'

'Some of it you could get from *Thom's Directory*. Like a list of Jews in Clanbrassil Street. Some of it you couldn't.

Like which ones have got real money and which ones have got friends in Fianna Fáil. You could move on to the Dáil members Keller treated for syphilis, and people in government who wouldn't squeak too loudly if the IRA found a way to get rid of Dev. I haven't memorised it all if that's what you're worried about. But it's in a simple enough shorthand. Anybody with decent German could read it.'

'Does it identify Keller's informants?'

'A lot of them probably. He's very thorough.'

There was nothing more to say. He knew what they really wanted. It wasn't about what Hugo Keller might have passed on to Adolf Mahr in the way of information; it was about where the information came from. It would be a list, another list of people. People who could be trusted and people who couldn't. And one day it might be about who was arrested and who wasn't. The smell of all that had been in his nostrils too long. He'd had enough of it.

'You've got what you want,' said Stefan.

'Is Miss Rosen going back to Palestine?' Cavendish asked.

Stefan was surprised. 'Why would that interest you?'

'It doesn't, but it interests you I imagine. I don't know if she's finished what she's doing for the Haganah, but I'm reliably informed she'll be lucky to get through London without British Intelligence putting a tail on her. When she gets to Palestine it's unlikely she won't be arrested and questioned by the Mandate Police. Not the Gestapo, but well worth her knowing.'

'Who told you that?'

'I talk to all sorts of people.'

'Does that include British Special Branch?'

'Please, Sergeant, you've got to draw the line somewhere. But don't think they're beyond exchanging information with German Intelligence, or the Gestapo if it suits them. Obviously she's drawn attention to herself.'

'I'll tell her. Thank you.' He smiled, remembering that first day in Pearse Street. 'I've questioned her myself. I'd say good luck to whatever colonial hack draws that straw.'

As he stood up to leave, Cavendish frowned.

'What did you make of the Nazis?'

'Make of them?'

'In their natural habitat.'

'They didn't surprise me, Lieutenant, if that's what you mean.'

'That's what's surprising, the fact that there's nothing surprising about them. They tell you who they are. They tell you what they want. They tell you what they're going to do. And when they do it, everyone's surprised.'

Not everything in Hugo Keller's notebook was in the biscuit tin Stefan had handed over to Military Intelligence. As he walked up Grafton Street and on to Stephen's Green, he was heading for Robert Fitzpatrick's house in Earlsfort Terrace. The letters the monsignor had written to Vincent Walsh were still in his pocket. He arrived as the bookshop opened. An elderly man told him that Monsignor Fitzpatrick was at Mass at the University Church and, though Stefan didn't ask, he also told him that Sister Brigid had been taken ill. The man seemed very worried, because the illness had come on so suddenly and he didn't even know where they'd taken her to be treated. Sister Brigid's abrupt illness didn't come as any great surprise to Stefan.

He left the house and walked back to Stephen's Green and the University Church. The Mass had ended now and he passed the last Mass-goers as he moved through the atrium of the long, narrow building. Angelic figures directed him into the blaze of marble and glass that was the nave, each one holding a scroll. 'Sanctus, Sanctus, Sanctus, Domine Deus Sabaoth.' Holy, Holy, Holy, is the Lord of Hosts. Above the altar, in a half dome of blue and gold and red, the Natural World paid homage to God's creation. At its centre sat Our Lady Seat of Reason. Robert Fitzpatrick knelt at the altar rail. His head was raised up to the Virgin above him, though his eyes were tightly closed. Stefan sat in a pew at the back of the church and waited for him. After a few minutes the monsignor rose from his knees and bowed his head. He crossed himself and turned to leave, but as he walked forward he saw Stefan Gillespie get up and step into the aisle in front of him, blocking his way.

# 23. Westland Row

'I don't think we have any more reason to speak to each other, Sergeant.'

'I think we have, Monsignor.'

'That's not my understanding. You certainly have no business here.'

'It won't involve anything God doesn't know already.'

'My sister has done nothing. It's a lie.'

'You think so? She told Seán Moran to get your letters from Vincent Walsh. When his Blueshirt pals buggered it up she sent him back to shut the poor bastard up for good. And when you told her to send a taxi car for Father Byrne, to bring Susan Field to hospital, she sent Seán instead, to clean up the mess. You do know why Vincent wouldn't let go of the letters? He'd got the wrong end of the stick. He actually thought he was protecting you, Monsignor.'

It was difficult to read what was going on in Robert Fitzpatrick's head. For some seconds he simply stared at Stefan. His face was white. There was something almost ferocious in his eyes; it could have been rage or despair. Then, quite abruptly, it was gone, and there was nothing. It was as if a light had been switched off. His face relaxed into a look of calm, bland disdain.

'There really is no more to say, Sergeant Gillespie.'

'I don't care what you tell yourself, Monsignor. I don't care what you believe. I'm not here for that.'

'Then why are you here?'

'Because I need your help.'

'And what makes you think I'd want to help you?'

'I'm sure you will. They can put a lid on a lot, but not on me. I haven't finished with you.'

'You disgust me!'

Robert Fitzpatrick stepped past Stefan. He gave him a look of withering contempt. Stefan grabbed him. He turned the priest round and held him by the lapels of his jacket, pulling him close and gazing angrily into his eyes.

'You need to talk to me. You really do, I promise you.'

He let him go. Fitzpatrick didn't move.

'Do you know who Father Anthony Carey is?'

The priest was puzzled. The name meant nothing immediately.

'He's a curate in Baltinglass, but that's not it; he's in your Association of Catholic Strength. I think he's a man you would probably know, Monsignor.'

Fitzpatrick answered warily, slowly, but he answered.

'Yes, yes, I think I know who you mean. But I don't understand –'

'Your Church is trying to take my son away from me, because of him. And he's your man, isn't he?' Stefan explained what had happened. He didn't need to go into detail. It all made sense to Robert Fitzpatrick. In fact there was nothing about it that seemed in the least bit unreasonable to him. The contact he had had with Stefan Gillespie now gave him every reason to believe that Father Carey had been doing what any decent priest should have done.

'This isn't any business of mine.'

'You can make it your business.'

'Why should I? Why would you imagine I'd even consider it?'

He would have said more, but he stopped. Stefan was smiling.

'Because I've got the letters you wrote to Vincent Walsh.'

Fitzpatrick froze. He had thought there was nothing to this other than more unpleasantness, but the letters were different. Whatever the detective knew about their content, he still believed they had disappeared along with Hugo Keller. It hadn't occurred to him that they were in the hands of this man who had done so much damage and caused so much pain. But the priest's sense of who he was, his sense of his fundamental invulnerability, was still there.

'Are you trying to blackmail me?'

'Yes, I am. I'm glad you understand that, Monsignor.'

'I see. And what are you going to do with these letters?'

He had found a smile, a half-smile, from somewhere. He was still stronger than this policeman. He had too many friends. No one would listen.

'I'm going to do more than Herr Keller, I promise. I know a man who knows a man in London who's in the market for that sort of thing. Journalist might not be the right word for it. He works for the *News of the World*. Nobody would ever publish anything in Ireland, of course not, but it's still quite a story; buggery, abortion, unexplained deaths. And who knows what they'd come up with? Maybe they'd find some other fellers out there who remembered you. What would you do, sue? It would be some case. And they're not so delicate with priests at the Old Bailey. One way or another you'd be finished in the Church. And I'd forget any plans you might have about sainthood.'

It really was blackmail, plain and simple. And there was nothing Robert Fitzpatrick could do about it. Blackmail is only ever as effective as the blackmailer's determination to carry through his threat. The monsignor only had to look into Stefan Gillispie's eyes to see that he meant every word he said.

'I'm done speaking for the dead, Monsignor Fitzpatrick. Now I'm speaking for myself. You will help me or I'll make it my only purpose in life to destroy you.'

*

An end was needed to the whole affair, but it was difficult for the Garda Commissioner and the Minister of Justice to find one. Among the few people who knew the story there were already different versions. Even Stefan's version had its versions. There was the version for Ned Broy, the version for Dessie, the version for Susan's father, the version for Hannah. The version he gave her was close enough to the truth, but didn't contain everything. What the Commissioner told the Minister and what the Minister told anyone else was something else again. There were certain things that could be done. Sister Brigid Fitzpatrick took a sudden decision to spend the rest of her days behind the impenetrable walls of a contemplative order of Carmelite nuns in County Limerick. She would never leave. She understood what had to be done although she would never feel any need for her daily prayers to be prayers of penitence. She would shut her life off from the world for the same reason she told Seán Óg Moran to kill: to protect

437

her brother and allow him to fight the mystical war that would save mankind.

Monsignor Robert Fitzpatrick, who had done nothing of course, would continue to proclaim the conspiracies of Jews and communists, and there were many who heard him sympathetically within the Church. His ideas were, after all, not wrong in themselves; they simply needed to be voiced less stridently. Not everyone could warm to Adolf Hitler, and there were certainly some unpleasant aspects to Nazism; but the real enemy was still red, not red and black; the hammer and sickle not the swastika. And with democracy on its last legs, something had to bring order to the chaos of secularism and immorality it would leave in its wake. The Nazis came down on their opponents hard, no doubt about that, but these were hard times. And if Adolf Hitler did keep talking about eradicating Jews, why would anyone want to take all that bluster literally? The man was a politician after all. The Church didn't have to like Herr Hitler to know that for now the future was with him. There was a longer game for the church to play than any Thousand Year Reich fantasies. It wasn't as if Robert Fitzpatrick didn't understand that. He spoke with the voice of the age. And somebody had to. Among the carpenter's tools were axes and hammers as well as fine chisels; now was the time of the axe and hammer.

Nevertheless, whatever version of the story Ned Broy and the Garda Chaplain told Archbishop Edward Byrne, at the archbishop's palace in Drumcondra, it was felt that Monsignor Robert Fitzpatrick would benefit from several years away from Ireland, researching his book on the Mystical Body of Christ at the Gregorian University in

Rome. The need for all this new research came upon him almost as rapidly as his sister's illness on her.

*

The day after Stefan Gillespie's conversation with Robert Fitzpatrick in the University Church, he saw Hannah Rosen for the last time. They both knew it would be the last time and neither of them wanted to spend an evening talking about that, or worse trying to pretend there was something else to talk about. Instead they sat in the darkness at the Gate Theatre and let other people speak. It didn't matter what the play was. It happened to be *The Taming of the Shrew*. It had the benefit of being long, but although it carried no special resonance for them, nothing that was about love felt easy. They would both have preferred an unhappy ending. However, they needed to be together and the Gate was a place to be that made silence something they could share. As they left the bar after the performance Micheál Mac Liammóir was heading towards it, out of costume now but with traces of make-up still on his face. He recognised Stefan and stopped, smiling.

'The thin detective! And how's the fat one?'

'He's not a great one for the theatre, Mr Mac Liammóir.'

'Did we scare him off?'

'There's not much that scares Dessie.'

'But it can be done.'

Stefan laughed. 'This is Miss Rosen. Hannah, Mr Mac Liammóir.'

'A pleasure, my dear.' He took her hand. He turned back

to Stefan, lowering his voice. 'Did you ever find out anything about the boy, Vincent?'

'We didn't.' It was an official lie. He didn't like it any more for that.

Mac Liammóir looked at him harder. It was difficult not to feel he knew more, or at least that he already suspected there was more to know.

'Well, we saw him off, just after Christmas. Eric Purcell was going down to Carlow to the funeral. I don't know how he cudgelled the details out the mammy but he did, and in the end a few of us decided to take the train as well, chums from the theatre and other assorted reprobates. I'd always wanted the chance to sing the song, so I did, on the train. "Up with halberd, out with sword, on we'll go for by the Lord, Feach MacHugh has given word! Follow me down to Carlow!" I'm not entirely sure Carlow has recovered yet.' He spoke more softly. 'If his mother and father didn't know him, I hope they knew there were people who cared about him, and loved him, it was a lonely end.'

When they left the Gate and walked down O'Connell Street towards the river it wasn't a journey they enjoyed, but they still didn't want it to stop. What Hannah knew about Susan's murder now was nearly as much as she could know. She seemed almost less angry than Stefan about the wall the state had already built around Monsignor Robert Fitzpatrick and Hugo Keller and Father Francis Byrne and Vincent Walsh and Brigid Fitzpatrick, and Susan Field too. She knew there was no further to go. There wasn't the resolution public justice should have brought, but she could do no more to repay the debt she owed to her childhood friend, except for one thing. She could live. For the moment she was thinking about the other dead body on Kilmashogue, the man she knew nothing about, who had died in the same way her friend had, for the same reasons, for nothing at all it seemed to her.

'I'd forgotten about him, Vincent Walsh,' she said.

'I'm glad not everybody has.'

'His parents don't know what really happened?'

'There's no one to tell them.'

'There's you.'

'Not everyone's like you. Not everyone wants to know.'

'Do you believe that?'

'There's a time to stop. I believe it's not my business any more. '

Somewhere that business that wasn't his was Hannah too. He didn't want it to mean that, but it soon would. They walked on again in silence.

'What will you do?' asked Hannah.

'My suspension's over, as of next week. I'm thinking I'll get out of Dublin and go back into uniform. When Ned Broy's thanked me for keeping my mouth shut about everything a few more times, I'd say he'll be glad to see the back of me. I think a lot of people will. He owes me a favour, so he can send me down to Baltinglass. Maybe I've got used to being at home after all these months.'

'Is that what you want?' She didn't altogether believe him.

'I don't know what I want. I think it's what I owe Tom.'

'That's not the same thing.'

'It's close enough,' he smiled. 'There are things you can't have.'

'If there was any point talking about it, Stefan –'

'I know that.'

441

'It doesn't mean I haven't thought about it. I have.'

'I'd have hoped so.'

'I've thought about it a lot.'

'That's the difference. I don't need to think about it.'

'Please don't, Stefan –'

'I think if we were going to find a way to be together we'd have done it, Hannah. I think with you, if I need to ask at all, then there's no point asking.'

They had reached the Liffey. Dublin was quiet now. They stood on O'Connell Bridge, watching the grey stream of water move towards the docks and the sea. There was no moon, only cloud and the city's lights below it.

'I wanted to change my mind. I can't. It's not easy to say that.'

'I know my psalms. I sang them as a boy at St Patrick's. They stick in your head, whether you want them to or not sometimes. "If I forget thee, O Jerusalem." That's the one that's been sticking. I might be able to compete with Benny and the oranges, but I can't compete with three thousand years of memory. I don't know the man, but I know it's not him you're marrying.'

She could have been angry with him, but too much of it was true.

'I wasn't sure what I felt when I came back, Stefan. I wasn't sure what I wanted. I mean when I first got home last year, before I met you.'

'And now you've met me, you're sure. Thanks,' he laughed.

'No, being in Europe made me sure. Danzig made me sure.'

'This isn't Germany. It never will be.'

'I don't know what it is.'

'You're Irish. You don't mean that.'

'And you're a policeman. If they sent you to Clanbrassil Street to fill a truck with Jews and take them to a concentration camp – would you do it?'

'That couldn't happen, you know that.'

'People like Monsignor Fitzpatrick would stop it, you mean.'

'He's not the Catholic Church.'

'No. But perhaps he's more of it than I want to live next door to.'

Stefan said nothing, but he knew she was still waiting.

'You didn't answer my question. What would you do?'

'I hope I'd refuse to do it.'

'You hope?'

'I wouldn't do it. Don't you know that?'

'You'd walk away?'

He nodded, but he knew it sounded like evasion, not principle.

'You think walking away would be enough?'

'No.' He couldn't say otherwise. He remembered Danzig too.

'I don't think so either. That's what I've learned, I suppose. I need to be where someone picks up a gun, not where people turn their backs.'

'Well, you've got the money for them.' It was a stupid thing to say, but her words had hurt him. They hurt all the more because she was right.

'You think we shouldn't defend ourselves, Stefan?'

'I didn't mean that. I'm sorry. But I can't fight any of this, Hannah. I want to talk to you about how I feel, about you and me. You want to talk about the world turning itself upside down and inside out. How do I deal with that?'

'I need a place to stand, Stefan.' She took his hand and smiled, looking up at him tenderly. 'I've always wanted to make up my own mind about everything. My parents never did, or my grandparents. As far back as you want to go. Everything that happened to them was someone else's decision. Sometimes whether you lived or died depended on nothing more than other people's moods, that's all. And it doesn't feel any different now. I don't want to live like that. I can't. I never really intended to go to Palestine. It was Susan who was the Zionist. She used to irritate me because she was always so sure about it. I didn't want the label. But my label's in my blood.'

'So is it for her as well?'

'Is what for her?'

'Palestine.'

She didn't respond, then she shrugged. 'I suppose a part of it is.'

'You're going to live Susan's life too?'

'If I can.'

She looked at him with something like defiance.

He smiled. She was still the woman he had met at Merrion Square.

They started to walk on, holding hands. As they reached Burgh Quay she put her arm through his and held him closer to her. They turned left along the Liffey. He could feel the rain beginning. It wasn't heavy; it was what it always was, the soft, grey, constant rain of Ireland.

'We won't see each other again,' he said.

'I know.' She held his arm tighter. 'I'd like a drink, Stefan.'

'There's nowhere open,' he smiled, 'it's Dublin, remember?'

She stopped. She was crying. He pulled her to him and held her.

'It's what I have to do. Can't you understand? I just want to live!'

At Westland Row Annie O'Neill produced a warm bottle of sweet white wine they didn't ask for and didn't want. She'd been drinking. As she left them she pushed a key into Stefan's hand. 'No one's in the front double.'

*

The next morning they dressed with a familiarity that reminded him for a moment of Maeve, taking no real notice of one another. It wasn't a painful memory. What was painful was that within a very short time this would be another memory. Hannah was aware of it too. As they walked out of the hotel into Westland Row she kissed him, quite abruptly, and then shook her head as he started to say something. She didn't want him to speak. She turned and walked away towards Lincoln Place. He stood looking after her, remembering the woman he had first seen in Merrion Square as he sat in a smoke-filled car with Dessie MacMahon. She moved with the same self-assurance. He knew now that sometimes she had to work hard at that. He smiled, hearing Dessie's words the second day they saw her. 'She's back, your dark-eyed acushla.' He waited, watching her move through the crowds going to work along Westland Row until she was gone. She didn't look back. He turned the other way and walked down to the junction with Pearse Street. The tram took him past the Garda station and Trinity College and then along the Liffey and the Quays to Kingsbridge, to catch the train to West Wicklow.

Later that day Stefan stood in the door of the farmhouse. Tom and his grandfather were driving the cows in from the fields for milking, as they did every evening. There were fresh flowers from Helena's garden on Maeve's grave. He had taken them up that afternoon with Tom. The swallows, back barely a week themselves, were feeding excitedly over the farmyard. He watched his son run out of the milking parlour, chasing the sheepdog. Three hills looked down: Keadeen, Kilranelagh, Baltinglass Hill. They were safe.

# 24. Baltinglass Hill

There was never any record of an interview with Garda Seán Óg Moran. After the night in Dorset Street with Stefan Gillespie and Jimmy Lynch, he stayed at home. Those were Jimmy's orders. The broken rib was slow to heal. The Garda doctor saw him three times and was in no hurry to declare him fit for duty, even when his own doctor said he was fine and getting back to work was exactly what he needed. But Seán Óg was in no great hurry to return to work himself. His life had been spent doing what he was told; if he was being told to stay at home, he was happy enough doing it for a while.

Most mornings he walked along the Grand Canal from the little house in Warren Street to the Church of St Mary and St Peter in Rathmines for Mass. Every three or four days he'd go to the library to get books for his children. The rest of the time he was either drinking in McGee's or trying to turn the patch of ground at the back of the house into the garden he had always promised his wife. He had bought a lot of seeds, but other than that progress was slow. Afternoons were devoted to the garden, and most afternoons, when he came home from McGee's, he slept. But a start had been made anyway, with the seeds. By next summer it would be done.

As May turned into June he was growing uneasy. He hadn't seen Jimmy Lynch in two months. He'd have thought Jimmy, of all people, would have dropped into the pub, or taken him for a game at Christy Thompson's Billiard Rooms. Jimmy had told him to keep his head down of course, and that was fair enough, but the other business would be forgotten now, surely. He'd never heard another word about it and the Garda Síochána was still paying him. It was maybe time to think about going back to work. He was five days into a novena at the church just now and he went to St Mary's every morning to recite the rosary. Next week, when he was finished, he'd go into town and see the lads in Special Branch for a drink in Farrelly's. But that was next week. Today he had the novena to think about. He put his rosary in his pocket and kissed his wife goodbye, in the way that people do when they've been married a long time – hardly noticing but never forgetting. His two children were with him as he left the house, a boy of six and a girl of eight. The six-year-old held his hand. Peadar Hayes had told him in McGee's the night before that he'd some African marigold plants he could have for the new garden. He'd get those on the way back from the pub and plant them that afternoon. The kids could help him after school.

When they reached the Grand Canal Seán Óg turned right towards Rathmines and the children turned the other way to go to school. He saw Eddie Sullivan's horse and cart pulling into Martin Street. Eddie didn't stop when Seán Óg bellowed after him, to ask when the fuck he'd be delivering the turf he'd promised. He'd be delivering it when he had the fucking time, and he made a mental note that would be when he was clearing his yard of the broken, wet turf from last winter nobody wanted. Moran could never be arsed to pay and he expected an extra load every time because he was a policeman. 'Well you'd want to keep on the right side of me, wouldn't you, Eddie?' That was always the joke, and Eddie always laughed and went away thinking did he really need to keep on the right side of the great gobshite?

The swans on the canal were noisy that morning. Seán liked the swans. He thought they were lucky. Sometimes he counted them while he walked along, just for something to do that he had the habit of doing, and because he thought the more there were the luckier they were. There weren't very many that day as he crossed over the road to walk along the towpath, and they were scrapping and squabbling the way swans do sometimes. He wasn't particularly aware of the two men coming towards him as he approached Kingsland Parade. They crossed on to the towpath as well.

There was something about one of the men he thought he recognised. He knew a lot of people. It was maybe someone he hadn't seen in a long time, but he knew him, he definitely knew him. There was a half smile on the man's face. Was he thinking the same thing? There was a smile on Seán Óg Moran's face too, as the first bullet hit him. He didn't fall. He was a big man. The second bullet hit him in the head and he was dead before his body hit the ground. The two men walked quickly across the road again. A black car pulled out of Martin Street. And then they were gone. The only sound was the hissing and snarling of the swans Garda Moran hadn't finished counting.

It was reported as an IRA assassination and Seán Óg Moran's name would go down on the Garda roll of honour. President Éamon de Valera said he died for his country.

And he did. There were some things it was better his country didn't know; if the president didn't know either it made it all the easier. He could never be put on trial for what had happened but something had to be done. Just as Special Branch looked after its own, it cleaned up its own mess too. If the men on the towpath didn't know Garda Moran, the man driving the car did. It was Detective Sergeant Jimmy Lynch.

When Eddie Sullivan finally delivered the load of turf to the house in Warren Street it was the best he had; and he never did ask to be paid for it.

*

It was a bright, hot day in August. Stefan Gillespie was walking along the main street of Baltinglass with Tom. There was a job to do that he didn't want. It brought the world outside into the small West Wicklow town in a way only he could understand. The night before he had read Hannah's letter again. It had arrived from Tel Aviv the week before. He had written to tell her what had happened to Seán Óg Moran, not with any sense of satisfaction but because he had to. It was only right. But it was clear she felt no less uncomfortable than he did about the mess of lies and evasion and, finally, stark brutality that had been served up as some kind of apology for justice.

*It's an end, but not much of one. I don't know what I expected. Something honest, I suppose. Instead there's just another kind of murder. Or maybe it's the same kind of murder, because there's something else to hide. We deserved more than that, even the man who killed*

*my friend deserved more than that. After everything*
*that's happened I'm not as good as I thought at an eye*
*for an eye. I think I wanted to leave all that in Danzig.*
*People feel it here too. Darkness, I mean. We're all*
*looking at the light and just hoping the dark goes away.*

As Station Sergeant in Baltinglass, Stefan used every opportunity to escape from the barracks in Mill Street. He had
a limited appetite for the kind of peace and quiet that kept
him sitting in an office processing the mountain of paperwork that just doing nothing seemed to generate. The
pleasure of being at home with his son was one thing; it
was what he had fought for. But there was a lot less pleasure
in the four dark walls of the front office at the Garda station.
There were no detectives in Baltinglass, however, and in
their absence he did his own detective work; it kept his
mind from seizing up and it got him out of the station. It
suited Inspector Riordan, who didn't like detectives coming
down from Naas and poking about in his domain. If his
sergeant could keep them at bay so much the better. An
afternoon out of the station should have been what Stefan
wanted on a day like this, but he wasn't going to enjoy the
appearance he had to make on Baltinglass Hill

The Archaeology Department of UCD had been exca-
vating the passage tombs on the upper slopes of the hill
throughout the summer, and today the director of the
National Museum was visiting the site. In a town where
not much happened, Adolf Mahr's arrival was a big event.
Local dignitaries would be out in force. And as Inspector
Riordan was in court in Naas all day, Stefan would have to
represent the Gardaí. His knowledge of the archaeologist's
extra-curricular activities in the Nazi Party left him with

no desire to be among the enthusiastic hand-shakers, but he had no choice.

He had walked up to the site several times that summer with Tom, who had just about worked out what archaeology was and had now decided he wanted to be an archaeologist when he grew up. He had been digging holes all over the farm for the last two months and the bedroom he shared with his father was filled with rusty iron and broken crockery. Stefan didn't want to make any more of Mahr's visit than he had to, but once Tom got hold of the news that the most important archaeologist in Ireland was coming it was impossible to tell him he couldn't go to the site with his father.

There were several cars parked by the lane that led up towards the summit of Baltinglass Hill, but what Stefan saw first was the motor coach. A swastika pennant fluttered on the bonnet; several more hung on the insides of the windows. Adolf Mahr hadn't only brought his archaeological hat to West Wicklow. The German community in Ireland had its own Hitler Youth branch now and they were down on a day trip to see the dig. It was the first time Stefan had seen a swastika flying since leaving Danzig. The world of missing sheep and poached salmon suddenly felt further away. The one that filled the newspapers and the wireless was in front of him again. He took Tom's hand. Tom grinned up at him. 'I like their flag, don't you, Daddy?'

At the top of Baltinglass Hill there was a wide ring of heaped stones that had once supported a great cairn over a passage grave. Three thousand years ago it would have been visible for many miles, like a pyramid. The cairn had been dismantled long ago, though its stones were to be found in the Iron Age earthworks that surrounded the hilltop and in the hundreds of field walls that spread out across the countryside below. Inside the ring were the quarried pillars and slabs of the tombs that were being mapped and scraped and dug by the students from UCD. Adolf Mahr stood in front of the wall of stones, with a dozen archaeologists on one side and a group of children and teenagers on the other. The boys wore the brown shirts and shorts of the Hitler Youth; the girls were in white blouses and dark blue skirts. A swastika flew beside an Irish tricolour. The great and good of Baltinglass looked on approvingly. Sheep grazed indifferently at the edges of the crowd. Stefan and Tom joined the onlookers. It was a long climb and they were sweating.

Stefan saw the Church of Ireland minister, the Reverend Fisher, standing with Father MacGuire; the two men were laughing. From behind they were almost indistinguishable in their black suits and black hats.

Father Carey had been gone for two months now. His bishop had been surprised to receive an abrupt note from him in May to say how concerned he was that pursuing the issue of Tom Gillespie and his Protestant father might cause divisiveness in the community at a level he had not anticipated. He had to question whether the case was good for the Church after all. The note was so unlike the single-minded, bull-headed aggression that had filled the curate's previous letters that the bishop could hardly believe it was from the same man. Divisiveness was Anthony Carey's stock-in-trade. He had certainly never shown the slightest regard for the Protestants in his community before. Clearly something had happened. The bishop didn't know what and didn't much care. He had been backed into a corner by the turbulent curate and his friends in the Association of Catholic Strength. There was an appetite for putting Protestants in their place that he was a lot less enthusiastic about than some of his younger priests. So it was with considerable relief that the bishop called the Church's lawyers and told them to find a suitable resting place for the file on Mr Gillespie and his son. He also decided it was high time Father Carey had his own parish. He had no vacancies himself, unfortunately, but he noted that other bishops did. The curate wasn't missed in Baltinglass. If nothing else it meant the parish priest and the Church of Ireland canon could go back to playing chess with each other on Fridays, as they always did before Father Anthony Carey's arrival.

At the Pinnacle, on the top of Baltinglass Hill, Adolf Mahr's voice fought the wind that always blew there, but his presence was more important than what he was there to say. He slipped from English into German and back, even though most of the German children spoke English too. The onlookers liked that. It made the half-heard words feel somehow universal.

'Prior to the coming of megalithic civilisation, around five thousand years ago, the north and west of Europe was inhabited by isolated and primitive tribes of hunter gatherers. We don't know how the newcomers came to Ireland, by boat from Iberia or from Britain, but it is their skill with stone that left the first marks of civilisation on our landscape. They still stand on our hillsides today, these tombs and monuments that needed sophisticated organisation, technical expertise and huge resources in manpower. Who were these people? We have no idea. These are their only memorials. We will never know the language they spoke or the gods they worshipped. As they displaced the tribes before them, so they were displaced by the next wave of invaders, who brought bronze and then iron to Ireland. We don't know whether they were extirpated or enslaved or simply absorbed by the Celts who finally claimed this island for their own. We may feel sadness sometimes, looking at these remains, for they are wonderful things and we should cherish them, but history is unsentimental. It is like nature. It obeys similar natural laws. The strong will survive; the weak will disappear.'

The German Stefan heard wasn't quite the same as the English. In German it was the strong race that survived and the weak race that disappeared. He didn't applaud as Adolf Mahr concluded with a few words in Irish to thank the local community for its support. Then, unexpectedly and delightfully for everyone there, with a nod and a smile from Mahr, the German children started to sing. The music was Schubert's, the words Goethe's. It had been one of his grandmother's favourite songs. 'Über allen Gipfeln is Ruh.' Over mountain and hill all is still. 'In allen Wipfeln spürest du kaum einen Hauch.' Through all the trees scarcely a breeze; in the forest there is no birdsong. Wait, wait, before long you will find peace.

There was more applause, and people moved forward to chat and shake hands all over again. Stefan had had enough. He took Tom's hand and started to walk away. As he did the Reverend Fisher and the parish priest turned towards him. 'Marvellous, Stefan, don't you think?' said the Church of Ireland minister. There were tears in his eyes. Those young voices had touched something inside him; perhaps it was the memory of his own youth. He lowered his voice. 'There may be a lot of things we don't like about Herr Hitler, but my goodness, there are things we could learn.'

Father MacGuire smiled. 'Probably great craic as long as you don't want to sing a different tune, wouldn't you say, Sergeant?'

Stefan nodded. 'I'd say so, Father.'

Tom was pulling at his hand. As he looked round he saw that Adolf Mahr was walking towards them, smiling at the priest and the minister. 'Thank you for coming, gentlemen. It's quite a climb. But worth it for the view.' They exchanged a few words about the view and the rain that usually meant there wasn't one, before the director of the National Museum stretched out his hand to Stefan.

'Thank you as well, Sergeant.'

Stefan had no option but to shake his hand.

'There's no need to thank me, Herr Doktor Mahr.'

The polite but unsmiling look and the oddly correct German unsettled Mahr. It seemed out of place. Something about the policeman was slightly familiar. He looked down at the small boy beside him and smiled warmly.

'Are you interested in archaeology?'

'I know it's where we came from.'

'It is indeed,' laughed the director. 'Good boy!'

He reached out and tousled his hair. Stefan, who was holding Tom's hand, instinctively pulled him away. It was done without thinking; he didn't want Mahr touching his son. The German was puzzled. He felt the hostility.

'Do we know each other, Sergeant?'

'No, we don't know each other,' said Stefan coldly.

As he walked away with Tom, the archaeologist watched him, now more puzzled than before. He paused for a minute, unable to remember why Stefan seemed familiar, then almost immediately he forgot about him and turned back to the queue of people who were waiting to shake his hand.

Stefan and Tom walked east from the Pinnacle, looking at the high, flat top of Keadeen and the Wicklow Mountains beyond. Within minutes the tip of Baltinglass Hill was out of sight behind them. The people were gone. There was only the rough grass and the gorse and the view across the fields towards the farm below Kilranelagh, and a few crotchety, grumbling sheep fanning out in front of them as they walked down the gentle slope.

'Were they all killed?' Tom was thinking hard.

'Who?'

'The people who lived here once. Who built the stones.'

'I don't know. Nobody really knows what happened. I don't suppose all of them were. I've always thought they're still here in some way.'

'Like ghosts?'

'Not like ghosts. I just mean . . . in us really. Well, we all come from somewhere. But if you keep going back to our grandparents and our great-grandparents and our great-great-grandparents for thousands of years, well, we probably all come from everywhere. Does that make any sense?'

Tom frowned. He wasn't really sure it did. Stefan smiled.

'But is this where we belong?' asked the boy.

'Well, there isn't anywhere else, so I'd say so, wouldn't you?'

Tom nodded. That seemed to make all the sense he needed.

They carried on down the hill. The wind had dropped now and they could feel the warmth of the sun. Tom still held his father's hand. Hannah's letter was in Stefan's mind again. He thought of her last words. 'There's not a lot of light. It's what makes it special. Thank you for giving me some of yours. I won't forget.' He wouldn't forget either. She had given him her light too.

Tom suddenly let go of Stefan's hand and started to run down the hill, faster and faster, scattering the bleating sheep ahead of him, and sending a pair of larks chirruping up out of the gorse into the clear, evening sky. He was shouting and laughing, just because he wanted to shout and laugh. And as Stefan chased after him, he was laughing as well, and for exactly the same reason.

# A Tale of Two Treaties

*The Free State: Ireland in the 1930s*

After almost eight hundred years of first Norman, then English invasion and occupation, including the union of Britain and Ireland that had been in place since 1801, the Irish Free State (Saorstat Éireann) was established as a self-governing dominion of the British Empire on 6 December 1922 as a result of the Anglo-Irish Treaty that had ended the War of Independence in 1921. For about one day the Free State comprised the entire island of Ireland, but then six counties in Ulster exercised their right to separate themselves from it, as Northern Ireland, and to remain part of the United Kingdom.

The Treaty's failure to give Irish Republicans a united Ireland, with no links to Britain, meant that the country was plunged into civil war, with anti-Treaty forces in Sinn Fein and the IRA taking up arms against the Free State despite an election that had approved the new government. The Civil War lasted over a year. It was characterised by great brutality on both sides as men who had fought together against British rule murdered each other. Éamon de Valera, who had been President of the Irish Republic

459

during the War of Independence, became the anti-Treaty political leader. Michael Collins, the most notable pro-Treaty leader, was killed by anti-Treaty forces in 1922.

By 1923 the anti-Treaty forces were beaten. De Valera argued for a truce, but the military leadership disagreed; the IRA dumped its arms, refused to recognise the Free State, and descended into internecine splits and failed bombing campaigns. For ten years the Irish Free State was ruled by the pro-Treaty party, Cumann na nGaedheal (Party of the Gaels). Meanwhile, de Valera had accepted there was no future in armed struggle. He left Sinn Fein and established a new political party, Fianna Fáil (Soldiers of Destiny). In 1932 he won a majority of seats in the parliament (Dáil). There was fear that Cumann na nGaedheal would not give up power. It had established a paramilitary wing, the Army Comrades Association, better known as the Blueshirts, modelled on what was happening in Italy and Germany, to defend the party against Fianna Fáil and a resurgent IRA. There was street fighting at political meetings but the ACA was not a serious threat to democracy, and it never really adopted a fascist ideology. Ireland's democratic instincts and institutions were strong enough, as was the loyalty of its young police force, An Garda Síochána (Guardian of the Peace), and its army. A 1933 march on Dublin, planned by ex-Garda Commissioner Eoin O'Duffy, never happened, though it gave de Valera the opportunity to ban the Blueshirts.

De Valera then adopted the policy Michael Collins had died for: the Free State wasn't freedom but it was the freedom to achieve freedom. By 1937 he stripped away most of the Treaty elements that tied Ireland to Britain, including references to the English king as King of Ireland. His new constitution claimed the whole island of Ireland, but recognised de facto partition. Incorporated into it was the special position of the Catholic Church; Catholic teaching on women and the family was an important element in the constitution and civil divorce was illegal.

Adolf Mahr came to Ireland from Vienna in 1927, first as Keeper of Antiquities at the National Museum, then as its director. His later role as Gauleiter (leader) of the Irish Nazi Party wasn't unusual in Europe, nor was the activity that went with it – keeping a close eye on anti-Nazi 'subversives' and acquiring information that might be beneficial to Germany. In the build-up to the Second World War the Germans got a lot of things wrong as well as right. In Ireland they failed to recognise the complexity of the relationship with Britain. The influence of 'physical force' Republicanism was overestimated as was its ability to be a serious terrorist threat to Britain. Antipathy towards England had a familial quality that Germany simply didn't see. It might make it impossible for Ireland to fight a war at Britain's side, but it would not translate into a popular will to support Britain's enemies in such a war. There were those in German intelligence who believed it would.

The Free City of Danzig (in Polish, Gdańsk) was two years younger than the Irish Free State. It was established on 15 November 1920, in accordance with the Treaty of Versailles that marked the end of the First World War; as the treaty that laid the foundations for the Second World War it proved even more poisonous than the one that established Saorstat Éireann. It forced Germany to give up territory (in the map above the red line marks the 1919 German border); it demanded crippling reparation payments in the midst of worldwide financial collapse; it mixed nationalism up with hatred and humiliation and despair; and it rolled out a red carpet for Adolf Hitler.

Danzig had been a German city for eight hundred years, though its hinterland contained Polish and German popu-lations. It had always had a tradition of independence, initially as a member of the medieval Hanseatic League of city states; but even as it had shifted back and forward between the kingdoms of Prussia and Poland it had maintained its own traditions and laws. Only in 1871 had it become, for a brief period, part of a united Germany. Now it had independence again, along with a liberal constitution watched over by a League of Nations High Commissioner. But ninety-five per cent of Danzigers spoke German and saw themselves as Germans; as German nationalism became angrier and more vociferous in the financial chaos of the twenties and thirties, more and more Danzigers felt the Treaty of Versailles had penalised them, as it had the rest of Germany. They felt they had been forced into an 'arranged marriage' with Poland, a country they believed was occupying ancient German land – and wanted theirs next.

The result was the growth of the Nazi Party in Danzig, mirroring Hitler's rise in Germany. In 1933 the Nazi Party took control of the Free City. In Ireland democracy offered the freedom to achieve freedom; in Danzig, as in Germany, it was a tool to end freedom. Opposition was repressed and eradicated. The only dissenting voices were the League of Nations High Commissioner and the Catholic Bishop. With appeasement throughout Europe and Nazi policies driving Germany, nothing would stop the Nazi juggernaut, but for a short time Seán Lester and Edward O'Rourke stood their ground.

Seán Lester was League of Nations High Commissioner in Danzig from 1934 to 1936, at the height of the Nazi rise to power. Before becoming a diplomat he had been a journalist and a member of the Irish Republican Brotherhood; he joined the Irish Free State's civil service with its establishment in 1922. In Danzig he fought a hard diplomatic battle to hold the Nazi government in check. He had the peculiar honour, during his years as High Commissioner, to be known as 'the most hated man in Nazi Germany'. After his departure Nazi dominance in the Free City increased and in 1938, despite the presence of the last High Commissioner, an Enabling Act finally abolished all opposition parties and Nuremberg racial policies placed Danzig's Jewish community utterly outside the law. From that point it was only a question of time until Danzig turned into a trigger for war.

Lester became the last Secretary General of the League of Nations. He sat out the Second World War in an empty Palace of Nations in Geneva, knowing that if Germany won he was on a Nazi death list; as the League of Nations fell apart he had prevented it becoming a tool of German domination in Europe. In 1946 he was the man who handed the vision of peace and cooperation that had been the League of Nations over to the newly formed United Nations. His retirement in Ireland was quiet and uneventful, first in Wicklow, then in Galway. He is one of the twentieth century's greatest Irishmen, but he is barely known in Ireland. Being too anti-Nazi once carried the taint of being too close to Britain.

Count Edward O'Rourke was appointed Bishop of Danzig in 1922. He was forced to resign in 1937 as a result of increasing conflict with the Nazi authorities, although he was under as much pressure from the Vatican itself, which did not want to antagonise Germany. His successor, Cardinal Carl Maria Splett, a native Danziger, became little more than a puppet of Nazi policy. Edward O'Rourke's ancestors had fled Ireland after the battle of the Boyne and had subsequently become Russian soldiers and aristocratic landowners. His family lost its estates after the Russian Revolution in 1917. He died in Rome in 1943, having fled Poland when the Germans invaded. Like Seán Lester he was on a Nazi death list. As one of the Catholic Church's most prominent opponents of Nazism, Edward O'Rourke has also been largely forgotten.

In the streets of Gdańsk's old town now you see much of what was there in 1930s Danzig. So successful has the rebuilding been that it is hard to believe it was almost totally destroyed at the end of the war. Its reconstruction was an extraordinary achievement by a Polish nation that lay in ruins everywhere. Yet Gdańsk is a city of ghosts. The people who originally built it have disappeared from its history.

# Acknowledgements

This is a work of fiction, but many books, over many years, have played a part in telling the story, too many now forgotten. But there are a few that should be mentioned: Herbert S. Levine's *Hitler's Free City*; Paul McNamara's *Seán Lester, Poland and the Nazi Takeover of Danzig*; Gerry Mullins' *Dublin Nazi No.1: the Life of Adolf Mahr*. What I have right I have from them; what is wrong is my own. Seán Lester's papers in the League of Nations archives have given a sense of who the man was and how he thought that has made me confident about speculation in ways I could not otherwise have been. I could not have written about Dublin's Clanbrassil Street without Ray Rivlin's *Shalom Ireland*, which is a precious document of record of Ireland's small Jewish community. A very different document, and one that makes for hard reading, is Denis Fahey's *The Mystical Body of Christ in the Modern World*; this book was published in 1935, and it is enough to say that it carried a bishop's imprimatur at the time. The story Tom listens to on the radio is Patricia Lynch's *The Turf-Cutter's Donkey* (1934). Directories of the period have been a special joy: in particular *Thom's Directory of Ireland*. Also invaluable was *The Irish Times Archive*, where I could sometimes find that things I had made up had happened. It is impossible to write about the Free City of Danzig without mentioning the website *www.danzig-online.pl*. It is an extraordinarily rich collection of documents and photographs for anyone interested in the Free City.